No More Mr. Nice Guy:

A Family Business Novel

No More Mr. Nice Guy:

A Family Business Novel

Carl Weber

with

Stephanie Covington

www.urbanbooks.net

Urban Books, LLC
300 Farmingdale Road, NY-Route 109
Farmingdale, NY 11735

No More Mr. Nice Guy: A Family Business Novel

ISBN 13: 978-1-60162-091-0
ISBN 10: 1-60162-091-8

First Mass Market Printing January 2019
First Trade Paperback Printing September 2016
First Hardcover Printing February 2016
Printed in the United States of America

10 9 8 7 6 5 4 3

Distributed by Kensington Publishing Corp.
Submit Orders to:
Customer Service
400 Hahn Road
Westminster, MD 21157-4627
Phone: 1-800-733-3000
Fax: 1-800-659-2436

No More Mr. Nice Guy:

A Family Business Novel

Carl Weber

with

Stephanie Covington

Dedication

This is dedicated to Zoë and Dylan

Prologue

I piloted the G550 down the runway, lifting her off the ground and into the morning sky out of sheer force of habit. My real attention was focused on the beautiful young woman I'd just left behind, her outstretched arms still waving at me from the ground. Even when she ceased being a tiny pinprick in my view, I couldn't stop thinking about how much I loved her, how I already felt incomplete without her, and how much I couldn't wait to finish this job and get back to her. I'd only been in love twice before in my life, but my feelings for Paris were more than my feelings for all the other women combined.

My next thought came to me in an instant, as if it were hovering in the back of my mind all along. The thought was simple and life-altering at the same time. When I arrived in New York, I planned to make an appointment to meet with the private jeweler at Tiffany's on Fifth Avenue and buy an engagement ring. When it came to Paris, only the best would do, and I intended to spoil her in ways she'd never known. That, of course, was going to be a near impossible task, since she was born with a platinum teething rattle, but that was what love made men do: the near impossible.

"This is 34699, calling base. Unc, are you there?" I shouted into my headset over the heavy crackle of static. We had gotten in the habit of using ham radio signals, because they were unlikely to be listened to by law enforcement or criminal enterprises. "This is 34699. Are you there?"

"Where the hell else would you expect me to be?" my uncle replied in a raspy voice. I could hear just enough to know that he had recently woken up, probably next to some beautiful young woman. I smiled at the thought. I hadn't realized how much I missed his foolish behind.

"I'll be landing in Manchester in about two hours. Going to need you to pick me up. We got a lot to talk about when I get there," I announced.

"So we got another job?" Willie answered back, and I could hear the excitement in his voice. "Must be real big if you're calling my sorry ass this time of the morning. It's about time you put the band back together."

I chuckled. "Yeah, we're going home to New York."

"New York. I like the sound of that . . . I hope," he replied. It was probably dawning on him that this meant the job was bigger than he had originally assumed. "How long we staying?" he asked tentatively.

"Four to eight weeks," I said in code, knowing he would understand that it meant less than forty-eight hours on the ground.

And he did. "I'll make arrangements for a charter from here to Teterboro Airport. We can be in the air within five hours of you landing. I've got your go-bags packed and ready to go. I'm figuring you're gonna wanna see Lora before we leave."

"There's no doubt about that." I sighed happily, bringing the plane around in hopes of getting one last glimpse of Paris. "How's she doing?"

"She's doing good. I'm sure she's laying around here somewhere playing with those damn rats you brought her," he said with a laugh.

"Will you stop calling them rats! Those are dogs. Very expensive miniature Dobermans, I might add, and she loves them."

"Niles, I'm from New York. I used to drive a cab for a living. I know a damn rat when I see one. Y'all just putting collars on them." He knew his comments would get under my skin. Willie had always liked to push my buttons, but I knew it was all in good humor.

I didn't answer him, because my mind was suddenly somewhere else. Something was wrong, I quickly checked the controls panel, but nothing seemed out of order.

"What the fuck is that noise?" I mumbled to myself, the vibrating static growing more intermittent.

"Everything all right?" Willie asked.

"I don't know, but I hear some type of humming." I took a quick look around the cockpit, noting that it was empty except for my bag. I always flew light.

"Shit, Niles, you think it's the plane?"

"Everything seems all right," I answered, but I knew anything out of the ordinary on a plane had to be checked out right away. One little miscalculation could mean death. I put the plane on autopilot and unstrapped myself from my seat, still wearing my wireless headphones.

I walked to the back of the plane, stopping at the carry-on bag I'd brought onto the plane.

"What the fuck!" I shouted. There was no doubt the humming was coming from within the bag.

"What?" My uncle's voice crackled over my headphones, but I ignored him as I reached down to open the bag and investigate.

"Niles! Niles! Niles!"

"Unc," I finally replied, staring down into the bag. "Yeah."

"There's a girl. Her name is Paris," I murmured, getting choked up. "She's really pretty, Unc. Really pretty. She goes to some fancy school outside of the city of Paris, but she's probably from New York."

"Yeah? What about her?"

"I love her, Unc. I love her like no woman I've ever loved before." Tears began to run down my face as I tried to wrap my head around the situation I suddenly found myself in. "But if for some reason I don't make it, I want you to kill that bitch!"

"I don't understand. You love her but I should kill her? Niles, what the fuck is going on?" There was fear in his voice. I think he understood more than he was admitting to himself at the moment.

I looked down at my bag and all those warm thoughts turned dark and frozen with the realization that Paris was not the person I thought she was. "Because that bitch is trying to kill me. She put a bomb in my bag."

Niles Monroe

1

Five years earlier

"Sargent Monroe, my name's Frank Bush. This is my colleague, Lance Rodgers. Sorry we had you waiting so long at such a late hour, but our business is twenty-four/seven. We had to put out a small fire with our guys in Afghanistan," the salt-and-pepper haired man said, offering his hand.

"Not a problem." I shook their hands, but I knew they were full of shit about the reason for making me wait the last hour and a half. That move was straight out of the Marine's sniper school playbook for testing a man's patience. "And call me Niles. I no longer wear Uncle Sam's stripes."

Bush, who sat across from me, was probably a retired Army officer. His partner, Rodgers, was a well-built brother. He was definitely Army, probably Delta Force like me. Neither of them carried themselves as if they'd seen any real action in quite some time.

"So, Niles, I have to admit I'm impressed. You've got quite a resume," Bush said, looking up from a folder. Their company, Dynamic Defense, LLC, a defense contractor, had flown me up from Fort Bragg for a consulting job interview after hearing from my commanding officer that I had just retired from the Army and was looking to settle back home in New York. "Six years special forces with the Rangers, two in the Night Stalkers. Airborne, and you graduated top of your class in sniper school. You've had quite the career."

"Thank you." It was obvious these boys had done their homework, and I was glad. Nothing I hated more than having to toot my own horn. People who bragged about themselves always made me wonder what they were hiding.

Rodgers, who was sitting on the edge of the desk, leaned in close to me. "That was some first-class shit you did down in Syria. How the hell did you carry both of them out without being seen? That must have been fifty fucking klicks."

I was about to react, but Bush jumped in. "What I wanna know is how you made that shot in Qatar last year. What was that—four hundred feet against the wind?"

"Four-fifty to be exact. But both those missions were classified." The fact that they knew about top secret missions was making me suspicious.

"Yeah, and so was the one in Colombia, Cuba, and the one in Taiwan, but who's counting? Bottom line is you're real good at what you do, and we can use your services. How's two hundred grand a year to start?" Rodgers asked.

The way they were staring at me made me think they were expecting an immediate yes to their large offer, but the whole situation was making me feel uneasy. I was starting to think this was some kind of set up, and there were few things I hated more than being blindsided.

"How the hell do you know all this?" I stood up.

"Hey, have a seat and I'll explain." Bush motioned to the chair. "This is a big company with a lot of friends and resources. We don't just pay anyone two hundred thousand dollars. We needed to know everything about you. How else are we going to utilize your skills in the field correctly?"

"What exactly do you mean by utilize? My CO told me that I was interviewing for a consulting job. This sounds like wet work."

"You are a remarkable soldier, Mr. Monroe. Why would anyone waste your talent consulting?" Bush said matter-of-factly. "Hey, I know it's a little overwhelming, but don't worry. We're the good guys."

He was trying to reassure me, but I was no longer so sure I was interested in the job. I didn't try to hide my skepticism, and Rodgers picked up on it, jumping in to try to convince me.

"Look, kid, Uncle Sam taught you well and gave you a very valuable set of skills," Rodgers added. "We can help you put those skills to work and make you a wealthy man in the process. Two hundred grand to start ain't nothing to sneeze at, and when you add in the bonus money, you could easily clear three, four hundred thousand your first year."

"You show us your worth, and the sky's the limit," Bush added, leaning back in his chair confidently. No doubt they assumed a brother like me would jump at their ever-growing salary offer.

Well, I had learned a long time ago that all money ain't good money, and to kill for my country was one thing, but to kill to put money in my pocket wasn't an option. It would just make me a thug.

"Thanks for the offer, gentlemen, but I'm no soldier of fortune. And to be quite honest, after what I've been through the past few years, a desk job sounds pretty good to me. I just want to lead a normal life." I took a step toward the door.

"Niles." Rogers' commanding voice stopped me.

"Yes?" I spun around on my heels to face him.

"Guys like us don't lead normal lives."

"Well, I'm sure as hell gonna try." I walked out the door.

Bruce

2

"Please! Please, no!" Lydell Washington pleaded as Majestic clamped a giant hand around his neck. I almost felt sorry for Lydell as Majestic removed him from the back of my Navigator and dragged him out into the open. I'd seen that deadly look in my best friend's eyes before, and all I can say is I wouldn't have wanted to be Lydell. "You know I'm not no snitch. I swear I didn't say shit."

"That why you been hiding from us?" I asked, emerging from the shadows of my truck with one of my signature mint toothpicks between my lips.

I glanced down the Robert Moses Causeway to make sure we were still alone. I'd known Lydell most of my life, and, up until a few days ago, I'd thought he was one of my friends. A lot had changed in the past three days, and most of it was no good.

"That why you disappeared after getting caught with that package?" I asked Lydell. "That why your ass is not in jail and standing in front of us?"

Dude looked like he was about to shit himself.

"You think you can snitch on us and get away with it?" Majestic's deep, growling voice made him appear even bigger than his six foot six, 350-pound frame. My man was so damn big he looked like a handsome refrigerator.

"I don't know what you're talking about," Lydell cried. "I swear I would never talk to the cops about you. That goes against everything I stand for. You cats are like family. Whoever told you that shit is a liar."

I had to give it to him. He said the shit with real conviction, but I still knew it was a crock of shit, because I'd gotten the information from the source myself. I spit out my toothpick and stepped up in Lydell's face.

"You calling me a liar, motherfucker?"

"Naw, Bruce, man, I'd never do that." The way Majestic's meaty hand was clasped around his neck, I was surprised he could even get the words out of his mouth, but then again when you're fighting for your life, I guess you find all kinds of ways to get your message across.

"Then why you been hiding?" Majestic asked, the veins on his neck throbbing the way they always did when he was furious.

We'd surprised Lydell when we busted up in his girl's uncle's house about midnight. Little did his dumb ass know that I'd been fucking his chick just as long as he had. I just wasn't stupid enough to make her my girl. She hadn't even hesitated to call me when she found out where he was hiding. I guess we know who'd been fucking her better over the years, don't we?

Lydell shook his head, or at least that's what it looked like he was trying to do, but like I said, he was limited in his mobility by Majestic's massive hands. "Majestic, me you, and Bruce, we're like brothers, man." Lydell coughed, struggling to catch his breath. "I've followed you to hell and back. I'm a loyal dude. You gotta believe me."

"I wish I could, but I can't let you take us down. We ain't dealing in nickel and dime shit no more now that we're with El Gato. This is the big time, and Bruce and I got too much to lose. You shoulda kept your mouth shut, Dell," Majestic explained calmly.

In one smooth move, he lifted Lydell up off his feet like a paperweight and dangled him over the guardrail of the bridge. Of course, Lydell's ass went crazy.

"Please! Please, Majestic, man! You're the godfather of my kids. You can't do this, man. We family. Shit, please don't do this! I don't wanna die." Dude was crying like a little bitch.

"You better stop moving or I'm gonna drop you for sure. It's a long way down."

Lydell glanced down at the water, and reality set in quick. All of a sudden, he was as stiff as a board. I mean he got real still. Majestic turned and locked eyes with me. A look passed between us that, had Lydell seen it, would have made him even more afraid.

"What you think we should do with him?" Majestic asked.

"We do all go way back," I reminded him. "But, on the other hand, you know how I feel about snitches."

"Come on, Bruce. Don't do me like that, brother," Lydell pleaded. "How many times have I saved your ass over the years?"

"That's all good, but here's my problem: You disappeared after getting knocked with a package."

"That don't mean I snitched."

"Maybe, but my people at the First Precinct and the Suffolk DA's office say you're the witness against us for the Johnson brothers hit we did for the Duncans a few years back. Somehow they found the bodies and have a witness to connect us to it. Problem is, nobody knew about that shit but the three of us." Lydell's eyes grew wide.

"Now," I continued, "since the cops are looking for me and Majestic, that only leaves you. Do you know how that makes us feel to think that you would turn on us? And what's really pissing me off is that you keep lying about it."

Lydell finally recognized that his bullshit lies weren't going to work. "A'ight, a'ight, look. I ain't had no choice. I got three strikes. They were gonna lock me up for good if I didn't talk," he sputtered.

"We all got choices!" Majestic yelled in his face. "You should have just done the time, man. We would have got you a lawyer and taken care of your family."

I turned to Majestic, twisting my lips. "Man, you was right. Drop this motherfucker."

"With pleasure." He let go of Lydell, and we watched him fall, screaming all the way down. He hit the water with a loud splash, and then there was silence.

I glanced over my shoulder to make sure there hadn't been any late-walking witnesses, then gazed down at the water again until the circle where Lydell had disappeared stopped rippling and the water was calm.

"What if he's still alive? I've seen white kids jump off this bridge a dozen times," I said, but that only made Majestic laugh.

"Yeah, but they could swim. That Negro's from the projects. He ain't never learn how to swim. His black ass is down there sinking like a rock." Majestic belted out a deep belly laugh.

I shook my head, agreeing, then put the whole incident out of my mind. I was already thinking about our next stop. "A'ight, now that Lydell's out the picture, you sure about this?" I questioned because once we did it, there would be no changing course.

"Positive." He smiled like it was no big deal, although we both knew this shit was a huge deal. Had it been anyone else, I would have tried to talk him out of it, but there wasn't another human being on the planet I trusted more than Majestic.

We got back in the car and headed toward Lindenhurst, Long Island, where I pulled up in front of Suffolk County's First Precinct.

As we headed inside past all the blue uniforms about to start their morning shift, the balding desk sergeant stood up and approached us.

"Can I help you?" Guess it wasn't every day two well-dressed black men stepped through those doors. They were used to the low-level criminals that are featured on the local news every day.

Majestic took a step closer to him like he was about to shake his hand. "Yes, my name's Majestic Moss, and I hear there's a warrant out for my arrest."

Bridget

3

"Good morning, Ms. St. John. My name is Nadja. The deputy director has told me so much about you. Is there anything I can get you? Coffee, tea, a cold beverage perhaps?" The perky Persian woman with a little more T and A than the job required greeted me as soon as I stepped off the elevator. She seemed awfully eager to meet my needs, so I guessed my reputation preceded me.

"Fuck the pleasantries. Where is Jonathan?" I barked, rolling my eyes.

"Excuse me?" Nadja stiffened with shock, her face flush with embarrassment.

"Look, don't act all offended, honey. You want to make it around here, you not only have to be smarter than them, but you better learn how to cuss like a sailor, fight like a man, and screw like a rabbit. That's the only thing these Neanderthals understand." I shook my head as I realized that I had actually rendered her speechless. This one wouldn't be here long. Way too weak.

"Now, where the hell is Jonathan?" I repeated.

"He's in observation room C. Follow me." She ushered me into a room where Jonathan sat with two tech geeks, wearing headphones and studying individual computer monitors. When I entered the room, the geeks stayed glued to their monitors, but Jonathan took off his headphones and turned to me.

"Bridget St. John." He smiled, undressing me with his eyes. "You're looking exceptionally good. Why don't you let me take you to breakfast? I have a few things I'd like to run by you."

"Cut the bullshit, Jonathan." I dropped my briefcase on a nearby desk. "What was so damn important that you had to drag me all the way down here at three in the morning while I'm in the middle of an assignment?"

"Breakfast with me not enough? You used to love when I made breakfast—and I love the way you cook my sausage." He gave me a lecherous smirk.

I took a deep breath. Some men should never have the opportunity to get really good pussy. They just can't handle it. Jonathan was one of those men. He completely confused casual sex for a relationship. Sure, we may have fucked back in the day, but there wasn't anything serious about what we had. As far as I was concerned, we were just passing time.

"Look, its late," I spit out. "I don't have time for your games, so get to the point or deal with the director, because fucking with me when on assignment is a no-no and you know it!"

"Relax. I've got something to show you that I'm sure you're going to wanna see." He turned back to the monitor like he was ready to get to business, but he couldn't hide the fact that he was pouting like a little boy "There used to be a time when you could take a joke."

"That was a long time ago, when I was your assistant and I didn't know better." I wanted to get the hell out of there before I followed through on my desire to cause him some bodily harm. "I run my own division now, and I don't have to laugh at your stale-ass jokes anymore. You should remember that." I glanced over at the newbie Nadja, desperate to make a good impression. It was hard to believe I was once that naive.

"Well, if we're going to be putting things on the record, then maybe you should remember exactly who recommend you for your high and mighty new position," Jonathan said.

"Yeah, yeah, and if I hadn't killed Miguel's brother Santos, you wouldn't have made assistant director. What does this have to do with me being here?"

He hit a button on his computer, and the fifty-inch flat screen on the wall lit up, revealing a closeup of an exceptionally handsome, light-skinned brother probably in his late twenties or early thirties. He was quite the physical specimen.

"So, what do you think?" Jonathan asked.

"He's cute. I think I'd like to fuck him. Is that why you called me all the way down here, to introduce me to potential sex partners?"

I saw his anger rising, but he quickly recovered.

"Not exactly. I was hoping tonight was going to be our night," he continued, raising his eyebrows a few times suggestively. Men were such damn children.

"Why are you wasting my time? You can bet your ass the director's going to hear about this." Interrupting an operative on an assignment for some nonsense crossed a real line. I snatched up my briefcase and headed for the door.

"He's the guy who took out Akbar in Syria last year, Bridget." His words stopped me in my tracks. In no time, I was back in front of the screen to get a better look.

"He took out Akbar?" I asked, admiring this fine brother for much more than his looks now.

Jonathan hit a button, pulling the camera back on the subject to reveal the room where he sat. Frank Bush, the head of recruiting, was sitting in front of him, along with Lance Rodgers, a man I despised. Lance was the head of field operations.

He and I had started with the company around the same time, yet we couldn't have been more opposite. While I worked my ass off in the field with Jonathan, Lance brown-nosed his way up the ladder, so to speak.

"His name is Niles Monroe, and he's our top recruit. As you can see, Lance is interviewing him right now." He handed me a folder, and I began to thumb through it. I'd never seen anyone with a more impressive jacket.

"Iraq, Syria, Sudan, Hong Kong, Colombia, this guy's off the charts. He's the real deal," I replied.

"Without question. I've had my eye on him the past three years. He's just become available."

"I hope you're not planning on giving him to Lance," I said as I continued to study his folder. "This guy's special. With the proper training, he could be one of the best." I tried to remain professional, but I was sure my hatred for Lance was coming through. Still, I meant every word I said. This Niles Monroe had true superstar potential.

Jonathan shook his head. "No, this guy's out of Lance's league. Truth is, I'm thinking about giving him to you to train." He paused with a slick grin. "If you're nice to me." I could tell he was holding something a little too close to his vest, so I remained silent to see if he would give it up.

"What do you think?" he pressed. "You're always complaining that you're a one-woman show. Now you have a chance to have our top recruit. With a guy like him under your wing, your career could skyrocket."

"You're kidding me, right? You're giving him to me?" From what I had just read, this guy was better than seventy-five percent of our recruits, and he wasn't even trained. Yes, I was certainly intrigued, but this was not the kind of gift Jonathan would just hand over to me. I'd spent a long time lobbying and pleading for help only to get the bottom of the barrel, so I was suspicious. Jonathan and his team kept all the best recruits for themselves. Now they were offering me their best? Sure, I knew Jonathan wanted to fuck again, but even I didn't think the goods were worth giving up an asset of Monroe's caliber. "What's the catch?" I asked.

"None. He's yours if you want him."

I studied Jonathan like a poker player looking for tells. "And I'm supposed to believe that? What's the catch?" I repeated.

"Dinner and drinks at my place." He intertwined his fingers behind his head, grinning like Cheshire cat as he leaned back in his chair.

"I didn't ask what I have to do to get him. I asked, what's the fucking catch?" How green did he really think I was? If I had been more of a people person,

I could have easily taken his job and run this division. "What are you not telling me, Jonathan?"

"Nothing. The guy's done everything in his file. I swear."

I leaned closer. "You want dinner and drinks and everything that comes after, then you better tell me what I want to know. What's not in that file?"

"Fine. The guy is something of a hothead. He does not play well with others, and my guys work as a team. But more importantly—"

"Oh, there's a *but*?"

"But, like someone I know, he doesn't exactly follow orders to the letter. The fucker's got a conscience, and he's morally objected to missions in the past." He finally divulged the guy's Achilles' heel.

For too many years, my main problem had to do with taking orders from idiots like Lance masquerading as bad-asses from their secure positions as bonafide paper pushers. It was hard to take orders from people who never had to risk their own lives.

"That I can deal with," I concluded. "So now what?"

"Now comes the tough part. You have to convince him to join the team. He thinks he's interviewing for a consulting job."

The guy stood up, and I didn't need sound on the monitor to know that he was upset. Still, Jonathan reached to the right of the screen and hit a button so that we could hear what they were saying.

"Thanks for the offer, gentlemen, but I'm no soldier of fortune. And to be quite honest, after what I've been through the past few years, a desk job sounds pretty good to me. I just want to lead a normal life." He took a step toward the door.

"Niles, guys like us don't lead normal lives," Lance countered.

"Well, I'm sure as hell gonna try." With that, Niles Monroe was out the door.

Jonathan turned to me. "I guess you're up." He pointed to the hall, where Niles was passing by our conference room.

I hurried into the hallway, determined to catch up with him at the elevator bank before he left the building.

He was even better looking in person. When he turned to notice me standing beside him, I gave him a smile. He must have liked what he saw, because as he pushed the down button and we waited for the elevator to arrive, I saw him surreptitiously checking me out. I had him by about 8 years—maybe more, but from the way he was grinning, it was obvious he knew a real woman when he saw one. *Yes*, I told myself as the elevator doors opened, *he's going to be fun to train.*

When we stepped onto the elevator, I pushed the button for the lobby and then turned to him. "Excuse me, Mr. Monroe. My name is Bridget St. John. Can I speak with you for a moment?"

He raised an eyebrow. "How do you know my name?"

"I'm a field supervisor for the company."

"I should have known." He sighed, shaking his head.

"Mr. Monroe, you're an extremely talented man. If you'd just give me five minutes—"

"Look." He cut me off, frustration evident on his face. "No offense, but I don't want to talk to anyone from your company anymore. I'm done."

"I do work with them, but I'm not them. If you come and work for me, then I'm the only person you'll have to ever deal with. That way you can see for yourself that we're not all alike."

"You want me to take a job killing for you—right?"

I said nothing, because I couldn't deny what he was asking.

He continued, as if my silence had answered for me. "Then I don't want to work with you or anyone like you. I got plans for my life, plans that don't include killing anyone. My killing days are over," he said as the elevator arrived in the lobby. He stepped out and strode with purpose out of the building.

I stood there watching him leave. This Niles Monroe was really the most interesting person I had met in a long time. His mind seemed to be made up, but then again, I could be a very persuasive woman with a lot of resources at my disposal.

Niles

4

The sun was shining through the windows of the cab as it exited the Southern State Parkway headed toward Wyandanch. I'd just left that waste of time interview with Dynamic Defense and was staring out the window like some lost tourist visiting for the first time. The neighborhood I'd grown up in didn't look anything like it had when I left ten years ago, straight out of high school. It had undergone a real transformation, I thought, as we passed a strip where a small row of stores had been torn down to make way for commuter parking lots and the new apartment building and shopping complex next to the Long Island Railroad station.

Despite the new buildings and the urban renewal, some things would never change, and as far as I was concerned, Wyandanch was one of them. When we turned off Straight Path down Long Island Avenue, I spotted ten or fifteen drug boys standing in front of the convenience deli like it was lunchtime and they were giving away free sandwiches. I swear they were the same dealers who used to stand around there when I was in high school. You could put lipstick on a pig, but when it came down to it, it was still just a damn pig. I guess you could say the same thing about Wyandanch.

"What's going on?" I asked as we turned up my block and the cab came to a complete stop. The driver began babbling in Hindi, pointing at the police cars and an ambulance blocking the street. I wish I could say it caught me off guard, but in my hood, the police were always showing up to carry someone off to jail, the morgue, or if they were lucky, just to the hospital.

"Just pull over. I'll walk the rest," I instructed the driver.

"You sure?" he asked, though he looked relieved as he stared at me through his rearview mirror. This was supposed to be a hardened NYC cabbie, but it was obvious he was scared shitless.

"Yeah, my house is just up the block." I glanced at the meter then reached into my pocket to pay the fare. I was going to let him keep the change, but then snatched it back when the son of a bitch popped open the trunk and gestured for me to get my own bags. I don't even think the trunk was all the way down before he pulled a U-turn and gunned it down the street toward the Southern State Parkway.

With my knapsack over my shoulder and two duffle bags in my hands, I made my way up the block toward home. I hadn't imagined I would ever wind up back here for an extended period of time. Hell, I'd only been back to visit about five times in the past ten years, but here I was, me and all my worldly possessions, along with no job and no prospect for a job. I could have done another tour and stayed in the Army, but I decided it was time to come home, or at least close to home. Truth is, I had really been counting on that consulting job so I could get a place in the city and still be close to my mom.

Speaking of Mom . . .

"You fucking devils!" An eerie voice shrieked loud enough for half the neighborhood to hear. "I'm going to kill all of you!"

"Shit," I cursed.

I'd been through hell and back as a soldier for my country, but that scream put more fear in my heart than any of the shit I'd seen in the military. You see, that scream wasn't just random. I'd heard it many a night while growing up, and it told me one thing: The commotion was coming from my house. I broke out into a full jog.

"You fucking devils! Stay the fuck away from me!" The voice continued to get louder the closer I got to my house.

By the time I got to the edge of my mother's property, there was a gang of nosy neighbors standing outside the house. I made my way through the crowd to the stoop, where I was stopped by a cop.

"Sir, you're gonna have to stop right there," the cop stated, blocking my entry.

"This is my house. Those are my people inside." I dropped my bags, staring him down, but he stood his ground. Based on my military training, I knew there were at least two dozen ways I could take him down and get past him, but I didn't want to do that if I didn't have to.

"Don't touch me!" The voice came from the house again. "I'll kill you all!"

The cop looked back at the house like he might be needed in there. What he didn't understand was that he had just as big a problem standing in front of him.

"Sir, we have a mentally ill person in there with a knife. I need you to stay back for your own safety."

"Look, officer, I'm the only one who is going to be able to defuse this situation. Now, let me pass, please, so I can help you. Those are my family members in there." I looked past him to his sergeant, who was standing in the doorway with his gun drawn

"The devil! You're all devils!" She kept repeating. "I'll kill you all!"

"Let him go, Stanford," the sergeant announced, and the cop finally let me pass.

As I walked by the sergeant at the front door, he told me, "You better do something quick or we're going to have to take matters into our own hands. You don't want that."

"No, I don't," I told him.

I entered the house to see a room full of very intense-looking cops. All of them had their guns out pointed in the direction of a panic-stricken man, who had his hands raised in submission beside a deranged, knife-wielding woman. The man was my uncle, Willie, my mother's younger brother and caregiver. The woman was my bipolar mother.

"Sir," an officer shouted at Willie, "I'm going to need you to step out the way and let us handle this."

"I'm not going to let you shoot my sister," Willie answered.

"Get out! Get out of my fucking house, you demons!" my mother screamed, stabbing at the air behind Willie, daring them to come closer.

"Lorna, please! Please! You're not making this any better," Willie pleaded, but she was too far into another realm to be able to comply.

Seeing me, Willie's face flooded with relief. "Niles, man, please help her! Please, man, if she don't calm down they're gonna kill her."

"They aren't going to kill anyone," I declared, stepping into the line of fire. Like Willie, I held my hands up so that the officers understood my passivity as I moved further into the room. Last thing I needed was a trigger-happy cop to make me another casualty in the ongoing war between the cops and people of color.

I turned and stared at my mother as she stabbed at the air with the knife. Unfortunately, seeing her in this state wasn't a rare occurrence. It was actually the reason why I had joined the Army and gone overseas. I loved my mother more than anyone in the world, but eighteen years living with a bipolar parent had almost sent me to the nut house along with her.

"Ma. Ma," I called out to her, my voice calm and coaxing.

She turned to me, her eyes glassy in that way that let me know she hadn't really seen me yet. "Willie! Get these devils out of my house! They're trying to poison me!" she shouted, flailing her hands and waving the knife around.

"Ma!" I raised my voice a little, hoping to jar her out of her current state. She froze for a split second. I took that moment to move toward her, waiting for her to recognize her only son. "Ma, it's me, Niles."

"Niles?" A spark of recognition glinted in her eyes. She glared at me hard, but then her face began to soften. "Oh my God. Niles? Willie, it's Niles."

"I can see that." Willie's voice was flooded with relief, but I noticed that he still kept his hands raised. He wasn't taking any chances with those officers. "Now give him the knife."

"Niles." Ma smiled and reached out her free hand to touch my face. "My Niles is home."

"Yes, Mama, your Niles. I'm home now. Home for good."

She kept grinning at me like I was a little boy, until one of the cops moved behind me. That set her off again, and she leaped in front of me, gesturing toward the cops.

"Stay behind me, baby. These are the devil's demons. They must've found out you were coming home, and they're going to try to take you to their master." She looked like she might attack them at any moment.

I tried to place myself between her and the cops, who looked even more confused than before, but she wasn't having it. She was like a mama bear protecting her cub.

"Don't fucking move!" I shouted at the cops then turned to my mother. "Ma, take a good look at them. Those aren't devils. Those are angels in disguise. Can't you see it?" My tone sounded light and sing-songy—nothing like how I felt.

She shook her head. "No, baby, those look like devils."

"Look closely and you'll see it." I began to massage her shoulders, hoping to loosen her up and also make sure I could stop her if she attacked one of the cops.

"You know, I think I'm starting to see it."

"Of course you are. They're right in front of your face."

My mother glanced from me to them and back before her face broke out in a sweet smile. "Niles."

"Yeah, Ma?"

"Those angels really should get better disguises, 'cause they are ugly as hell."

I laughed, and as she lowered the knife, I guided it out of her hands.

Keisha

5

"I know you ain't wearing that shit tonight. That boy done bought you a closet full of clothes, so you ain't wearing that shit." My mother drilled me with her shrill voice. She snatched the outfit out of my hand and rolled her eyes at me.

I loved my mom to death, but sometimes I hated her just as much. She had a tendency to play fashion police every time she knew my son's father was coming around.

"You know he likes for you to show off that caramel skin and those sexy-ass curves you got from me." She was feeling herself as she switched her way over to my closet and pulled out a tight-fitting halter top and some short-shorts. "Look at this shit. These still got the damn tags on them."

"If I put that on, he's going to be all over me tonight and you know it." I sucked my teeth as she waved the revealing outfit in my direction. "Whose side are you on anyway? You know he wants another baby."

She looked at me over her sunglasses. "I'm on the side of having a roof over our heads. Besides, if I had a man that treated me as good as he treats you, I'd be working on giving him more than one baby."

"Then why don't you fuck him?" I shot back, tired of her being his full-time cheerleader. She smirked at me, and I knew that if he gave her even the slightest chance, she would sleep with him. My mother was only fourteen years older than me and closer to my sons' father's age than I was.

"Well, I certainly would treat him better than you do. You have no idea how good you got it."

When I first met my sons' father, I was just out of high school: young, dumb, and looking for fun. He was fine as hell and drove a Land Rover. All the girls wanted him, which, of course, made me want him even more. Well, when it was all said and done, he chose me. Back then I didn't know who I was or what I wanted. I was just a kid who wanted to be popular, and being with him made me just that.

I can't lie. It was fun for while, at least until my son was born. Once I got pregnant, everything changed. Now I was a grown-ass woman with a baby daddy and a child, but I wanted something more out of life. I wanted to go to college and get my degree and make something with my life, but he wasn't having it. He didn't want me to do anything except take care of his son and wait for him to come fuck me. I felt like a prisoner, but as far as my mother was concerned, I should be happy as long as he was giving me money.

"Let me ask you a question, Mom. Would you be kissing his ass so much if he wasn't paying your car note and cell phone bill?" I snapped, annoyed at how many times I'd had to sit by and watch her gush over him, taking his side in every argument like he was her son—or her husband, for that matter.

"You young girls don't know shit. You think a man like him just gonna come along again 'cause you something special? Please. It's not going to happen. He's the best thing that ever happened to us, and if I were you, I'd remember that before he gets sick of your ass and finds somebody new. Damn, that boy's a great catch."

"He's a controlling pain in the ass." I pouted.

"Man pays the bills, he's got a right to say what goes on in his house. I don't see your ass handing him the keys back."

There wasn't much I could say to that. Now you know why I hated her sometimes.

She placed a hand on her hip and handed me the outfit. "Now put this shit on and stop playing games."

The doorbell rang, giving me the break I needed from my mother. I went racing from the room, not wanting the sound to wake up my son, MJ. Of course my mother followed right behind me and stood over my shoulder like this was her house as I opened the door.

"Giirrrrrlllllll, wait till you hear this!" Jasmine Peterson, my wild and ghetto fantastic girlfriend shouted when I opened the door. She was wearing one of her favorite catch-a-man outfits: a skin-tight burgundy dress with matching heels, hair fresh off the Asian beauty supply shop shelves, and a huge grin on her face. "Matter of fact, you need to sit down before you hear this shit."

I glanced over at Tanya Brown, my next door neighbor, who was standing next to Jasmine with a concerned look on her face. They both stepped inside. Tanya didn't put it out there like Jazz, mostly because she didn't have to. Unlike Jasmine, Tanya was smart, natural, fine, and employed as a home health aide. She was thirty-five years old but looked younger than me. I liked her because she was more like a big sister than a friend. She also didn't take any crap from my mom.

"Hmph! You bitches always gossiping," my mother muttered under her breath. She knew my baby daddy didn't like my friends, so she decided she didn't like them either. He was worried that I'd see how much fun they were having and want to join in. That wasn't that far from the truth these days.

"Stop playing games, Jasmine, and tell me."

Jazz kept doing some dramatic movements with her hands before she spilled the tea. "Guess who got arrested?"

"Who?" I was anxious for some dirt that didn't include my baby's diaper.

Jasmine started rolling her neck and looking around like she was thinking about moving in.

"Dammit, Jasmine, who?"

Tanya burst out with, "Your baby daddy!" ruining Jasmine's big reveal.

"You lyin'!" My mother jumped in the middle of them.

"If I'm lying, I'm dying, Ms. Smalls," Jasmine snapped. "That shit is all over the block. Majestic and Bruce got locked up for murder."

"Wow!" I couldn't believe it. It felt like a weight had been lifted off my shoulders and I had been freed from prison myself. "You know, I guess there really is a God."

"What the hell is that supposed to mean?" My mother snatched my arm. "Do you know what this is going to do to me—I mean us?" Suddenly all eyes were on my mother. "You need to go down to that precinct wherever they got him and see what you can do to help get him out."

"Mommy, you must have fell and bumped your head, 'cause I ain't going nowhere." I gave her a look like she was smoking rocks or something. "I been with that man for six years, and the last two I've been completely miserable. Not that you care. This is like my get out of jail free pass." I threw my hands up in celebration.

Tanya raised her hand to meet mine in the best high-five I'd given in what seemed like years.

Jasmine was already onto the next thing. "C'mon, girl. We need to go party."

"Shit. You got that right. I know exactly what I'm gonna wear," I said as I started for my closet. "My mother just picked it out. Isn't that right, Mom?"

"Not for you to be strutting around some other man!" my mother shouted at me like she thought I was still a child she could control. "You ought to be worried about who's gonna pay your bills." She said it firmly, like she thought that would shut my party down.

"I'm gonna get a job, Mama. Isn't that what normal people do?"

"I swear to God you better find some good sense and get down there and help that man get out of jail." She kept at it, obviously worried her meal ticket was over.

I fixed my eyes on her. "Not tonight. Now that his ass is the one locked up, I'm free, and I'm going to party. And you are going to watch your grandson. This is not open to debate," I told her as I turned and strutted toward the bedroom, with my girls following my happy dance down the hallway.

Majestic

6

I had walked up to the desk sergeant in the First Precinct and smiled like I'd won the lottery, not the least bit concerned about the decision I was making. "My name's Majestic Moss, and I hear there's a warrant out for my arrest."

The man had to lift his head to get a good look at me, since I towered over him. "Majestic Moss. . . ." He looked back down and typed something into his computer. Whatever came up on the screen had him spooked, because he jumped up, whipped out his gun, and pointed it at me like I had just threatened him. Of course, his actions incited the other half dozen cops in the room to pull their weapons out and point them at Bruce and me. "Hold it right there. Don't you move a fucking muscle."

"I wasn't planning on it," I replied, raising my hands very carefully.

"What's going on?" one of the cops asked the desk sergeant.

"These guys are both wanted for murder. Slap some cuffs on them and get 'em in the back."

I glanced over at my man Bruce, who was usually cool, calm, and collected under the worst circumstances. Even he looked like he was having doubts about my decision to turn ourselves in. Not that I could blame him. A half dozen guns pointed at your head will put doubt in anyone's mind, including mine.

Within seconds, Bruce and I were cuffed and escorted into the back of the precinct, where we were placed in separated interrogation rooms. I waited in that room for six hours before a salt-and-pepper-haired man in a cheap suit finally came in.

"Majestic Moss." He gave me a self-satisfied smile as he took a seat in front of me.

"Detective Wright. Good to see you again." I nodded my head in acknowledgment, sitting back in the small-ass chair they'd provided.

I'd known this fuck since I was a teenager, when he was a beat cop patrolling the streets of Wyandanch. He'd been trying to nail Bruce and me ever since we were kids slinging rocks for Mr. Magic and Bobby Dee. Now that we'd finally hit the big time and he was about to retire, he wanted our asses even more.

"Do you know how long we've been looking for you?"

He didn't sound pleased, and that made me laugh. The cops just didn't get it. This was my town. No way was I going to get found if I didn't want to.

"You must have not been looking very hard, Wright, because, as you can see, I'm a pretty big guy. I'm not hard to miss."

He shrugged his shoulders nonchalantly. "Well, it doesn't really matter, does it? I'm going to be able to find you any time I want for the next twenty years." He started laughing, as if he knew something I didn't.

Little did he know, the joke was on him.

"It's not every day a wanted felon turns himself in and saves us the trouble and manpower of finding him,"

"Well, I think the felon part is a little premature. I'm an innocent man until I'm proven guilty, remember? Why else would I turn myself in? I'm sure once my lawyer gets here, I'll be going home."

He leaned back further in his chair, the smile still plastered on his face. "You ain't going anywhere. I got your ass dead to rights on two murders, and by the time my partner gets finished listening to Bruce sing in there, I'm sure we'll have you on multiple counts."

"Really? And exactly what murders did I do?" I leaned forward and chuckled.

"More than I wanna think about, but we got you dead to rights on the Willie and Lamar Johnson murders. You and Bruce shot them in cold blood, right over there by the landfill in West Babylon."

Damn, I thought, it was a good thing we hadn't left those bodies in that landfill.

"Hmmm, that doesn't ring a bell. I don't even know a Willie or Lamar Johnson, and neither does Bruce. Do you have a body or a murder weapon, or perhaps . . . an eye witness to collaborate this fabrication? 'Cause this sounds like a setup to me." I tipped my chair back to lean against the wall.

"Oh, we've got a witness all right. We've got one hell of a witness."

"You sure about that? When was the last time you spoke to that witness? Maybe they've recanted their story."

Wright was not a stupid man. He read between the lines, and his eyes narrowed to angry slits as he glared at me. "Have you messed with my witness, you piece of shit?"

"I'm just saying you can't always rely on the word of a man like Lydell Washington."

"You fuck!" He jumped up, his chair clattering to the floor. "I never mentioned Lydell Washington's name."

"Oh, really?" I said with a smirk. "That's interesting. Maybe I was just thinking of all the piece-of-shit people who would lie on me. You do realize that Lydell's at the top of that list, don't you?"

Wright's face was bright red as he leaned over the table, looking ready to spit fire.

"Come on, Wright. Do it. Throw that pension of yours down the drain," I taunted.

I was sure he wanted to smack the shit out of me, but he resisted when I gestured toward the camera in the upper corner of the room.

"Yeah, I didn't think so, 'cause if you touch me, I'll own Suffolk County literally and not just figuratively."

He pointed a crooked finger at me. "This isn't over, Majestic. This isn't over by a long shot."

As he turned to walk out of the room, I said, "It is if I say it is, detective."

Willie

7

Niles and I walked into Sugar's, a small local bar and grill on the West Babylon side of Straight Path, after spending most of the day getting my sister out of police custody and into South Oaks Hospital in Amityville. Neither of us had eaten more than a candy bar, and I for one was starved, not to mention the fact that I could use a stiff drink after all that damn stress.

"What can I get for you gents?" the waitress, a short dark-skinned woman with huge tits, asked.

"Gimme a burger, fries, and a double shot of Henny on the rocks," I replied, taking in the ample view. "Oh, and make sure they don't put no cheese on my burger. I'm lactose intolerant like a motherfucker. I'll be farting all night."

Niles laughed. "Make that a burger and Heineken for me. I'll take cheese on mine."

I gave him a pat on the shoulder. "It's good to have you back, nephew. From an ex-Marine, I just want you to know I'm proud of you. Your mama is too."

"Thanks, Unc. If it wasn't for you coming home when you did, I wouldn't have been able to leave. I appreciate you taking care of Ma all these years."

"Wasn't like I had a damn choice after they shot my leg up with friendly fire in the first Gulf War." I'd been a Marine for almost ten years when a stupid sergeant used real ammo on a training exercise and shot me in the leg. They gave me a purple heart and an honorable discharge, but that was the end of my soldiering. Still, I guess my military service had made an impact on Niles. He swore that my being a soldier was half the reason he joined the Army.

"Besides, that's my big sister. She took care of me before you were even born. It was the least I could do."

"Well, I appreciate it nonetheless," he said.

The waitress placed our drinks in front of us. "Anything else I can get you gentlemen before I bring out your food?"

I wanted to say she could give me her phone number, but the way she was smiling in my nephew's face like he was Valentino or something, I knew I didn't have a chance, so I just picked up my drink and took a sip.

When the waitress walked away, I turned to Niles and asked, "So, what you gonna do now that this consulting thing done fell through?"

He shrugged, taking a sip of his beer. "I don't know. I saw a couple of billboards in the city for the NYPD. And one of the cops at the house said the Suffolk County Police are looking for minority recruits."

"Shit, Suffolk County Police are always looking for minorities. That's why half of us are locked up," I joked halfheartedly, sitting back in my seat. "I'll be honest with you, Niles. I never figured you for a cop, but it makes sense with all that military training you done got. Shit, you could probably be SWAT."

"What?" He put down his drink and stared at me.

"If you're willing to be a cop, why'd you turn that job down with Dynamic Defense? Shit, two hundred grand a year is a lot of bread to walk away from. I mean, to be honest, all they're asking you to do is the same shit you was doing for Uncle Sam the past ten years, but they're willing to pay you handsomely to do it."

"Yeah, but when I was in the Army, at least I could pretend I was doing it for my country. With these guys, who the fuck knows what their real agenda is? Look, Unc, I got no regrets about turning them down. Something just didn't feel right."

"I hear ya," I said, nodding my understanding even though I really didn't get it. That boy was walking away from a shitload of money. Money only a crazy man would walk away from.

"I will tell you one regret I have about not working with Dynamic Defense."

"Oh, yeah? What's that?" I asked. The boy had a mysterious grin on his face all of a sudden.

"That woman Bridget. I wish I had gotten her phone number. Unc, she looked like something straight outta one of one of those women's magazines: professional yet sexy."

"She was that fine, huh?" I tried to form an image in my mind.

"Mm-mm-mmmph. Was she." He shook his head slowly. "I'm not in the habit of paying for pussy, but I'd pay to get some of that. Sex with her is probably a once-in-a-lifetime experience."

"Damn, what you trying to say? She got some bucket list pussy?"

"Something like that." He raised his glass and I tapped mine against his, giving an informal toast to the bad-ass beauty of this woman Bridget.

The waitress brought our burgers over, and we dug in, not speaking again for a while as we filled our empty stomachs.

About halfway through the meal, Niles threw me a curve ball. "So, Unc, what happened to your cab?"

I should have figured he was gonna bring that up sooner or later. I exhaled loudly and dropped my head, not really wanting to discuss it. I'd bought a cab with money the government gave me for getting shot up. Made a pretty good living driving it, too, until I got two DUIs and they took my hack license and impounded the car.

When I admitted that to Niles, I could see he wanted to comment, but he held his tongue.

"I know it was stupid," I said, "but dealing with your mother drove me to drink."

Niles nodded his head. "Yeah, I can imagine. Taking care of Ma can be stressful. But, Unc, you gotta stop that binge drinking, man. You're gonna kill yourself."

"Yeah, I know," I replied then downed half my drink.

"Look, don't worry about money," Niles said. "I got a little something stashed away. We'll be all right until I land something."

I lifted my head, mustering up what little pride I had left. "Look, Niles, I don't want you spending your money on me. I don't need your charity. Shit, I'm a veteran. I got a pension, and I'll find myself another job soon. You can't be the only Monroe man who is employable."

"I hear you, Unc." He picked up his beer and clinked it against my drink. "Besides, what the hell are we talking about all this depressing shit for with all these fine women up in here? Five o'clock to your right."

I followed his gaze over to three women who were turned away from us as they moved toward a booth. From my vantage point, I knew exactly which one of the three had caught his interest. I laughed, nudging him playfully.

"Damn, she's right up your alley, ain't she?"

The woman he was looking at turned toward us. She was a very pretty light-skinned woman with a small top and large, shapely hips. Niles had always been an ass man, and this woman had ass for days.

"Don't act like the one on her right isn't up yours," he said.

I studied her friend a little closer. "Oh, yeah, she got some big-ass titties."

Niles and the curvy sister locked eyes, and from that moment on, it was as if everything and everyone in the room went spinning and faded away. I swear to God he couldn't hear or see anything but her.

"Niles. You okay, man? Niles?"

He lifted his hand casually to silence me as she approached.

"Well, well, well. If it isn't Ms. Keisha Smalls." Niles broke into a broad grin as she sashayed in front of us.

"Niles Monroe." She had left barely an inch between them, both of them standing there grinning like two fools. "Aren't you a sight for sore eyes."

"You're not so bad on the eyes yourself." The poor boy was cheesing like a little kid.

"You two going to get a room? Because if not, I'd like you to introduce me to your pretty friend over there in the purple dress." By now I was on my second drink, so if I said something stupid, I would blame it on the alcohol. "I'm Willie, by the way." I offered her my hand, and she tore her attention away from Niles long enough to shake it.

"Keisha." She smiled at me, but her thoughts were obviously still on Niles. "Sure I'll introduce you—if your friend buys me the drink he's been owing me for almost six years."

I glanced at Niles, and he nodded. "Sure. We'll buy you ladies a couple of drinks."

Keisha twisted around in the same spot, like a young girl standing nervously in front of her high school crush. "Then I'll go get my friends. I'll be right back."

I nudged Niles as she walked back to talk to her friends. "Damn, she got one hell of a doo-doo maker on her, don't she?"

"Where the hell do you come up with this stuff?" Niles shook his head, but he couldn't help but chuckle.

"I don't know. I just say what's on my mind. The women seem to love it. They say it's refreshing." I finished off what was left of my drink. "So what's her story? It's pretty obvious you got some kind of connection."

"Who? Me and Keisha? Man, Nia introduced us a while back, and we should have got together, but either one or both of us was always getting into or out of a relationship."

"Well, you obviously never forgot about her," I said.

"Yeah, there was just something about her."

"Yeah, she got a phat ass," I joked.

"She's more than just a phat ass, Unc. It's very possible Keisha's the one that got away."

"Well, don't let her get away tonight, 'cause I wanna get with her friend. You see the tits on that broad?"

Niles tapped my arm to shut me up as Keisha approached.

"Y'all want to join us?" she asked.

Before Niles could even settle the tab, I was already across the room, introducing myself to her friend. By the time he arrived at the table, I had settled between the two women, who were introduced to me as Tanya and Jasmine. They were Keisha's best friends, and she had dragged them out to celebrate—only they wouldn't tell me what they were celebrating.

"I'll tell you right now," I said to the girls. "I like to drink and I like to laugh, so if y'all don't like to have fun, tell me now and I'll carry my ass."

"Laughter is good," Jasmine replied.

"But drinking is better," Tanya added.

I thought Tanya was pretty from afar, but she looked even better close up.

Niles slid in next to Keisha. She leaned in closer and pressed her body against his side.

"So how are the Marines treating you?" she asked.

"It was the Army, and I'm done with all that. I'm home for good now," Niles replied.

"Wow, that's great. So how's your sister Nia? I haven't seen her in a long time. I used to run into her, but then . . ."

"She got strung out," Niles replied, and the poor girl just shut up abruptly.

"She was in pretty bad shape last time I saw her," Keisha said sadly.

"She died of an overdose two years ago. I didn't get to make it back for the funeral. I was in Afghanistan," Niles replied. "I didn't even find out until a month later."

"I'm sorry to hear that." Keisha placed a hand on top of his in a move that was either comforting or flirting. I couldn't tell which.

The waitress walked by, and I stuck out my hand, smiling at Tanya the whole time. "You know what? I think it's a good time for us to order some drinks."

Niles

8

"I win!" Keisha's friend Tanya proclaimed happily as she slammed her shot glass down on the table just before Willie did his. This was their second round of shots, and I was pretty sure Willie was letting her win. The two of them were getting along like old friends.

"Damn, that was close. Three outta four?" Willie challenged, signaling for the waitress to bring them another round. He draped his arm around Tanya's shoulder and turned to me and Keisha. "You two want some of this?"

Keisha rubbed up against me. "No, I'm pretty much a lightweight. I drink any more and I might not remember what happened in the morning."

"And we definitely want you to remember what happens tonight." I eyed her flirtatiously.

"So what are we doing here? Let's blow this Popsicle stand. Shit, I got a bottle of white Hennessey I been waiting to crack open for just such an occasion. Y'all wanna go back to the house?" Willie asked.

Keisha glanced over at her girl as if Tanya was the real decision maker. Tanya leaned her head against Willie, giggling. "Sure. Sounds like fun."

"Now that's what I'm talkin' 'bout. Let's get the hell outta here." Willie smiled so wide I could see every tooth in his mouth.

We stood up and were about to head out the door when a thuggish young dude shouted at Keisha.

"Yo, Keisha! What the fuck you doing here? You supposed to be at home watching MJ!" he barked. He was about fifteen feet away, flanked by two other wannabe gangstas who were at his side, and they were closing ranks fast.

"He's home with my mother. Don't come in here acting like you got ownership on what I'm doing, Rodney," she snapped at him. She was giving him attitude, but I was close enough to sense the fear his presence had brought.

"Is there a problem?" I whispered to Keisha. The last thing I wanted to do was to get in the middle of other people's domestic issues, but I stepped in front of Keisha just in case something jumped off.

"No, there shouldn't be," she whispered. I sensed that if this asshole hadn't been glaring down at us, I could have gotten the full story. "But let's get outta here before he starts drinking and makes it one."

"And who the fuck is this nigga?" Rodney asked, jerking his head in my direction.

"He's a friend of mine, and let's get something straight. I don't report to you. Now, you need to take your ass and sit it down somewhere," Keisha said.

"I don't know who you think you're talking to, but you wouldn't be talking this shit if Majestic wasn't locked up." He reached for her wrist. "Come on. I'm taking your ass home."

I snatched his arm before he could put a hand on her. "Don't touch the lady," I said, my voice laced with the threat of violence.

"You got a motherfuckin' problem?" He snatched his hand back. His shouting had caused the entire bar to fall into a quick silence in anticipation of some action. Wouldn't be the first beat down this bar had ever seen.

"No, I got no problem, but you will if you try to put your hands on her again."

Keisha placed her hand on mine, trying to stop things before they got out of control. "Come on, Niles. He's not worth it."

"Who the fuck is this nigga? Sir Lancelot? Keisha, you better tell him something before his ass ends up pushing up daisies."

I took a deep breath and let it out slowly, feeling myself ready to snap. People like Rodney always had to make things difficult for themselves. Willie saw that I was reaching my breaking point.

"Look, why don't you fellas go over to the bar and have a drink on me? Ain't nobody looking for trouble. Trust me. Y'all don't wanna get hurt," Willie said calmly.

Rodney wasn't backing down. "What you trying to say, nigga? You bitches wanna take it outside?" He laughed with his boys like it was the funniest shit they'd ever heard.

"Trust me. You don't want to do that," I warned him.

"The fuck I don't. Bring your ass outside," Rodney yelled, jumping around all pumped up by his backup.

"Yeah, that's right. Take his ass outside and fuck his ass up, Rod." The thug on his right egged him on.

Well, damn, if these dudes weren't going to give up, I decided, then they left me no choice but to give them what they were asking for. I gestured to the back door.

Keisha took hold of my arm. "Niles, don't. He doesn't fight fair."

"It's all right. We just gonna go out there and talk like gentlemen. Isn't that right, fellas?" I leaned over and gave her a kiss, partly because I had wanted to do that since I saw her, and also because I knew it would send Rodney over the edge.

"Yeah, we gonna talk all right." Rodney slammed his fist into his palm.

"Okay, gentlemen, let's go outside and have our talk." I took off my jacket and started walking toward the back door.

"Aren't you going with him?" I heard Keisha ask Willie.

I had to laugh at his response, the last thing I heard before I walked out the back door.

"Nah, he can handle this. Trust me. I'd just be in the way. "

We walked outside into a dimly lit ally. Rodney, who was standing between his two friends, didn't waste any time. He rushed at me wildly, telegraphing his punches from a mile away. It didn't look like I had to worry about any formal training on their part.

I side-stepped him, sending my fist crashing into his stomach and knocking the wind out of him.

"Had enough, punk?" When he couldn't answer, I taunted him with, "Oh, I'm sorry. It's kind of hard to talk when you can't breathe, isn't it?"

I was tempted to hit his ass again, but there was really no need. His ass should have gotten the message. Besides, dude still couldn't even catch his breath. I almost felt sorry for his weak ass.

"Now, I don't know what the fuck is going on between you and Keisha, but while I'm around,

you keep your hands to yourself. We clear on that?"
I said.

One of his boys grabbed me from behind. Big
mistake on his part, because I hit him twice with a
bolo punch aimed at his throat.

"Damn, I know that's gotta hurt," I said.

He grabbed his throat and fell to his knees.

"But not as much as this." I gave him a swift kick
to his jaw, and he fell backward.

I spun around to check on Rodney and came
face-to-face with the third dude, who had picked
up a pipe of some sort. I'd been nice to the first
two, but I wasn't going to play games with this guy
holding a weapon.

Wait for it, I told myself as he came closer. *Wait
for it.* As soon as he was close enough, I dropped to
the ground and swivel-kicked his legs from under
him, grabbing the pipe out of his hands before he
hit the ground.

"You deserve this shit," I told him, smashing the
pipe into his ribcage three times. I heard something
crack, so I was sure he wasn't getting up anytime
soon.

Click. Click

I froze for a second when I was caught off guard
by the distinct sound of a bullet being slid into the
chamber of a 9 Glock. I turned around cautiously
to see Rodney pointing a gun at me.

"Yeah, motherfucker," he said cockily, pointing the gun at my chest. "Let's see what that Bruce Lee shit does against this nine. Now, drop the pipe."

"I guess Keisha was right. You don't fight fair."

"Ain't no such thing as a fair fight. Either you win or you lose. Now, I said drop the fucking pipe."

"You ever kill anyone, Rodney?" I asked.

I think my question confused him, because instead of spouting off at the mouth, he went silent. "I only ask because the gangsta way you're holding the gun sideways gives you a thirty percent less chance of hitting your target, even at this range."

He tried to straighten out the gun, which gave me just enough time to whiz the pipe at him and duck to my left, in case the gun went off. Instinctively, he raised his hand to protect himself. I was on him like white on rice, landing a swift kick to his chest that allowed me to wrestle the gun from his hand and point it at his head.

"So, Rodney, what d'you think? Is it a good day to die?" I took out a piece of gum and popped it in my mouth to calm my nerves. Now it was my turn to show him exactly who he was fucking with.

Keisha

9

I hit the button on my phone, ignoring my mother's call as I took one last look at myself in the bathroom mirror. She'd been blowing up my phone for the past half hour like she knew exactly what I was doing and who I was about to do it with. Normally I answered her calls, but I didn't feel obligated this time, because she had refused to watch my son when I told her I was going out. I knew she was pissed when I dropped him off at my grandmother's house and kept it moving.

"You all right?" Niles asked as I stepped out of the bathroom.

I nodded, suddenly too nervous to find my voice, especially since the only man who had seen me naked in the last five years was Majestic.

"'Cause we don't have to do anything," he said. He looked at me with kind eyes, and it just made me more sure that I wanted to do this.

"No, I'm all right." I giggled nervously, feeling like a virgin standing so close to him.

He wrapped one hand around my waist and brought me closer to him, all the while searching my face for answers. "Talk to me, Keisha." His voice sounded so earnest; deep and sexy, like something out of a movie. If I had been wearing panties instead of my birthday suit, they would have been sopping wet by now. That's how much he turned me on.

"It's just that I've only been with one person for the past five years, and well . . ." I trailed off, and he waited patiently for me to gather my nerve to continue. "I can count all the men I've slept with on one hand and still have a finger or two left." I was worried that he would prefer someone with a whole lot more experience.

"So you're not easy. I know that, Keisha. You don't think I remember all those fast girls you hung out with? You and Nia were the only ones always stuck in your books," he reminded me, staring into my eyes with the kind of desire I had only dreamt about. I don't mean the "I want to fuck the shit out of you" stuff, either. His eyes were saying simply "I want you," and that meant something, because this was a man who could have any woman he wanted.

I shook my head, still unable to believe that I was standing here like this with him. "Look at me. It's been less than four hours, and I'm already naked in your shower, about to do all kinds of things." I felt myself blushing. Man, I was really ruining this moment with my hesitation.

Niles didn't seem to mind, though. He lifted my chin so that my eyes met his. "Hey, we can go at whatever pace you want, Keisha. I don't need to rush this."

I felt myself damn near melting. The more he put the ball in my court, the more I wanted him. Hell, I knew enough from my own life and from watching my single girlfriends to know that men don't just back away to check your feelings when you're both butt naked. Most of them do whatever they can to close the deal. Niles was different, and that's why I wanted to be with him.

I reached up and kissed him like I'd been imagining for all those years when I was way too young for him to really notice me.

"Unless you think I should get dressed and leave?" I teased as I pressed my body, hot with desire, against his letting him know that I would do no such thing.

"You sure?" he asked me again, although we both know he'd already gotten my answer.

"I'm not very sure about a lot of things these days, but this . . ." I slipped my tongue in his mouth and proceeded to move us past the talking stage and into the doing stage.

Niles took both my hands in one of his and raised them above my head as his mouth moved from mine to my neck. By the time he reached my ear and nibbled on it, my body had heated up like an electric furnace. He released my arms and took the soap, rubbing it all over my body until he'd worked both the soap and I into a frothy lather.

When he handed me the soap, I was more than happy for my turn. That man had the kind of chiseled Adonis body you only saw on television. This was some next level shit that I couldn't believe was happening to me.

"C'mon." Niles swooped me up and carried me into the bedroom, where he put me down in front of the bed. First he toweled me off. Then he opened his suitcase and pulled out a bottle of lotion and began to rub it over every inch of my body until I glistened. When he turned me around to lotion my ass, he started rubbing his hands up and down my inner thighs, making me moist and sticky. Then he dropped down on his knees and began to lick and suck on my inner thighs, moving closer and closer to my horny center.

Everything in me was begging for this man to be inside of me. His greedy tongue found its way to my sweet spot, and I went weak. He proceeded to lick and suck on my clitoris until my legs started to shake.

"Oh, Niles. Niles." I grabbed hold of his head as his tongue darted in and out, flicking across my clitoris. "I'm going to fall. Please. Please," I begged him, but he was unrelenting as an orgasm took over my body. "No. No. No. I'm . . . oh. Oh. Niles. Niles. Please. Please."

I knew I looked like a complete mess, but when I opened my eyes, Niles was staring at me with a satisfied grin on his face.

"That was beautiful, Keisha."

"I've never come standing up," I admitted, trying to contain the smile on my face. Man, he just did something to me.

"Well, I'm not done with you." He picked me up and laid me down. "Don't move," he said in a way that was so tender that I did just as he asked. He got a condom, and as he put it on, he started kissing me hungrily.

"Please, Niles. I need you," I purred, writhing on the bed as he climbed on top of me.

"I need you too, Keisha," he said, blowing my mind. Then he leaned down and started to lick and suck my pussy again, getting me wetter. He lowered himself on top of me, and I palmed his ass cheeks and pulled him toward me. I couldn't remember ever feeling as good as the moment he fully entered me. It felt like I'd been waiting for this forever.

I moaned and threw my head back as he spread my legs apart in order to go deeper inside of me. His hand cupped the back of my head as he brought my lips to meet his, our bodies rising and falling in unison.

He must have turned me every which way but loose, and I loved every moment of it. Instead of being fucked, I felt like I finally understood what it meant to have someone make love to me. This was no sex as a competitive sport, with me making sure he got his. I'd never had a man pay as much attention to my needs as Niles did, as he brought me to orgasm over and over again. When I thought it was the last orgasm, my body would surprise me with yet another one.

In between the orgasmic waves, he would stop and kiss me, staring deep into my eyes. It was as if he wanted me to know that he was present and this wasn't just fucking. I don't know how many times that man made love to me before I fell into a deep sleep, cradled in his arms, happier than I'd been in years.

Bridget

10

"C'mon, you black bitch. Who's your daddy? Tell me. Who's your daddy?" Sebastian smacked my ass repeatedly as he screwed me from behind.

If only his lovemaking skills were on par with his ego. Not only did the man have no skills whatsoever, but he had a teeny weenie to boot. I stifled a yawn halfway through the act. He reached out and grabbed me by the back of my neck. I took this as a sign it was time to put on an Academy Award–winning performance on faking an orgasm so he could release himself.

"Oh, shit, daddy!" I squealed dramatically, twerking my hips like his was the best dick I'd ever had.

Sebastian and I had been playing this game for almost three weeks, so I considered it all in a day's work. What he didn't know was that when he told me about his nephew Rashaan's plans to sell weapons to Iran, this had become my last day on the job.

"Give me that big old dick. I'm about cum all over you." I moaned loudly.

"That's right, you black bitch. You love this big dick, don't you?" He continued bragging in his eastern European accent about his fantasy mega penis.

As he pumped away like an excited teenager, I pushed my round, juicy ass further into his crotch, knowing it would get him even more turned on.

"Oh, my goodness! It's so big I don't think I can take it anymore!" I shouted, stifling my laughter. I knew that all my praise would make him light up like a damn Christmas tree. Men were so damn predictable when it came to sex. As long as you made them think they were the best you ever had, they were happy little boys.

He roared like some type of conqueror. "I always had a thing for you black bitches. You all must come out of the womb knowing how to fuck." He just kept up with that black bitch bullshit. If he didn't get this over with soon, I was going to have trouble not slapping the shit out of him.

"My turn now." I slid away from his dick and flipped him over, which probably shocked the shit outta him, considering I weighed 135 pounds and he weighed well over two hundred.

"What are you doing?" he asked.

Instead of answering, I grabbed hold of his balls and squeezed them in my hand just enough to get him into the whole pain/pleasure thing. I'd seen it work on guys in the past, but this fool went nuts.

"I love it, you black bitch," he groaned.

"This is how I like it." I climbed on top of him with my spiked thigh-high boots pressing against him. I lowered myself until I was lined up perfectly with his hard cock.

Sebastian's eyes grew wide as I slid his dick inside of me. Yeah, that was more like it. He may not have known what to do with that pencil-size prick of his, but I sure did. Now it was my turn to ride him.

"Oh, shit!!" He hollered as I began to buck up and down on him like an expert.

I increased the tempo on top of him, as my tongue ran around the rim of his ear, sending his body shivering in delight.

"All right, motherfucker. Who's your mama?" I demanded as I rode his little-ass dick like he was a bucking bronco.

His head was already bobbing up and down in expectation, so it didn't take him long to whimper a response. "You."

I clamped my muscles down on his dick, showing him what twelve years of yoga, five hundred squats a day, and no babies could do to your goodies. He damn near jumped out of his skin. "Say it again. Who's your mama?"

"You are. You're my mama. Damn, that felt good. Do it again!" he begged.

A superior smile expanded across my face. "And whose dick is this?" I clamped down again.

"Yours! It's yours. It's your dick, mama! Nobody but yours. Shit, that feels so good." I swear to God he sounded like a virgin getting his first taste.

"You know what, Sebastian? You're a real prick." I clamped down again, reaching into the garter hidden in my boot.

He was too busy enjoying himself to see what I was doing, so when I whipped out the long, narrow blade and slipped into his ear canal, causing an instant bleed, he didn't know what had hit him. He was dead within seconds.

"Fucking bastard. Nobody calls me a black bitch and gets away with it." His fate had already been sealed, but talking shit, well, that was just the icing on the cake.

Now that he was dead, the easy part was over and the hard part began. It was time to clean up the mess. Well, at least the forensic mess.

I removed the condom from his shriveled-up penis and then got up to get dressed.

"Fuckin idiot got blood on my boots," I snarled as I inspected my shoes. I wiped it off with a concoction I carried with me in a spray bottle. I then sprayed Sebastian's body. This shit was good, and it would break down any DNA I might have left behind, just in case some bored forensic detective or a lab rat decided to do their job and get all CSI on a girl.

I went into the bathroom to wash my hands and my private parts then threw the washcloth and condom in a Ziploc baggie, which I placed in my purse. I pulled off the blond wig and hazel contacts, then put on the tight black dress I'd worn earlier, along with a beret and a large pair of sunglasses. Even with the disguise, I didn't plan on taking the elevator or going out the front door, in case there were surveillance cameras in the lobby.

I grabbed my trench coat off the back of the chair. Just as I went to open the door to leave, my phone rang.

"Hello," I answered curtly when I saw the number.

"Ms. Saint John, this is Nadja. The assistant director would like to speak to you. Please hold." I really wanted to curse this dumb-ass bitch out, but I knew this wasn't her doing, so I held my anger for the person responsible.

"Bridget." Jonathan's voice came on the line.

"Jonathan, what the fuck are you calling me for? I'm on assignment." I stared back at the mess

Sebastian's blood was making as it soaked into the mattress. "You're going to have to start respecting protocol."

"Yeah, that's what they keep telling me. Look, some interesting developments have come up. I think you need to get down here right away." He said it nice and smooth, which immediately made me suspicious.

"Uh-huh, and what is it? I don't have time to play Twenty Questions with you. I'm in the middle of something." I glanced over at the bed again.

"It appears an opportunity has presented itself regarding Mr. Niles Monroe. Now, how soon can you get your sweet ass down here?"

"Shit, why didn't you say that in the first place? I'm on my way." I took one more look around the room, grabbed my bag, and headed out the door.

Willie

11

"C'mon, fine mama, won't you back that thing up. Back that thing up!" I sang out loud as Tanya's ass moved provocatively toward my face. As soon as she backed it up close enough, I wrapped my lips around her clit, sucking on it like it was a peach pit and I wanted to get that last bit of nectar out of it.

"Uh!" Tanya groaned as I ran my tongue repeatedly along her throbbing love button. There was nothing I liked more than eating a woman out, and this woman's honey pot tasted like nectar from the gods. My jaws were putting in the work as she started grinding against my tongue, increasing the friction until I could feel her trembling. "Shit! Shiiiit! Don't stop!" Tanya hollered

Moving my face away, I licked my lips. "You like that, huh?"

"You know I do," she said playfully. "Not only because it feels good, but 'cause it's the only time I can get you to shut the fuck up. Now, put those cute lips of yours to use and make me cum, baby."

"Oh, you got jokes?" I shot back, lifting my head so I could stick my tongue deep inside her pussy like a mini dick.

I was fucking her with my tongue so good she started to grip the headboard, her body rising and falling in ecstasy. Once I had her ass squirming around, I clamped my lips right back around her clit.

"Ohhhh, shit! Willie, what are you doing to me?" she hollered.

I brought her to the edge of orgasm and then stopped cold, lowering my head. Boy, the look she gave me could have frozen some ice cream.

"What are you doing?"

"What do you mean?" I asked like I didn't understand her salty expression.

"Why'd you . . . Why'd you stop?"

"Oh, you thought I was gonna let you get yours without me?" I joked, shaking my head. "This ain't one of them equal opportunity fucks where you get yours first and then I have to wonder if I'm going to get mine. The way this works, I get mine, and then if you're nice, maybe you'll get yours."

Tanya rolled off me and burst out laughing so hard she forgot she had been on the edge of an orgasm, which was exactly my point. Plus, I really liked that she got my humor already. She was laughing so hard she could barely talk.

"Oh, I get it. You're fucking crazy!" She reached out and took hold of my dick, stroking me until I was rock hard and ready. Then she stopped. "How about nobody gets any and I take my ass home?"

"Huh? You ain't going nowhere." I straddled her, kissing and sucking on her nipples, first the right one and then the left, until all she could do was smile up at me like I was her fucking Prince Charming. "I like you, you know that?"

"I like you too," she whispered sweetly, her eyes holding my gaze.

"Damn, you're sexy." I worked my way back down between her legs and made sure she was nice and wet before I climbed on top of her.

She moaned as my hard dick penetrated her and then I worked my way deeper inside. "Shit!" she cried out, causing me to pull back.

"You all right?" I checked.

"Yeah, it's good, but damn, you're big." She giggled, clearly happy to discover how much I'd grown in size since her first glance at my dick.

"Yeah, well, I'm just getting past the part that ain't never been used." I laughed at my own joke about her fucking men with tiny dicks, and, of course, she couldn't help but join me.

"Stop!" she said, laughing with me, until I went a little deeper inside of her and the look on her face turned serious—and pleased. "You're funny; I get it. I like it. It's why I'm here with you right now, but no more talking. You got something to say, let your dick do the talking. Just fuck me, please."

She reached up and brought my face to meet hers, and we kissed, our tongues coming together hungrily. We held each other's gaze as our bodies melted together, and damn if she didn't lock her pussy lips around my dick, adding friction as I slid in and out.

"Ummmm!" I murmured, in the zone as the two of us went at it, enjoying the hell out of this new connection. I could only begin to imagine the sex we'd have in the future if it was this good the first time.

We were going at it buck wild, both of us hot and sweaty and enjoying the fuck out of fucking, and I swear I was on the countdown to cumming.

Bam! Bam! Bam!

The sound of someone pounding at the door made me freeze mid-stroke.

"You hear that?" I glanced over at my clock radio. It was damn near 3 a.m. Who the fuck could be at the door at this hour?

"Yeah?" Despite being pinned underneath me, she tried to look out the window. Her demeanor completely changed. "You ain't got no woman, do you? Please tell me you ain't got no crazy woman. I like you, Willie, but I ain't gonna be no side chick."

"Hell no, I ain't got no woman! You ain't got no man, do you?"

"No, I swear I'm single."

"That's good, 'cause you got some good damn pussy, but it ain't worth fighting over." I was dead serious, but for some reason she started to laugh.

"Well, for the record, good dick is hard to come by, so I might have fought for you." This time it was me cracking up. It was good to finally meet a woman with a sense of humor. I was really starting to like Tanya.

Bam! Bam! Bam!

"Dammit! Let me go see who the fuck this." I hopped up and threw on my boxers.

As I walked out my first floor bedroom, I winked at Tanya, who was covering herself with my shirt. I wasn't sure who was at the door, but I was gonna get rid of their asses and get back to her quick.

When I got to the front door, Niles was coming down the stairs in his briefs.

"What's going on?" he asked.

"I don't know." I shrugged then hollered through the door, "Who is it?" Nobody ever came to this door at this time of night, so I was really hoping like hell it wasn't something to do with my sister. I just wanted to get back to fucking the hell out of Tanya, and I was not happy about this interruption.

"Open the door! It's the police!" a masculine voice ordered.

"What the fuck are the police doing here?" I turned to Niles, who looked just as confused as I was. Turning back to the door, I pulled the shade to the side and saw six uniformed officers. I opened the door immediately, because these Suffolk County motherfuckers had no problem knocking it down, and I was not about to give them just cause.

The first officer through the door, a burly, bald-headed fucker came at me, gun in hand. "You Niles Monroe?" he demanded, raising his gun so it was pointing dead center in my chest. Man, I'd already had my fill of cops pointing guns at me that day. The other cops just stood in the doorway, scowling and blocking our exit.

"Hell, no. Not me. I'm not Niles," I shot back, shaking my head. I glanced over at my nephew, standing two steps below Keisha, who was draped in his sheets, looking wild-eyed and scared.

"I'm Niles Monroe, Officer. What seems to be the problem?"

Niles had barely gotten the words out of his mouth when the cop with the gun in my face turned it on him. His fellow officers tackled my nephew.

"Niles, don't resist," I pleaded as the cops pinned him to the ground and put him in handcuffs. This had to be some type of misunderstanding, but one wrong move and this could have turned into Ferguson, Missouri.

"What the hell is this all about?" Niles asked amidst the confusion.

"It's about murder," a barrel-chested detective announced as he walked in the house. "Make sure you read him his rights, boys. We got this one dead to rights."

"Murder?" I repeated, feeling like someone had punched me in the gut. I listened to them Mirandize my nephew, who was the closest thing I had to a little brother. Niles looked stunned, too, as they lifted him off the floor.

"I didn't kill anybody," Niles protested as they jerked him around roughly.

"Tell it to the three guys in the morgue," the detective answered.

I turned to Niles. "Don't say shit until you have a lawyer." The last thing I wanted was for him to wind up another statistic.

"Can I get my shoes?" Niles motioned toward his Jordans that were parked next to the front door.

"I got 'em." The detective picked them up as they perp-walked my nephew out of the house.

"Shit! What the fuck was that?" Tanya's voice reflected the shock and horror we all felt in that moment.

Keisha came over to me. "He didn't really kill anybody, did he?"

"I sure as hell hope not," I answered, but truthfully, I didn't know.

Niles

12

"Darius Thompson, Rodney Moss, and Shakim Paul. Those names mean anything to you?" Detective Fuller, the cop who had arrested me, pelted me with the names. He was sitting in a chair across from me, waiting for an answer.

I'd been in the interrogation room for the better part of an hour when he finally walked in carrying a manila envelope.

"Nope. Can't say that they do." I stared straight at the wall above his head.

"Why don't you make it easy on yourself by telling me the truth? We know you did it." He leaned across the metal table to look me in the eye, as if that would convince me to change my story.

"I told you, I'm innocent. How many times I gotta tell you that?"

"You do understand that you're in a whole lot of trouble."

I was starting to feel like I was banging my head against a wall. "Look, this is just a big misunderstanding. I didn't kill anyone."

"Oh, yeah. Were you at Sugar's Bar and Grill last night?" he asked.

"Yes, I was, but—" I was prepared to explain myself, but he cut me off.

"So you're trying to tell me that you didn't have an altercation with any guys last night?" Fuller cracked open the manila envelope in front of him, took out three photos, and laid them down on the table so that they were facing me. "Recognize these guys?"

I looked down at the pictures of Rodney and his two friends. Or rather, their corpses.

"I asked you a question. Do you know these men?" He pierced me with a stare that felt like he fully expected me to lie to him.

"Yeah," I admitted. "That's Rodney and his friends."

"And how exactly do you know Rodney and his friends?" he asked.

"They were being disrespectful to a lady friend of mine at the bar last night. I took them outside and taught them some respe—" I stopped myself before I said anything incriminating, but, of course, he'd noticed.

"But you showed them." He smiled, nodding his head up and down like we were sharing some kind of secret.

I looked down at the pictures again. "No. Yes. I mean, it wasn't like that."

"So, Niles, why don't you tell me what it's like? 'Cause I have three dead bodies and you were the last person to see any of them alive."

"Obviously I wasn't the last person to see them alive, 'cause I didn't kill them," I countered, my head starting to spin.

Someone tapped at the door before opening it. A young officer approached Fuller and set a Ziploc bag down on the table between us.

"You wanted this after it was logged into evidence."

"Thanks, Officer." Fuller acknowledged the cop before he turned and left. He picked up the package in his hand, gripping it so that I could see the outline of a gun.

"Any idea where this came from?"

"It's Rodney's." I couldn't believe I'd been stupid enough to leave the gun behind after our fight.

"What if I told you that it was the murder weapon?" I could feel the detective watching me, weighing my reaction, but I wasn't about to give him what he wanted. I showed no response. "Are we going to find your prints on this gun, Niles? 'Cause once CSI wipes it for prints, I won't be able to help you."

"I swear I didn't do this. Yeah, I took the gun from Rodney, but I threw it in the Dumpster. I didn't use it." Deep inside of me, I was shaking, but my military training had taught me how to remain calm if captured by the enemy, and from where I was sitting, this was the enemy.

"So you didn't do anything to them?"

"Sure, I roughed them up a little, but they were alive the last time I saw them. How many times do I have to tell you that?"

"They look a little more than roughed up to me," he said, reaching down and picking up the photos to study them. "Look, I know these guys. Especially this piece of shit Rodney. There could be real repercussions to you killing him. He has more connects inside the prison system than he does outside."

He spoke like he actually gave a shit, but I knew that it was all just an act to lower my defenses. I sat there, staring at the detective, seeing my life spiraling down right in front of me.

"I didn't kill nobody!" I shouted, tired of being blamed for something this heinous. I'd only been back a day and half, and the threat that I was experiencing was as real as anything I had dealt with in a war zone.

"The evidence says otherwise," Fuller shot back.

I dropped my head into my hands, exhausted, with my defense falling onto deaf ears.

Bridget

13

When I opened the door I saw him, half asleep, exhausted but still defiant, sitting at that interrogation table. It almost made me chuckle the way these bare rooms were made to insure the highest amount of intimidation and the least amount of comfort. They were so archaic and barbaric that it was impossible to get comfortable; but, of course, that would defeat the purpose. I knew that he had been there for the better part of six hours as they grilled him mercilessly about the murders.

"Niles," I spoke, gently waking him.

His eyes were cast downward toward the floor, and I could feel them on me as he worked his way from my high black Louboutins, up my leg to the skintight pencil skirt and tight blouse I wore, until he arrived at my face.

"So we meet again," I said.

"You!" he spat out the words, leaving no doubt how he felt about my presence in that room. His dislike for me almost rose up in waves, as his nostrils flared open.

"Yes, Mr. Monroe. It's me."

"What are you doing here?" He seethed, watching me now, fully awake and fully alert. He glanced around the stark room, no doubt wondering how I had gotten into the room, especially without the detective being present. I knew exactly what he was thinking. He tensed up, studying me silently as he tried to put the pieces of the puzzle together in his mind.

"You did this, didn't you? You set me up." His rage was palpable, and if I were anywhere else, I would have actually worried about being alone with him at this moment; but I knew that he was smart. Too smart to take any chances. The fact that he was handcuffed to the table didn't hurt either.

"I can see why you would think that, because I am a woman accustomed to getting what I want, but let's just assume that I didn't have anything to do with your being here."

"So you're saying you want me to work for you bad enough to murder three men? How sick is that?" he asked, ignoring my comment.

"I'm not admitting to anything. Truth is, like the police, I believe you did it; but unlike them, I think you've done the world a huge favor. I read their police jackets, and they were trash." I moved to the chair across from him and sat down.

"I'm not talking to you anymore, so please leave." He glared at me.

"Niles, I'm not so sure that you understand. I'm the only friend you have at this moment."

"You are no friend of mine, so leave!" he fumed, gritting his teeth.

I turned to look at the door and then back at his angry face. "If I do what you want and get up and walk out that door, what do you think would happen to you? Who is going to believe that you are innocent? A discharged special forces soldier just back from the war, angry at the world, and pissed off about a girl?" I waited as the truth of my words sank in. The defeat was immediate. His shoulders deflated and he stared down at the floor. "If I walk out of this building, they're going to lock you up for a very long time."

"So I'm fucked!" he spat out.

"Not necessarily. I can get you out of here. I know a lot of people in very important places, and lucky for you that could work to your benefit. I mean, if you are willing to strike up a friendship with me, I can make this entire nightmare disappear."

I waited and watched as the Niles Monroe I had met in the hallway a day earlier returned. His chest puffed out. He was in control, and he was mad.

"Oh, now I get it."

"And what exactly do you get?" I pushed, wanting him to spell it out.

"That you want me to be your bitch. That me turning down your offer and walking away pulled your lace panties into a bunch and made you even more ruthless than I imagined you were yesterday. That you, Ms. Saint John, are the definition of a first class *bitch*." He sat back, watching to see how his words had affected me.

I smiled. "I've been called worse. In fact, I've been called a lot worse just today. But you still have not given me your answer," I reminded him, ignoring all the emotional gymnastics. People hated to be cornered, and he was no different. It was a shame that he was so furious, but I intended to use that same aggression and anger that he was directing at me, and make it work for me.

"I'm not doing it! If I have to spend the rest of my life in jail then so be it. I'm not letting you bully me into something I don't want to do." He fumed in his anger, but I was past the point of worrying about that. For Niles Monroe, I had become the lesser of two evils. I knew it, and so did he. It was only a matter of time before he accepted his fate.

I decided to try a different approach. "And what about your mother? She's bipolar, isn't she? In need of constant care," I reminded him in my matter-of-fact way.

At first he seemed surprised, but that disappeared quickly.

"She's in a state-run hospital right now, right?"

"Of course you know about my mother. You and your organization have done your homework. Find the vulnerabilities first. Got it. Bravo!" he announced without the slightest hint of celebration. Yeah, this guy was saying and doing everything that I would have had I been in his position.

"This job will provide you with the ability to make sure that your mother is in a first-class facility, with doctors who know her and state-of-the-art treatments and comfort, not this state-run, low-rent situation she's in now."

I hoped learning that he would now be able to provide for his mother would lessen the defeat. Obviously, she'd come off her meds, had a psychotic break, and had been hospitalized again. From the police reports, she'd been hallucinating and pulled a knife on two law enforcement officers.

"So this is about my mother? Wow. That is low, but not any lower than you setting me up in order to get me to come work for you."

"Niles, I am a businesswoman, and I only want what is best for my business. From where I'm sitting, this arrangement will be a win-win for both of us," I informed him. Hell, I knew he was pissed, but emotions were just a waste of time in the work that we performed, and I only hoped he'd be able to set his feelings aside and do the job. "So, do I make the call and have this all go away, or would you like to stick to your self-righteous anger?" I asked.

He glanced from me to the door, then back at me. While I waited for his answer, I only hoped he was as smart as everyone had led me to believe.

Majestic

14

After two days of being forced to wear that scratchy-ass prison-issued orange jumpsuit, it felt damn good to be on fleek again in my dark blue Hugo Boss suit, starched white Armani shirt, and sterling silver Gucci loafers as I headed to my bail hearing. They'd let my man Bruce out yesterday on an R.O.R—release your own recognizance—trying to give me the impression that he had snitched on me, but Bruce was smart enough to get the word to Andrew Goldman, my pit-bull attorney, so I wouldn't accuse him of any bullshit.

Once inside the courtroom, I turned toward the back of the room, but all I saw were a whole lot of strangers. Not one familiar face separated itself from the throng of onlookers crowded into those four rows of hard wooden benches. They were all waiting for other cases. No one was here for mine. Where the fuck was Bruce, my mother, and my baby mama?

"What the fuck! Where is everybody?" I griped under my breath at Goldman, who was about to either earn his extravagant hourly fee or my wrath. It felt good to be out from behind bars, but I needed to know that freedom wasn't some pipe dream.

"I don't know. I called Bruce last night to tell him about the hearing, but he seemed a little preoccupied. I'm sure he'll be here," Goldman replied.

Hell, it was his job to make sure that shit ran smoothly. He should have made sure my people had their asses in that front row, no questions asked. In his defense, though, I hadn't even expected to be standing in this courtroom before my trial got underway. Originally I thought I would be released within twelve hours, like Bruce had, but then twelve hours stretched into two days. That was when I found out I was going to have to attend a bail hearing. They had sprung that little gem on me late last night.

"He better be here," I muttered.

"Majestic, keep it down." Goldman motioned to the black female judge named Ellen McDougall seated on the bench, reading through the paperwork he'd given her. I was familiar with her, and I knew she didn't play. His warning reminded me that this wasn't the world I controlled, but one in which I needed to appear redeemable.

"You think this is really going to work?" I whispered to Goldman, who smiled and nodded his head.

I glanced over at John Hightower, the prosecuting attorney. The frown on Hightower's face suddenly had me feeling a little cocky. The guy looked like his shirt had been buttoned up a little too tightly, which told me he wasn't feeling all too confident about his case against me.

When he noticed me looking at him, he glared openly, but I couldn't be mad because we would always be on opposite sides, like cops and robbers or cowboys and Indians, and as long as I was on the winning team, life was good. If that cheap-ass Men's Wearhouse discount suit was all he could afford for his hard work, then I had definitely chosen the right career.

"Gentlemen." Judge McDougall finally put down the paperwork and addressed the lawyers. "After reading Mr. Goldman's motion, I'm going to need the prosecutor's office to provide a witness to corroborate this evidence," she advised.

Hightower's face turned crimson. He looked ready to blow. "Our witness has disappeared, Your Honor, and the other witnesses we have refuse to come forward in fear for their lives and the lives of their family members. You see, Mr. Moss is not only a murderer, but—"

"Your Honor, I object! My client has not been convicted," Goldman interjected.

Hightower looked satisfied that he'd landed a blow to my character in front of the judge, and he looked over at me like he was trying to send me a message with his smirk. Man, this dude was lucky we were meeting in a courtroom and under these conditions, 'cause anywhere else and his ass would be dead. I did not allow anyone anywhere to disrespect me.

The judge raised her hand. "Save it, Mr. Goldman. Mr. Hightower, due to the lack of evidence, we can no longer hold Mr. Moss on these charges without a corroborating witness," she announced without the slightest hint of relief in her voice. "So I'm dismissing the murder charges."

I reached out ready to slap palms with Goldman and let him know that a huge bonus would be included in his check.

"However, Mr. Moss!" Judge McDougall's harsh tone interrupted me. "While you may look at this as a reason to celebrate, I would not order the welcome home balloons just yet, if I were you. I am going to continue to hold you on the felony marijuana charge for which you failed to appear in 2012."

"But, Your Honor, you just said that the charges my client is being held for are dismissed," Goldman reminded her.

She ignored him and spoke sternly to me. This broad definitely didn't like me. "Mr. Moss, you've been in and out of my courtroom a dozen times, and yet again, you're skating on a technicality. While there is nothing I can do about that heavier sentence, you will be held on the felony marijuana charge."

"Your Honor, I object," Goldman said again. "My client has already been behind bars for the past two days, kept away from his son on trumped up charges. I'd like to make a motion for an R.O.R, or at least bail until trial."

"Motion denied. Due to his lack of appearance on these charges, I consider Mr. Moss a flight risk." The judge smiled, and I knew something was wrong. "I can offer Mr. Moss six months or a speedy trial, but we both know how backed up the courts are, don't we, councilor? Six months might just end up being a year, or perhaps eighteen months."

"Your Honor, this is very unorthodox," my lawyer shouted, throwing his hands up in exasperation. No doubt he was thinking about the bonus he would no longer be getting.

The look the judge served Goldman would have destroyed a lesser attorney, but he was used to being threatened, so it didn't faze him in the least.

"If I were your client, I would take that deal and not push it. There are a few other charges that can be associated with this case, such as intent to sell and distribution. Do you understand?" Judge McDougall challenged Goldman.

"Yes, Your Honor. Can I have a moment?" requested Goldman. The judge nodded, and my lawyer turned to me, speaking quietly. "Take the deal. I might be able to win eventually, but she'll have you waiting on trial for a good fifteen months, and she's not going to relent on bail."

"Well, gentlemen?" the judge interrupted.

"I could do six months standing on my head," I bragged before Goldman could say a word. I was feeling real pleased with myself.

"Well, thankfully for the people of the State of New York, you're going to do that six months as a ward of the state," Judge McDougall snapped before banging down the gavel and putting an end to my case.

"I'm sorry. She seems to have something out for you," Goldman said as he started gathering up his papers from the table.

Out of the corner of my eye, I saw someone approaching the table, and I turned to see Bruce standing there. I wanted to say "Better late than never, motherfucker," but he looked so stressed I held my tongue.

Goldman turned to the bailiff, who was prepared to escort me out of the courtroom and back to the jail in Riverhead. "Can you give them a moment?"

The bailiff nodded and took a step back.

"Where you been, man?" I asked Bruce.

"I have some bad news," he said with his eyes cast down toward the floor.

My stomach dropped. "Nothing happened to my son, did it?"

"No, no, he's all right. It's your brother Rodney."

"What about him?"

"He was shot the other night behind Sugar's bar."

I felt myself getting lightheaded, as if all the oxygen had left the room. "Shot by who? Who killed my brother, Bruce?" My little brother was a fuck-up, but he was my family.

"I don't know yet. I was in here with you until last night. I got ten grand on the streets. I'm working on it."

"Well, work fucking harder!" I snapped then quickly backed up, remembering who I was talking to. If anyone was on my side, it was Bruce. "Hey, bro, sorry. I'm just pissed." I lifted my shackled hands.

"No problem, man," Bruce replied. "Don't worry, though. Rodney was like my little brother too. I got this." I could tell by the look in his eyes that he meant every word.

"Bailiff, please remove Mr. Moss from the courtroom." Judge McDougall pointed at me. Next thing I knew, two COs were on either side of me, leading me out of the room. I was overwhelmed with emotion and seriously felt the need to hurt somebody, but I knew that I couldn't risk getting any more time, so I played it cool.

"Bruce, I wanna know who killed my brother!" I shouted as the officers pulled me from the room. "Find that motherfucker!"

Niles

15

I opened one eye and listened intently, pretending to be asleep when the door to the interrogation room opened. It had been almost an hour since that bitch Bridget had smugly walked in, trying to persuade me to make a deal with the devil. This time it wasn't her entering the room, but a six foot tall male cop who should probably leave the donuts alone. He hadn't come into my sightlines yet, but I could tell his height, gender, and weight by sound of his shoes on the tile floor.

"Hey, Monroe, naptime's over." The black officer was now standing in front of me. He wasn't wearing a gun, and even handcuffed I could have taken him out within seconds, but I'd decided to wait until they took me outside to transport me before I'd make a break for it. That way fewer innocent people would get hurt. Once free, I'd make my way out of the state and then the country, although I hated the idea of not saying good-bye to my mom and uncle. Or Keisha, for that matter.

The officer unhooked my handcuffs from the table and led me out the door, down a corridor, and into an office. Detective Fuller was in there, sitting behind a desk. To his right was another white man who carried himself like he was the boss. Both men stared at me with undisguised disdain.

"I don't know who you are or what your story is, Monroe, but you can't go around killing people," Fuller started. He sounded as frustrated as I felt.

"Not your problem or your concern, Detective," Bridget snapped from a chair in front of them.

What the hell? I thought. She must have been some type of ninja or something, because I hadn't even noticed her sitting there until she opened her mouth.

"This is way above your pay grade, and you're being well compensated to keep your mouth shut."

Fuller eyed her, tightening his lips. This guy did not like to be told what to do, but Bridget obviously didn't give a shit.

"Can we get rid of those?" She pointed at my wrists, lacing her voice with just enough arrogance for him to get the message that she was in charge.

Fuller motioned for the officer to take off my handcuffs.

"I'm going to need that gun. Oh, and any other paperwork related to him or this case." She smiled, working overtime to taunt him with whatever power she had used to effortlessly free me from his grasp. Not only did she do this all effortlessly, without a hint of hesitation or doubt, but this chick had the nerve to smirk openly at him.

He looked up at his boss, who nodded his head. Reluctantly, Fuller handed her the gun and a file sitting in front of him. She took them, but not before taking a quick survey of his desk.

"Is your notebook in here, Detective?" she questioned. I had to admit that as pissed as I was at her, it felt good to see Fuller being the one worked over for once.

"Yes, everything is there." He shot her a look full of hate. If it were legal, he would have punched her in the throat.

"I don't need to remind you that no one can know he was ever here, so take a minute if you need to double check." Bridget leaned against his desk and folded her arms across her chest as if to say she had time to wait. It took everything for me not to burst out laughing as I watched Fuller squirm.

"Look . . ." He started to protest, but one raised eyebrow from Bridget shut him down.

"Fingerprints in here?" she asked, motioning to the file.

He took a deep breath, obviously struggling to calm himself down. "Yes."

"And all the files have been fully scrubbed from both the server and the hard drive?" She continued to grill him. Clearly she had done this before. "I'll have our people go behind you, but I just want to be sure."

His boss finally spoke. "Yes. My people know exactly what they're doing, Ms. St. John."

With that, she looked over at me. "Okay, Mr. Monroe, I'd say we're ready to go." She strutted past me and out of that office without so much as a single glance backward.

I couldn't resist looking back, though, because I was hoping to see a defeated look on that detective's face. What I saw wasn't exactly what I had been expecting, but it almost made me laugh out loud. Something had caught his attention, and it was like he had already forgotten about me. He was steady watching Bridget's ass like he wished he had gotten a chance to interrogate those two round globes to the fullest.

Click-clack, click-clack!

I listened to Bridget's spiked heels hitting the tiles as we marched through the station. Every head swiveled in her direction, and few cops even bothered to disguise their interest. Man, talk about being invisible. Not one person noticed me walking behind her. Every cop, male and female, kept their eyes glued on Bridget until she was out the door.

Outside, a uniformed driver stood holding the door to a Rolls. She slid into the car, while I stood there gawking like some country bumpkin. This was definitely some next level shit.

"You waiting for an invitation, Mr. Monroe, or do you plan on walking?" she questioned, sticking her head out the door, which the driver was still holding open for me. I went around to the other door, still somewhat in shock over what this woman had just pulled off.

I shrugged. "I'm coming."

"As you can see, I kept my side of the bargain," she said as I settled in beside her. "Now, can I count on you to keep yours?"

"For now," I answered, still unable to commit to much more than that. The whole night had been too surreal.

The driver headed toward my house in Wyandanch without any direction from me. I guess she really had no doubt I'd go along with her plan. Yeah, Bridget St. John was clearly used to getting her way and would do whatever it took to make it happen.

She held up the file she'd gotten from the detective. "You do understand that this file and gun can be given back to the cops at any point."

I stared at her, realizing that I may not have a choice, but I did have certain needs she had to address before I would fully commit. "And you need to understand that you promised me more than just my freedom. I want my mother to get the best health care available. I want her out of that facility and in a private one as soon as possible," I said, laying down the first of my demands.

She snatched her iPad out of her bag and typed something onto it. "Handled. Anything else?"

"Yes. Explain to me how all this works again, and more importantly, how I'm going to be paid for doing your dirty work."

This little Q and A didn't seem to faze her at all. On the contrary, she seemed impressed.

"You will work exclusively for me, and your job description is whatever the fuck I say it is, until I deem you ready to go out in the field alone. You will be given a particular dollar amount for every assignment you complete. I would expect that if you listen to me, by the end of the year you're going to be a very wealthy man, Mr. Monroe."

The driver pulled up in front of my house, and I could see the neighbors gawking already. Willie was standing on the steps.

"I guess that's a small price to pay for selling my soul to the devil."

"So is that what I am? The devil?" She smiled.

"Something like that." I stepped out of the car.

She rolled down the window as I strode up the walkway toward the house. "We start work Monday morning. I'll pick you up at seven a.m. sharp. We have a lot of work to do, so don't keep me waiting."

Keisha

16

I was in the midst of frying some chicken for dinner when I heard the doorbell. I let my mother get it, because I was sure it wasn't anybody important. Actually, my hope was that it was Tanya with some news from Willie about Niles. As much as I had tried, I could not get him or the fact that he'd been arrested for murder out of my head.

I turned to see Tanya standing at the entrance to my kitchen, looking mortified.

"What's wrong?" I asked, wishing my nosy-ass mother would go somewhere, instead of standing behind Tanya like Inspector Gadget.

Tanya took a deep breath, as if what she was about to say was painful. "You're never going to believe this, but Rodney's dead, and so are his two friends." I knew she wanted to say more, but she glanced over at my mother, who was hanging on her every word. When our eyes locked, words were not needed, because I was sure we were both thinking the same damn thing: *Niles killed them.*

"No. Not Majestic's brother Rodney!" my mother cried out in disbelief. "Stop lyin'!"

Tanya just rolled her eyes in my mother's direction, shaking her head. We had been friends a long time, and she knew my mother was a real piece of work. "Anyway, like I was saying, Rodney and his two friends are dead."

"You sure?" I asked, not wanting it to be true.

"Sure as I'm standing here," Tanya replied, going in my fridge to grab a child-size Sunny D. She opened it and put the plastic container to her lips. "His baby mama Tisha's out there on the block, whooping and hollering like they was married."

I wasn't Rodney's biggest fan, and he sure had pissed me off at Sugar's, but I didn't want anything like this to happen to him. "Have you spoken to Willie?"

"Nah. He's supposed to call me tonight."

The doorbell rang again, so I took the opportunity to get a moment alone to pick Tanya's brain. "Ma, can you get that?"

As soon as my mother was out of sight, I walked up on Tanya, my nerves on high alert. "You think he did it?" I whispered harshly.

Tanya nodded her head slowly. "They found their bodies behind Sugar's. Who else could it be?"

I returned to my frying chicken. "I don't know. I just don't want to think about him that way. He doesn't seem like a murderer."

Tanya looked at me like I had two heads. "Exactly what does a murderer look like?"

"Majestic," I snapped back quickly.

We laughed halfheartedly, enjoying the momentary break in the tension.

Suddenly, we heard my mother yelling at someone. "Who the hell are you?"

Tanya and I rushed from the kitchen.

"Whatever you're selling, we ain't buying," Ma ranted.

I hurried down the hall to find Niles standing in the doorway with a bouquet of red roses clutched in his hands. I turned toward, Tanya who gave me an encouraging smile.

"Ma!" I yelled.

"What?" She whipped her head around and sneered at me. "I'm just trying to make sure this boy understands that you got a man."

I rolled my eyes, wanting to strangle her right then and there. "I don't have a man. I'm single and you know it."

"Um, I sure hope your man knows that," she shot back, always needing to get the last word.

"Debra, why don't you and me go check on that chicken?" Tanya grabbed my mother by the arm and tugged. "C'mon."

As my friend helped me get rid of my mother, Niles stood there patiently. He looked damn fine, even better than I remembered, and once my mother was finally out of earshot, I moved closer to him.

"I'm glad you're all right," I said, enjoying the heat of his body next to mine. "I was worried about you."

"Sorry about that. But I swear, Keisha, I didn't have anything to do with those murders."

"I believe you," I told him. "I don't think you'd be standing in front of me if the police believed that you did."

He pointed out the door. "Can we go for a walk and talk?"

"Sure," I answered, glad to get away from my mother and her wrath. She drove me crazy with her commitment to Majestic, no matter how much janky shit he did to me.

Niles reached out and took my hand as we headed down the street. "I'm sorry I didn't come straight here once they released me, but I was so tired I had to get some sleep." He looked at me with intensity, as if he needed to know that I was listening. Once he knew he had my full attention, he continued. "I also wanted to tell you in person that I didn't have anything to do with Rodney and his friends getting killed."

"Okay. You already said that," I answered, not sure why he felt the need to repeat himself.

He laughed nervously. "Keisha, I like you."

"The only thing I'm asking is for you to keep it real with me."

"That's what I'm doing. That's why I'm here." He put a reassuring hand on my shoulder, giving me the sweetest look that did a lot to thaw my resistance.

We walked a little bit in silence, and then I stopped at the corner. It took him a moment to realize that I was no longer next to him, but when he noticed, he doubled back and joined me.

"Um, you're standing here why?" he asked just as the yellow school bus pulled to the curb in front of us. When the doors opened, MJ came flying out.

"This is the reason." I took MJ's hand and started leading him and Niles back toward the house.

"How was school?" I asked my son.

"Mommy, we have to do homework," he whined, clearly not pleased with kindergarten. "I have to write ten things that begin with the letter G. Ten whole things." He sighed like the weight of the world was on his shoulders. Homework meant he couldn't just kick back and do nothing but play video games on his iPad.

"Can you say hello to my friend Niles?"

MJ looked up, finally noticing that I wasn't alone.

"Hello," he said quietly to Niles. I could tell that he was still distracted by the homework.

I guess Niles caught that too. "Why don't you tell me some things that begin with the letter G? Like, what's that next to the pavement?"

"Grass!" MJ shouted victoriously.

"Uh-huh, and what color is it?" Niles asked.

"Green!"

This went on until we reached the house, with Niles throwing him all kinds of easy clues.

"Tell Grandma to give you a snack," I told MJ as we reached the front door.

"Grandma! That's another G word!" MJ announced right before he raced into the house, yelling, "Grandma, I know nine words that start with a G!"

We both cracked up at that kid and the crazy amount of energy he had.

"I can see you have your hands full, but if you can get a babysitter, I would love to take you to dinner. And I will handle both." He was looking into my eyes with that sexy stare of his, and suddenly Friday was feeling way too far off.

"You think I got my mother here for no reason?" I joked. "Did you already forget how annoying she is?"

Niles took that opportunity to lean in and kiss me. "I got to get on home, but I'll call you about dinner."

"Promise?" I tried not to sound desperate.

"Yeah, I promise," He nodded.

When he left, I felt like I was walking on air—until I entered the kitchen and saw my mother glaring at me.

She ordered my son away. "MJ, go play in your room."

She waited until he was gone to lay into me. "So, he the one who killed Rodney!" she said, shooting me a dirty look. "You know you just setting yourself up for trouble, girl."

"Why you gotta be listening to my business?" I shot back. "All up in the Kool Aid and you don't know the flavor," I said, repeating one of her annoying sayings back in her face. "Besides, he didn't do it."

"You lucky I'm listening, 'cause you too stupid to stay out of trouble, and that boy is trouble. You think Majestic ain't gonna find out?"

"There is nothing for him to find out. We're not together. God! Just let me live my life!" I was screaming at her at this point. I didn't give a shit that she was my mother. I'd had enough of her trying to control my every move.

"Uh-huh. Just wait. Chickens always come home to roost." No doubt she thought she was giving me some sage advice, but she didn't know what the hell she was talking about. She never did.

The doorbell sounded again. I cursed under my breath when I peeked out the window and spotted Bruce's car in the driveway. Apparently my mother had seen it too.

"See, I told you. You playing with fire. What would you do if Bruce had caught that guy in here?"

"I'ma go check on MJ," I said, stomping away to get a moment's peace from her badgering me. At that moment, everyone could just go to hell as far as I was concerned. There was no way I was about to let my mother, Bruce, or even Majestic get in the way of my relationship—or whatever this thing was with Niles. All I knew was it was something that I wanted.

Bruce

17

With Majestic locked up for the next six months, it was my responsibility to handle not only my side of our business, but his side too, which included knowing exactly what kind of numbers our various businesses were doing, who was shorting us, and who needed to be dealt with immediately, permanently, and sometimes both. There were parts of his job that I liked better than others. My least favorite was dealing with all his hormonal-ass women. The only one I didn't mind so much was his baby mama, Keisha. Out of all his bitches, she always kept it real.

"Hey, Bruce." Keisha's moms answered the door wearing a halter top and booty shorts. Her big-ass nipples were standing at attention, 'cause the chick wasn't wearing no bra and didn't seem to care.

"What's up, Ms. Smalls?" I looked down at her through my mirrored sunglasses, sucking on a toothpick. "Keisha home?"

"Why you keep calling me Ms. Smalls? I told you before my name is Debra." She leaned closer to me and ran her hand over my arm suggestively.

"I'm just tryin' to show you that respect as Keisha's mom, that's all."

"Fuck that. I had Keisha when I was young. I don't want you to respect me as her mother. I want you to respect me as a woman." She spun around in those short shorts, displaying her perfect, juicy, heart-shaped ass.

"Like what you see?" she asked flirtatiously.

I gave her a quick once-over, having to admit to myself that I did like what I saw. She was a thicker version of her daughter, and I liked them thick. Too bad she was Keisha's moms, otherwise I might have stopped by to tighten her phat ass up.

"No doubt. I like what you working with."

"Then why don't you take me out so I can show you exactly what I'm workin' with? That is, unless you're not into grown-ass women," she said, challenging me.

Her brazenness made me laugh. "Nah, I like my meat seasoned, 'cause I'm not into giving lessons. My women have to know what they doing."

"I heard that!" She laughed and stepped out of the way to let me enter.

Keisha appeared at the end of the hallway with MJ on her hip. "Ma, what are you doing?" she snapped.

"I was trying to do this handsome man before you interrupted me," Debra answered a little too sweetly, and I could see Keisha roll her eyes like she was embarrassed by her mother's behavior. If you ask me, she should have been proud that her mother could still work it.

Keisha stomped up to us and passed MJ to her mother, essentially cock-blocking anything that might be going on between us. "Ma, could you put him down for a nap? He's tired but fighting it." It was clear from her tone that she wasn't asking Debra to do it; she was telling her.

"Hey, little man." I rubbed MJ's head and then pretended to box with my godson, who giggled at the play.

Reluctantly Debra took her grandson to his bedroom, but as she switched her ass down the hall, she looked back over her shoulder and locked her eyes on me. Yeah, I was definitely going to have to practice some restraint.

Keisha busted me, slapping my arm. "Stop looking at her like that. That's my mother. It's weird."

I fixed her with my own stare. "Well, your mother better stop playing with me, 'cause I'ma fuck the shit outta her ass one of these days. And you seen what happens after that."

Of course she jumped to her mother's defense. "My mother ain't one of your hoes, Bruce, so you better remember that."

"Yeah, well, she just put in an application. If she keep fuckin' with me like she been doin', I won't have no choice but to put her in the rotation," I warned smugly.

"Don't play with me, Bruce." Keisha sucked her teeth and directed more attitude my way. "What are you doing here anyway?"

I took out the bankroll of hundreds that I always kept at the ready, peeled off fifteen, and handed them to her. "Majestic wanted me to give you this and to let you know that while he's away, you and MJ ain't gonna have nothing to worry about."

She took the money and slipped it in her pocket. "So you think this is it? He going away for good?" She sounded curious, but she sure as hell didn't sound heartbroken.

"I don't know," I lied. Majestic and I had decided not to let anyone know he was only in for a short period of time, because we wanted to know just who we could trust on a lot of levels. Sure, I could handle things forever if I had to, but we both understood that we worked better as a team. "You know the system. Now that all these jails are privately owned, they always looking to keep us behind bars."

The look she gave me said a lot. This bitch was hoping Majestic was going away for a very long time. "I just want to know if I can move on with my life."

I let out a sigh. "Look, Keisha, let me give you some advice. As long as that man's alive and you have his son, you belong to him. So take this money, go get you something cute to wear, get your hair done, and go out to Riverhead and let him see his son this weekend. Anything else you got in your head is just gonna cause you a world of hurt."

"Bruce, Majestic doesn't own me," she said defiantly. "He can't tell me what to do anymore."

"I'll tell you what: He may not own you, but I bet you take your ass down to that visit on Saturday. I bet you that. 'Cause if you don't, this house you living in and that car parked out front will all be a distant memory."

She didn't reply; just nodded her head. The one thing I could say about Keisha was the girl had smarts. I could see why Majestic kept messing with her all these years. She had something these other girls didn't. She wasn't your usual girl-from-the-hood type of bitch. She could probably be a teacher or run a business, but Majestic was not down with her being smarter than him, so her full-time job was being his baby mama.

"You heard about what happened to Rodney?" I asked, getting to my other reason for stopping by.

"Yeah, I'm sorry to hear about him. I was planning on taking MJ to see his grandmother tomorrow. You heard anything about any arrangements?"

"Saturday, but listen. I need you to keep your ear to the ground, 'cause we're looking for anything that could help us find whoever did this shit. You ain't heard anything, have you?"

"Nah, I seen him at Sugar's for a hot minute, but that was about it." I could swear I saw something in her expression that bothered me, but it passed as quickly as it came.

"Well, if you hear anything, give me a call."

Keisha nodded her understanding. "Thanks again for the money."

"Anything you or MJ need, just hit me up. I gotta bounce and check out some leads on this Rodney thing. You a'ight?" I double-checked.

"Yeah, I'm good." She was looking past me at the door like she couldn't wait for me to leave.

"Tell your moms I like those shorts she was wearing," I said just to get under her skin.

She cut her eyes at me and slammed the door behind me. As soon as that door shut, I could hear her yelling at her moms from the other side. I had to laugh, 'cause I knew the two of them were going at it about me.

By the time I got in my car, I had all but forgotten about them. All I wanted to do was find the person who had killed Rodney and deliver the same fate to him.

Niles

18

"Mr. Monroe." A tall, stocky, fiftyish black man wearing a dark suit approached me from the sidewalk as I exited the house. He looked totally out of place, but also like he could handle himself. Something told me he had been in plenty of places way more dangerous than the streets of Wyandanch.

"Sorry I didn't have a chance to introduce myself the other day. My name is Winston," he said as I met him on the walkway.

"Nice to meet you, Winston." I shook his hand.

"Ms. St. John is waiting in the car," Winston informed me as I followed him to the black Rolls Royce parked at the curb. A crowd of school kids and their parents waiting for the bus had gathered near the car. It wasn't every day that they got this close to a vehicle costing twice as much as most of their houses.

Winston opened the door for me, and I climbed into the back seat, noting the irony of my situation.

The other night I was being shoved into a police car, and now I was being invited into a luxury vehicle by a private chauffeur. It almost made me laugh, except that I didn't have much of a sense of humor lately. I didn't have any idea where they were taking me, and the lack of control made me feel some kind of way. I was not exactly fearful, because I'd faced life and death situations before in the Army, but I felt uncertain. I was venturing into unknown territory.

Bridget was tapping away on her iPad. She barely glanced up as I slid in next to her.

"Where are we going?" I asked as Winston pulled away from the curb. I hated feeling like a kidnap victim.

Bridget stopped working on her iPad just long enough to say, "Mr. Monroe, I can assure you that no harm will come to you, for you are too valuable an asset to me." Then she went right back to work.

"Well, you did work extra hard to make sure I had no choice but to work for you." I spat the words out, not giving a fuck.

She finally closed her iPad and turned to give me her full attention. "I can assure you that this rage you are feeling will be put to better use. We have a lot of work to do to train you for your new position. But first things first." She reached into a large bag and handed me a thick manila envelope.

I took it, but I wasn't in any rush to see what it contained. It wouldn't have surprised me if they were papers she needed me to sign, giving her total control over my life.

"Aren't you going to open it?" She had the nerve to smile at me like we were friends.

"Ms. St. John, we are not cool, and this is not some buddy movie where we are going to turn into best friends. You are blackmailing me, and unless you read me wrong, you should know that I'm not cool with that."

"I understand, but maybe you will be cool with what is in that envelope. At least it's a start. I promise you that it won't bite." She smiled again.

Fine. I realized I was going to have to pick my battles with this woman. I let out a frustrated sigh and opened up the envelope. Five large stacks of hundred-dollar bills were fit tightly inside, along with a wallet and an iPhone.

"Still think I'm blackmailing you?" she teased.

"What the hell is this for?" I pulled them out, and I'm not gonna lie; I probably looked like a bozo staring at all that money.

"Whatever the hell you want it to be for." She laughed, sitting back in her seat smugly. "You are going to need to look and act like you are completely comfortable in the world of the rich, famous, and criminal elite. Now open up the wallet."

I had to do a double take when I opened it and saw the Visa and American Express black cards neatly tucked in the flaps, along with a Bank of America platinum debit card.

"The account attached to the debit card has a hundred thousand dollars in it," she said.

"And this?" I lifted the iPhone.

"That is an iPhone with satellite capabilities. It also has an electronic scrambler on it." She took the phone from me and pushed a few buttons before turning the phone in my direction. "This app activates the scrambler. It will give off a fake GPS location, and you will be able to make secure calls. I've taken the liberty of programming my number, Winston's number, and the assistant director Jonathan Green's number into it. Only call Jonathan if there is an emergency and you can't reach me."

"I see. What else do you have in store for me?" There was no denying that she had my interest.

"I was thinking maybe we'd give you a makeover." She reached out and touched the fabric of my suit and frowned. "You're looking a little shabby in this cheap suit, Mr. Monroe."

"Wow, you don't hold shit back, do you?"

"Not in my job description," she replied, leaning so close to me that I could smell the perfume rising off her skin. If I didn't know better, I would have sworn she was about to kiss me. Instead, she whispered in my ear, "Now, this is the part of the job I think you are going to really enjoy, if you are capable of putting your hostility aside." She pulled away from me. "And if not, I really don't give a fuck."

We spent the rest of the ride in silence. I was still fuming about the way Bridget carried herself with such a superior attitude. It was hard to imagine myself taking orders from someone like this. At the same time, the money, the credit cards, and the tech gadgets had me curious. Most importantly, I knew that if I wanted to provide a better life for my mother, I had no choice but to try to make this work, no matter how much Bridget got under my skin. By the time we pulled up in front of what appeared to be an art gallery in Soho, I had made the decision to stop fighting this and wait to see exactly what Bridget St. John had planned for me.

"So you're going to buy art?" I joked as I followed her inside the door in the alley of someplace called Michael Andrews. Upon entering, I realized that I had been wrong about this being an art gallery. Red-and-gold brocade wallpaper covered the walls. The room held marble coffee tables and a deep, rich sofa. It looked more like an old-fashioned gentlemen's club.

"Bridget, it's so nice to see you again." A dapper-looking Frenchman in his late fifties dressed in an expensive pinstriped suit greeted us. He and Bridget air-kissed a few times in the European way.

"Pierre, this is my new protégé, Niles Monroe. I need you to work your magic and design him a complete new wardrobe. Something stylish and chic, yet conservative."

Pierre, clearly the owner of the establishment, shook my hand then stepped back, eyeing me from head to toe in a way that made me slightly uncomfortable.

"You've brought me a lot of clients over the years, Bridget"—His eyes wandered over me again—"but nothing like Monsieur Monroe. His physique looks like it has been chiseled by the gods. He was made for my clothes. I'm going to have so much fun with him."

"Fantastic. I knew I'd brought him to the right place." She glanced at me and, noticing my discomfort, gave me a smirk. She turned back to Pierre and instructed, "He will need six suits, shirts, ties, and all the trimmings for fall. Another six in your spring and summer weights."

"Well, of course he'll need a cashmere coat. Oh, and I'll have to send one of my personal shoppers out to Saks and Bergdorf's for a leather jacket, boots, wingtips, and more casual attire. How does that sound?" He asked Bridget, the two of them studying me as if I were a naked mannequin. I kept my eyes on the ugly-ass wallpaper, refusing to look at either one of them.

"Sounds perfect. By the time we finish with him, Niles Monroe will be one of the best dressed men in New York," Bridget said.

As the two of them continued to speak about me like I wasn't there, I walked over to a small table where I found the company brochure. I almost choked when I saw the price of one suit. It would set you back a couple of grand for the most basic style, and this woman had just ordered twelve—plus the trimmings, whatever that meant. What the hell was I getting myself into?

Willie

19

I watched in awe from the porch with a shit-eating grin spread across my face as Niles slipped into the back seat of the Rolls Royce in front. My nephew was something else. I was proud of him for refusing to become a soldier of fortune for Dynamic Defense, but he must have really impressed them during the interview, because he told me they came back and offered him the consulting job after all. In less than forty-eight hours, he had gone from being falsely arrested to being hired by a fancy consulting firm that was escorting him around town in a luxury car.

By the time the car turned the corner, however, not only had my smile disappeared, but I felt like someone had sucker punched me in the gut. How the hell could I look at myself in the mirror after watching my nephew get up and go off to work with his hustle strong, while I had essentially turned into a no-account bum? Hell, I didn't even have the excuse of watching my sister anymore. Along with this new job, Niles had managed to get her transferred to a top-rated facility in the Bay Shore, where she was getting the same kind of care as those rich white people.

"See you tonight?" Tanya came out the door from behind me. She kissed my cheek, and I wrapped an arm around her, hugging her to me. Her sweet voice made me feel just a little bit better, but it was short-lived. As soon as she said good-bye and I was alone with my thoughts again, my mood plummeted. I wanted to try to make something happen with Tanya, but she was the kind of woman who deserved more than an unemployed, unmotivated loser by her side. It was time for me to stop making excuses, get off my ass, and get my life back together.

I got off of the Long Island Railroad in Jamaica and walked down to the Queens impound yard over on Atlantic. By the time the guy located my car and processed my payment, I'd pretty much worked through most of the money I'd managed to save up, but if I was serious about working, I needed my cab. Now I had to go to the one place I'd been avoiding: my old job a few miles away.

"Monroe, what you doing in here?" Mr. Friedman, the old Jewish guy who ran the Metro Cab Company barked when he saw me get out of my cab and enter his office.

"I thought it was time we had a talk," I answered, taking a seat in front of his desk so he couldn't ignore me.

He looked over his black-rimmed glasses and focused on me. "Sorry, Monroe, but we can't afford any more liabilities. The insurance is already too damn high. We out here competing with Uber, Lyft, the gypsy cabs, and God knows who else."

At one time, Friedman and I had been pretty cool. He liked me—until I got one too many DUIs. I hoped that old friendship would still count for something as I begged him for this favor. "I would not be here bothering you if I were still a liability. I'm getting my act together, and the only piece missing is a J.O.B. I really need to work, man. Please."

He studied me a minute before he responded. "I can't just put you back on the road. You're an insurance nightmare."

"Mr. Friedman, you've known me for eight years, and during the first seven I was one of your most reliable drivers. You told me that yourself."

"Yes, and then you fucked it all up when you took to the bottle," he said, looking at me like I had disappointed him all over again.

I stared across the desk at him, hoping that somewhere inside him he would find an ounce of sympathy. "I'm begging you to give me one more chance."

He studied me quietly for a minute, and I could tell he was wrestling with his decision. Then I saw his expression soften, and I felt a spark of hope.

He sighed. "The only way I know for you to get your hack license back is sign yourself into one of those alcohol programs and stay sober for three months. If you can do that, I'll make a couple of calls."

"Woo-hoo!" I jumped up and came around the desk, extending my hand to him. He didn't take it.

"Monroe, this isn't going to be easy," he said gruffly. "You have to complete the program, take mandatory tests to prove you're sober, and you have to attend those meetings. This is past the point of me being able to take your word."

"I understand," I said, and I honestly did. I had really taken advantage of his kindness in the past. "And I want to do it. I want to get sober, not just for this job, but for my life." It wasn't until I said those words that the reality of their honesty hit home. I was ready to change.

"Until you do that, you will be uninsurable," Friedman said. "We can't assume that kind of risk, not even for you, Willie, so I wouldn't mess it up if I were you. In other words, this is your last shot."

"I will not let you down," I assured him, feeling better and more hopeful than I had in ages.

Majestic

20

"Baby, please, I need you to come see me. I'm gonna go crazy in here if I don't see you, boo. I'm mad lonely." Some young dude was damn near crying into the phone as the line of inmates waiting for the phone wrapped down the hallway. Two prison guards stood off to the side, watching his pitiful ass, ready to react if those in line got out of hand.

I cut to the front of the line, serving him the kind of attitude that made most of my fellow inmates shake in their boots. "Get off the phone!" I growled, letting him know that his life could depend on him giving the right answer.

He bitched right up, just like I expected, stuttering into the phone, "B–b–baby, I'll call you tomorrow." He hung up and handed me the receiver as a sign of respect. The inmates waiting behind him stayed real quiet as I made my call. That was the kind of respect I was used to, and I expected nothing less.

I dialed 0 and followed the prompts to make a collect call.

"This is a collect call from the Suffolk County Jail at Riverhead," the automated voice spoke when Debra answered. "Will you accept a call from . . ."

I inserted my name. "Majestic."

"Yes. Yes. We accept!" Debra damn near shouted. She sounded pretty excited to hear from me.

"What's up, Deb?" I asked, already feeling salty that Keisha, who hadn't visited me once, hadn't answered her own phone.

"Nothing. How you doing, Majestic? I was real worried about you." She'd always been my biggest fan. "They treating you all right?"

"This ain't nothing but a thing," I told her. "What I really want is to talk to my little man."

"Oh, he right here. Let me get him." I could tell that she turned her head away from the phone, but her voice was still too damn loud in my ear as she hollered to my son. "MJ, your daddy's on the phone. Come talk to him."

I could hear my son running to answer the phone, and then I heard his voice on the line.

"Hey, Daddy!" He sounded so happy to be talking to me. I could just imagine the big smile on his face, which put one on mine.

"You a'ight?" I asked.

"Mm-hmmm. Where you at, Daddy?"

For a kid his age, I was sure that my sudden absence made no sense at all. I ain't gonna lie; it made me a little emotional.

"Daddy's away for a little bit," I told him, pissed off that Keisha hadn't even bothered to make up a lie to help the kid deal with my absence.

"But where? I wanna come see you," he told me.

"I wanna see you too, little man, but I'm at a camp for grown-ups. No kids allowed," I said, although every part of me wished he could come visit me. "I should be home soon, okay?"

"Okay," he answered, but I could hear the disappointment in his little voice.

I had to get off the phone quick before my emotions got the best of me. With all these dudes in the line behind me, I couldn't risk being seen as no emotional little bitch. "Be good, son. Let me talk to your grandma."

"K. Bye, Daddy," he said then handed the phone back to Debra.

"Where's Keisha?" I asked not so nicely.

"She's out at the grocery store," she said hurriedly, and something in her tone made me not believe her.

Before I had a chance to tell Debra I knew she was full of shit, a guard approached and motioned to let me know that I had a visitor. I'd have to deal with Keisha's triflin' ass another time.

"Tell her I called and that I expect her to be at my next visit on Saturday. And tell her to bring my son," I said, changing my mind about not letting him see me locked up. "Look, I gotta go."

I hung up without waiting for Debra to answer and strutted past all the guys waiting for the phone, headed into the visiting room.

Bruce stood up as I approached. "Hey, man. Good to see you."

We did a little handshake then a quick half-hug before sitting down to face each other.

He jumped right in with the reason for his unexpected visit. "I think I got a line on who killed Rodney." He waited for the information to hit me.

"Who?" I seethed between clenched teeth, trying to contain myself.

He looked around to make sure no one was eavesdropping, and then he spoke quietly. "Rodney's baby moms, Tisha, said he had some beef with her ex, DaQuan Braithwaite, and a couple boys from Sonny Williams' crew a couple of nights before he was killed."

This was not good news, but it made sense. Sonny Williams was an old school cat that ran one of the toughest crews on Long Island. Shit, the Bloods and the MS13s might have gotten more airtime, but Sonny's crew did way more real damage. Like us, they were also connected to the Duncan family and the Black Mafia.

"You verify any of this?" I asked.

"Yeah, DaQuan definitely had a confrontation with Rod, and your brother was talking a lot a smack. Shit, most motherfuckers wouldn't talk, especially with everyone knowing you in here."

I leaned in close. "You need to handle this."

Bruce nodded calmly. He knew exactly what that meant, even if I didn't use more plain language. I couldn't risk incriminating myself, and there was no telling who might overhear our conversation, no matter how quiet we were trying to be.

"What about Sonny?" I asked. Then something came to me. "No, Sonny just landed up in here. I'll deal with him. Either he's going to be part of the problem or the solution. That's up to him, but either way I don't really care."

"That's what's up," he answered, rising. "I'll let you know what I find out."

The two of us locked eyes. "Just let me know you handled it."

Bridget

21

I rose up from the bed, anxious to get into the shower and scrub off the afternoon's work. In other words, I wanted to act like this shit had never happened, despite the fact that the sex was some of the best I'd had in the past year. He did, after all, know how to work the stick. If only he weren't so damn clingy.

I could feel his fingers gently touching the soft skin on my ass. His dick wasn't going to be worth shit for at least another fifteen minutes after what I'd put on it, but he was one of those men who liked to cuddle. I didn't have time for that. I needed to get back to my day job.

I stepped forward, moving toward the shower to escape his grasp.

"We're even," I spat out unceremoniously, done with owing anybody anything—especially him. I stopped, waiting for him to acknowledge my words.

"For now." Jonathan leaned up on one elbow, giving me the once-over as his expression revealed his lecherous thoughts.

"For now, my ass," I shot back. "You got laid, and now Niles is mine. From this point forward, my debt is paid and we are done."

Jonathan raised his hands in temporary submission. "So how is the new recruit? It's been two weeks. He living up to expectations?"

"Better. He's breezed through most of his classes, killed every psychological exam we've given him, and his gift for languages is extraordinary. I can't wait to start training him in the field this week." I was excited about how well things with Niles had been going. Something must have shown on my face, because suddenly Jonathan's mug flooded with distaste.

"You seem to have taken a real liking to Mr. Monroe." He plastered on a fake-ass smile, but I'd been doing this too long to let him manipulate me.

I shrugged it off as he got out of bed and approached me. "Yeah," I said, "he's a great recruit. He should be a real asset to the company when I'm finished with him."

"Uh-huh," Jonathan said, rubbing a hand along my arm. "He's young and obviously easy on the eyes, but let's not forget that he's my gift to you, and just as I give it, I can take it away." He placed his hand over my breast, squeezing my nipple gently. "So, St. John, have you fucked him yet?"

"I would tell you to kiss my ass, but you've already completed that task. And for the record, let me assure you that you don't own me or control me. What I do in my own time is my business, and I really don't care if you don't like it," I snapped at him, knowing that watching me with an attitude was his favorite foreplay.

"You haven't answered the question."

I lobbed another question back at him. "Have you fucked that new assistant of yours yet? What's her name? Nadja?"

Jonathan straightened up and his face turned red as he pulled his hand from my breast. "No. Nadja's the daughter of one my Far East counterparts. She's on loan to us. Her father asked me to show her the ropes."

"Is that what you call it these days, showing her the ropes?" I snickered. "When I was your assistant, we just called it fucking."

He threw his head back and laughed. "Damn, you're hot when you get all hostile. Look what it's doing to me." He pointed at his penis, which had risen back up and was standing at attention. Not what I wanted to see. "Why don't you come back here and take that anger out on my cock? I know you want to," he murmured, running his hand up and down his shaft.

"We are done, Jonathan." I hated the fact that he thought he could just fuck me whenever he wanted.

"Does this look done? I'd say he's just getting started." He gave me a commanding look that told me I didn't have an option.

If this had been a few years ago, when I was his assistant, he would have been correct. I would have been out of options, and I would have climbed right back in the bed with him and did exactly as I was ordered. Things were different now. I was not obligated to take those kind of orders from him anymore. I was damn good at my job, and I refused to be reduced to a piece of ass. No one but me was in control of my body.

"I will repeat myself once more, Jonathan. We're done."

I headed to the bathroom to wash his stink off of me. He let me go, but he still had to get the last word.

"Bridget." The tone of his voice stopped me in my tracks. "We are never done. And that—" He waved a hand to indicate that he was talking about my body—"is always going to be mine."

Willie

22

"Congratulations, Mr. Monroe." The director of the Suffolk County Alcohol and Drug outpatient treatment facility shook my hand after I'd completed all of the paperwork and fully enrolled in their ninety-day program.

I liked this guy already. I had come into the place really nervous, but when he shared the story of his own struggle with alcoholism and how he'd managed to turn his life around to help others get sober, it put me at ease. In his words, "When it comes to sobriety, you can't keep it if you don't give it away."

"So, I will be here on Monday morning for my first session," I agreed. That was the plan he'd laid out for me.

"And you will attend thirty meetings in your first thirty days, where you will get that form signed by the secretary of the meeting. This includes a random breathalyzer test three times a week to make sure that you are staying sober."

I shook my head. "Yes, sir. I'm really looking forward to a new life as a clean and sober person."

"It works if you work it. Like I said earlier, this program isn't magic. You will get out of it exactly what you put into it. People come in here and make all kinds of excuses, but the ones who succeed are the people that take complete responsibility for their sobriety, and that includes all of their past actions. Cleaning up the wreckage of your past is the only way an addict can stay sober and have a future. Mr. Monroe, I certainly hope that you are one of the people who can work this program." He handed back my insurance card.

As I tucked it in my wallet, I felt like something had already changed in me. "Mr. Walker, I can assure you that I'm done drinking and using anything that gets in the way of me living my life. My nephew just returned home from the service, and I'm so proud of him, but I want to make him proud of me."

"All right. Then I'll see you Monday at ten for our first group meeting," he told me as I stood up to leave. "Oh, and Mr. Monroe, a lot of people leave after signing up, and then they immediately go out and have what they think will be their last drink, drug, or whatever. A lot of those people never make it back here."

"Yeah, well, that's not going to be my story," I promised him.

When I got to my car carrying the AA big book, a meeting list, and the agreement I'd signed, I really did intend to be one of the success stories, although I had to admit I was already feeling a bit shaky at the thought of an alcohol-free life.

I had been in there for a few hours, and it was close to six. Tanya would be home from work by now, and I had the urge to go see her. She always made me feel better without even knowing how bad I'd actually been feeling. Something about that girl just did it for me.

I sent her a text: You around? I was thinking of stopping by. Maybe we can grab a bite.

C'mon over was her immediate response.

I already felt a whole lot better as I drove over to her place. There was nothing better than a woman who wasn't afraid to let you know she was into you and didn't play games.

Her place was in a rougher part of Wyandanch, actually worse than the projects, but I knew it was all she could afford on her part-time salary. She was looking for another position, but it was hard out there, and she was grateful for the job she had.

I texted her again. Need anything?

I always wanted to be the gentleman, except when it came to the bedroom. Then I didn't play by anybody's rules.

Her response put a big smile on my face. Bring yourself. You're all I need.

By the time I arrived at her door, any semblance of worry I'd had about putting my life back together slipped away, and I was feeling like I could conquer the world. She opened the door wearing a huge smile and a sexy-ass baby doll dress. She threw her arms around my neck and kissed me, and I was more than happy to return the favor, holding onto her waist as we moved inside her apartment.

"Damn, girl, you're really making me miss you, and I just got here."

"I'm glad you decided to stop by," she said, grinning up at me.

"Not nearly as glad as I am," I told her as I took her hand and led her over to the couch. I wanted to talk with her, connect, and not just get down to the sex business. I already knew we were good in bed, and now I wanted to make sure I was right and that we were good outside the bedroom.

As soon as she sat down, she popped back up. "Where did I put my manners? I have a bottle of red zin in the fridge. Let me pour us a couple of glasses. Shake off this Friday thing and get into the TGIF mode."

As soon as she mentioned the wine, I felt myself salivating for a taste. Just a little taste. But then I started thinking about what Mr. Walker told me about that last drink, and I knew that if I let myself drink a glass, it would only be the first of many this weekend. Suddenly, I knew that I didn't want that. I wanted to show up to that place on Monday, and that meant not taking any risks.

I put my hand on her arm, slowing her down. "Nah, you have a drink. Actually, I made the decision today that if I'm going to be the man I need to be for myself, for my family, and for you, I'm gonna need to stop drinking. I want to get my job back, and one of the conditions is I have to complete this alcohol program for three months. Truth is, I want to stop drinking 'cause it hasn't led to anything positive for me."

Tanya looked down at me and gave me the sweetest smile. "Cool. If you're not drinking, then I'm not drinking."

"Really? You don't have to do that."

"I know, but I want to," she said as she sat down beside me again. "Besides, there are a whole lot of other things we can do together that are much better."

I found myself looking deeply into her eyes and thanking God.

"How did I get so lucky? Already you're make this decision a lot less hard." This girl was almost too good to be true. She was making me feel things I hadn't felt in a long time.

"Maybe I'm the lucky one." Tanya turned serious. "Look, I'm not some naïve little girl. I been out there, and most guys I meet are full of shit. They got all kinds of other women and way too much baby mama drama. Soon as they start talking, I can tell everything out of they mouths is just secrets and lies. Or they want to control me and tell me what to do, like I'm twelve and ain't been running my own life for all these years. I mean, it's rare to meet a nice guy. The other stuff is extra if you have a nice guy who ain't screwing everything that moves or try'na take advantage of you.

"Willie, you make me feel good about myself, and that's important. When I call you, I know you're happy to hear my voice, and when you say you're going to do something, you follow through."

I swear her words made me puff up with pride, something I hadn't felt in a long time.

I took her hands in mine. "We're both lucky."

The kiss she laid on me only confirmed what I already knew: This girl was a keeper.

Bridget

23

Niles had passed almost every test we'd given him with flying colors, proving to many that he was better than most of our agents before he'd even taken on an assignment in the field. However, I wasn't training him to be better than most agents; I was training him to be the best agent, so it was time to show him how the job really worked, or better yet, how I expected it to work. That lesson was never easy.

I'd brought Niles to the Shops at Columbus Circle, intent on killing two birds with one stone. First, a lesson on sub-diversion, and then another kind of social lesson would follow. However watching him struggle with his first assignment had me quickly running out of patience. I hung back and watched him attempt to do it again. Fail. Fail again. Epic fucking failure! Did I mention that patience was not my strong suit?

"Shit!" He seethed under his breath, rubbing his neck after a woman smacked him upside the head for touching her inappropriately.

"See, you're not paying attention." I actually laughed out loud when he walked back over to me, which only made him angrier. Like him, no one would ever accuse me of playing well with others, probably because I found most people inept. "Perfect opportunity to get that runaway temper under control, Niles. You have to stop caring what other people think of you."

"That's easy for you to say. You didn't just bomb a simple test for the twentieth time today," he snapped, though I knew he was more pissed off by his own ineptitude than by my teasing.

"Easy? Is that what you think? None of this is easy. For your information, it took me three months to master that simple task consistently, and that was after I worked at it every fucking day," I admitted. "So if you think you're supposed to be perfect in two and a half weeks, then you need to check your ego."

"Three months? Nah, you're messing with me."

I supposed I was flattered that he considered me so talented, but he needed a reality check so he would stop getting frustrated every time he didn't get something right the first time. "Do I really look like I'm messing with you? Mr. Monroe, I intend to ride you hard, and I'm not going to show any mercy, so if I were you, I would grow a tougher skin. Hell, I thought you project kids were tough."

"Oh, fuck you! I'm not from the projects," he protested. "I grew up in a house just like you. And I promise that if it took you three months to do it, then it'll take me a month. You got that?" he said, stepping up to the challenge just like I wanted him to.

"I hear you. Now let me show you how to do it," I told him in a not so pleasant tone. This wasn't friendship; it was business, and nothing bothered me more than anyone getting in the way of me handling mine.

"Let me try again. I can do it!" he said, his eyes blazing. Obviously this boy did not like to fail at anything. I really was going to have to teach my new associate how to handle his emotions. "Bridget, I can do it," he said again when I didn't step out of his way.

"Just relax. I want you to watch and learn," I whispered as I moved away from him and walked through the doors of Sephora. The makeup and beauty emporium proved to be the perfect place for this lesson. There were lots of customers, and the place was full of mirrors, with people poised to catch everything. Picking up a tube of Bobbi Brown mascara, I held it next to my eye, as if I were checking for the color. Then I walked over to three women who were basically playing with lipstick. I slid past them, leaving something behind for each one of them. I turned to Niles and headed out of the store, but only after I was sure he had seen my handiwork. Each of the three women had a tiny red dot of paper stuck dead center on the back of her neck, and not one of them had noticed a thing. Niles gave me a look like he refused to be impressed, but I knew he was.

"You have to concentrate and use an easy touch. Not everything is about brute force," I chastised.

"I could have done that," he said, pouting. Such a man. They always hate to be outdone by a woman. Well, he would have to get used to that, because I was so much better at my work than most boys.

"No, you couldn't and you didn't, but you will before I am done with you," I assured him, expecting another smart-ass reply.

"Hopefully that will be soon," he said.

"Well, if you keep fucking up, then I won't have any need for you and you can go back to jail and live out the rest of your life. I hear you can get a degree and everything Upstate." I knew I shouldn't have said it, but I needed to motivate him.

"You think you know so much about me? Well, you don't. Jail doesn't scare me," he said, his voice full of bravado.

"Maybe not, but your mother spending the rest of her days in Creedmoor sure as hell does. And as far as what I know; I know that you don't belong in Wyandanch any more than I belong in Arkansas on that little farm. I get that you're not happy with how this went down, but I don't have time or interest in any more excuses or apologies. If you want the life and the freedom that this job is going to afford you, then you have to let go of this piss-ass bitterness and be willing to learn from me. What I can promise is that you will not be disappointed. You will be prepared in every way possible for the job at hand."

I stepped away to give him—well, truthfully, to give me a moment. I really needed this guy, but there was no way I could do this without him wanting to be a part of it. He needed to commit fully so that I could help him get to the next level.

"Okay. What's next?" Niles asked as he came to stand next to me.

"Right this way," I told him, concealing just how relieved I was.

He trailed me up the escalator to the fourth floor. I stopped at the doorway to Thomas Keller's Per Se, one of the highest rated restaurants in New York. It was a foodie paradise, and this was where I planned to help refine Niles's palate. I stepped back and allowed him to open the door, and we went inside.

"Ms. St. John, welcome back. Right this way." The hostess led us through the restaurant and into the private dining room. It was here that I planned to help Niles prepare for his work with me. "Mr. Flaubert will be with you shortly."

After she left, Niles turned to me, looking confused. "You're taking me out to eat? I thought you had more work for me to do. Why are we wasting time at lunch?"

"In this position, you will be entertaining and entertained by world-traveled individuals. If you use the wrong fork or suggest the incorrect wine with a meal, it will blow your cover, and that slip could cost you your life. Those are not chances we are going to take. Mr. Flaubert is one of the best etiquette specialists in the world. He has been a butler for some of the royal families in Europe, but with all the nouveau riche in America, he does quite well here. Afterward, Andre, the sommelier, will teach you everything you need to know about wine."

"Are you kidding?" He seemed to think I was playing some kind of joke on him.

"The people that we deal with are not just common criminals. Many of them are well-bred, international criminal masterminds. In order for you to infiltrate these businesses, you need to appear as worldly and untouchable as one of them—like James Fucking Bond, if you need a visual. That means you will learn to eat, drink, and live as if you were born with a twenty-four-karat golden spoon in your mouth. Learning to love certain delicacies may prove harder than you ever imagined. Trust me. Try eating cow balls with a smile on your face. I know it sounds disgusting, and it was, but I did it. I hadn't even tried sushi when I got this job, and now, the rarer or the rawer the better."

"You're serious?"

"Yes, you weren't hired simply because you know how to kill people, Mr. Monroe. Lots of people know how to kill, and they're not as hard to convince. Your IQ test numbers qualify you to join Mensa, and your aptitude to read people beat mine, which is off the charts. So you see, some would say that you were firing on all pistons."

He didn't say anything, but I noticed an immediate change in his body language. He sat up straighter, as if he were mentally preparing to do this. I'd spent the day wondering if I had made the right choice, but something told me that Niles Monroe was born for this position, and once he accepted it, his potential would be limitless.

Keisha

24

Jasmine and I had spent most of the day getting my hair, nails, and feet done for another date with Niles. It was almost time for him to pick me up, and I was just about ready when I felt my mother's presence hovering in the doorway. I tried to ignore her and finish what I was doing, I swear I did, but her continuously loud sighs were becoming more aggravating by the second.

"Where's he taking you?" she asked all nasty and mean.

"I don't know, but then again, I don't really care either. I finally have a man who wants to take me out and treat me nice," I said.

"Well, I'm not happy about this." She folded her arms and reminded me for about the hundredth time that Majestic was her favorite person on the face of the earth.

"Look, you done made yourself clear, and so have I. This is me doing me, and I don't need your approval. If you haven't figured it out, I'm a grown-ass woman. You live with me, not the other way around. If you don't like it, you can leave." I knew that would hurt her, and it wasn't like I was happy about insulting my mother, but I was getting sick of her shit.

"Fine. But don't come crying to me when this shit blows up in your face and Majestic kicks your ass for cheating on him." She sounded almost like she was looking forward to witnessing that day.

"You would like that, wouldn't you?"

She sucked her teeth and stared me down. "Sometimes a good ass-whipping is exactly what a woman needs to get her priorities straight."

"You know what, Mama? I think you actually believe that." I shook my head, feeling a little sorry for her.

"I do. There were plenty of times I needed my ass whipped," she said and my mouth dropped open. "I just never had anyone with as much money as Majestic doing it."

I shook my head, unable to deal with her anymore. I felt bad that she seemed to totally lack self-esteem, but I was also pissed that she wanted to see me tied down to someone who would beat my ass too. What kind of a mother wishes that for her daughter?

"Can you check on MJ, since you're supposed to be watching him?" I was desperate to get her out of my face with her steady stream of negativity. Once she walked out, I cranked up the music because I needed it to shift my mood after dealing with her ugliness. Nicky Minaj was the shit the doctor ordered. By the time the doorbell rang, I was flying high with anticipation of the night ahead.

The skintight bebe dress with the dropped ruffle at the knee and the snakeskin Jessica Simpson heels I chose to wear had every part of my body on point, but not in a hoochie mama way.

"Wow!" Niles's whistled when I opened the door and he took an appreciative trip up and down my body with his eyes.

"Wow yourself," I said, checking him out too. If I had thought I was going to be the best dressed person on this date, I was dead wrong. He was wearing a tailored black suit that looked like it was made for his body.

Although we talked almost every day, I hadn't seen Niles since our date two weeks earlier. Well, what a difference two weeks make, because Niles looked like he'd been transformed into a super-model. I swear I was getting hot and bothered just looking at him. I grabbed my purse and slammed the door before I dragged him into my room like some desperate, sex-starved ho.

A black Town Car sat at the curb, an older white man in a suit standing beside it. He opened the door as we reached the car. I turned to look at Niles in awe. I had no idea he got down like this. No one else I knew in Wyandanch showed up for a date in a chauffeur-driven car. Shoot, plenty of people I knew didn't even own a car.

Niles winked at me, enjoying the surprised expression on my face.

Twenty minutes later, the driver pulled in front of The Lobster Café, one of the nicest seafood restaurants in all of Long Island, according to the critics at Newsday. Of course I'd never been there before. Places like this weren't Majestic's style. He liked anyplace with large portions and buffet items he was already familiar with.

"I hope this is okay. A colleague from work brought me here, and I thought you would like it. I can vouch for this place. The food and wine are excellent," Niles said as we looked over the menus. There was something different about him, something more confident and classy than I remembered. It was like he had matured five years in the two weeks we'd been apart.

"You're kidding, right? This is the fanciest place I've ever been to in my entire life," I admitted, feeling like the most unsophisticated date ever.

The entire dinner was amazing, like something out of a fairytale. The restaurant was on the water, and even at night I could see the ripples in the water, shimmering in the moonlight as boats passed. We sat there for hours talking, eating, and just having a good time.

Niles had ordered for both of us, and he made me close my eyes before I took the first bite. I'd never tasted food so sophisticated on my palate, words my date had used earlier when he explained our dishes to me. I tasted flavors I didn't even know existed. These were certainly foods my mother had never cooked, and they weren't on the McDonald's menu, which was one of the only restaurants I'd eaten at as a kid. The wine was to die for, too.

"That's steak? Like, why does it taste that good?" I gushed as I popped my eyes open and saw the meat, charred on the outside but red, barely cooked on the inside. I had never eaten meat that raw, so it surprised me that I enjoyed it so much.

"A good steak is supposed to be eaten char rare, or black-and-red," he told me, sounding like some kind of expert.

"I would have never ordered it that way," I admitted as I took the fork from him, cut off another piece, and popped it in my mouth.

Something told me that Niles could teach me things I didn't know about a whole lot of subjects.

All night we had been on the same page, and some-thing told me that the rest of the night would not be any different. The longer we sat there talking, the more I wanted to show him something too: me, butt naked and writhing on top of him.

"I want you," I said as we rode away from the restaurant.

Niles rubbed his hand on my leg and up my thigh. Then he placed his hand between my legs, making me want to groan. I expected him to reach for my panties, but he pulled his hand back out and moved me closer to him.

"Your place or mine?" he asked.

"Mine," I replied.

Niles instructed the driver to take us back to my house. I fell back against the seat, a goofy smile on my face, because I knew that it was only a matter of minutes before we arrived at my place.

We'd just pulled down my block when my stom-ach started doing flips. I almost threw up all that wonderful food I had eaten when I saw the black Navigator parked in front of my house. "Oh my God." The words slipped out of my mouth, unin-tentionally alerting Niles that there was problem.

"What's wrong?" he asked, but then he spotted Bruce's truck sitting in front of the house. "Who's that?

I could hardly breathe, let alone talk. All I could think of was crazy-ass Bruce seeing Niles.

Somehow I found my voice and pleaded, "Just go to your house, please, Niles. Tell the driver not to stop at my house. Please. We can't stop at my house."

Niles cut his eyes, studying me. He did not look happy, and I could imagine the thoughts going through his head. I was relieved that he didn't confront me, but instead did as I'd asked and directed the driver to keep going.

He leaned forward and got the driver's attention. "My man, swing by where you picked me up instead."

As we passed the truck, I stared at big-ass Shorty sitting behind the wheel. Bruce sat next him, talking on his phone. In the back seat were two of Majestic's meanest hard-asses, Pooh and Freddy G. I didn't know what the heck they were all sitting in front of my house for, and I wasn't ready to find out. Thank God for tinted windows.

We rode in silence for a while, but I guess Niles couldn't take it but for so long.

"You all right?" he asked, and I realized every muscle in my body was still tense.

"No. I'm not," I confessed.

"Who were they, and what was that all about?" Niles watched and waited for me to continue.

"I haven't been completely honest with you," I answered. "My son's father is not a very nice person, and those were his people in that car."

Niles's face revealed his concern and his anger. "Maybe we should turn around and have a talk with those gentlemen."

"No! God, no!" I said in a panic, feeling like I couldn't breathe again.

"I thought you two weren't together," Niles said, picking up on my reaction. He was so observant of every move and every word. If anything more developed between us, I would surely never be able to hide my feelings from him.

"We're not together, but it's complicated." My own words sounded hollow, but they weren't a lie, that was for sure.

"Complicated how?" he pressed.

"He doesn't want to let go, and he's nobody to be played with, Niles."

"Neither am I," he said confidently. I was sure that if he knew what I knew about Majestic and his boys, he wouldn't have been quite as cocky.

"Niles, those guys aren't Rodney and his friends. They're killers, and they enjoy what they do. Especially that crazy-ass Pooh."

He folded his arms, ignoring my warning. "Well, you can't duck and dodge them forever. Sooner or later you're going to have to make a stand."

Suddenly I wished I was a kid, like my son, and I could just stick my fingers in my ears and act like I didn't hear him. I didn't want to ever have to make a stand against Majestic and his thugs, although I knew that if I wanted this thing with Niles to work out, then one day I would have to.

Bruce

25

After picking up a stash of guns Majestic kept hidden in Keisha's garage, I drove out to Amityville to look for DaQuan. There was a bar called Odell's, right off Route 110, where all the dope boys and wannabes hung out. I decided to hit it up as soon as we rolled into town. Odell's was more like an institution, and I'd spent quite a bit of time with Majestic in that place back in the day.

As soon as I got out of the truck with Pooh, Fred, and Shorty, this scrawny cat with a fake gold grill standing next to the door said to his mini-me friend, "Oh, shit. That's Bruce." As we got closer, he shouted, "What's up, Bruce?" He was a little too familiar for a motherfucker I didn't remember ever laying eyes on.

"Do I know you?" I growled at the fool as I looked him up and down dismissively, shutting him down just like the maggot he was. He snatched open the door and stepped aside as we entered without saying another word. His mini-me friend kept laughing at his ass the whole time he was fronting.

Odell's was the kind of comfortable neighborhood hangout that entertained at least two generations at any given time. It had a killer jukebox and a back room with a pool table that was always in rotation. There wasn't much of an age limit, and since everybody specialized in minding their own business, a lot of shit went down on the regular.

The bartender, Harold, a guy I'd gone to school with and whose grandparents owned the spot, broke into a smile as I entered and met him at the bar.

"My man Bruce. What's going on, brotha?" We slapped hands. "Sorry to hear about your man Majestic. Let him know I asked about him."

"I sure will, Harold."

"Cool. What you fellas drinking? First one's on me." Harold knew this couldn't be a social call for me to roll in here this deep. Everyone on Long Island knew if Majestic and I brought Pooh's crazy ass out, it wasn't meant to be social and somebody's ass was about to get got.

"Nothing right now," I told him. "We're looking for someone. You seen that dude DaQuan Braithwaite around here lately?"

Before he could answer, Synthia, a cocoa-colored little shorty with a banging body and a fierce head game I hit every so often scooted up to me, poking her titties out like she wanted me to reach out and grab them. She had a man, but so did most of the chicks I fucked with. It was easier to keep them in line that way, and much less of a headache.

"Hey, Brucey," Synthia cooed, cozying up next to me, completely oblivious to the current vibration.

"Look, I'm here on business, so go sit your ass down." I didn't even bother to look at her. My tone of voice told her everything she needed to know.

"No problem, daddy." She hustled back to wherever she had come from.

Harold and the boys busted up at how under control I had these bitches.

Harold leaned close to make sure I was paying attention and gave a slight nod toward the next room. I waved to my guys, and we moved past the people getting their drink on, until we reached the back room. DaQuan and another guy, a redbone with freckles, were playing a game, while all their boys stood around watching and taking bets on the winner.

"DaQuan!" I called out right as he was about to take a shot.

He flipped the ball over the stick, causing it to land with a thud across the table, instead of sinking perfectly into the hole. "What the fuck is wrong with you?" he snapped, gripping that pool cue like he was about to do something, until he turned and saw that I was the one who had called his name. The wind went out of his sail, and he backed way the fuck up.

"Oh, shit. Bruce, what's up, man?"

"What's up my ass, motherfucker. Let's take a walk."

He took one look past me at Pooh, Shorty, and Fred, who all flanked me, blocking the door and any chance of an exit.

"Uh, for what? What's the problem?" Dude looked like he wanted to shit himself.

"Rodney's the problem. Word on the street is you had beef with him. Now he's dead. So that says we need to talk." I pointed at the front door.

His eyes doubled in diameter. "Bruce, I ain't have shit to do with that."

"You can tell me all about it on our walk," I said calmly, trying not to make a scene in front of witnesses.

"Nah. I don't think so," he said, shaking his head quickly. "I ain't taking no walk with you. I already said I ain't had nothing to do with Rodney. You wanna talk, we can talk right here." His eyes traveled the room, checking to see that his boys were all there to back him up.

"No, I think the conversation would be better outside." The bass in my voice grew stronger, letting him know that I was running out of patience.

He started to get twitchy as he spoke, which wasn't a good sign, because I was sure he was carrying a gun. "I know what happens on these walks, and I ain't walking nowhere with you."

Shorty took a step closer to him. His nickname was ironic, considering he was at least six foot six.

"Then I'm gonna carry your ass out of here, you lying piece of shit." Pooh's crazy ass leapt past us and slammed a pistol repeatedly upside DaQuan's head, causing him to crumble to the floor in agony.

"Get that nigga's piece," I ordered.

Pooh reached down and found it as Shorty picked DaQuan up off the ground and slung him over his shoulder.

"I swear I'm innocent. I swear."

You'd think one of his boys or somebody would come to his defense, but hell, we might as well have been ghost considering the amount of attention we got as we left Odell's. Nobody said shit.

Twenty minutes later at the Wyandanch landfill, Shorty dropped DaQuan to the ground like a sack of flour. We'd given him a pretty good beating on the way over, but this fool would not crack.

"Tell me the truth!" I glanced at my watch and realized I was supposed to be somewhere in ten minutes, so as I stood over him I pulled out my gun to inspire him to talk soon.

"It wasn't me!" he shouted, but at this point I was pretty sure he knew what I was about to do. Surprisingly, he sat up straight and looked me dead in the eyes. "I didn't kill Rodney. And to tell you the truth, I didn't like Rodney and was glad somebody got him, but that somebody wasn't me. If it was, I wouldn't lie on it. I'd tell you why I did it. Everyone knows he was living off his brother's rep. Rodney was a pain in the ass. "

"Yeah, but he was our piece-of-shit pain in the ass." Without allowing him to take another breath, I pumped three bullets into his chest.

Pooh knelt down and checked his wrist to see if he had a pulse. He shook his head, and we headed back to the car.

Fred spoke up for the first time that night. "Yo, boss, you think he was telling the truth? He sounded pretty damn sincere."

I stopped dead in my tracks, giving Fred a look that could have chilled the devil himself. "Who the fuck are you, Nancy Drew all of a sudden? Ain't nobody paying you to think. Just shut the fuck up and get in the damn car!" was what I said to him, but I had to admit to myself that I had been thinking the same damn thing.

Majestic

26

The library went deathly silent as I entered, with the majority of the inmates either looking past me or trying hard not to see me at all. There were the bold few who nodded to let me know that they were on my team, or at least not against me. Riverhead already housed quite a few brothers who already worked for me or wanted to when they were released, so I had more than enough muscle behind me to deter anyone from getting bold and doing anything stupid.

"Majestic?" Sonny was a tall, lanky guy ten years older than I was, and one of the heads of the South Side Crew.

I sat down across from him so we could be face-to-face. There had to be close to seven other South Side brothers hanging close by, and each one of them was now focused on me.

"Sonny," I greeted him, the whole time keeping an inner dialogue going about how I needed to keep my cool.

"To what do I owe this visit? You looking for a good book?" he asked. Rival enterprises, including gang members, usually steered clear of each other inside jails, same as on the streets, unless they were looking for trouble. A couple of his men moved closer so that they were within an arm's distance from grabbing me.

"Need to have a sit-down with you." I lifted my shirt and flipped over my waistband so he'd trust that I wasn't holding.

He waved his hands in front of me, locking eyes with his guys so that they'd back off. "That won't be necessary. Men on our level prefer not to get our hands dirty, am I right? I know that if you are coming for me, there is no way you'd come to this side of the building alone."

I nodded. Like I said, rivals stayed in their lanes unless it was something serious, and this was the way to address those things.

"There's some shit we need to discuss," I said politely, particularly because all of his men were watching, and the last thing I needed to do was show any sign of disrespect. These young cats, like my brother Rodney, had to learn that there was a protocol that needed to be followed if we were to coexist.

Sonny motioned to me, and I followed him out of the library and into the long corridor. "Let's go somewhere we can have privacy." The two of us headed through the heavy door and into the common area that led to our cells. By the time we reached his cell, damn near everybody in the jail had heard about our meeting. I had to give it to Sonny; he definitely protected his back with this move. If he wound up dead or injured, the first person they fingered would be me.

A big, burly motherfucker about my size, with death in his eyes and ham hocks for hands, sat up from the bottom bunk when we entered. You know it's real when you got your own bodyguard as your cellmate. I wasn't sure what Sonny was in for, but he must have been expecting a long stretch.

"Eddie, give us a moment." And just like that, Eddie humped his gigantic ass out of there, leaving us alone.

Sonny sat down on the bed and offered me a chair.

I sat down and began, "Not sure you heard, but my little brother Rodney was killed recently."

"Yeah, I'm sorry to hear about your brother," he responded, not taking his eyes off of me. "He talked a lot of shit he couldn't back up, but so does my son Troy. These young kids are gonna be the death of us."

"Tell me about it. But speaking of your son, doesn't he hang out with that kid DaQuan?"

Sonny's eyebrows shot up. "Yeah, they're friends. What about it?"

"Word on the street is that DaQuan and one of his partners killed my brother," I told him, trying to keep any trace of anger out of my tone.

"I can't speak for DaQuan, but I can assure you that none of my people or my son hit your brother. Unless, of course, there was a personal beef between your brother and some of my people that I am not aware of that could have escalated."

I wanted to call bullshit on his answer, because there wasn't much a boss didn't know about his underlings. People climbing the ladder loved to rat out their comrades in the hope of rising above them.

"If you want, I can talk to Troy and DaQuan to see if they had anything to do with it. I can make that happen."

"Sonny, there ain't no talking to DaQuan. My man Bruce took him out last night." I leaned my chair against the wall, letting him digest what I had said. "The only real question is, was your son Troy involved? And if he was, am I going to kill him or not?" Sonny studied my face. I made sure my expression left no doubt about how serious I was.

"Are you threatening me, Majestic?" He sounded concerned.

"No, you've known me long enough to know I don't make idle threats. I'm asking you, Sonny, because Vegas Duncan asked me to, and also because I'm sure you know the truth. Now, did your boy have anything to do with my brother's death?"

"No," he said, not with fear or concern, but with certainty. "He didn't have anything to do with it because he's a coward. My son is a straight-up pussy. He may hang with thugs like DaQaun, but he doesn't have the stomach to do what they do."

Well, that wasn't the answer I had expected to hear. "A'ight, I'm gonna accept that for now, but, Sonny, if I find out different, Troy's a dead man, and so are you." I got up from my seat and walked out of his cell but before I left I said, "Oh and Sonny, we are not on the same level."

Niles

27

I'd just arrived on the steps of the New York Public Library, and between the building and the grounds, it was teeming with people. I actually smiled when I saw Bridget sitting next to the cement pillar that held up the lion. After spending the weekend with Keisha, I had a newfound respect for how money could change one's life and the advantages of working with Bridget and Dynamic Defense.

"Look at you, all happy and spry. You look ready for work," Bridget said, handing me a cup of coffee. "I guess getting laid agrees with you, although you might wanna get an upgrade. Keisha's a little ghetto for the image we're trying to give you, don't you think? Not to mention she carries a lot of baggage."

Bridget's words caught me off guard, stealing a little bit of my joy. How the hell did she know about Keisha? I was pissed off at the thought that my employers were still watching my every move, but I recovered quickly, remembering who and what I was dealing with. Looking up at her nonchalant expression, I came to the conclusion that I didn't even want to get into it with her, so I ignored her prying into my private life so I could concentrate on the work at hand.

"Yeah, I gave it a lot of thought. I'm ready to do what I need to do to get the job done."

"Good. You have a lot of potential, Niles. Let's put it to good use." She stood up, and I followed her down the steps and into the park, where lots of people were having lunch or moving through the park to get to their next destination. She found a bench, and we both climbed up and sat on the top.

"All right, so what are we doing? Surveillance, botany, bird watching?" As far as I could see, nothing was happening, but then again, you could never tell with Bridget. She was like Mr. Miyagi from *The Karate Kid* with her unorthodox teaching methods.

Bridget reached in her pocket and pulled out a sheet with a bunch of blue dots on it. I looked down at the dots, the only test I just could not pass for some reason.

"It's been a month. Time for you to put your money where your mouth is. That is, if you think you can do it." She smirked at me, which only made me more intent on getting it right, just to wipe that look off her face.

"How about a thousand dollars?" she challenged.

I took a deep breath then cracked my neck as I stretched, biting my bottom lip. "Make it two thousand and you've got a bet." I took out a piece of mint gum and stuck it in my mouth like I didn't have a care in the world. Inside, I was hoping I wasn't about to lose two thousand hard-earned dollars.

"You're awfully confident." She looked pleased.

"I've been practicing."

"Humph! Okay, let's see what you got. So, you see those three women right there?" I followed her eyes until I saw three twenty-somethings off in the distance moving toward us. She handed me the paper. "Let's see if you can hit the target at least once without being detected. Hit two and you win the bet."

I took the paper. "Nah, I'm gonna hit all three or you win the bet," I told her then got up and slowly moved in their direction.

I made a subtle motion toward the long-legged redhead dressed in an attention- getting black mini skirt and motorcycle boots. It happened to be one of those beautiful spring days in New York, when it hit 80 degrees and everybody got half naked in Central Park. People were out in full force to soak up the sun, especially the suits taking a lunchtime stroll before they headed back inside the stale-aired office buildings off the park.

I palmed the tiny blue circle and moved stealthily through the crowd, until I was right next to them. Swiping my arms up, I grazed the back of her neck before bringing my hands back to my sides. *Yeah, I got this,* I thought as the woman turned and checked me out, no doubt alerted by my close proximity. Instead of ignoring them, I smiled flirtatiously and moved closer.

"Afternoon, ladies." I smiled wide, like I was about to ask one of them to the prom. "Beautiful day, isn't it?"

Their flirtatious smiles told me they had no inkling of what had just happened. "Y'all have a nice day," I said as I passed by them. I leaned against a tree and watched as they passed Bridget, who got up from the bench, cracking the fuck up.

"What the hell am I going to do with you?" she asked, still chuckling. Not only did I hit the target behind one woman's neck, but I also put stickers on each of the nipples of the second woman, and right between the crease of the third woman's camel toe.

"How about you pay me?" I laughed, sticking out my hand.

"How about I give you something better than two grand?" She smirked seductively.

Ten minutes later, we were in the Rolls, headed west on the Henry Hudson Parkway toward the George Washington Bridge.

"Where we going now?"

"Well, remember how I said you are going to need a complete makeover?" she asked, giving me a once-over that made me feel uncomfortable. I thought I was killing it in my new custom-made suit.

"Yes?" I hesitated to say more, wondering if this was going to be something I liked—not that it mattered, because I knew I didn't have a say in the matter.

"Let's just say that what I'm about give you is very personal and will make you happier than you've been in years," she answered cryptically before turning her attention to her iPad.

We crossed the GW and got on Route 1–9, into the heart of New Jersey. When we exited, I glanced over at Bridget, who looked way too pleased with herself. She still said nothing to me, until we pulled into a BMW dealership.

"Winston and I can't drive you everywhere, so I think it's time we got you some wheels," Bridget informed me when she finally spoke.

She exited the car, leaving me with my mouth hanging open. I got out and headed straight for the M3 convertible in cherry red, the dream mobile parked in a sea of Beamers. I ran my hands over the pristine paint job, noting the fine lines and excellent workmanship. Damn, if those Germans didn't know what the hell they were doing, 'cause this ride was tight. It made me wonder what the next test would be as I started running possible scenarios in my head.

"This is me," I boasted to Bridget, who had followed me over and was watching me with a pleased expression.

"You like that?" she teased. "You would really look good in it. That is, if you were getting the kind of car that made every single person you passed stop and stare." Her tone told me everything I needed to know.

"But it's fast and powerful. With a car like this, I can do damn near anything you need," I pressed, not ready to let my dream die.

"Attention is good, but you must attract the proper attention at the proper time. Always remember, class over flash. You remember that, and you'll be able to fit in everywhere. Go back to your sniper days. Would you want the enemy to notice you before you took the shot, or do you want to blend into the background? Like a sniper, in our line of work, that can be the difference between life and death." Her words were sobering because I knew they were true. There was no way I could fly under the radar in that car. Damn.

She waved to a well-dressed salesman and then motioned me over to a black 750i sedan, the mack daddy of cars. Whatever temporary loss I was feeling about that red car dissipated as I slipped inside this baby. Yeah, now this was everything: luxury, style, class, and a whole lot of power.

"We'll take this one. When can we pick it up?" Bridget asked the salesman as she opened the car door so I could slide in. "You've done well today, Mr. Monroe, and you deserve this car, but you still have a lot to learn."

"Yeah, I can see that," I replied, gripping the steering wheel.

Whatever this new world was I had just entered, it happened to be a hell of a lot more high-end than I was used to, but something told me getting used to luxury would be the easy part. Eventually I'd have to start killing people.

Keisha

28

"What do you think about this color?" I held up a body-hugging sea green dress for Tanya to give me a yeah or nay before I tried it on. She had her hands full, carrying the pile of clothes I had asked her to hold for me while I grabbed one more dress.

She leaned in to get a better look. "I like it, but you need to try it on. It's not about how it looks on the hanger. It's about making sure your man wants it on the floor."

"You got that right." I said in agreement as I headed into the dressing room. "Tanya, pick something out," I called out through the door. "Aren't you and Willie going out tonight? I'm sure he wants to see you all turned up."

"Well, he's going to have to settle for something out of my closet," she said in a snippy way that I didn't take personally because I knew she was stressed about money. "The way they keep fucking with my hours at that job, before I know it there won't be no hours left. Last week they cut me from forty to twenty-five, and now they're threatening to cut me even more. I don't know how I'm going to keep my place unless I find some other job."

I stepped out of the room in the dress, now more worried about my friend than how the dress fit me.

"That looks good on you." She beamed at me.

Tanya was the hardest working friend I had, so it pissed me off that the people at her job were taking advantage of her. She had loved taking care of people ever since we were little, so it made sense when she decided to go to school and get an associate degree as a medical assistant. She thought it would guarantee her steady employment, but I guess not.

"Let me treat you to a new outfit, and we'll get our hair and nails done. The whole thing," She was one of the few people I knew who never let anybody do things for her. She was the opposite of a gold digger.

Just like I expected, she shut me down. "Keisha, I can't let you go buying me things."

I cut my eyes at her. "Why? It ain't like it's even my money," I said with a laugh.

"Yeah, well, Majestic wouldn't take kindly to you spending his money on me. That money's for you and MJ."

"I ain't answering to him, and once this is gone, I'm not taking any more money from him. Besides, I don't hardly go nowhere anyway. You can be the first woman he spends money on who's not fucking him. Let me do it for once. Please," I begged. Tanya had always had my back for real, and right now she needed to be reminded how important she was to me.

She didn't look convinced. "Are you sure?"

"Yeah. Now, just pretend for five minutes that you're one more money-hungry chick," I joked.

"If I was, I certainly wouldn't be going all crazy for Willie, 'cause he ain't got a dime." She laughed. "But I really like him."

"Well, if he's anything like his nephew, he's a keeper. I wonder where they're taking us tonight."

I glanced over at Tanya when she didn't answer and saw that same worried look on her face she used to get when we were teenagers and had stayed out past our curfew. It started to make me nervous, so I asked her, "What?"

"Now, don't get mad. I'm not trying to ruin your excitement, but aren't you even remotely worried about Majestic finding out about Niles?"

"Fuck him. Hopefully they'll keep him in the jail for the next twenty years. Just because I have his baby doesn't mean that he can control my life," I said, taking a stronger stance because there was no way he could get to me. "Don't worry. I'm gonna tell him that we're over, and I mean it."

"We both know he's not try'na hear that. Let's face it. Majestic is cray-cray, and he's not going to let you ride off into the sunset with some other Negro," Tanya said ominously.

I shuddered, but I shook my head defiantly. "Niles is the best thing that's happened to me in a long time. I'm not about to let nobody, including my baby daddy, ruin it."

"You realize we're not talking about some nice, sane guy with common sense? We're talking about crazy-ass, shoot-and-ask-questions-later Majestic and his Deputy Dog, Bruce. Oh, and lets not even bring Pooh into the mix."

"Yes, I know." I sat down in the dressing room and stared at her. "I can't just walk away from this. I'm falling in love with Niles. I know you probably think it's too soon, but it's like I've always been in love with him. I'm not ready to give him up."

Tanya stared at me. "Maybe you won't have to. Maybe Majestic will fall madly in love with one of those other women he's with and let you go. Maybe he'll get somebody else pregnant."

I shook my head. "He won't do it. Over the last year, I've heard stories of women trying to get knocked up by him, but he's smart. For some reason, he chose me to bear his child. While we were dating, he begged me to have his baby. If I had known he was fucking all those hoes, I would have never agreed to it, but you know how charming he can be when he wants something. He made me think I was the only woman in the world and not just the one at the front of his harem. With Niles, I would never worry about him cheating."

"I know. That's how I feel about Willie. He's so kind and interested in my life. He says he wants to help me, even though you know I won't let him. It's really nice to have a man want to put that kind of focus on only me."

"Course I know your ass wouldn't take it." I laughed at her. Tanya was such a good girl.

"Well, if we're married, that's different," she said as calmly as if she were discussing accessories for our dresses.

"Marriage?" I shouted out in total shock.

"Well, there is something about him. I don't know. It's just that when I look down the road, I can see a future with him," she said, grinning like a lovesick teenager.

"Me too. That's how I feel when I think about Niles," I said quietly, but instead of being excited, I was starting to feel a sense of dread.

Bruce

29

I entered Phil's barbershop on Straight Path in Wyandanch, stepping right into the barber's chair. My boys Fred and Pooh posted up in two chairs on either side of the shop, while Shorty stood by the door.

"You want the regular?" Eddie, my barber, checked as he tied a smock around my neck to catch the hair. I'd been coming to Phil's ever since I was six years old. My moms would drag me down there every Saturday so he could cut all my hair off. Back then Phil, the owner, was the only barber. Funny thing is, I ain't let Phil touch my hair since he fucked up Majestic's fade when I was thirteen, but me and his son Eddie have been strong ever since.

"You know what?" I told him. "Take just a little more off the top. I been so busy I can't get here as often."

"Okay. So how's Majestic holdin' up? I was real sorry to hear about his brother. Please send him my condolences," Eddie said.

"Yeah, he took Rodney's death real hard. It's tough for him not being around for his family, especially at a time like this, but he's all right. Quiet as it's kept, his sentence just got reduced. He'll be home sooner than you think."

"That's good. Real good. Folks start to act up when they think they can get away with it. I'm glad he's coming back. Hell, you two are my best customers," Eddie gushed.

Shit, when Majestic was out, Eddie would clear the shop whenever we came in. Of course, the way Majestic tipped him made it worth it. We could talk business in the shop, and nothing ever got out. Eddie was a real stand-up guy.

"Yeah, he's gonna need your skills as soon as he's released. You know he likes to keep it together," I said, giving Eddie a fist bump.

"Hell, all the pussy that guy gets, I don't blame him." He laughed. "Don't want to have it in your beard and shit."

We both looked up when a disheveled woman in her early forties came into the barbershop. Shorty stopped her, but we could both hear her getting loud with him. Raised voices always caught my attention. You had to be ready in case some shit jumped off. Shorty, convinced she wasn't a problem, left the woman and came over to us.

"Yo, that lady says she needs to talk to you, Bruce. Something about she knows who really killed Rodney. What should I do?" he asked me.

I glanced in the mirror at Pooh, who was waiting for my response. I nodded, and Pooh sent Shorty over to retrieve her. Girlfriend looked tired, like she had just aged a decade. She had bags under her eyes, and they were red and puffy-looking, along with a real sadness. She looked like she might be on that shit.

"Ok, ma, what's this about you knowing who killed Rodney?" I already knew who killed Rodney, but I wanted to hear her out. I raised my hand to tell Eddie to give me a moment before I addressed this crazy-looking bitch.

"That I can't say, but I know who didn't kill him, and that's DaQuan Braithwaite," she said. Her voice was a bit shaky, like she was fighting to hold it together. I glanced at Shorty, giving him a *What the fuck is this shit?* look.

"Is that right?" I sneered, about to tell her to get the fuck out of my face, but no matter how old I got, I didn't like disrespecting women that were close to my mother's age.

Immediately her expression hardened. "You fucking killed him, didn't you?" she screamed, making me sit straight up in the barber's chair.

"I didn't kill Rodney!"

"No, you killed DaQuan. Everybody knows that, and the whole damn block is talking about it. Said you blame him for killing that boy Rodney that lives over on Eighteenth."

"I hear you. Now, do you have any proof, or are you just coming at me with some bullshit rumors? 'Cause I can't do nothing about rumors!" I said, returning her glare. She was really starting to piss me the fuck off.

"Well, for your information, that was three weeks ago, and my boy could not have killed nobody three weeks ago," she insisted.

"Look, I know how it is. No mother wants to think the worst of her own kid, and you're not any different. I'm sure that since your son was dealing drugs, there were a whole lot of people who wanted to see him dead. Drug dealers make a lot of enemies in their line of work." I turned to Shorty. "Will you get her the fuck out my face?"

I turned away from her. At least that way she could slink out with some semblance of her dignity.

"But my son was not around that day. He wasn't. I swear!" she shouted, grabbing my arm desperately to get my attention.

I snatched my arm away and turned back to her. "What you try'na say? 'Cause you ain't said nothing that makes me convinced that your son is the only innocent dead man in Wyandanch," I snapped at her. "How can you be so damn sure that your drug dealing son wasn't a murderer?"

"I know because he was stuck on Rikers Island. They caught him with some weed, and it took me over a week to get the money to post his bail. Rodney was killed on the eighth, and my son was locked up on the seventh and didn't get out until the tenth—the same day you killed him. So it couldn't have been him."

She reached into her waist to grab something and came out with a pistol. Shorty jumped up and snatched the gun out of her shaking hand. It made her fall back and down to the ground. I was about to get up and stomp the bitch, but Eddie raced over, grabbing the woman up then putting on quite the show.

"You crazy bitch! What the fuck is wrong with you? Trying to kill somebody in my place of business. Get out! Get the hell out of here! And don't you ever come back! You stupid whore!" Like I said, he put on quite the show, and probably saved her fucking life. I'm just not sure if he did it for the woman's sake or the sake of his shop, but he shoved her out the door.

She left, but not before turning her attention onto me one last time. "You murderer! You will pay for this!"

I pointed my finger as I eased back in the chair. "And you better leave before your ass is joining your son, bitch!"

Keisha

30

"Morning, beautiful." Niles awakened me with a gentle kiss on the lips after a phenomenal night of sex, which can only be described in further detail as epic.

"Good morning." I kissed him back, opening my eyes to take him in. He was standing there looking sexy as hell in a fluorescent green-and-black tank top and black running shorts. "How long have you been up?"

"I don't know. Probably since around five. I wanted to get in a workout and a run on the beach before we head home."

I stared at him in amazement. A run and a workout after the work we put in last night. Damn, I really was dating Superman.

"Does this mean we gotta go home?" I groaned, hating that our fantasy vacation weekend was ending so soon.

Niles had surprised me with a weekend getaway to a luxury resort on the edge of Montauk. Now, don't get me wrong; I'd been to nice places before, but no place compared to this.

"We can come back anytime you want. Just say the word," he told me.

"Promise?" I wanted to pinch myself that I was here with this guy telling me it didn't have to be a one-shot deal.

He ordered a room service breakfast and then took my hand. "C'mon. Let's take a shower." He led me into the bathroom, then into the shower, and of course, we made love. By the time we'd toweled off and were wrapped in our thick white robes, the busboy arrived with our breakfast. One bite of the Belgian waffles and lobster hash, along with a taste of Niles's steak and eggs had me fiending for our next visit.

"I want to take you somewhere special," Niles said cryptically. It didn't matter where, as far as I was concerned, because at this point, I would go anywhere with him.

He led me out of the room and down the stairs of the beachfront hotel, and in a moment we were walking barefoot on the sand. I was feeling like someone out of one of those romantic movies. The entire weekend had been perfect. We barely talked as we strolled the private beach, taking in the beauty of our surroundings.

I played the details of our weekend over in my head. I couldn't believe that I lived ninety minutes away and had never come out here. I assumed only the rich got to enjoy this place, but Niles had reminded me earlier that the view was free. It didn't take nothing but a car and some gas to get here.

"Um!" I closed my eyes for a split second so that when I reopened them, the view would be even that much more electric. "I could stay here forever."

"Yeah, me too." He tugged on my hand. "It's this way."

We began to walk up a path to a place called the Wellness Center. For a minute I thought it was some kind of spa, until I noticed that it was a fancy medical facility. Niles led me through the building and down the hall, stopping outside a room. He opened the door, and the first person I saw was Willie, sitting next to a window. Jesus, did he have some kind of breakdown? Poor Tanya. I wondered if she knew.

"Where's . . . Ma!" Niles called. Before Willie could say anything, Niles's mother came out of the bathroom. Even though it had been years since I'd seen her, I would have recognized her anywhere.

"Who's this?" She pointed to me. I moved further into the room to stand close to Niles, and suddenly I felt a little self-conscious.

Willie answered for Niles. "That's Keisha. You know Keisha. She was a friend of Nia's when they were in high school. You remember?"

She motioned for me to come closer.

"Oh, yeah. I remember you. You were that nice girl, but your mother was a hoochie-mama," she said. She had insulted my mother, but it was weird because her tone was so kind, like she didn't even realize it was a rude thing to say. I didn't take offense, because I knew that Niles's mother had some issues, but I also knew she had a good heart.

"I'm sorry to hear about Nia," I said. "She was a nice girl. Sometimes, especially where we come from, people are just waiting to take advantage of nice girls. It wasn't your daughter's fault. She just fell in with the wrong crowd and we lost touch."

She placed her hand over mine. "Honey, I'm glad you got out all right," she said, and my heart broke a little. As much as I loved my mother for being my mother, she was nothing like Niles's mom.

"Yeah, I think your son is glad, too, from that smitten look on his face." Willie chimed in, making us all laugh—except Niles.

"So, you like it in here?" Niles checked with his mom.

She took a look around. "Well, if I had to be in one of these places, this is the nicest one I've ever seen. The food is real good, and the doctors come and see me every day. I see the same doctors every day, so I don't have to keep explaining my case. That's real nice."

"Good. I'm happy. As long as they're treating you well, that's all I want. Willie, can I talk to you a minute?" He excused himself, and then the two of them stepped outside.

"So, tell me, Keisha. You like my son as much as he likes you?" Niles's mother came straight out and asked me.

I nodded. "Yeah, I like him a lot. He's different than the other guys I've dated. A real gentleman," I told her.

"Yeah, he's always been special," she agreed, but not like she was bragging on her son, just telling the truth.

"Yeah, and he's real good with my son, too." I gushed about him, but I couldn't help it, because that man had my nose wide open.

"You have a son? How old is he?"

"MJ is five. He's the love of my life." I pulled out my phone and scrolled through to show her pictures.

"That's a cute boy. Reminds me of Niles at that age. I'm glad. My son has always been so serious.

He needs someone to remind him to slow down. Kids will do that."

"Yeah, I like them together," I said. "Can I bring you anything? I can bring magazines, books, food? Anything. I don't live that far away."

"You just take care of my son, and when I get out of here, I expect to meet this MJ."

Niles and Willie came back. "What are you two talking about?" Niles asked with a little playful suspicion in his voice.

Before I could answer, his mother spoke up. "We were having girl talk. I like her." She pointed to me. "I like her a lot."

Niles took my hand. "Me too, Mom. I like her a lot too."

Willie rolled his eyes. "Keisha, you better not mess this up, 'cause my sister don't think anybody is good enough for her son." He and Niles started laughing, and I couldn't remember the last time I'd felt this good.

Niles

31

"I want you to look at these pictures, pick out your target, and handle your business without anyone knowing you did it. Do you understand?" Bridget said sternly, handing me an envelope as we exited the car on Fourteenth Street.

I opened the envelope and glanced down at the pictures, memorizing the face of the individual before handing back the envelope. I'd been training with Bridget for almost three months now, and although I hated to give her credit, I'd be lying if I said she hadn't taught me a hell of a lot.

She instructed her driver to meet us a couple of stops away, so I followed her down into the crowded subway station and onto the F train platform. This was supposed to be my final exam from her one-woman boot camp. Pass this test and I'd be a full-fledged agent for the firm.

Once on the platform, I reached into my pocket and pulled out the pack of gum I always kept on hand. She furrowed her brow as I stuck it in my mouth.

"What the fuck's with you and the gum?"

"An old trick I learned as a sniper. It helps to keep me relaxed."

She rolled her eyes, but I could already feel my blood pressure lowering as I chewed.

"So I can concentrate on the task at hand," I said.

"You just better be ready," she snapped. "I've got a lot of time and money invested in you, and people are watching."

"I got this," I replied.

She slipped me a clear dot affixed to a tiny slip of paper. "One dot, one target. Let's see if you can pass the test."

I nodded at her then moved stealthily through the throngs of people, making a point not to connect with anyone as I looked for the mark. I took a seat on one of the newer-looking subway benches and searched the incoming crowd. It was still pre–rush hour, but in about twenty minutes, this place would be wall-to-wall bodies.

That's when I spotted him, a thirty-something blond man dressed in a smart charcoal business suit. He had two bodyguards who were close, and a third who stood about ten feet away. That one was supposed to be inconspicuous, but thanks to Bridget's training, he was anything but. I got up and slowly moved in their direction, freeing the dots from the paper. I had to admit it felt good to be very blasé about something that had stressed me the fuck out a few months ago.

Across the platform, I spotted Bridget watching my every move. Trying to ignore her, I moved across the platform, my heart beating fast. A moment ago I felt full of confidence, and now, with one simple look from Bridget, I wondered if I could pull this off. Shit!

Out of the corner of my eye, I took in the target and everyone around him, especially the two bodyguards. *You can do this, Niles,* I told myself. Shit, I had wiped out a room full of men holding military grade weapons, so a little dot should have been nothing. With every step, I reminded myself of who I was and why I was doing all this. During my military career, I had accomplished missions that dwarfed this simple task, yet I was still worried about completing this one successfully. Mostly, my ego couldn't handle Bridget thinking I was an incompetent.

Shit, shit shit! From the way he was eyeing me, it looked like the third bodyguard had spotted me coming. He would be easy to take out, but that wasn't the mission. One dot, one target.

I scrambled to come up with another approach, and then it came to me. It was time to play tourist.

I headed for the bodyguard instead of the mark, which seemed to surprise him.

"Excuse me. Do you know if I'm on the uptown side of the tracks?" The bodyguard stared at me for a moment, probably assessing whether I was a threat, and then nodded. "Good. Thanks," I said then stepped in front of him. Now I was between him and the other bodyguards, but still not close enough to the mark.

"One minute," I heard someone say as the overhead sign flashed the amount of time left before the next train would be arriving at the platform. That gave me less than a minute to do this, or else they would be gone and so would my chance. At that moment, an attractive woman passed in front of them. I took that opportunity, swiftly planting my mark on the back of my target's neck just as the light of the train peeked through the tunnel.

I turned back to the third bodyguard. "Hey, you know where I can get a newspaper around here?"

He shook his head and scowled at me, clearly annoyed.

I walked away, toward the newsstand on the other side of the platform, then I looped around and returned to Bridget, happy as a mofo, until I heard a woman let out a blood-curdling scream.

"Somebody call a doctor!" a man shouted. "Is anyone a doctor? This man needs help."

I turned to see what all the commotion was about, but my arm was suddenly jerked in another direction. My muscles tensed, because my instinct was to protect myself from whoever had grabbed me, but I turned to see that it was Bridget tugging at my arm.

"Let's go," she commanded as the train arrived at the station and total chaos ensued. She handed me something that looked like an aspirin. "Take it. Take it now!"

"Oh my God, I think he's dead!" another woman with a Spanish accent screamed.

"What the fuck is going on?" I kept looking back to see, and she kept jerking my arm, pulling me in the opposite direction, toward the train.

"Don't worry about him. He's dead. Now, take the fucking pill unless you want to join him." The look she gave me told me everything I needed to know, so I did what I was told.

We got on the train, and as it pulled away and passed the commotion, I saw that the dead man lying on the platform was the mark I had placed the sticker on. His three bodyguards were looking around, confused. I turned from the man to Bridget, who looked completely unfazed, as if she had nothing to do with that dead body.

"That man is dead. I killed him, didn't I?" I whispered.

She nodded her head.

"Fuck! I thought this was a test."

"It was a test. You passed." Bridget smiled, her voice smooth as butter as she calmly led me off the train at the next stop and out of the station, as if the shit that had gone down was all in my imagination.

I couldn't understand how she could remain so emotionless. This wasn't the same as being in Afghanistan, where you had a clear image of the enemy, who was most likely aiming a weapon at you or holding a grenade. At the very least, you knew your enemy belonged to a terrorist organization that wanted to kill Americans. I knew absolutely nothing about the man in the station; he was just a guy waiting for a train. He could have been completely innocent. I had no information about him to inform me one way or the other, and it had my head spinning, wondering what the hell I had gotten myself into and how, or if, I would be able to get out of it.

Her car and driver sat at the curb waiting for us. Winston had already gotten out and had the door open by the time we reached the Rolls. Once we were inside, I turned to her, ready to let her have it.

"What the fuck was that? You set me up for murder again!"

She held up her hand to silence me while she addressed her driver. "Winston, can you roll up the window and put on the music?"

Once the divider was firmly in place and reggae music piped through the car, Bridget turned to me.

"So tell me?" I shouted, not willing to play anymore of her games.

"First off, when there is another person present, you are never to assume that they are privy to the same information as you. You keep your mouth shut until I tell you that you can speak! Do you hear me?"

"This was fucked up, even for you, Bridget." I looked down at my hands. "How come I'm not dead? I touched the sticker."

"Because the toxins in the poison take longer to penetrate the tough skin on your hands. Eventually you won't have to take a pill. You'll build up immunity to it, like me."

"I doubt it."

She gave me a smug grin then picked up her iPad and hit a few buttons, like this shit happened every damn day.

"What the hell are you smiling about?"

She lifted up the iPad and turned the screen toward me. "You just got fifty thousand dollars deposited into your account. Congratulations."

"Did you even know that guy? Was it some fucking joke to you?" I seethed, wondering what kind of fucked-up psychopath I had gotten myself entangled with. "Bitch, you must be out of your mind. That was an innocent man."

Just saying that word out loud made me realize that this situation had really gotten to me. I hated to call a woman the B word, and yet I couldn't think of a more suitable title for Bridget at that moment.

"Let's get one thing straight. Do not call me a bitch again. You will not like the results. And that man you're freaking out about because you think he's so innocent? Let me assure you that Mr. Hannes Baumgartner is not some regular guy. He's a German terrorist here to cause major damage to our infrastructure. His little tour of the subway wasn't because he wanted to go across town. See, Germany wants America to lose all its allies, while pretending to be almost as neutral as Switzerland. You may not get it at this moment, but you will soon learn that nothing I do is done lightly or haphazardly."

My blank stare was the only response I could supply. What I did understand was that I had crossed the line from trainee to full-fledged paid killer, and like it or not, there was no going back.

"Well, maybe you'll get this." She handed me a knapsack.

"What's this?"

"Look in it."

I opened the knapsack and then looked to her for an explanation before I would remove the contents.

"Those are all the files the cops had on you—and the gun with your prints. They're yours. I'm giving them to you."

I took out a folder and the gun, glancing at her skeptically. "Why?"

"Because you're good, probably the best this agency will ever see when you're fully trained. I know this is hard to believe, Niles, but I want you to be my partner, not my hostage. Partners have to trust one another. You can't trust me if I'm holding this over your head."

Bruce

32

Majestic was on the warpath about Keisha not coming to see him, so instead of sliding up into this spicy Latina piece I was messing with in Brentwood, I had to switch gears and head over to deal with Majestic's baby mama. Don't get me wrong. I didn't blame him, because if I had been the one locked up and one of my girls pulled this, I might've caught a second case. Shit like that was the reason I never had no children or baby mamas. I needed to be able to cut a bitch off quick, and I wouldn't want my kids to be no liability.

I got out of the car and went to the door, my hand still clutching my cell. Prison was a joke when it came to contraband. Majestic had a cell in Riverhead, and he was waiting for me call. As soon as I stepped up to the door, I dialed his number.

"Yes?" Keisha answered the door all sassy, like she thought being polite was a goddamn option when she saw it was me at the door.

"You know Majestic's been calling you for days, so how come you haven't been picking up? He's hot, Keisha." I tried to warn her, but she just stood there looking salty in her sweats, twisting up her mouth at me like she didn't give a fuck. Man, I wished for one minute he had been the one ringing the doorbell.

"I'm not in the business of repeating myself, Bruce, so there ain't no reason for me to speak to him," she said.

In response, I handed her the phone. Majestic had been listening to her every word. She looked down at my hand but wouldn't take cell, still acting like she didn't want to be bothered. I shook my head and hit the speaker on the phone.

"Yo, Majestic, you on speaker!"

"Woman, I been locked up in here for four fucking months and you ain't brought your ass to visit me once. What the fuck you think this is?" He barked the words at her like he hoped they would choke her.

She hesitated for a split second, and I fully expected her to fall into line and promise to be at the jail the following weekend. What she actually said shocked the shit out of me.

"I told you before you got arrested that I wasn't happy with our relationship and that I wanted out. I'm sorry it's got to be like this, but we're over. You need to get that through your thick skull."

She had the balls to tell him this over the phone, but no way would she say that shit to his face. I was standing there waiting for all hell to break loose.

Majestic's voice thundered through the phone. "What the fuck did you say to me? I don't give a fuck what you want. No. I give less than a fuck what you want. Everything you have and everything you are is because of me, and you better fucking remember that. You lucky you got my son, or I'd have Bruce throwing your shit out my house right now." I knew he wanted to tell her that she was lucky to be living, but the walls of the fucking prison cells always have ears.

She rolled her eyes like he could see it, and then doubled up on the attitude. I didn't know when this bitch had become so fearless. I was starting to think she had a death wish as she continued to defy him.

"Majestic, let it go. We're done and there is nothing you can do to change my mind. Oh, and this is my house. You may have paid for it, but you put it in my name to hide it from the IRS, remember?"

"Done? We're done when I say it's done, you ungrateful bitch. You better bring my damn son up here to see me today. I'm not playing with you, Keisha."

He wasn't kidding, but she just kept at it like she had some kind of choice.

"I am not bringing my son into a prison." she shouted back at him.

"Bruce, take me off speaker."

I put the phone to my ear. "Yeah. Speaker's off," I told him then listened to his instructions. When he was done telling me what he wanted, I almost felt bad for Keisha. I hung up and turned to address her.

"Go get MJ ready and go get dressed. Put on something sexy that will make my boy happy."

She mad-dogged me, holding her ground. "I'm not doing it."

Calmly, I repeated myself. "Go get MJ ready and get yourself dressed. Put on something really sexy that'll make Majestic forget what a bitch you've been to him lately, and maybe your ass will have a chance."

She shook her head.

"You really think this is a game, don't you? Well, let me give you a word of advice." I spoke slowly and calmly. "He ain't gonna be in there as long as you think. And he ain't giving you any more money if you don't let him see his son."

"I'll take MJ to see him."

I turned to see Debra, all made up and looking good, standing in the doorway. Damn if that woman wasn't looking better and better. She had on a short jean dress and heels, with her hair done up. Even if she wasn't as fine as her daughter, her easygoing disposition gave her extra points, putting her way ahead of that rude-ass daughter of hers.

Still full of fire, Keisha jumped bad with her mother. "You're not taking my son nowhere. I don't want him visiting no jail. Isn't it enough that damn near sixty percent of all men in prison are black? I don't want him to grow up thinking that's his future, so if the best I can do is keep him from ever visiting a prison, then I'm fine with that."

"That boy needs to see his father, and he ain't gonna care if it's in a prison or a goddam amusement park." Debra spat the words at her daughter, earning major points from me. This woman did not appear to be backing down.

"See, Keisha?" I said. "Why can't you be like your mama? She knows how to treat a man, and when a man wants to see his kid, you take him. Too many of these fathers out here don't care about their sons, but when one does, you women got to be the one causing trouble and making it hard for him."

"If your daddy ever wanted to see you, I woulda taken you anywhere," Debra told her daughter, who was looking pissed since we'd ganged up on her.

"That's not a place I want my son to see his father, all locked up behind bars like an animal in a cage," Keisha explained.

Debra stared her down like she was willing to go head-to-head. "We don't always get what we want. At least Majestic will know that some of us are there for him. That man deserves some support, and if seeing his son is going to help him do his time, he deserves that."

"Yeah, and you wouldn't want to lose your meal ticket." Keisha sucked her teeth at her mother before storming into the other room and slamming the door.

"Let me get my bag and get MJ together, Bruce," Debra said before disappearing into one of the bedrooms.

"I'll be right outside."

I stood on the steps, thinking about how stupid Keisha was. That wench had no idea the can of worms she'd just opened, but at least my boy would get the chance to see his son.

Willie

33

"Now, I hope none of you take this the wrong way. . . ." Mr. Walker paused, staring out at the twelve graduates sitting in the small makeshift auditorium along with the staff, friends, and family. I'd made a choice not to invite Niles or Lorna to the ceremony. I hadn't even bothered to tell them about it, because I knew Lorna would have a hissy fit and insist on coming to support me. I guess I figured I'd gotten myself into this mess and it was up to me to clean it up.

"When you each take your ninety-day chip and certificate of completion, I hope to never see you again," he finished, and the entire room burst into laughter, especially those of us who were graduating. I certainly hoped to never have to come back to this place again. I knew that I didn't have another chance left in me, so I planned to make the best of this one and keep myself sober.

Sitting there watching my fellow alcoholics walk to the podium, take their chips and certificates, and say a few words, I almost couldn't believe how much my own life had changed in the past three months. Not only had I not touched a drink, but I'd also managed to get a girlfriend as a sober person. Drinking just wasn't a thing anymore, and I couldn't wait to take my certificate down to Mr. Friedman and get my cab back on the road. I owed it to myself, but just as much, I owed it to Niles.

"William Monroe." I heard my name called out, and I walked up to the front of the room, where Mr. Walker stood at the podium.

"Thank you. All I ever wanted was a chance, and this place gave me one. I know it's only been ninety days, but I'm excited about the life I have in front of me. I couldn't say that when I walked through those doors and signed up for this program. It works if you work it." I took my chip and certificate and accepted the hug Mr. Walker offered.

I stepped off the podium, surprised to see a smiling Niles when he approached, offering his hand. "Congratulations, Unc."

"How . . . how'd you find out about this?"

"Let's just say my new job has me privy to a lot of information I probably shouldn't know," Niles said with a smirk. "I'm just wondering why you didn't tell me. You know I would have been here for you."

"Yeah, I know, but this was something I had to do on my own, for me. But I'm glad you're here," I admitted. It was nice having someone in my corner show up for me.

"I understand," he replied, gesturing toward the door. "Come on. I'll buy you lunch. I know this hot sushi spot over on Jericho Turnpike. Their spicy tuna is to die for."

"Sushi? Since when did you start eating raw fish?" I asked as we walked to the door. I was a Popeye's kind of guy myself.

"With my new job, I have to try new things because I deal with people from all walks of life. I can't afford to be close-minded. Sushi is an acquired taste, but trust me. Not everything there is raw."

I followed him to his car, a new BMW. He nonchalantly flipped me the keys.

"What are these for? You giving that to me?"

He laughed so loud that other people in the parking lot turned to stare. "Have you lost your mind?" he said to me. "Hell no, I'm not giving you my car. I just wanted to know if you wanted to drive."

"Do you even have to ask? Heck yeah, I wanna drive," I replied be-bopping over to the driver's side. It was a well-known fact that I was a car guy. I slipped behind the wheel of Niles's ultimate driving machine, and man, it was like I was at home.

"I know you're excited about going back to driving your cab," he said as we headed toward Jericho Turnpike, probably noticing my goofy, ear-to-ear grin. It was more than just the fact that I was driving again that had me smiling, though. I was ready to be self-sufficient again, and getting my hack license back was the first step—or so I thought.

"Maybe driving a cab isn't the most logical next step," Niles said.

"Huh? I'm ready to work," I assured him.

"And that's why I need to talk to you," he said, his tone suddenly serious.

"What do you think of the car?" he asked. "How's she drive?"

"Man, this baby is like new pussy. I could lay up in her all day."

"The real question is, could you drive her all day?"

I raised an eyebrow. "What are you saying?"

"Well, I have a little situation. . . ."

In his brief hesitation, all sorts of scenarios ran through my mind. I was so used to being a fuck-up that I wondered if I had done something wrong.

"Everything okay?" I checked nervously.

"Yeah, I'm good. I'm real good, but I lied to you, Unc, I didn't take that consulting job like I told you." He really didn't sound remorseful.

"What are you talking about? How could you not have a job? What about all the new clothes, the money, and more importantly, what about this car?" I didn't understand why Niles would feel the need to lie to me, and I was disappointed that he had. After all, his success was the reason I had decided to get myself together, and now I find out it might have all been based on a lie? Not cool.

"No, it's not like that," he said quickly. "I do have a job . . . but it's not doing consulting."

Now I was really concerned. Come to think of it, Niles had been awfully secretive lately. Whatever he was doing must really be terrible.

"Okay?" I pulled the car over to the side of the road then sat back and waited for him to continue, my head spinning.

Niles put his hand on my shoulder. "Unc, I need your help," he told me in a whisper that made the hair stand up on the back of my neck. My sister's child was not the type to show a vulnerable side, so he must be in some real trouble.

"Nephew, I'm here for you. I'm always going to be here," I assured him. No matter what he had done, I would never turn my back on him. He had to know that.

"Okay," he said, "but what I'm about to tell you, you can't ever tell anyone. Not even Ma. Shit, especially not Ma." He stared at me, waiting for me to acknowledge that I understood.

"Sure, sure, Niles." I nodded, wondering what the fuck the big secret was. "You can tell me anything. What's going on?"

He looked around as if someone might hear what he had to say. "Unc, I'm not a consultant for Dynamic Defense. I'm an operative. I do wet work for them."

It took a minute for what he'd said to sink in, but when it did, everything became clear. "Wet work. That's just another name for assassin, isn't it? This all has to do with those murders at Sugar's that night, doesn't it? I was wondering why they released you so fast without a lawyer."

The pieces started to fall into place. That night at Sugar's had to have something to do with this, because after that night, things had been moving pretty quickly for my nephew. He'd become a lot less talkative and lot more secretive.

"Niles," I asked, "did you kill those men?"

"No, but somebody sure as hell wanted it to look like I did so Bridget could come swoop me up outta jail like a super hero." Niles's face tightened.

"Bridget. Bridget. Why do I know that name? Oh, shit! You talkin' about the chick with the bucket list pussy." My mouth opened wide when I realized what he was talking about. "You think she set you up?"

"Maybe not directly, but she or someone in her camp sure as hell did. She waltzed into that interrogation room and everyone snapped to attention. They weren't happy about it, but they released me in a hurry once she showed up. She made it clear that the only way I could repay her—and make the murder charges go away—was to come work for her.

"Once I passed all their tests and they transformed me into what they wanted me to be, Bridget handed me all the evidence against me and offered me a job," he said. "I'm not gonna lie. With those murders plus all Ma's medical bills at the Wellness Center, I didn't really have a choice. I took the job."

I turned and stared at my nephew, scared for him. "Niles, you know I've been around for a while and I've seen my share of shit. I'm tellin' you this don't sound like any defense contractor I've ever heard of. This sounds like a—"

He cut me off. "A CIA or NSA front?"

"Well, yeah."

The look he gave me told me I wasn't far from the truth.

"Jesus, Niles, what the hell have you gotten yourself into?"

"Unc, I really don't know, but I'm gonna need your help if I'm ever gonna get out of it."

I cleared my throat nervously. I wanted—no, I needed—to help Niles, but I hoped to God this didn't fuck up my newly won sobriety. "What can I do?" This was all moving way too fast, and here I was agreeing to it. Just like Niles, I really didn't have much of a choice. He was my family.

"I need you to watch my back. I need you to be my right hand until I can figure this all out."

"What about your girl Bridget? What's she gonna say about all this?"

"Nothing. In my new position, I'm gonna need to hire a driver. Someone I trust and someone who can keep a whole lot of secrets and handle business if the time arrives."

"Someone like a retired Marine sergeant?" I chuckled, reaching out and gripping the steering wheel. "I don't know what to say," I mumbled.

"Just say yes." He held out his hand to me. "There is no one I trust more than you in this world, Willie, but you should know that this job is dangerous. It's not working on computers or in an office. It's working with and taking out some very dangerous people. You may be called upon to take a life to save my life—or your own."

I couldn't wrap my head around this just yet. Niles was working some kind of top-secret job, and he was offering me work to watch his back? It sounded mysterious, it sounded dangerous, but as crazy as it seemed, being his driver actually sounded like fun.

"Okay, yeah," I said. "I'll do it, but on one condition."

"What's that?"

"You gotta take me shopping. I can't be rolling around in this whip dressed like this, with you in the back seat."

He laughed. "I guess lunch is going to have to wait. Let's go shopping."

"That's what I'm talking about," I said as I put the car in gear and sped away.

Majestic

34

As I stood in the transition room waiting to change out of my prison garb to go home, a C.O. handed me a bag containing the outfit I had worn when I entered. Damn if I wasn't ecstatic to be putting on something other than that ugly orange polyester-blend jumpsuit. I grabbed my navy pants and slipped them on, along with the slightly wrinkled, form-fitting Italian dress shirt. The Gucci loafers were timeless, and I knew I looked good, but sliding into my Italian leather jacket was the moment that made me feel like I was actually going home.

"Good luck and hope to never see you again," the guard said as I passed. I was sure he'd said that same line a thousand times to every person who'd exited on his watch. The only difference between me and most of the others was I knew I'd never walk back in there.

When the buzzer sounded and a heavy metal gate clanged open, I was one step closer to getting back to my old life, the one where I was the HNIC. I took a deep breath. Even the air smelled better on this side of the gate.

"Damn, your ass look like you got bigger," my man Pooh called out. He was standing next to a brand-new, tricked-out Escalade with flashy twenty-twos. Bruce was standing next to Pooh, grinning from ear to ear, with that trademark toothpick between his lips. They both looked happy to see me. I gave them both some dap and pulled each one in for a brotherly hug. These two were my dogs. I could count on them for damn near anything.

I whipped open the door and peered inside. "Where's my son?" I grumbled. I expected my orders to be followed to the letter, which meant my son needed to be there.

Bruce looked me straight in the eyes. "Sorry, partner, but she wouldn't let me bring him."

"Is that right?" I snapped, my hands balling into fists reflexively.

"You know, Keisha is full of excuses these days," Bruce replied.

"She's full of shit. I know that, but I got something for Ms. Keisha." That girl had a holiday while I was locked up, but now that I was out, she needed to step back in line or get snapped. "She don't know I'm coming home, do she?"

"Nah." Bruce shook his head. "I figured you'd want to keep that on the low."

"You figured right."

We got into the truck, and Pooh headed up the island. I spotted the mahogany box on the back seat next to me and reached for it, smiling. It had everything inside that I needed. I put on my diamond-encrusted Cartier, pinky ring, and my thick gold chain. I picked up my LV money clip and saw that it was fat with hundred-dollar bills. Bruce had even gotten me the new iPhone and transferred all of my information.

"You good?" he asked.

"Real good. Now all I need is to get me some ass and I'll be one hundred."

Bruce and Pooh shared a look.

"You wanna go see Keisha?" Pooh asked.

I gave him the stink eye. "What? Hell no. Let's go find us a couple freaks. I bet you two been tearing shit up since I been locked up. Time for me to catch up."

Bruce tried to hide a grin. "Yeah, shit was live, but I spent most of it trying to keep things together."

"Yeah, I know. You was holding down shit like a motherfucker, but you ain't gotta hold that weight by yourself no more. I'm back, bro, and I'm ready to let niggas know."

"That's what I'm talking about." Bruce held out his fist for me to bump. "Look, I got a couple of Puerto Rican freaks over at the crib, buck naked and waiting. Why don't we take that ride so that you can get your shit off?"

"Man, that shit is like music to my ears. I'm so backed up y'all probably gonna have to peel them bitches off the bed when I'm finished with them," I proclaimed, sitting back in the chair. "Then we're going to deal with that bitch Keisha. She got all the way out of pocket. She needs to be reined in, and I'm just the man to do it."

Bridget

35

Niles matched my 9 mm shot for shot with his .45 at the Westside Rifle & Pistol Range in New York City. He made a point to have his bullet land within centimeters of wherever mine had pierced the target each time.

"You do know that you don't have to prove anything to me anymore. We're partners. I've already conceded that you're a better shot than me." I watched as his next five bullets obliterated the paper target, sending it flying to the floor. "That kill shot you made yesterday in Dallas was incredible. Hell, even the director's talking about it."

"You didn't hire me for my looks or charm," he responded in a deadpan, securing his weapon. It was easy to see that Niles was the real deal when it came to his marksman skills, but he was still holding back in ways that I needed him to let go. Sure, he'd accepted the job, but the resentment he held toward me was still there, and it was more than obvious. It was spilling over in every area, but I needed him to let go and trust me. We had a lot of work to do, and his attitude contributed to things not moving as swiftly as they needed to go. He'd made two of the most incredible kill shots I'd ever seen in the past two weeks, but our work wasn't always going to be long distance. Most of the time it was up close and personal, and for that I needed a partner I could trust.

"You may not believe it right now, but one day you're going to see that I am not the enemy," I told him as I removed my goggles and we began to pack up our weapons.

"So what? You think you're a friend?" He smirked at me as all of his annoyance arrived right there on the surface. I wasn't about to play this game with him.

"Yes. I want very much for us to be friends. This job isn't like your normal nine to five. It requires you to be able to put your life in my hands and vice versa. At some point, whether you know it or not, you are going to need me."

"What are you trying to say? You want us to be besties? Like girlfriends? After all, we already went shopping together and we have shared a few meals, and without me even telling you, you managed to know everything there is about me." He said the last part with more than a little disgust in his voice. "So what's the next level—friendship? Friends with benefits? Like, I can come over to your house and we sit together on the couch and watch old movies, or we go drinking together before we fuck?" he snapped in my face, intent on letting me know that he didn't see that happening—despite the fact that I did.

"Yes, all of it," I agreed, challenging him. I decided to go with this. He was no more serious than I was being, so I decided to give him a taste of his own medicine.

"Oh, so now we're not just working together, but we're also fuck buddies?" He actually threw his head back and laughed loudly.

"Wow, I'm not used to a man finding the idea of fucking me so funny. Usually the reaction is a bit more . . . shall I say, grateful," I purred, moving closer to him, making a point to invade his private space. All of the flame of his argument extinguished with that one move.

"Whoa! That's because it's never gonna happen!" He backed away from me as if I were carrying some deadly disease. That, admittedly, was like a smack in the face, but I would never let him see it. As a matter of fact, it only made me more determined to prove him wrong.

"Don't flatter yourself, Mr. Monroe. I may be a flirt, but I am far from serious. I wouldn't waste my personal understanding of the *Kama Sutra* on a young man like you. It's too dangerous. Every one of those positions is mind-blowing, and I'm an expert at them all. Despite the fact that you're athletic and good-looking, the jury is still out on whether you're even a decent fuck, let alone worthy of my skills," I told a shocked Niles, who, had he been a few shades lighter, would have turned bright red.

For the past few weeks, I'd been buttoned-up with his fine ass, but I could see how that may have contributed to him being unwilling to relax and let go of his anger. So, I had to meet him on a more visceral level.

"The absolute last thing I need is to have you fall head over heels in love with me. The director would kill me."

"What? You think I can't sleep with you without getting all googly-eyed? That I'm too inexperienced to handle you?" he scoffed, growing testier by the second, which was exactly what I wanted.

"That's exactly what I'm saying, Niles, so you don't have to worry about me even going down that road. What lies between my legs has taken out some of the most powerful men in the world. Giving some to you would be like giving a stick of dynamite and matches to a child: just plain irresponsible."

There is a great psychological side to sex. Both men and women are conditioned to want what they cannot have, and I had just taken all my pussy off the table. Funny, before this conversation, he had probably never thought about me that way, but now he wouldn't be able to stop thinking about me, because I had just dealt his fragile male ego a harder blow than any woman he'd ever met.

Niles glared at me. "You are so lucky I have a girlfriend."

"That's your pride talking, Niles. This isn't some game where you place a sticker on the back of a woman's neck. Look, you're a great asset to the company, and I'm ecstatic about having you as a partner in the field, but as a bed partner, well, not so much. Most pretty boys have a tendency to be soft." I gave him a sympathetic smile. "No offense. We are who we are." I finished my speech and went right back to business as if the conversation had never happened. "So, you ready?" I grabbed my things.

I made a point to walk in front of him as we exited the shooting range. Nothing like giving an unobstructed view of what you just took off the table to make a man's head explode. By the time we entered the parking garage, I could see that Niles was even more suspicious of me.

"What are you doing this weekend? I'd like to go over our next assignment." *And perhaps a little more.*

"You know I can't do anything this weekend," Niles replied as we got into the car.

"Oh, yeah. You're moving Mom. You're a good son."

"I try, but it's not that easy when your mother's bipolar," he admitted, sounding worried. Every time he mentioned his mother, he went from being shut down and almost cold, to vulnerable and kind of adorable.

I studied him, softening inwardly as I went from adversary to ally, but I didn't say anything.

"What?" he barked, no doubt noticing the way my eyes lingered on him.

"Hearing a guy talking about his mother that way will never get old. In fact, you need to use it when you want to hit that emotional note with people we're dealing with. It will help to get them to lower their guard. This is very good."

"Really? Is everything about work with you?" he said. This damn guy was wound so tight he couldn't even recognize a compliment when he got one.

"What? Maybe I am guilty of taking my work too seriously, but then the alternative in this business is usually death. Look, I just need to make sure that you're on board. You're on your way to being one of the best operatives I've ever come across, but you still have a lot to learn. I need to know if I can count on you in the field."

"Don't worry about me; worry about yourself! I'll take care of my end," he said, his voice back to sounding clipped and slightly hostile. If it had been anyone else at this point, I probably would have bailed and sent him back to Jonathan, but the problem was that he was as good as he thought— probably better, which meant in the long run that I needed him more than he needed me.

Patience did not come easily to me, but instead of getting snippy, I just sat back and watched him stroll across the parking lot and disappear into his car.

Niles

36

"I'll circle the block until you get back," Willie told me as I got out of the car and walked toward the Hotel Pierre. I glanced down at my watch. It was ten minutes to five, and we'd been waiting for over an hour. Protocol said that I was supposed to wait at least another half hour, but my gut told me that when Bridget didn't emerge from the hotel, our mission was blown and I had to go in after her.

Bridget had given me strict instructions in case I needed to make this move, and after all my years and missions in the military, I sensed that something was not right, so I was on my way, with my gun tucked neatly in its holster. I paid close attention to everyone and everything around me as I headed through the lobby of the hotel. There were two guys that looked like they could be trouble, but one was talking on the phone and the other was waiting for instructions. Neither seemed to notice when I stepped onto the elevator.

I pressed the button for the twelfth floor, hoping like hell no one else got on, because I didn't want to waste any more time. When the doors closed, I turned my back to the security camera and screwed a silencer onto my gun.

As I exited the elevator, a dumpy Latina house-keeper grabbed supplies from her cart parked outside a room. She eyed me with interest, and I passed her, giving just the right amount of attention to know that she had turned in my direction.

I stopped in front of room 1216, discreetly removing the DO NOT DISTURB sign then pretend-ing to check my pockets. Feigning embarrassment, I sighed, turning to her for help.

"Excuse me. I think I left my key in the room. Is there any way you can let me in?" I asked, turning up the wattage on my smile.

"No, I'm sorry." She shook her head, getting flustered as I stared seductively at her. "I can get in a lot of trouble. We're not supposed to let people into their rooms."

"Really?" I took a few steps back toward the elevator. "You're really going to make me go all the way down to the front desk?" I frowned as if she'd deeply saddened me. "It's always the pretty girls who disappoint."

She looked down both sides of the hallway, still worried. "Okay, but I can get fired if my manager finds out," she said, still worried.

"It'll be our little secret," I told her as she unlocked my door. "I really appreciate it," I said, holding the door cracked.

As she went back to her cart, I watched her, sticking a fresh piece of gum in my mouth before I slipped into the room, pulling the gun out of my waistband, ready for action. Thankfully I didn't meet any resistance, but across the room was Bridget. She was naked, gagged and handcuffed to the bed face down. She looked really bad.

Her eyes widened as I came toward her and removed the gag. "Thank God. He's in the bathroom," she whispered. I could hear the shower.

"Come on. I'm getting you outta here."

"No. We've got to complete the mission." Bridget was like no solider I had ever encountered. Despite being physically and probably sexually abused, she was still worried about completing her mission. "You have to take him out, Niles.

"I'll get him once I have you free," I replied, looking on the nightstand for the key to her handcuffs. I ended up finding the key in a pair of pants that were hanging on a chair near the desk.

"Niles!" She screamed, but she didn't have to. I saw the guy just as I turned around to toss the keys to her. He had to be some kind of aerialist the way he came flying at me, knocking the gun from my hand.

I might have lost my gun, but I was far from losing the battle. I went after him with everything I had, landing a chop across his neck and sending him down to the ground. Bridget had barely finished uncuffing herself when the adjoining door slammed open and two burly men rushed into the room, guns blazing, ready to do battle.

One quick glance at Bridget and I could see she wasn't prepared for this—but I was. Diving to the floor, I picked up my gun and pelted a round into the first guy. His partner ducked out the of way and rose up with his own weapon in hand. Just as he went lunging at Bridget, I pumped two well-placed bullets in him, ending any chance of him rising up again.

What I didn't plan on was that the original target would recover so quickly, because now I was looking up at the barrel of his .45. Fortunately he didn't pay attention to Bridget, who stuck her boot knife into his neck so hard that blood started gushing everywhere. He fell to the ground, and she kicked him repeatedly in the groin. Whatever he'd done to her must not have been pretty.

"Bridget! Bridget!" I shouted. "You can stop now. He's dead."

"Well, that wasn't exactly how I planned it, but at least the mission is accomplished," she huffed, grabbing her clothes as if nothing had happened.

"You all right?" I asked, trying to avoid watching her get dressed.

"Yeah, he liked it rough. Caught me off guard with that S&M shit. I don't know what I would have done if you hadn't shown up. Nice save."

"Don't praise me yet. We still have to get outta here," I said as I headed for the door. "You ready?" The housekeeper's cart was there, but she was nowhere to be found, which was not a good sign. She had most likely heard the commotion in our room.

As we darted out of the room and headed for the stairs, the elevator doors opened and we barely escaped. The two men who had been on the phone downstairs came barreling out, no doubt called by their now-dead colleagues.

"Call your driver and tell him to get to the hotel exit on Forty-fifth Street," Bridget ordered when we hit the seventh floor.

I called Willie and told him where to meet us. A few minutes later, Bridget and I burst through the hotel's side door. I can't tell you how happy I was to see Willie sitting at the curb.

"What the fuck is that?" Bridget chastised. "Why is he driving a cab? I told you not to hire his drunk ass."

"He's driving a cab because nobody in New York City is going to notice a cab riding around a hotel. Now, get in so we can get the hell outta here."

As we got into the car, another door opened and the two bodyguards rushed into the street in front of the car, guns pointed at us. Willie took off like a bat out of hell, slamming the car into both men and sending them ten feet in the air.

After about a mile, he pulled over, jumped out, and ran around the back. I heard the trunk slam, but it was still a minute before he got back in.

Willie slid behind the wheel. "I had to put the plates back on." He sounded really proud of himself.

"That was brilliant thinking, Willie," Bridget told him, surprising the hell out of me.

"Yeah, I figured if you were running then there might be someone behind you who we didn't need to be able to find you," Willie answered.

I would have to pat Willie on the back later, but right now my head was spinning with what had just happened. "I told you in the beginning that I didn't like the idea of you going in there alone, but you insisted," I said, expressing my frustration.

"Fine. You were right. That what you want to hear?" she challenged me.

"If we're really partners, then I need you to trust that I have your back," I snapped at her, throwing her own words in her face.

"Okay. I got you," she said, her tone as apologetic as I'd ever heard it.

"Okay then," I agreed.

"Something tells me we need to give your driver a bonus for his quick thinking," she said loud enough for Willie to hear.

"I like the sound of that, boss," he quipped, laughing. "Or should I say bosses?"

Majestic

37

I had to admit it, it felt damn good to be hugged up with someone soft and beautiful, with curves in all the right places. We slid into a booth in the back, and Harold insisted on buying our first round. Of course, he knew I wasn't leaving here without giving him a tip large enough to justify tossing some regulars out of the booth to give it to us.

"Damn, sure put it on my ass back at the house," I said to Hazel, a stripper who got her name because of the color of her eyes. I'd been fucking with her for at least a year.

Now that I was home enjoying my freedom, Bruce and I had decided to head over to O'Dell's and have a couple of celebratory drinks with a few honeys. Not getting any pussy for six months sure made you appreciate it when you finally did.

Hazel batted her eyes at me. "I told you to take me out of rotation and make me a wife. You know I'm a keeper."

"Yeah, well, we'll have to see about that," I lied. Since she'd been so good to me, pulling out all her skills, I didn't want to burst her bubble.

"Majestic, you need to go 'head and let me have your baby. Just imagine how pretty our babies gonna be," she said like that was gonna cement the deal.

"Baby, are you out your fucking mind?" I moved so I could get a good look at her face. The bitch was dead serious. I already knew the look Bruce had on his face before I saw it. He was try'na keep a straight face. "What I tell you about that baby shit before I got locked up? I already got a baby mama, and I ain't interested in being Lil Wayne or any of them other fifty-baby-mama motherfuckers. Play your fucking position and I'll keep you around. Otherwise, it's a long way back to Bellport."

I glanced over at my man Bruce. "You hear this shit?"

"Shorty already know how I feel about that baby shit." Bruce cut his eyes at Leelee, the pretty half-Asian chick at his side, and she nodded obediently.

"Yo!" I raised an eyebrow toward Bruce to get his attention. A brother had walked in dressed in jeans and a polo shirt. He was obviously trying to fit in, but he had cop written all over him.

As the dude approached us, Bruce pulled out his wallet and removed some cash. "Ladies, y'all take this and hang out by the bar till I tell you."

Leelee took the cash, and they scooted over to the bar.

"Can I help you, officer?" I asked the man, sitting up straight in my seat, my arms stretched across both sides of the booth.

The man looked around at the other patrons. He frowned, looking down at his outfit. "I'm not wearing a uniform. Why'd you just call me a cop?"

Bruce gave him a snort. "Man, you got *pig* written all over you. Ain't nobody in here wearing a polo shirt, or Levis jeans, for that matter."

"And the biggest giveaway is those cheap-ass skips you got on your feet." I laughed.

"I take offense to that," he replied a little too loud, and for a second it appeared we were at a standstill. "My shoes ain't cheap." Then all of a sudden, he burst out laughing. Bruce and I joined in.

"What's up, Pete? How's it going, man?" I stood up, shaking his hand and smiling at one of our most reliable business associates. In our line of work, it helped to be in bed with the boys in blue.

"Me?" He pointed to himself. "How you doing, man? It's good to see you out here in the world."

"Man, you ain't saying nothing but the truth. I can do the time, but I prefer to be doing me, and me prefers to be free," I told him in response.

"I know that's right," Bruce chimed in as Pete took a seat in our booth.

"You come to have a drink, or you here on business?" I asked.

Bruce reached into his jacket and took out a heavy envelope and slid it to Pete, who was almost salivating to get his paws on the monthly payout. I can't lie, though. He deserved it this month. It was him who told Bruce about Lydell's treachery in the first place. Without his heads up, both of us would have been doing twenty years.

"Thanks, gentlemen." He pocketed the cash-filled envelope.

"We're always happy to help out the boys in blue," Bruce joked with him. Pete saluted.

"And the boys appreciate the donation. I'm gonna let you guys get back to your lady friends." Pete stood up to go, but then he turned to Bruce.

"Oh, and that other shit you had me look into—those dates checked out. DaQuan Braithwaite was locked up on Rikers on April seventh."

"What the fuck are you talking about?" I asked, the bass growing heavy in my voice as I turned and faced Bruce, who didn't bother to hide his guilty look.

"I asked Pete to look into a rumor that DaQuan might have been locked up the day Rodney died."

Pete glanced from me to Bruce and back, deciding he didn't want none of this. "Like I said before, I'm gonna let you brothers have some privacy. Call if you guys need anything."

I wasn't ready for him to go just yet. "Hang tight over at the bar for a minute, Pete," I told him. Pete knew that if he wanted another envelope next month he should do as he was told, so he went to the bar and sat down.

As soon as he was out of earshot, I leaned across the table. "What the fuck, Bruce? When was you gonna tell me this shit?"

"I was hoping there wasn't gonna be anything to tell, but DaQuan's mama been running her mouth to anyone who would listen that I killed her kid. That he was innocent because he was in jail. So, I hit up Pete 'cause I didn't want some guilty motherfucker out here running free if I popped the wrong person."

He paused when he was finished explaining. I stared him down but made no comment, which I knew would have his nerves on edge. Good. I needed him to feel uncomfortable. He was my right hand man and all, but I didn't want him to think for a minute that it was cool for him to make a move—any move—without discussing things with me first. My silence had the desired effect.

"I'm sorry, man," he apologized nervously, "but I didn't want you having more shit to worry about until I was absolutely sure."

"I got you," I replied, nodding my head. I glanced over at Pete and summoned him back over to our table.

"I need you to take a closer look at Rodney's case," I told him when he got up from the bar and came over to us. "I wanna know everything there is: suspects, witnesses, everything. It's worth twenty grand to me. Can you do that?"

Pete broke into a wide grin. I swear there were fucking dollar signs dancing in his eyes. "Absolutely. For twenty grand I'll find out who shot Kennedy for you. Give me a week."

Bruce looked frustrated as Pete walked out. "I sure hope he finds something."

"I'm not worried about that. We gonna get whoever killed my brother, and that motherfucker is gonna pay."

Niles

38

"Where are we going?" my mother hissed, looking confused as she stared out the window. We'd just exited the Long Island Expressway and even before she'd opened her mouth, I knew what she was thinking. I'd just checked her out of the Wellness Center after a four-month stay, and this wasn't the exit to our Wyandanch home. I was sure she thought I was taking her to a new treatment center, or perhaps an institution. Despite her recovery, my mother was still a little off and sometimes quite paranoid.

"It's a little surprise," I told her, holding back from explaining any more than I had to. I could see the worry appear on her face as she strained to figure it out. Her expression hardened, and I knew her thoughts had started to darken.

"You're taking me to another hospital, aren't you? I don't need another hospital stay, Niles. I'm fine. The doctor said the new medications are working good. Serious, baby, I'm fine. Please don't take me to another hospital," she rambled.

I reached across the seat, taking her hand. "Ma, I promise I'm not taking you to any hospital or doctor or anyplace like that. I'm taking you to a happy place. You're going to like where we're going. You gotta trust me."

"I do. I trust you, Niles. I'm tired. I just want to go home, take a bath, and lie down."

"Mama, you're gonna be able to do all of that," I assured her.

She nodded, looking around the car for the first time. She hadn't really paid any attention to it when she got in. She was too busy being concerned about leaving something behind at the center. If I had my way, my mother would never be going back to that place, despite how high-end it was. Hell, everything I was doing came out of needing to provide a better life for her, and I was happy to be able to do that.

"Where did you get this car?" she asked, her voice full of suspicion and concern. "Boy, are you dealing drugs?"

I burst out laughing. "No, Ma, I'm working as a consultant for a defense contracting firm. It's a really prestigious job, and, well, it comes with a lot of perks, like this car and a bigger salary than I ever dreamed possible. I was even able to hire Willie."

"Hire Willie? Doing what? Willie don't like to work that much."

"Driving this car. I have to meet with a lot of important people, and I guess they need me to impress them, so I have my very own driver." I laughed at the very idea of it. It sounded strange even to me.

"Yep. I'm about to be doing big things, Mama. So you don't have to worry about me. I'm going to be able to take care of you," I said, gripping her hand tighter.

I pulled into the driveway of a large colonial house, parked the car, and walked around to the passenger side to open Mama's door.

"Where are we? Those are pretty," she said, admiring the flower pots on the wraparound porch.

"Home, Ma. We're home." I grabbed her hand and led her up the steps.

The front door opened, and standing in the entryway with a huge grin on his face was Willie.

"Welcome home, Lorna," Willie said to his sister.

She looked shocked, her mouth hanging agape. She kept staring from one of us to the other. "What is this?" she asked.

"Ma, you always said you wanted to live in one of those big houses over on Pidgeon Hill Road. Well, I found us a really nice one. It even has a stable in the back for horses. You always said that you wanted horses. So you want to see your new home?" I asked as Willie stepped aside and we went in.

"Oh my God, this is so beautiful," she exclaimed and immediately started to cry.

Wrapping my arms around her, I pulled her close. "Mama, you don't have to cry. This is good," I told her.

"No, I think you're going to have to take me back to Wellness Center," she said as she wept.

"The Wellness Center? Why? What's wrong?"

"Because I'm hallucinating. This is all one big hallucination, isn't it? I don't understand. I'm taking my meds."

"No, Ma, this isn't a hallucination. It's real. All of it is real," I replied, squeezing her in a reassuring embrace.

"Real. This is all real. Thank God. I thought I was losing my mind again," she kissed me on the cheek. I felt her relax in my arms. "Thank you, son. Thank you."

"You ready to see your new home? Now, anything you don't like we can take back, and you can get what you want. All your clothes are in the closets, but you can also go shopping and get whatever you want," I told her all in one excited breath.

My mother started to walk around, taking in her new home like a kid in a candy store, going from room to room, nearly bursting with wonder and joy.

"Niles, I just have one question." She stopped and stared at me.

"What's that, Ma?"

She had a big, childlike grin on her face. "When are we going to get some horses?"

"We can go look at horses tomorrow, Ma. How about that? I promise."

"Thank you, baby," she gushed, continuing her childlike exploration from room to room.

I felt a hand on my shoulder and turned to a grinning Willie. "You did good, Niles. Real good."

"Yeah, but if you're gonna be my driver, we got to find a home healthcare worker. I got a list of companies from the hospital." I pulled out the paper with the information they'd given me at the Wellness Center when we checked Mama out.

"I may have someone," Willie told me. "Somebody we might be more comfortable with. Lorna ain't gonna want some uptight nurse in her house. You know how she is about people. Let me handle this."

"You sure?" I asked doubtfully. I wasn't necessarily comfortable relinquishing control of the situation. I mean, I loved my uncle, but Ma wasn't exactly in great shape when I first came home, and Willie had been the one in charge at that point.

"Trust me. I got this," he said with a clear-eyed gaze. That's when I realized that Willie deserved the benefit of the doubt because he was a different man than he had been a few months ago. He was sober now.

"Thanks. I appreciate it, Willie."

"Please, with all you do for us, it's the least I can do. You are a real good son—and you're not such a bad nephew either."

Bridget

39

There was nothing I hated more than having to justify my position to a bunch of paper-pushing, egotistical bureaucrats twice a year, but there I was, once again explaining myself to a group the company called The Committee. I'd completed the first half of my debriefing unscathed about ten minutes ago, and unlike most of the other times I'd been in front of The Committee, I felt good about it. As I walked back in for the second half of the meeting, I was actually looking forward to what I had to relay to the suits.

"Bridget." Jonathan caught me right before I walked through the double doors like he had some kind of GPS on me. He'd been off to the side during the break, flirting with that wannabe assistant of his, Nadja, who was starting to look at me as if she considered me a threat. I did not know how the hell he had gotten her clearance to be in a meeting like this. "How about dinner tonight?" he asked me.

"How about you kiss my ass?" I replied curtly, keeping it moving.

"Well, we can do that too," he whispered. Of course he stayed right there on my heels as I stepped my red bottoms into the secure conference room we'd been meeting in.

I ignored Jonathan, taking my place at the podium on the far side of the room next to the teleprompter. This wasn't your normal conference room. It was soundproof, swept three times a day for bugs, and had two-way monitors on the walls for the committee members who had to video conference and couldn't attend in person.

Today, though, most of the big wigs were in attendance, including the two big dogs, Director Douglas Bonaventura, who sat at the head of the table, and Senator Robert Stove, the chairman of the Committee on Homeland Security, who sat to Doug's right. The senator rarely ever made an appearance, so I knew this wasn't really about me but about Niles. Other than Douglas, Jonathan, and the senator, there were eight others seated at the conference table, and two on video cam. Nadja was the only other woman in the room.

I could always count on Douglas's support because he was a friend and mentor. I appreciated him, especially because he'd never tried to get in my pants.

"Gentlemen, are we ready?" I removed my paperwork from the leather valise I carried.

"Any time you are ready, St John." Douglas's voice boomed with authority. He glanced over in Jonathan's direction, and Jonathan scrambled to his seat. "I'd like to hear about our new superstar."

"Gentlemen, this is Niles Monroe, our newest operative and my new partner. Niles is the most efficient and effective partner I've had the pleasure to work with. It's only been a few months, and already he's taking risks and getting jobs done that men who've been on the job ten years are not prepared to handle." I hit a button on the prompter, and a screen behind me lit up with a picture of Niles. Each of the committee members opened up a folder that had been placed in front of them. "As many of you know, Mr. Monroe was a Special Forces sniper with an unprecedented kill record. He's the man that took out Akbar, and he now works for us."

All of a sudden, all eyes were on me.

I clicked the prompter, showing pictures of different dead men as I spoke. "Under my supervision, Mr. Monroe has taken out Hannes Baumgartner, the German who was planning to destroy New York's subway system; Muhammad Aabzaari, who was sent to the United States to recruit college students for ISIS; Tom and Wiliam O'Connell, two homegrown terrorists who planned on duplicating Oklahoma City in ten different states simultaneously; and Jomo Kibaki, number three on the FBI's Most Wanted list. Mr. Monroe's kill shots on the O'Connell brothers were like nothing I've ever seen before."

"How is that possible? It says here he's only been an agent for less than six months." Senator Stove's question was probably the same one half of the men in the room had been thinking. The only one who wasn't showing any reaction was Nadja, and that was because she had her head buried in Niles's file.

"Senator, I can understand your skepticism. Heck, if I wasn't there, I might not believe it myself; but I watched him complete each of his assignments," I said very frankly. "And to answer your question, it's possible because he's just that damn good."

"You honestly believe that?"

"Senator, when it's all said and done, this man may be this organization's and the nation's greatest asset." I glanced over at Jonathan, who looked like he was going to suffocate in his own jealousy.

"I like the sound of that." The senator sat back in his chair with a satisfied smile. Douglas nodded his approval.

"Now, I'd like to suggest—"

"It says here that his mother has mental illness and his sister died of a drug overdose, possibly suicide." I was interrupted by Lance Rodgers, the only brother in the room and the biggest Uncle Tom in the building. He pointed at the report in front of him. Everyone in the room turned to the page on Niles's mother and sister. "Should we be concerned about mental illness? Maybe we should have his mental health tested. We don't want a ticking time bomb on our hands, Director."

"Yes, his mother's bipolar, Lance, and his sister was a drug addict, but Mr. Monroe has never shown any signs of mental instability," I snapped, hating to be called to task by this paper-pushing prick. Lance was part of Jonathan's team, so I knew where that question was really coming from. I looked over at Jonathan, who smirked smugly.

"As a matter of fact," I continued, "he's been tested on all levels, and his scores have been off the chart. But if you'd like to take him out of the field and have him tested again, then who's going to handle the Wilcox problem? You? Somehow I doubt that, considering how your team handled the Tampa situation."

Lance's face turned red, and more than a few people laughed.

That's it, Bridget. Keep them off balance, I told myself.

"I don't think that's necessary. Mr. Monroe is well on his way to being one of our shining stars with your guidance, Bridget," Douglas said, sounding proud of me and the treasure I was handing to the agency. I stood there grinning like a proud mother—or maybe like a proud trainer, because I was definitely not Niles's mother.

"Well, I, for one, want to meet him," Douglas said to the obvious displeasure of some of the more insecure men in the room.

"And I'm sure he wants to meet you too, sir," I assured him.

"Director, since Mr. Monroe has already taken out six of our most recognizable targets, then I say we test his skills on our West Coast problem." Jonathan delivered this bombshell while smiling at me like he was handing me some fucking gift.

"What do you think, Bridget?" Douglas asked. I could see the hope in his eyes of eliminating a huge threat. Our West Coast problem was a man we called The Cat. He was a very dangerous arms dealer and smuggler connected to the Mexican Mafia. The Cat not only supplied terrorists with guns, but he was in some way responsible for half of the illegal weapons on the streets, along with a good portion of the illegal drugs. We'd been after him for years, but the man was elusive as a cat and just as hard to kill. He'd taken out at least ten of our best agents over the years.

"No." I shook my head emphatically. I had to control myself from trembling at the thought of them sending Niles to deal with him. "He's not ready for that."

"Why not?" Jonathan snapped. "If you're telling us he's our best, then we need to use him to take out our biggest threat. It just makes sense."

"Jonathan, he's not ready."

"What do you mean? How can he not be ready?" He slammed his hand on the conference table for emphasis, but I knew this was all an act for my benefit. Jonathan was just trying to get under my skin. "If he's not ready to handle The Cat, then what the fuck are you bragging about him like he's the Second Coming of Christ? Don't tell us how good he is unless you're willing to put him to the test—and that is the test."

"It's only been a few months, may I remind you. Sure, we could send him, but I want to make damn sure he's seasoned so that when he does go to California, he comes back alive. For fuck's sake, I almost didn't make it out of there when you sent me, in case you forgot," I seethed. There was no way I was ready to risk Niles the way he had risked me.

"Oh, now I see. This isn't about Monroe. This is about you and the fact that you almost got your-self killed trying to take down The Cat, isn't it?"

He glanced around the table with a triumphant expression, like he had busted me, and I wanted to strangle him.

"Fuck you, Jonathan." I let my feelings slip, but I didn't regret it. Now everyone in the room knew that this was personal. "I don't remember you running out West to confront that sadistic bastard."

"If I remember correctly," Jonathan shot back, "you volunteered for that assignment and went against a well laid plan to kill the man, in favor of your fucking dots." Jonathan was trying to embarrass me, but I wasn't going out like that.

"You know what? Maybe it's time I came out of retirement and showed you how it's done, since your boy's not up to it."

"Don't make me laugh. You told me yourself you have to have a real set of balls to be in the field. You've been behind a desk a long time, Jonathan. Don't come from behind it. You might find yours have shrunk quite a bit," I countered. In truth, he was a really good operative in the field, maybe the best I'd seen until Niles, but I wasn't about to admit that to him.

"What's that supposed to mean?" Jonathan had snapped back. "I busted my ass in the field for this company."

"Jonathan, no one ever questions your ability to do a great job," Douglas reminded him, and like a good dog, he backed down. "Bridget, this is not a place for personal attacks."

But Jonathan wasn't done.

"Why don't we leave it up to Douglas to make that decision, since he's the one in charge?" Jonathan challenged me like we were fighting over a bag of chips and not a man's life.

"Enough! This is not a pissing contest. We're talking about the safety and well-being of the American people," Douglas said, throwing me a bone. At least he understood. "You wanna test this guy, let's send them to handle Alexander. You take care of him, and it'll take a lot of pressure off my back and the senator's."

I stared angrily at Jonathan. "Consider it done, Director."

Willie

40

Niles had already given me the go-ahead, so I couldn't wait to talk to Tanya and see the look on her face when I gave her the good news. That woman was seriously working up to wife status, and I'm not just talking on Facebook. I'm talking the all day, every day kind of commitment. It had only been a few months, but I could already tell that she wasn't the type of woman you run into on the regular. She was ride or die, and after being down on my luck for so long, I liked having a real partner to share my good times with, especially when I knew she'd be there even if things got tough. She liked me when I didn't have a pot to piss in or a window to throw it out of, and in today's world, that's saying a whole lot.

"Where you taking me?" she asked as she got into the car with her overnight bag, all excited, like a little girl hoping it was a trip to FAO Schwartz. I'd told her to dress casually, but even in a pair of jeans, flats, and a T-shirt, she was turning me on.

"It's for me to know and you to find out," I kidded, using a favorite childhood comeback to tease her.

"This don't look like the way to your house," she said, trying to get a clue, but I wasn't budging. "Well, wherever it is don't matter, since I'm not working tomorrow. They said I might have some hours on Tuesday. I swear, if I didn't have to keep up my rent, I would just quit."

"Then quit. It's not like you're in love with that apartment anyway. Didn't you just tell me your neighbor had a break-in?"

"Yeah, I know it's not much, but it's what I can afford." She sounded frustrated.

"Hey, I get it. You see where I'm living," I reminded her, failing to mention it in past tense, since that would have given away part of the surprise.

"How far is it?" she pressed after I'd driven another twenty minutes.

I smiled over at her and took her hand. "Not far."

"You know the suspense is killing me."

"Baby, it's like me. Worth the wait," I joked as I ran my hand between her legs.

Tanya picked up my hand and held it in hers. "You better stop or you're going to have to take care of me right here in this car."

"Oh, I can do that and still drive." I waved my fingers in the air to remind her of how quickly I had made her come in the movie theater the other night.

She burst out laughing. "You are too bad, Willie. Least now I get the full appeal of dating an older man. You have tricks."

"And don't you forget it, because I'm not planning on letting you go." I could see out the side of my eye that she had brightened at that statement. I can't tell you how happy it made me to be with this woman.

We pulled into the driveway a few minutes later.

"What a beautiful house," Tanya gushed as we pulled up in front of the home Niles had recently purchased. "Who lives here?"

"I do."

She glanced over at me. "What?"

"Well, not alone. Niles bought it, but we moved in yesterday," I confessed, leaving out the part about the top-flight moving company who packed and unpacked everything, along with the furniture delivery.

"God, this neighborhood . . . it's just lovely." Tanya got out of the car. "Now I'm really not breaking up with you."

Now it was my turn to be surprised. "What? You were breaking up with me?" I sputtered.

"Gotcha! Next time don't surprise me." She laughed as she threw her arms around my neck and kissed me.

"Come on. I want you to meet my sister." We headed through the house to the family room, where Lorna sat watching Law & Order.

"Lorna?" I called to her as we entered. She turned, and her face lit up when she spotted Tanya.

"Willie, who is this young lady?" she asked as we made our way over to her.

"This is my girlfriend, Tanya," I told my sister, realizing it was the first time I'd ever referred to her as my girlfriend. I could see the surprise on Tanya's face and Lorna's.

"Come here and sit with me," she said to Tanya with a big, friendly smile on her face. Tanya took a seat beside her on the sofa.

"This is my favorite show," Tanya told her.

I went to find Niles, and by the time I returned, they were fast and furious friends.

"Did you eat anything for lunch?" I asked Lorna. "Or do you want me to fix you something?"

Tanya jumped in and volunteered. "I don't mind. I can cook something."

"No, I can run out and get us food." I tried to insist, but Tanya was already asking Lorna what she would like and hurrying into the kitchen, so I followed her. She was already in the refrigerator, which we'd stocked yesterday.

I interrupted her search. "I'm taking you to dinner to celebrate."

"That's fine, but what are we celebrating?" she asked.

"Your new job—that is, if you want it. It comes with benefits, aside from seeing me all the time."

"What new job?"

"Well, Lorna needs someone to be here to take care of her. We were going to hire from a service, but I told Niles that if you agreed, there was no one we'd feel better about in our house with Lorna."

Tanya slapped a hand over her mouth. "What? Willie, really?"

That's when Niles came into the kitchen. "Tell her to take the job," I told my nephew.

"Take the job. It starts at $650 a week, but we can raise it. Did you show her the quarters?" Niles asked.

"What?" Tanya looked like her head was about to explode.

"This is far from where you live, and when we're working, we need someone who is willing to work around the clock. You'll be compensated. There is a separate wing in the back, so you'll have your own apartment if you want it. That way you'll have total privacy when you're not working," I explained.

"So I'd live here?" she asked, sounding shocked.

Niles answered, "Yes. Some days we'll need that, but it's up to you if you want to keep your place. The apartment comes with the job."

Tanya walked over to the window and looked out. "So, I can live here? This beautiful neighborhood would be my neighborhood?"

Niles and I both answered, "Yes!"

"I'm in. Oh my God! I can't believe it. When can I move in?" She was jumping around like she'd just won the Miss America pageant.

"Whenever you want us to send the movers to your place. They will pack you up and unpack you," I said.

"I can't believe this. Does Lorna know?"

"We wanted to wait and see if you took the job first."

Tanya moved toward me and threw her arms around my neck. "Thank you."

"No, thank you." I kissed her.

Niles interrupted us, joking, "It's getting too sappy in here." He walked out, leaving me free to love on Tanya. I knew that my sister was lucky to have such an amazing woman looking after her, but that paled in comparison to how lucky I was to have found this special woman to call mine.

Keisha

41

Have you ever had what I call a come to Jesus moment? Where you feel like your entire life has come to an end, and all you want to do is just bury your head in your hands and fade away? Well, that's how I felt when I answered the door to find Majestic and Bruce standing on my stoop.

"Um, Majestic, you're home," I mumbled.

"That's right, I'm home. Now where's my son?" Majestic demanded. He pushed past me like I wasn't even there. Bruce, on the other hand, just stood there smirking at me. He didn't have to say what he was thinking. His facial expression said it all for him.

"You could have called and told me that you were coming," I snapped after taking a long, deep breath. If he thought I was going to put up with his bullying, he was wrong. One of the things I'd learned about my relationship with Majestic was that if you didn't stand up to him, he'd run all over you.

Majestic stopped and gave Bruce a look.

"Man. I told you she was out of control," Bruce commented.

"Shut the fuck up, Bruce. Ain't nobody talking to you." I turned all my anger toward him. I guess I wasn't quite ready to stand up to Majestic yet. "This is my fucking house, and you can get the hell out."

"No, Keisha, this is my fucking house," Majestic said. "I pay the bills here, and you might want to remember that, instead of giving me and my boy all that fucking attitude," he blasted me, going from room to room with me following behind him to make sure he didn't tear the place up. "Otherwise, you can pack your shit and get the fuck out right now. Now where the fuck is my son?"

I knew I had no choice but to let him see MJ, but I didn't have to pretend to be happy about it. "He's sleeping, so let me wake him up so he don't get scared," I told them. "Stay here."

Majestic ignored my direction and followed right behind me. "What, you ain't miss me?" He grabbed me around the waist and pulled me close.

"Stop, Majestic," I whispered, not wanting MJ to wake up with him all over me. I tried to pull away, but he had a death grip on me and was burying his head in my neck.

"Now we need to get busy giving little man a sister or brother."

"I'm not having another baby by you," I whispered harshly, feeling my stomach turn with fear and disgust. "Why don't you get one of those other hoes pregnant? You know the ones you got all over town," I reminded him.

"Keisha, you are my baby mama. I told you when you got pregnant that I want all my kids to have the same mother."

I gave him a look like he was crazy. "We're not together anymore!"

He threw back his head and laughed like what I said was funny as hell. In retaliation, he grabbed me by the arm and held on tight, giving me a cold and intimidating look before he threatened me. "We are together as long as I say that we are together, and if you value your life, you need to remember that."

He let my hand go, and I felt myself turn to mush, shaking in fear for my life. That didn't mean I was ready to roll over and give in to him, though. I'd always had a bit of a stubborn streak. I was enjoying my new life with Niles, and I didn't want to even think about going back to the way things were when I was under Majestic's thumb.

"I don't want to be with you anymore," I insisted. "Don't you want a woman who wants to be with you and can love you the way you deserve? You deserve to be happy, Majestic. I can't do that for you." I thought that would soften the truth that I didn't love or want him anymore.

Suddenly, his face turned into a monster's, and he went ballistic. "Bitch, I don't give a shit what you think you want or what you think I deserve. What you think and how you feel don't mean shit to me, and you want to know why? Because I will tell you what to think and how to feel—and don't be confused that I need you. MJ is small enough that I can get rid of you and find him a new mother like that!" He snapped his fingers to make a point. "Is that what you want?" He stood close to me, lifting his shirt to show me his gun. I knew not to push him, or he could make me disappear.

"Answer the fucking question," he said. "Is that what you want?"

"No."

"No what?" he growled.

"No, I want you," I lied. He didn't care if it was true, as long as I got back in line.

"Now go wake up my son and bring him into the living room," he demanded as he left the room. I had to fight to keep the tears from flowing, but the last thing I wanted was for MJ to see my crying.

I reached down and picked him up and held him close to me. I loved my son more than life itself, but his father was a whole other issue—one I would have to deal with, whether I wanted to or not, until I could figure out another way.

Of course Majestic insisted that I run out and get him and Bruce Chinese takeout. When I tried to take MJ with me, he shut that down and told me to go alone. God, I hated them.

When I returned with the chicken wings and fried rice, MJ was sitting on Majestic's lap, playing with his phone, as happy as he could be.

Majestic shot me a look that said *I told you so*.

"You need to relax," he said. "My son is happy to see his daddy," he bragged as I set the food down in front of them.

"Anything else?" I asked as I placed the two Cokes down.

"What about my little man?" he asked, pointing to the soda.

"He doesn't drink soda. It's not good for him. I'll get him a juice box." I headed into the kitchen and returned with the juice.

He turned to Bruce. "Told you she would make a good mother. Lots of those chicken heads would give their kids anything." Then Majestic focused on MJ. "You ready for a little brother or sister?"

I almost choked hearing that, but I knew to hold back what I wanted to say.

He turned his attention to me again. "You know I wanted to spend time with my son, but you wouldn't bring him to visit me."

"Well, I don't think jail is a good place to take a kid," I said, trying hard not to shout, because I knew it would scare MJ.

"Did you miss Daddy?"

MJ stared up at Majestic. "Yeah. Daddy, when I grow up, I want to go to camp too, just like you."

"Camp? Well, MJ, you're going to another kind of camp. You're going to college."

Majestic got that look on his face that let me know he was angry. "MJ, go find Grandma room and play with some of those toys Uncle Bruce brought you while I was in camp."

My son scooted off his father's lap and raced into the other room.

I called after him. "MJ, wash your hands first." That's when I saw an exchange between Bruce and Majestic.

Bruce got up and went into the room after MJ. I folded my hands across my chest, waiting to get scolded by Majestic, who was finishing a wing.

"You know how many women want to have my baby? 'Cause I make sure that you don't want for nothing, long as you take care of my kid. But everything here, including you and MJ, belong to me. You forget that again, and your ass will be on the street alone. You feel me? Now, you had your little fun while I was locked up, but Daddy is home now. You get that?" He reached out and grabbed my arm and twisted it. A red/purple welt rose up on my arm.

I nodded like I was supposed to. "Yes. Stop. You're hurting me. I get it!"

"Good." He let me go, but he never took his eyes off of me. "Now, I suggest you bring your ass over here and give me a warm welcome home."

I wanted to cry, but I knew I couldn't. Instead, I approached him and gave him a kiss, even as my stomach churned with disgust. When we broke apart, I thought that would be the end, but I was wrong. Majestic picked up another wing and started eating, which I took as a sign that I could leave.

I started cleaning the dishes off the table.

He gave me a cold look before he spoke. "Nah, put that shit down. Get over here," he said.

Reluctantly, I did as I was told, mostly because my son was in the other room and I didn't want to start fighting with Majestic now.

I stood in front of him, and he said, "Down on your knees and show me some gratitude for all I do for you."

"Are you serious?"

"Do I look serious?" he raised his hand.

"But MJ could walk in," I insisted as I backed away.

"Bruce got it handled, but if you're worried, then you should be quick. And do it just the way I like it." He stood up and unzipped his pants before sitting back down and continuing to eat. "What you waiting for—an engraved fucking invitation? And bitch, if you bite me, I swear to God I'll kill you and anybody closely related to you."

I lowered myself to the floor, pulled out his penis, and started to blow him like my life depended on it, because we both knew that it did. Niles crossed my mind while I was on my knees, and I felt like I was betraying him. Yet it would hurt my son if I got killed by this maniac, so I did what I had to do. I blocked Niles out of my mind.

Niles

42

"This is bullshit and you know it, Bridget." I couldn't disguise the frustration in my voice as I stared over at Bridget, who was in the back of her Rolls, nonchalantly inspecting her manicure. Even she had to admit that I was becoming more efficient at what we did, and in some ways I was even better at it than she was. That didn't mean she was willing to give me any credit.

"When are you going to stop babysitting me and let me go out on my own? Haven't I proven I can do the job?" I pressed.

She turned and glared at me. "Sure, you've proven you can be an effective killer, but there are ten-year-old boys doing that for Isis in Syria every day. How many times do I have to tell you this job isn't just about putting a bullet in someone's head? You're good, Niles, real good, and you have the ability to be one of the best operatives this agency has ever produced, but you still have a lot to learn.

I think tonight will prove that to you." She had this sarcastic way of complimenting me and then tearing me down at the same time that drove me insane.

She handed me a folder, and I thumbed through it, stopping at a black and white surveillance photo of a bearded white man in his late forties. "This our mark?" I asked.

She nodded. "His name is Alexander Renkoff. He used to be a CIA asset. Now he's a man with a conscience. On Monday, he plans to testify in front of the United Nations about United States crimes against humanity in Guantanamo Bay. We've been asked to discreetly make sure he doesn't make it to the UN."

"Why do we care about what happens to the CIA?" I asked, not exactly thrilled with the idea of killing someone just to keep his mouth shut.

"You know, for someone who spent most of his life as an Army grunt blindly following orders, you sure as hell ask a lot of questions. And for the record, this is way above your pay grade—and mine, too, for that matter. We have a job to do, and we're being paid well to do it. Let's just get the job done."

I sighed. "Okay, let's get it done. I'm willing to do whatever it takes to get the job done."

She smirked. "Are you? Because I'm going to test your ability to stay cool, calm, and collected under pressure, amongst other things, then turn around and test your moral compass."

"I love tests. I've always been an A student. You should know that, teach," I said, my voice full of cocky self-assurance.

"Yeah, well, you get an A in this, and even I'll be impressed, because this job isn't just about killing a mark. It's about getting to the target and not letting anyone know we did it. So don't fuck this up. I'm not the only one who will be watching." There was something about the way she said it that gave me concern, but I played it off the best I could. I didn't have a good feeling about this one, but taking care of my mother was my first and foremost concern, so I was going to do whatever I had to do.

When the car pulled up to the curb, Bridget nodded to Winston, and the two of us got out. We were greeted by two doormen who looked like Samoan wrestlers. They were standing guard in front of an inconspicuous building with no obvious signs, like an old school speakeasy. Bridget leaned in and whispered something to one of the doormen. He nodded to his colleague, who opened up the door.

"You two enjoy yourselves," the man holding the door said.

"Oh, I'm sure we will," Bridget answered, raising her eyebrows suggestively before taking my hand and leading me inside.

The moment we walked in, we were bathed in low lighting and classical music that gave the place a very high-end feel. A scantily clad woman promptly took our names and directed us to a private room that appeared to be a small locker room, like the kind you see at hotel spas. I really wanted to ask questions, but all that went out the window when I turned to Bridget and saw that she was already halfway out of her dress.

"Ummm, why exactly are you standing in front of me half naked?" I couldn't help the fact that my eyes were glued to her damn near perfect bare breasts.

"What does it look like I'm doing? I'm getting undressed. You need to do the same," she snapped like this was what we did on a daily basis. She let her dress drop to the ground, and all she was wearing was a tiny black thong, which she didn't hesitate to remove. Damn, I had to give it to her; the woman had an amazing body. One look at her Brazilian wax job and my dick jumped straight to attention.

"I don't think that's such a good idea. We have to maintain some type of professionalism, don't we?" I tried to sound sincere, but the last thing I wanted was for this egotistical woman to see me naked with a hard dick. It would just make her more arrogant than she already was. Even with my clothes still on, I had to turn my body away from her so she wouldn't see the tent in my pants.

"Look, Niles, I don't have time for your vanity. Now, get out your fucking clothes. You're wasting valuable time!" she snapped in a way that made me realize she was serious and I didn't have a choice. I followed suit, feeling like a fool as I stood in front of her, naked, with an erect penis. God, if Keisha knew about this, I thought, she'd kill me.

For a brief moment, Bridget stood there and stared at my package, nodding with a big-ass grin on her face, like she knew something I didn't. "Not bad, Monroe. I was really afraid you were going to have a little dick, but you got something a woman can work with. Not too big, but definitely not too small."

Without warning, she took hold of my penis, firmly leading me toward a door on the other side of the room, which she didn't hesitate to open. We were immediately inundated with music and strobe lighting. The place had the feel of a club, except that everyone in the room was completely naked. It took a moment for my eyes to adjust to the light; however, that's when I realized that not only was everyone naked, but most of them were engaged in some type of sexual act.

What the fuck? I guess the best way to describe it was that I was standing in the middle of a big-ass orgy.

"What the fuck is this place?"

"It's a sex club. Now, stay close and keep your eyes peeled for Alexander." She tugged on my dick, and I had no choice but to follow her into the room. Thank God for the crazy lighting, or everyone would have seen me blushing. The crazy thing is, despite how embarrassed I was, my dick remained hard the whole time.

A thirty-something-year-old redhead swept past us, stopping Bridget. "Oh, that looks like it could be fun." She looked downward, and that was when I realized she was talking about my dick.

Bridget smiled and said, "I know, right? I'm about to find out."

"Let me know. I'd totally take him in my ass."

Bridget smiled at the bold woman but, to my relief, kept on moving, still leading me by the dick as she searched through the crowd of freaks.

After about two or three minutes of people feeling on my ass and touching me like I was some type of plaything, I stopped dead in my tracks. This shit was getting crazy, and I wanted some answers.

"What the fuck is this place? And why the hell are we here?"

"We're here because Alexander's here. He never misses one of these parties. He can't help himself. He's got this thing about watching people fuck, so loosen up and keep your eyeballs peeled." Once again, she began to lead me around, looking at one freaky act after another as we searched the room.

"Bridget, over there." I motioned toward an upper level, and there was old boy, watching two people go at it while some East Indian woman sucked on his dick.

"C'mon." She led me over to the stairs, which were roped off.

"Sorry, VIP only." A beefy man in a G-string stopped us from going any farther. He pointed at his wrist. "You gotta have a green bracelet."

"Fuck!" Bridget tried to talk the bouncer into letting us up the stairs, but she was getting nowhere with him. "Come on," she said to me as she pulled me away from him. "There's more than one way to skin a cat."

She led me over to the center of the room, staring up at the VIP section until Alexander was in perfect view. Once there, she let go of my penis and stared at me seriously.

"This is where you earn your stripes, Monroe. Right here, right now, we find out if you're Jason Bourne or Maxwell fucking Smart. Are you ready?"

She reminded me of this really intense, no-nonsense commanding officer I used to have. You never wanted to let this guy down.

"Of course I'm ready," I said like this wasn't the weirdest fucking situation I'd ever been in. "What do I have to do?" I stood in front of her, chest out like a warrior ready to go into battle—but no way was I expecting this kind of fight.

She took a long breath then spit out a question. "Do you know how to fuck?"

The way she said it was all business, and not the least bit sexy.

"Huh?" I stared at her, my back kind of stiffening.

"I said, can you fuck? Are you any good with that thing hanging between your legs?"

"What kind of question is that?"

"Just answer the damn question. Do you know how to fuck? Can you put it down and make a bitch scream?"

"I haven't had any complaints, if that's what you're getting at. What the hell are you up—"

Before I could complete my question, she jumped up in the air, wrapping her arms around my neck and her legs around my waist.

"What the hell are you waiting for? Fuck me!" Bridget began to rock her back and hips in anticipation.

I whispered in her ear, "I have a girlfriend."

"Tell *him* that," she whispered back, gesturing toward Alexander before grabbing my hard dick and shoving it inside of her. Within seconds, it was engulfed by the warmest, moistest coochie I'd ever felt.

She held onto my neck and began to slide up and down. As much as I'd like to say I refused to participate, my dick stood at full attention, instinctively thrusting into her. My manhood had a mind of its own, even though my mind was racing with guilt about Keisha. I attempted to resist, making myself stand as still as possible as I tried to get my bearings, because clearly the little head was leading the big head.

"I can't do this. I have a girlfriend," I repeated.

"Do I look like I give a shit?" she cursed, continuing to slide up and down on my pole. She was doing something with her muscles; I can't tell you exactly what it was, but it sure as hell felt good.

"We've got a job to do, Niles, so man up and fuck me. It's the only way Alexander's going to come down from his ivory perch," she said, still ordering me around as she was fucking me like a pro.

I guess I should have expected her to do something like that the minute we walked in the door, but I hadn't. It hadn't even crossed my mind. I mean, call me naïve, but it's not every day you are asked to fuck your boss in the line of duty.

"God dammit, fuck me!" she growled.

That was the last thing I heard before I bit my lip and began doing exactly what she demanded. I didn't just fuck her. I took out all my anger, aggression, and frustration on her woman parts. Surprisingly, the meaner I got, the more she seemed to like it.

"That's it. That's it, fuck me!" she shouted, letting go of my neck and leaning back like she was riding a bucking bronco. I must say she was putting on quite a show, to the point that she was attracting a crowd, which was probably her point.

She rode me like that for a few minutes, then stretched her hands back to the floor in some crazy yoga position. "That's it, baby. Keep fucking. Now spin me."

"What?" I was still pumping away, but what she was asking seemed kind of crazy. Then again, nothing could be crazier than us fucking in a sex club to attract the attention of a horny ex-CIA agent.

"I said spin me around!"

Once again, I did what I was told, spinning her around in some wild Dancing with the Porn Stars fuck move. While we spun, I continued to fuck her hard and strong, despite the fact that I was getting dizzy as hell. The most ridiculous part was the dizzier I got, the more into it I seemed to be. "Yeah, that's it, baby. Fuck me! Fuck me!"

She let out a scream, which I think included my name. "Oh, shit, Niles! I'm gonna come! I'm gonna come!" At this point I was sweating like a pig, and like her, I'm about to come as well. Her body began twitching and writhing as her climaxed released, and when I say she released, I mean it. Come to find out Bridget was one of those rare women that they called squirters. "Fuck, I'm cooooming!" she screamed for both of us.

I slowed down, trying to shake the dizziness, only to see most of the club's crowd surrounding us. Believe it or not, those perverts broke out into a standing ovation, and the man leading the applause was none other than our mark, Alexander.

Bridget

43

"Aaaaaaaaaaaaah!" I was putting the finishing touches on my makeup in the locker room when I heard someone let out an ear-piercing scream from inside the club area. Then all I heard was a commotion and people scrambling like madmen, which told me that our mission had been a complete success.

After my freaky performance with Niles, Alexander had introduced himself then very politely asked Niles if he could fuck me. Niles, of course, offered no objection, and during our brief moment of intimacy, I placed a very special dot on the back of Alexander's neck. Unlike the dots that I usually used, this dot didn't kill the subject right away; instead, it caused a blood clot, causing the victim to either have a severe stroke or a heart attack.

Leaving the building promptly, I took a deep breath as I slid into the backseat of the Rolls, because my new dilemma resided with my partner, who, to be quite honest, had fucked me like a pro.

"What the fuck!" Niles snapped as he climbed in the car.

Winston closed the door, making his way around the car and into the driver's seat.

"Not now, Niles," I said with authority, reminding him who was boss. I could hear the ambulance sirens and wanted to get ghost as soon as possible. None of this could be traced back to us. The fact that there were so many prominent folks inside at the time guaranteed news coverage would be minimal, but I still didn't want to be anywhere near the place, in case some genius happened to find the dot, which was designed to have fallen off by now.

"Winston, let's get outta here," I said.

"You did that shit on purpose." Niles hit the button, raising the glass between Winston and us. He looked like he was ready to strangle me. "We could've hit that target anyplace else in the city, but you insisted we had to get him in the sex club. You know I have a girlfriend that I'm faithful to. Was this just some setup so I would screw you?"

I rolled my eyes. "Stop being so paranoid. And stop flattering yourself. You think you're so hot that I would go to those lengths to get with you? Please. It's just a part of the job, little boy."

He cut his eyes at me, and I realized I had wounded his ego. I decided to throw him a small compliment so he wouldn't be pouting all night long.

"Okay, fine. I will admit that you have skills, but the bottom line is we do whatever the fuck it takes to complete a mission. There wasn't any other way to get to Alexander. If we could have gotten his attention without our little performance, then I would have. And besides, you seemed to enjoy yourself. Can't we just look at the sex as a little bonus?" I couldn't hold back my smile as he glared at me.

"I have a girlfriend. You should have respected that," he responded, unable to answer my question or look me in my eyes. "I could have taken that guy out from a block away as he was leaving the club."

"No, you couldn't. It had to look like an accident, not an assassination. That was the job. He was the target, and this was the only way to get close to him," I hissed, getting more annoyed. I did not like to have my judgment questioned, especially by my underling. "There were two A-list stars, a couple of Fortune 500 CEOs, and a congressman in there, Niles. You think us walking in there clothed and shooting would have missed the news?"

"You couldn't have given me a heads up? Perhaps told me the fucking plan?" He pouted, refusing to be pacified. "We're supposed to be partners. You should have trusted me."

"If I had told you that you might have to fuck me to get the job done, would you have done it?"

He hesitated, giving me his answer without saying a word.

"Exactly my point. This job is about the job, and that's all."

"Not if it affects my life. I'm planning on marrying that girl someday."

A twinge of jealousy swept through me, taking me by surprise. He had been with Keisha over seven months now, and life was good—except when he had to go out and kill someone for his new job, or now, fuck someone he worked with. He really didn't want to mess up a good thing, which was amazing. It was rare to find a man who even recognized when he had a good thing. That Keisha was a lucky woman. I wondered if she knew it.

"I can't just go around fucking people," he continued, unable to let it go.

I scrunched up my face dramatically. "Boo fucking hoo. If your girl has a problem with you doing what your job requires, then you're just gonna need to learn how to keep a secret. Besides, be honest. You liked it, didn't you?

I teased. "You like the way I fuck, don't you? I'm super tight and really wet." In fact, I was getting wet now, just having flashbacks to our encounter in the club.

He looked flustered. I wondered if he was also having flashbacks. "That's not the point," he finally mumbled. "And this is not your life. It's mine."

"Niles, I know you love this job. How can you not? And eventually, you're going to realize that this job is your life. Until then, you need to grow the fuck up," I said, deciding that this discussion should be over. "Now, I'm hungry and I need a cigarette, because I like to have a nice smoke after I get fucked real good."

"So that's it?" he huffed.

"What do you want me to say? This is work, and work comes first. Now, you understand the job. Do you want to continue to complain about it? Because I can find someone else to do the job, but just know that we don't pay unemployment, and even if we did, it sure as hell wouldn't be enough to support your mama the way you want." I pulled out an e-cigarette, desperately taking a blissful toke.

"From now on, I'm told the total mission from the start, or else I walk," he said, as if he was actually contemplating quitting. I knew that would never happen, but I let him believe I was concerned he might quit.

I nodded to let him know I was giving in to his demands, allowing him to maintain the delusion that he had any true control over his situation now that he was employed by Dynamic Defense. Looking satisfied that I'd given in, Niles took the cigarette out of my hand and took a drag.

"So she doesn't mind you smoking?" I joked.

He threw his head back and exhaled, announcing with plenty of confidence, "When it comes to this job, what she doesn't know won't hurt her."

I suppressed a sigh of relief. For a minute, I had thought that I was going to lose him over this assignment. Now I was growing more certain that Niles was truly cut out for this job and me.

Keisha

44

I held onto a pillow, fighting back tears as Majestic stood on the floor by the edge of the bed, pounding me from behind like some deranged animal. His sweat was flying all over the place, and each drop that landed on me made my stomach turn. I was so disgusted by him. All I wanted him to do was finish so I could run to the pharmacy and get one of those morning after pills to prevent a pregnancy. I had hoped that giving him head that afternoon would keep him away for a while so I could figure things out with Niles, but he was back later on that night without Bruce and carrying an overnight bag. He'd been on me ever since.

In less than a day, the wonderful life I'd been living, where I was a single parent with a loving man in my life, had disappeared. Now it felt as if I were the one in a prison, except it didn't have the bars. Make no mistake about it: Majestic was my jailer, and that was the way he liked it.

He finally stiffened up and let out a few grunts before collapsing on the bed next to me. "Now that was some good shit. What you got to eat?"

"I don't know. What you want?" I said. The last thing I wanted to do was get up and feed him, but I also didn't want to set off his temper.

"I ain't had one of your cheese steaks in a minute. You got any Steak-umms?"

"Yeah." I pushed myself up from the bed, put on my robe, and headed down the hall to the kitchen, thankful that he didn't get up and follow me. If only I could have taken a shower to wash off all traces of his body on mine.

I had just broken out the Steak-umms and a frying pan when my mother came in the back door.

She looked over at what I was doing and broke into a huge grin. "Mm-hmm, thank God things are finally starting to get back to normal around here. I saw Majestic's car parked out front. While you're at it, can you make me one too?" she asked on her way into the bathroom.

The headlights of a car shone through the window as someone pulled into the driveway and parked behind my car. As he shut off the engine and the car's interior lights came on, I could see that it was Niles. I rushed to the front door like my life depended on it—which, in reality, it probably did.

"Niles." I opened the door and stepped onto the porch just as he was about to knock

"Damn, baby, you all ready for me?" Niles stood there in an expensive navy suit looking like something out of a dream, but I knew for me, the dream had turned into a nightmare. Before I could stop him, he reached out and grabbed me around the waist, pulling me close so that he could kiss me. I hadn't even taken a shower yet, so if I lingered in his arms long enough, he would have smelled Majestic's sweat on me.

"Stop," I snapped as I pulled away. "I need to take a shower."

His face broke into a devilish grin. "Why don't we take one together?" Niles said in that deep, sexy voice. He took a step toward the door, but I didn't move. Normally I'd be stripping off my clothes and racing him to the shower, but right now I was feeling sick, knowing that I had to get him out of there before Majestic came looking for me.

"I'm not feeling so good right now," I said, only half lying. "Can I call you later?" I needed him to leave, but he knew me too well, and he was having none of it.

"What's going on, Keisha? Talk to me."

"Nothing. I just need some time to myself. I'm not feeling so great. I think my period's about to start. I'm gonna go lay down and take some Motrin." I knew my lies sounded hollow, but all I could think of was how bad it would be if Majestic came out of my room and there was a confrontation. "I'll call you later and we'll talk, okay? I promise."

"Come on, Keisha. Don't lie to me. We both know you had your period last week." He shook his head, looking disgusted; but what else did I expect? I was so ashamed I couldn't even look at him. I sure as hell couldn't tell him the truth—that I was once again the property of my baby daddy, and if he wanted to live, he should stay as far away from me as possible.

"Niles, I can't right now," I told him curtly, hoping it would work and he'd finally leave. It felt like a clock was ticking down the seconds until Majestic showed up, and I couldn't risk it, especially with me standing here butt naked under my robe. "Niles, you're not getting it. You need to leave."

He threw his head back and laughed. "Keisha, stop playing with me. This ain't funny."

"And I ain't laughing. I can't see you anymore. It's over," I announced, steeling myself for his response.

"What I do?" He started breathing rapidly and the muscles in his face tensed up. Clearly, he was pissed. I had no choice but to rip off the Band-Aid.

"Niles, take the fucking hint, a'ight? It's over!" I said angrily, my fear driving me.

Just then, the door opened up, and my heart was in my mouth. I was so damn scared.

"Keisha." My mother stepped out and pulled the door closed behind her. She smirked at Niles as she continued. "Majestic wants to know what the hell you doin' and where are his cheesesteaks. I suggest you bring your ass inside and take care of your man."

"Majestic?" Niles repeated, staring directly at me. "Isn't that your ex?"

"Apparently he ain't the one who's an ex," my mother snapped. "Now come on in here, girl, before that man comes out here and you have more trouble on your hands than you already have."

"Niles, I'm sorry, but I have to go," I said, holding back tears.

I stepped inside, and my mother followed, slamming the door shut in Niles's face. I felt like I wanted to die, but I refused to let Niles get caught up in the crossfire of my sick relationship with Majestic. I had to protect him, even if he didn't understand, and I knew I couldn't tell him the full truth, because he was macho enough to want to fight Majestic. That kind of mistake would be his death sentence, and even if I couldn't be with Niles, I couldn't bear to see him hurt either.

Bruce

45

"Where the fuck is this guy?" I thought out loud to myself. I was sitting on some random street in Queens Village, across from a junior high school, with my car idling like some pedophile. Unless I was getting some ass, I never liked leaving the confines of Suffolk County. With everything Majestic and I had going on, I just felt safer there. I was a true creature of habit. Still, this was where he told me to meet him, so there I was.

I lifted my iPhone and dialed Majestic's number. "Yo, where you at?" I asked.

"On my way to my mother's to drop off my little man. Where you?"

"I'm still out here waiting on your friend," I said. Majestic had sent me out to gather some information about Rodney's death. "I'ma swing by and get you as soon as I hear what this dude's got to say."

I had learned real early in my business that most people come with a sticker price, and this dirty cop was no different. I just hoped he came through with the information we needed. I was getting sick of reaching dead ends.

"Yo, don't let him leave nothing out," Majestic warned.

"Don't worry; I got this." In my rearview mirror I clocked a Toyota truck parking behind me. Pete, the cop on our payroll, opened the door to my ride and got in.

"Sorry about that. I had to make sure I wasn't being followed," he said dramatically, like his ass had been watching way too many reruns of Law and Order.

"So what's up? What you got?"

"I got some really interesting shit, that's what I got." Dude was grinning like he'd brought me a prize.

"Uh-huh, and? Spit it out already. This ain't no fucking date." I raised my voice at him, growing restless. We were paying this guy too much money to be playing games.

"You were right. There was definitely some type of cover-up pertaining to Rodney's murder."

I nodded my head slowly. "Okay, okay, so you got the file or what?" I just wanted to read the shit and find out who we needed to exterminate, like, yesterday.

He shook his head. "That's just it. There was no file." He dropped the information in my lap like he was saying something, but I was hot, 'cause I wasn't hearing shit that was useful to me.

"What the fuck you mean there's no file? I thought you were in charge of the records room," I snapped at him. "That's what you said, right? 'I'm your guy. I can get my hands on anything.' If you think you gettin' paid for this bullshit waste of my time . . ." I fumed. This was not the outcome I wanted to bring back to Majestic. This sellout fuck-up was making it impossible for me to do my job.

"Look, Bruce, what I'm telling you is more valuable than a file."

"You expect me to buy this bullshit? Look, man, just because you a cop don't mean I won't smoke your ass for trying to take advantage."

"No, you don't understand. Shit gets lost all the time. Cops are notoriously lazy about filing stuff, but there's always some type of record: a notebook, a log book, or fingerprints. Something. Except in this case, there is no record. There's not even a fucking 911 tape. It's like it didn't even happen, which is crazy," he explained, getting all worked up. "First time I ever seen anything like this."

I glared at him, ready to toss him out of my car head first. "So you got nothing? Pete, I'm not the kind of guy interested in having a meeting that shoulda been a goddamn text message."

"No. That's not what I'm saying at all," he answered cryptically.

Man, I was getting ready to choke this mofo if he didn't stop dragging this out. Maybe he was trying to make sure I knew he earned his money, but he was moving closer to earning a beat down than getting his hands on the cash in my pocket.

"Well, fuck, spit it out!" I finally snapped at his ass.

His eyes widened in fear, but it was enough to loosen his tongue. "There was a lead detective assigned to the case by the name of Fuller. He interviewed whatever suspect or suspects he found. But check this out: there was no evidence of anything, not a single case. And this guy is known for being thorough."

"Uh-huh?" I said, now following this trail.

"So, I did my due diligence and went to one of the other detectives, who straight up told me, 'Pete, this is not your problem.' So now I'm really getting suspicious, because I ask about cases all the time. First time I get that for a response."

"Uh-huh?" Shit was starting to look like a cover-up to me.

"So I nosed around some more, and I found out that this shit was quiet on a really high level. I mean, it went up the food chain and then suddenly just dropped off. Silent."

"Okay, before you go all James fucking Bond on me, how do you know there was anything? What if this guy just didn't find any witnesses?"

"That's the thing. There would still be paperwork. This buddy of mine happened to be working that night and told me that initially they did pop someone for it, but again, when I went to do the research, no records. Nothing."

"And this Fuller? Where is he?"

"Gone. Retired not too long after the case." He finished his report with a goofy look on his face, like he was proud of the useless shit he'd just fed me.

"So tell me more about Fuller," I pressed.

He looked slightly guilty as he continued. "He was a really good cop."

I chuckled, letting him know I didn't believe there was such a thing. He didn't seem to care what I thought.

"Fuller was like one of my mentors," he continued. "A nice guy."

"Uh-huh. And how do I find this 'nice guy'?"

He pulled out a piece of paper and handed it to me. "That's his information—address, everything."

Five minutes later and five thousand dollars lighter, I was on my way to sit down with Majestic.

Niles

46

"You okay, boss? I know you back there thinking about Keisha."

Willie wheeled the BMW into the E-ZPass lane of the Midtown Tunnel, headed into the city. He'd been singing old school songs that were playing on the radio most of the ride, while I was doing what Willie said: thinking about Keisha and the fact that she so easily dumped me for her ex-boyfriend.

"I'm fine. And stop calling me boss," I snapped at him for no real reason at all.

"Look, man, I like Keisha, but you gonna have to let that broad go. You can't be pining over no woman while you're working on a mission," he advised me.

"I just don't understand what went wrong, Unc. I thought we were falling in love with each other. At least I know I was."

I could see him shaking his head up front. "You know how these women are about their baby daddies. There's something about popping out a puppy for a brother that gives them undying loyalty. She done made her decision. You need to leave that shit alone."

"You're right, but I just can't believe I was so wrong about her."

"Damon Dash said the same thing about Jay-Z, and look where that got his ass."

He laughed, but I didn't.

I needed to do something to put a smile on my face, so I checked my account online to see if my latest payment had been deposited. I definitely smiled when I saw I had over a quarter of a million dollars in my account in less than three months. Even better, Bridget had said that she was finally going to let me plan and do most of my contracts without her standing over my shoulder. She was still my handler and we were going to be partners on larger jobs, but for the most part, I was finally on my own.

Once through the tunnel, Willie drove four blocks into a nearly deserted parking garage and parked next to a plain white van. We'd already checked to make sure the cell phone reception was good two days earlier, when we dropped off the van.

Willie got out and opened the door to the van, pulling out the magnetic signs that he slapped onto the side of the van. I popped the trunk of the BMW and removed a bag containing work coveralls with a patch bearing the name of the same dry cleaning service that was on the magnetic signs. I put on the uniform, and I was ready to roll.

"Need anything else, boss?" Willie handed me some clothing on wire hangers covered by a black garment bag—my props to make it look like I was delivering dry cleaning. He also gave me an all-plastic, silenced gun in three parts, which I strategically placed in compartments in the garment bag before I got into the van.

"Happy hunting," Willie said as he climbed back into the BMW to wait.

"Yeah, this shouldn't take long," I told him. I was prepared for this. Uncle Sam had trained me well for this new life, and so did Bridget.

I drove the van a few blocks, parked in front of an expensive high rise on Park Avenue, and grabbed the fresh dry cleaning from the back. I put on a baseball cap and a pair of sunglasses to conceal my face before heading into the building. This wasn't your normal office building. It had crazy cameras, uniformed security, a metal detector, and armed guards who were supposed to look inconspicuous in their plain clothes.

After making it through security, I took an elevator up to the third floor, where a cute, curvy brunette receptionist and a beefy security guard watched me the moment I entered the office. He looked all business, while she looked like a potential bed partner, if that was what I was into at the moment. A quick glance around the room told me there were no security cameras, so it was safe to take off my sunglasses. I stepped up to the receptionist's desk and flashed her a smile just as the security guard stood up.

"Can I help you?" she asked.

I gave her my rehearsed line. "I have a delivery for Mr. Wilcox."

"I'll take it," the security guard said, coming from around his desk.

I took a step back. "I'm sorry, sir. This is Mr. Wilcox's tuxedo for tonight's Tea Party fundraiser. I have strict orders to place this in his hands."

"That's ridiculous. I take stuff for him every day," he scoffed at me.

"I'm sorry, but my boss will have my head if I don't personally place this in his hands. There was some kind of mix-up last time, and I'm supposed to assure it doesn't happen again." I tried to sound apologetic, hoping that my reason would resonate with him, one blue collar worker to another.

When it became obvious that he didn't give a shit what my reason was, I turned my attention to the receptionist. "You understand, don't you?" I asked her, my eyes roaming subtly along her body so she knew I found her attractive. It worked.

"Howard," the receptionist said, "you know how Mr. Wilcox can be. Remember what happened last time with his dry cleaning."

The security guard's face went pale as he picked up the phone and dialed an extension. "I understand that. Let me see what I can do."

I had to give props to Bridget. Hacking into Wilcox's email and seeing that his dry cleaner had screwed up his tux the last time was brilliant—maybe as ingenious as me sending Willie over to the cleaner's to pick up his tux as his personal valet.

"Mr. Wilcox, I have a deliveryman here with your tuxedo. He says you need it for tonight?" He finished the call before turning to me. "Sure, sure Mr. Wilcox. No problem. I'll send him right down."

"Sir, if you'll just follow me." He walked over to his desk, which was right in front of two very heavy doors. He picked up a metal detector. "I'm sorry, but I'm going to have to scan you for metal objects before you can come in."

"They already scanned me downstairs," I said, keeping a friendly tone.

"Sorry. Anyone who goes through those doors gets scanned," he said with no warmth at all in his voice. This guy was anything but friendly.

"Okay." I shrugged. "I ain't got nothing to hide. What the hell is this place, the CIA?"

"No, this is a conservative think tank and super PAC," he replied as he scanned me.

"Whatever the hell that is," I responded. That one got him to laugh finally. He turned and punched in a code, which opened the doors.

"Straight ahead, last door on the right."

I walked down the corridor of what seemed like a nice office. When I got to the end, I was greeted by a secretary, who buzzed me into Wilcox's office. I was surprised when the door opened directly into an office with views all over the city. Wow, this place was spectacular. A balding, middle-aged man involved in a phone conversation motioned for me to hang the tux in a closet near the door.

"You guys get the stain out of the collar this time?" he asked, placing his hand over the receiver of the phone to speak to me.

"Yes, sir," I answered, slyly checking out the surroundings. "I'm sure we did."

"'Cause I don't want to have to come in there and cause hell again," he barked before returning to the phone conversation. "You got that handled? Good. Talk later," he said, hanging up the phone. I'd pieced the gun together before he hung up. He looked surprised when he noticed I was still in the room. I guess he was used to his servants just disappearing when he was through with them. "Fuck you waiting for, a tip?" he snapped at me.

I stood silently, which seemed to confused him a little, but he tried to maintain his air of superiority.

"Don't bet on black. How's that for a tip?" He threw his head back, laughing at his own joke, and that was just enough time to catch him off guard.

"What the hell is this? Do you know who I am?" he said, still not understanding that the tables had just turned.

"Actually, Mr Wilcox, I do. You're the scumbag who's behind over a hundred million dollars in drug money that's secretly finding its way into the Tea Party."

His eyes grew wide with surprise that he'd been discovered, and then fear when I raised the gun.

"My sister died of a drug overdose, so I hate drugs."

Thunk, thunk, thunk. Three bullets to the chest and he was on the floor, the life draining out of him.

"I hate drug dealers even more."

I tucked the gun back inside my jumpsuit before heading out the door. On the walk back to the reception area, I pretended to be cooler than I felt. When the doors opened, my eyes went immediately to the armed security guard leaning against the reception desk.

"Sir," the receptionist called out as I passed. My heart started racing as I envisioned my freedom slipping away. Would my first solo assignment also be my last one? Bridget would be so disappointed in me.

I turned around, a big smile on my face. "Yes?"

"Everything go all right with Mr. Wilcox?" the security guard asked.

"Yes. Better than I expected," I commented as I stepped on the elevator with legs that felt weak from nerves. I slipped the sunglasses back on. Through the glass I could see that the van was less than one hundred yards away. Keep your head down and be cool, Niles, I told myself. All my energy was focused on getting off the elevator and out the door and into the van.

"It's done," I told Bridget as I left the building and spoke into the burner cell included in my kit. I knew I'd have to trash this one before I reached Willie and the BMW. I pulled over onto a side street and spotted a large trash bin. I smashed the phone, wiped it clean, and threw it away.

"My man!" Willie called out, the relief written all over his face when I parked next to him. "How did it go?"

"It went just the way we planned," I told him. He didn't need to know that for a minute there, my self-confidence had taken a deep dive. Now that the job was done and I was safely out of there, I was feeling invincible again.

Majestic

47

I was sitting in the car outside the barber shop where MJ had just gotten a haircut when my boy Pooh jumped in the car, shaking his head like he'd just heard some really fucked up shit. We were supposed to be headed to the city. There was a certain Puerto Rican honey I felt the urge to see—and by that, I mean fuck.

"Yo, Majestic, let me tell you about your girl Keisha."

MJ leaned forward in the back seat. "I wanna see my mommy," he said.

I shot Pooh a look. "You'll see mommy, later little man, we going to your Nana's house now."

Everyone was silent during the ride to my mother's house. I knew by the tone of Pooh's voice that whatever he had to tell me was not good, so I was mad before he even said anything. Pooh wasn't the type to make small talk, and MJ was in the back seat eating the lollipop they'd given him in the barber shop. When we got to my mom's house, MJ jumped out of the car and ran straight to her. That boy sure loved his Nana.

After kissing my moms and handing her a few bucks, I said good-bye to my son and got back in the truck with Pooh. We headed off into the city.

"I'ma head over to Carmen's," I told Pooh. "I'm sure she got a friend."

Pooh gave me a serious look.

"What? You got a problem with Carmen?"

"Nah, not with Carmen."

"Then what?"

"Like I was telling you when I got in the car, your baby mama is foul."

If most dudes had talked about my son's mother like that, I would have smacked the shit out of them, but Pooh was different. He wasn't really the type to talk about much of anything if he didn't have a point to make. "Why?"

"I can tell you right now you ain't gonna like this." He stopped like he needed to figure out how to spoon-feed me the information.

"Pooh, I ain't got time for the bullshit. Just fuckin' spill it." My voice sounded gruff, but I didn't like being treated like I needed to be protected. This was my world, and nobody better keep nothing from me.

"You know I just started fucking Keisha's friend Jasmine, right?"

"Yeah, congratu-fuckin'-lations, you and about ten other dudes. That bitch is a ho. What's the fucking point?"

"The point is that she told me that Keisha's been stepping out on you with some dude from Wyandanch ever since you got locked up."

My entire body tensed up. "What? What the fuck? I knew that bitch was acting mighty bold for some reason. Now that shit all makes sense."

"Yeah, well, that's just the tip of the iceberg. She also told me that her and Keisha were at Sugar's bar the night that Rodney got killed, and that dude got into an argument with Rodney."

I clenched the steering wheel to stop myself from putting my fist through the windshield. "Is that the nigga who killed my brother, Pooh?"

"Nah, I can't say that." He shook his head. "I asked her, but she said no. You can never tell with these bitches, though. Once I started asking too many questions about Keisha, she shut down like she didn't want to get her girl in trouble."

"Fuck. I need to deal with this right now." I turned the car around.

"Boss, maybe we should go into the city right now. You get to see Carmen, give yourself a little time to cool down." Pooh was no doubt worried I would kill that bitch for withholding information about my brother, but I needed to see her face when I asked the questions. The one thing I demanded out of everyone I dealt with—employees, family, friends, and the women in my life—was loyalty, and if I found out my kid's mom, of all people, lied about something this big, then nothing could save her.

"Pooh, if you don't shut the fuck up with that bullshit. . . . You supposed to be a killer and you sound like a little bitch."

Pooh was still playing fucking nursemaid when we pulled up. "Want me to go in with you?"

"I got this," I said as I jumped out of the ride and headed to the front door.

Bam! Bam! Bam! I banged on the door.

Keisha looked freaked out when she saw me. "Majestic, what are you doing here? I thought you was taking MJ to your mom's."

Without a thought, I balled up my fist and hit her square in the mouth, sending her violently to the ground. "What the fuck I hear that you was with some nigga at that bar the night my brother was killed?"

Bridget

48

"Good job. I'll make arrangements for the funds to be transferred into your account." I hung up my phone feeling satisfied and proud of my student. Once again Niles had done the impossible, taking out a man Jonathan's team had been hunting for almost a year. I'd have to do something special for him when he and Willie returned from Venezuela.

In the meantime I checked my hair and makeup to be sure they were still flawless before stepping out of the car. I'd always made it my business to look my best, especially when I knew I was going to be around another woman. Well, actually, Nancy wasn't just another woman. She was the one person I could tell everything to without worrying about what she would think or how she would use it against me. One thing life had taught me was that you can't trust just anybody with your secrets, unless they have multiple degrees, charge a grip to listen to you, and are bound by law to keep your business to themselves within reason. So sure, there were lines I skirted around in our conversations, but my time with Nancy was as honest as I allowed myself to be with anyone. Crazy thing is, I actually looked forward to it every two weeks.

"Bridget, how are you?" Dr. Nancy Young, the psychiatrist I had been seeing for the past eight years, greeted me as she opened the door to her Manhattan brownstone office. Nancy had no need for a receptionist because she had a very small practice, dealing with only a few celebrities, mobsters, and assassins like me. In fact, she was so exclusive she didn't even keep records on her clients or accept any type of insurance. She just did her job, which was to listen and help direct us through the bullshit we called our lives. "Nice to see you."

"Whatever. Let's get this over with. I have some shopping to do." I grumbled my usual greeting, but of course, she was used to my reluctance to admit how much I looked forward to our appointments.

"Shopping. Someone is trying to compensate for a bad week?" She studied me as we took our seats across from each other.

"No. Yes. I don't know. I'm stressed the fuck out." I wondered why I didn't just come straight out and tell her what was on my mind. I already knew that after all these years, she could read me better than anyone.

"Is this about Niles? Is he still angry with you?" Good old Nancy, always getting right to the fucking point. But what else did I expect? The reason she could afford that Mercedes she had parked outside was because she was so damn good at her job.

"Look, I know I told you that I had to lie to get him to take the job, but I really didn't have any choice. If I didn't, someone else would have. Besides, he's good at it. Really good. And he's made a ton of money. He should be thanking me," I said frankly.

Then she narrowed in on me. "And you believe that? You really believe he should be thanking you?"

"Well, yeah." I let out a sigh. "How often do you get an opportunity like this, to be trained by someone like me? I'm busting my ass for that man. Fuck! Why can't he just put it in the past so we can move forward?"

"Why should he? You're the one who lied; not him."

I gave her a confused look. I was not even sure we were talking about the same thing. "I'm not talking about the lie I told. I'm talking about last week."

"Last week? I'm not following you. You haven't told me anything about last week."

Jesus Christ, she was right. I was just rambling like a blooming idiot. I sighed, struggling to get the next part out.

"Fine. I might as well tell you. You'll just pick at me to death until I tell you the whole thing."

She sat back and silently waited in that oh-so-annoying therapist's way.

"We were on a job together last week, a very important job, and I kind of talked him into screwing me," I explained without any emotion.

"Talked him into it?" She looked like she wanted to laugh. "Bridget, you're not the type of woman who talks men—or women, for that matter—into sleeping with you. He either begged you or you found some way to manipulate the situation."

God, I hated that she knew me so well. "Okay, maybe I used my powers of persuasion to get what I wanted, but it wasn't like I raped him or anything."

Nancy's expression didn't shift in the slightest with this information. Hell, she'd heard a lot more scandalous stuff from me in the past. "Why'd you do that? You already know he has a problem with your manipulation."

I groaned, shrugging my shoulders. "It wound up being a way to save the job we were involved in. We landed at a sex club, and we had to make it look like we were into that scene. The only way to do that was to either have sex with others or with each other. I decided I wanted to fuck him."

"I see." She nodded. "So how'd that work out for you?"

I shot her that look you give your best girlfriend when you're about to get real. "It was great. The sex was amazing. Shit. It was probably the best sex I've ever had, and since you know I'm not anybody's virgin, that's saying a whole lot." I enjoyed a momentary flashback image of Niles pumping me hard and fast. "Not only did he have the equipment, but he knew exactly what to do with it," I told Nancy, sounding like a groupie at a rock concert. "Shit, I can't wait to fuck his ass again and see if it was a fluke."

"Sounds like you had a good time," she said in her best neutral voice. "So why are you so stressed? Is he becoming obsessive like some of the others?" For a woman who didn't write anything down, she sure as hell had a memory like an elephant.

I shook my head, lowering it in embarrassment. "Not even close."

She sat up in her chair. I refused to make eye contact. "So how do you think he feels about this?"

"He's pissed, but he's being professional, which is pissing me off even more."

She focused a little too closely on me. We'd just reached uncharted waters, Nancy and I. "Well, this is interesting. I never thought I'd see this day, but Bridget, I think you like him."

"Sure. What's not to like? He's smart, handsome, and incredibly good at his job. We have a lot in common." A smile escaped. "Hell, when he lets go, he's actually fun to be around."

"Do you hear the way you talk about him?" Nancy asked. "You don't just like him; you really like him."

I waved my hand to dismiss her suggestion. "Don't trip. He's a nice guy to work with and a really good fuck, but that's it," I said, fighting to maintain my innocence.

She smiled. "And that's all? Nothing else?"

"Well, yeah, that's all. I already admitted that the sex was fucking awesome, but it was just sex. It's not like we're getting married or even moving in together," I said glibly, hoping she'd let it die.

She didn't. "Oh, Bridget, you really don't hear yourself. Why can't you let yourself go and enjoy life?" She said it like it was the easiest thing in the world when, for me, it was harder than taking a human life.

"I don't know," I admitted, feeling the heaviness of that statement. "Why is it so godddamn hard for me? Maybe because every man who has ever wanted me doesn't even really know me. It's like that Marilyn Monroe quote: 'They go to sleep with

Marilyn and are disappointed when they wake up with Norma Jean.' "

"Is that what you think?" she questioned.

"It's what I know. Men see me as this tough-as-nails, badass bitch, and that's what they want. They like my not-gonna-take-any-bullshit-from-you attitude. They don't want me vulnerable, or, for God's sake, needy or acting like some basic bitch."

"And that's what you'd be if you were in love?" She always managed to use my words against me.

"Probably. I'm not superhuman. I mean, isn't that the whole point of a relationship, to let someone in? To allow another person access to your deepest, darkest self?" I said dramatically, making fun of her work.

"Yes, but it's more. We're in a relationship. You allow me to see you and to have access to your vulnerabilities. Why can you do it in here and not out there?" she asked gently, probing even deeper.

I laughed. "Because we're not fucking."

"No, we're not" she responded, sounding amused. "I'm not letting you off that easily. What if you started to like this guy? Would it be so awful to let him in?"

"Yes. If I started to like him, it could affect everything. What if I had to sleep with someone and I had this boyfriend? Could I even do it? Would I suddenly morph into some straight-laced chick and not be able to do my job? Probably. And I don't think I'd want to do a lot of things the job requires. I don't know if I can have a relationship and have this job," I admitted.

She watched me, not speaking for a moment. "And this job is worth you not having a full life? Is it worth not ever being in love? Is that what you're saying? "

"Ugh!" I groaned. "I used to love my job: the thrill, the excitement, the satisfaction, and just knowing that I was really good at something. I could count on it. I loved that."

"Loved?"

Hearing the word repeated back to me made me realize I'd said it in the past tense.

"Yes, but lately I don't know. I'm not so sure that I'm cut out for it anymore." I confessed a fear to her I'd never voiced out loud, and just hearing myself say it shifted something.

Then she went back to the beginning. "So when you had sex with this guy and it was the best you ever had, were you able to let yourself go?"

"Well, yeah," I said meekly, not sounding like myself at all.

"And do you think that has anything to do with this revelation?"

I really didn't know how to answer, so I just stared at her as she continued.

"Do you think your feelings for this guy are changing your feelings for your job?"

My head was spinning when I finally answered lamely, "I don't know!"

Nancy leaned back in her chair and focused on me. "I think you do, and I think this guy may be getting in there—that place that you decided a long time ago to wall off from the possibility of feeling anything more than a passing fancy."

"That's ridiculous," I scoffed. "I haven't known him long enough to feel anything more than excited about the dick. That's all. It's a new, exciting dick," I thundered, desperate to be let off the hook. Why wasn't she just agreeing with me?

Keisha

49

I could feel my face beginning to swell as I blinked my eyes open, trying to stay conscious. I'd never felt that much pain in my life, and I'd given birth to a ten-pound baby. Grabbing my throbbing face in my hand, I stared up at Majestic's blurry silhouette feeling nothing but hatred. I had no idea what I'd done to cause this much anger, but I nearly peed myself when he leaned down, his fist balled in a knot, ready to strike me again.

"What did I do?" I cried, praying he would have mercy on me.

"It's what you didn't do. Why didn't you tell me you were at the bar that night Rodney got shot?" For a second, I was so glad MJ was not there, because if he was scaring me, my child would have been terrified.

"I was there, but the last time I saw Rodney he was alive," I said, trying to defend my actions and hide the ones he didn't yet know about. I placed a hand on the wall, standing up on shaky legs.

"Don't fucking lie to me, Keisha." He raised his hand high in the air.

"I'm not lying. I don't know anything," I cried out, trying to manipulate him into taking pity on me. "It was packed in there."

That's when I glanced over and saw my mother standing in the doorway with a smirk on her face. I just knew she was dying to say, "I told you so." Majestic was standing over me like he was going to kill me, her daughter, and she was standing there like he was rubbing my feet.

Majestic leaned threateningly in my direction. "Keisha, you fucking skating."

I avoided eye contact. "I told you I don't know anything. See, this is exactly why I don't want to be with you anymore," I snapped back at him. Yes, I was scared, but being treated like an animal also pissed me the fuck off.

I couldn't help but notice the malicious glint in his eyes as he answered. "You ain't got no choice in that matter."

God, I hated the fuck out of this man, and with the exception of MJ, I wished I could go back in time and make a different choice.

"What do you want from me?" I fumed, knowing he could slap me down again for being so combative, but suddenly, I almost didn't care. I hated being at his damn mercy all the time.

"I want you to stop lying and tell me what the fuck happened that night."

"I was there. I just said I was there, but it was a weekend night, and the place was crowded, so I don't know what happened to your brother." That was as much as I wanted to tell him. If Majestic knew that I was with Niles that night, I'd be as dead as Rodney.

He took a step closer to me. "So, did you see my brother?"

"Yes. I saw him."

"And what?" His voice exploded at me.

I took a deep breath. "He was popping all kinds of shit. Talkin' 'bout I needed to leave and go home and take care of MJ. You know Rodney."

"And he was right."

I shot him a hostile stare. "He's not my daddy, and neither are you."

Majestic pointed his finger at me as a warning. "You got one more time with your bullshit. So what else happened that night? Who was this nigga I heard you was with?"

I tried not to hesitate, because I knew if I did, he'd hit me again. "He was just this dude from the Army. Me and Tanya was gaming him and his friend for drinks." I toned down my attitude and tried to look sincere.

"And this dude and Rodney had beef? Did he kill my brother?"

"No, more like Rodney had beef with him and everyone else in the bar. But he didn't kill your brother. He left the same time as us, and Rodney was alive."

"You better be telling me the truth." He seethed in that way that shook me to the core, but I tried to play it off like I wasn't affected.

"I'm not. I swear," I said, raising my hand like a pledge.

"Next time you need a drink, buy a bottle and stay your ass home," Majestic said before he headed out the door. I almost collapsed onto the floor with relief that maybe, just maybe, he believed me.

"Why didn't you tell him the truth about you and that boy?"

I turned to see my mother's smug ass challenging me, her hands folded over her chest like I was supposed to answer to her now.

"'Cause it didn't have nothing to do with Rodney being dead!" I shouted at her for always trying to start something. "Why the fuck did you just stand there when he hit me?"

She sucked her teeth. "Shit, have you taken a good look at your face?" she asked as if I had a mirror in front of me. "I'm sorry, but there wasn't no need in both of us getting our asses kicked."

Majestic

50

Before I got out of Bruce's car in front of the modest house, I checked the rear view mirror and saw that Pooh, Eddie, and Shorty had pulled up in an SUV behind us. Although I like to handle business personally, Bruce liked to bring muscle to the party so the two of us didn't have to get our hands dirty.

"Let's do this," I said to Bruce as we both got out of the ride, the other guys following us.

"What you want us to do?" Pooh whispered when I rang the doorbell and there was no movement in the house.

"There's two cars in the driveway. Somebody's gotta be home," I answered. "Eddie, go check the back."

He went to check, then came back, giving me a thumbs up, so we followed him back there. We stepped through the decorative gate to find a middle-aged white couple lounging by the pool, reading the Sunday Times and sipping on mimosas. Hell, I almost hated interrupting such domestic fucking bliss.

"What the fuck!" The man jumped to his feet when he heard the gate close and saw us.

"Isn't this special? Beautiful place you have here." I smoothly delivered this line, knowing it would convey the right tone of threat and confidence. The man reached to his side as if he was going for his firearm. "Nowhere to strap a gun when you're wearing a bathing suit," I said with a laugh.

His wife started covering up, throwing a towel over her swimsuit like we were a pack of pussy-hungry rapists, desperate to get a piece of her middle-aged ass.

"Who the hell are you? And what the fuck are you doing here?" he yelled, trying to convey some type of confidence. Obviously, he was used to being in charge and putting people like us behind bars—except this was a new day, and things were a lot different, which he was about to learn.

I snapped my fingers at my men, and they all moved closer.

"You do know I'm a cop," the white man said, like that was going to stop us.

"Yeah, I'd heard that." I sat down in a chair and nodded to Bruce, who sat down next to me. "Matter of fact, that's exactly why I'm here, Detective

Fuller, because you're a cop." At the mention of his name, he finally showed recognition that we had the upper hand, and he definitely had a problem on his hands.

"They say when a crime's been committed, you should go to the police," I taunted. "Well, I'm here to report a crime."

Detective Fuller looked damn near apologetic. "I'm sorry, but technically I'm not a cop anymore. I'm retired. You might want to call 911 or go down to your local precinct. I'm sure they'll be able to help you."

I leaned back and put my hands behind my head like I was settling in for a long visit. "Retired, huh? Yes, I think I heard that too."

That's when Eddie pulled out a pistol and pointed it at Fuller. His wife went ballistic, so Pooh grabbed her, pointing his piece at her head.

"If you don't shut that bitch up, things are gonna get a whole lot worse around here, real fast," I warned Fuller. Oh, the look of pure helplessness was perfect. I almost wished I had the time to take a picture, but, of course, I couldn't risk the evidence falling into the wrong hands. Boy, did I love seeing a pig utterly helpless for once in his life. I could only imagine the number of brothers he'd had in this same situation.

Fuller called out to his wife, and then he started begging. "Bonnie! Please, please. Don't hurt my wife. You're not going to hurt us if we cooperate, right?"

"No doubt, Fuller. I just want information about my brother." I gave him a little smile, which seemed to be enough to calm the bitch down.

"Sir, I'm sorry about your brother, but I can't be of any help. I'm not a cop anymore, so I don't have the access like I once did," he said, full of false sincerity.

"Then maybe a name will bring back your memory. His name was Rodney Moss . . ." I noticed him freeze and his eyes went wide. Bitch better not tell me he didn't remember after I saw it right there on his fucking face. "And you should have no problem remembering him, since it was your last case. You did put in for your retirement the day after his murder, and from the looks of things, you doing all right. Maybe better than all right for a retired cop."

The good detective got all jumpy and overly solicitous. "Oh, yeah, I remember now," he said as his memory came flooding back. "He was killed in an alley. Shame that we never caught his killer."

"Is that a fact? Because that's not what I've heard. I heard you arrested somebody and let him go," Bruce snapped.

I motioned to the wife, and Pooh grabbed her up by the neck. Of course, she screamed.

"Leave her alone!" The detective shouted like he really wasn't understanding that he had no control.

Eddie slammed his gun against Fuller's head, and he went down like a paper weight. Fuller groaned and started to rise, only to find the pistol pressed against his temple. The wife was finally smart enough to keep her big mouth shut now.

I glanced down at him, my expression as cold and lethal as my men's guns. "You gonna tell me what I want to know?"

"Look, I'm telling you I don't know anything," he swore, except we both knew that he was lying. I nodded to Pooh, who picked up the wife and plunged her head straight into the pool and held it down. Hell, if he wanted to let the bitch drown, then no problem.

"Nooooo!" Fuller screamed, although he was still not offering up any information. He tried to grab for her, but Pooh pushed her head down deeper into the water.

Fuller finally caved. "All right. All right. I'll tell you what you want to know. Please, please pull her up! Please." He stared toward his wife as Pooh pulled her up, gasping for air.

"Talk!" I warned him. If he wanted to test me, he'd see that the threat of drowning was nothing.

"There was a guy. I don't remember his full name other than Monroe, or even if that was his real name. What I do know is they took his file and erased all the records of his existence. The brass told us not to say anything, but the next day there was fifty K in a shoebox in my locker with my retirement papers. I got the hint."

I could see that he was afraid of whoever the "they" was he'd just told me about. I glanced over at Bruce, who I could tell was thinking the same thing.

"Who erased the files?" Bruce asked.

Fuller shrugged his shoulders. "I'm not sure. I wanna say they were FBI or CIA, but I'm not sure. All I know is they had all the bosses scared to death, and that's saying something."

"That's not enough." I nodded to Pooh, who immediately dunked the wife again.

"No!" the detective hollered in response.

"You think I'm playing? I'll drown this bitch just as much as look at her."

He shook his head. "I swear I'm telling you the truth. I don't know who they were. But the woman in charge, I'll never forget her."

This sounded promising. I raised my hand, and Pooh pulled her from the water, sputtering and shaking.

"Why's that?" I questioned him.

Before he answered, Fuller glanced at his drenched wife, embarrassed. "Because she was beautiful. The kind of woman nobody forgets."

"In other words, you wanted to fuck her." I laughed. He didn't reply; he just lowered his head. "You happen to remember the name of this hot piece of ass?"

"Yeah," he answered. "Her name was Bridget. Bridget St. John."

Bridget

51

I stepped out of the car and headed into my Manhattan condo while Winston retrieved my shopping bags from the trunk. A few seconds later, I stopped, letting him catch up to me so that he could open the door to the lavish lobby. We entered, stopping at the elevator banks so I could retrieve and wave my keycard.

When the elevator bell chimed, I reached for my packages and said good night to him.

"You sure you don't want me to carry these upstairs?" Good ol' Winston was always trying to make my life flow easier.

"No, I could use the workout," I kidded with him. He handed half of the packages to me, but I could tell he had something to say. "What's on your mind, Winston?"

He looked around the lobby, making sure no one was eavesdropping. "Ma'am, Bridget, I know this may be out of line, but . . ." He began tentatively, but we'd been together so long that I knew whatever he had to say to me had been well thought out if not rehearsed. Winston didn't speak much, but when he did, it was necessary and usually helpful.

"Winston, nothing you say is ever out of line. You're like family. Hell, you're closer to me than family. More like my second dad. So speak freely."

"Thank you for the kind words, ma'am, but I think you're in danger of crossing a very dangerous line with this one." Winston looked worried, which was saying a lot considering what we did for a living.

"What exactly are you talking about?"

He handed me the Ermenegildo Zegna shopping bag, "You've never gone shopping for any of them after their initial training. Why are you doing it now?"

"It's just a couple of shirts, a sweater, and a tie." I glanced down at the bag. "It's no big deal."

Wilson straightened his back, wearing a frown on his face. "I'm sorry, but I'm going to have to call your bullshit on this one." He pierced me with a serious expression. "This is a very big deal. This man is taking you off your game. It could get you both killed."

"I'm fine, Winston. I swear."

"No, you're not. I see the way you look at him. You want him like no other."

All my defenses flatlined. "Okay, okay, do I think about fucking him? Yes. Probably more than I should, but it's fine. You don't need to worry."

"Too late for that," he admitted, which made me love him even more than I already did. He was always there for me in a way my family had never been. "The only way to get past this is to admit how you feel, to yourself and to him."

"Winston, it's not what you think, so stop worrying. Go and have yourself a good night. If I need to go out, I'll take the Porsche," I insisted, basically forcing him to give me the rest of my shopping bounty.

"All right," he said reluctantly. "Have a good night. Just think about what I said."

That's the only problem with working with the same people for a long time. They fucking know you.

Loaded down with all my bags, I opened the door to my apartment, dumping the bags. I looked out the window and smiled. I never got tired of my penthouse view of the East River.

"Finally!"

I jumped out of my skin when I heard the voice of someone in my apartment. I reached automatically for the gun strapped to my inner thigh, but then I saw who the voice belonged to.

"What the fuck are you doing in my apartment?" I shouted at Niles, who was lounging comfortably on my Italian leather sofa, looking finer than I remembered.

He rose and came toward me. "I'd say you trained me well."

"Well, you could have gotten yourself killed," I barked at him, more to hide my excitement at how glad I was to see him.

I took a good look at him. Frankly, close up he looked like shit.

"I need a new assignment," he said.

"What's going on? You just finished an assignment. Take a few days and relax." I was concerned. Those bags under his eyes were a telltale sign.

"I need a distraction," he said, going back to the couch.

"Why don't you take that girlfriend of yours on a trip to the islands and blow off a little steam?"

"No can do. We broke up," he said. "Well, she broke up with me."

"I'm sorry, Niles. I didn't know." I stayed calm, but inside I wanted to jump for joy. How the hell did that woman fuck up such a good thing?

I guess he felt the same way. "Fucking came out of nowhere," he said.

I went over to the bar, poured a couple of shots of bourbon, then handed one to him as I took a seat next to him.

"Look, Niles, I'm sorry. I know how much you liked her, but it's probably for the best. We already fucked, and in this job, you're going to have to do that again. I'm not sure a girlfriend would fit with your job description."

He fixed me with an intensely suspicious stare. "Did you have something to do with Keisha breaking up with me? Do you have something to do with her ex being released?"

All I could do was laugh.

"Seriously? Wow. You give me way too much credit. I may be capable of a lot of things, but I can't make a woman fall out of love with you." I wasn't about to admit that the idea of trying to make that happen had already crossed my mind.

"Look me in the face and tell me you didn't know about him being locked up."

I stared him right in the face. "I did, but what your girlfriend didn't tell you was that he only had six months."

"What? That's not possible. She told me he had twenty years."

I raised my eyebrows, not wanting to suggest out loud that his girlfriend was a fucking liar. "Guess she was mistaken," I said.

"We're supposed to be partners," he shot back. "Why didn't you tell me he was released?"

"It was none of my business. Why didn't your girlfriend tell you?"

He chose to ignore that question. "So I need some work. I have to stay busy." He downed the shot and put the glass on the table. Then he got up and went to stare out the window. I got up and followed him.

"I'm sorry this has you all upset, but there will be plenty of work to keep you busy."

"Good. The more the better." He sighed, running his hands over his head in obvious frustration. It actually made me feel bad for him, no matter how hard I tried to block those feelings.

I put a hand on his shoulder and was surprised by the jolt of electricity that went through me. There was some serious chemistry between us. I wondered if he felt it too, and decided to test the waters.

"I know you've heard this before, but the best way to get over someone is to get under someone else."

He didn't answer for a few seconds, and I took my hand off his shoulder. I was almost expecting him to turn down my offer, and it was pissing me off. Then he took a step closer to me, and I could feel his intensity.

"Is that an offer?" he asked.

My work phone started ring before I could answer him.

"Hold that thought," I said as I went to answer the phone.

"Hello."

"Bridget, this is Jonathan. I'm texting you an address. I need you to come to right away." Before I could tell him to, 'kiss my ass,' he said, "This is a code Alpha-Omega," then hung up without waiting for a response.

"Shit," I mumbled, trying to get my head together.

"Everything all right?" Niles asked.

"I hope so, but I have to go," I said, hating to have to say it. I could feel his heat from across the room, and all I wanted to do at that moment was rip his clothes off and get busy. But duty called. "Lock the place when you leave, okay?"

Niles

52

During the entire ride home from the city my mind was only on Bridget. There was no doubt that if she hadn't received that phone call, we would have ended up in bed. Damn, if that woman didn't have me feeling like I could lift a whole lot of weights or do something superhuman. The question was, how did I feel about that, especially with us being partners and her ice-cold demeanor most of the time? I was glad I was pulling in the driveway so I could talk to Willie about it. He would already know once he saw my face that something had gone down. I never was good at hiding things from my uncle.

"Hey, Niles, your mother is taking a nap." Tanya jumped up as soon as I came into the living room, because sitting right there between her and Willie was Keisha. This girl didn't even have the decency to face me though.

Willie got up and took Tanya's hand. "We gonna give you two a minute." Ignoring my raised eyebrows and funky attitude, the two of them hustled out of there quick. Keisha still hadn't looked up at me, which was making me even madder than just seeing her in my house.

"What are you doing here?" I snapped, pissed that I had to have one moment of my day interrupted by her. When she finally turned her head toward me, I took a step back and just stared at her. Somebody had beaten the shit out of her, leaving her eyes puffy, with black and blue marks and scars all over her face. I quickly reminded myself that Keisha and her face were no longer my problem.

She bowed her head as she came over to me. "I need to talk to you."

"Then talk so you can get the hell out of my house—then do me a favor and don't come back."

"Please don't be mad at me," she said breathlessly. "It wasn't my fault. I swear."

This bitch must have confused me with someone who still cared. "Really? So . . . you coming to answer your door while you got your baby daddy laid up, or you fixing him a nice plate then telling me to leave and slamming the door in my face. What part of that is not your fault?" I seethed, overwhelmed by the memory and suddenly feeling like it had just happened today.

She tugged at my sleeve, pleading with me. "Niles, please listen." I snatched my arm away from her. She looked really pitiful, but I was beyond caring. This woman had broken my heart and treated me like shit, and now she wanted me to act like it was some kind of mistake? Naw, I was the one who had made a mistake by ever trusting this unfaithful bitch. If she had bruises all over her face, it was her own fault for going back to that asshole in the first place. Still, I felt something deep inside of me, something like pity and concern for her well-being, and I wanted her to leave before it escaped and she thought it meant I forgave her.

"Keisha, I swear you need to leave!" I took her arm and led her down the hall and out the front door, but she was relentless.

"Niles, don't do this. I need to talk to you. It's life or death, and that's not a joke." She had big crocodile tears rolling down her face, like that was going to soften me up.

"Please. You look like somebody already tried to smash your face in, so you a whole lot closer to death than me," I retorted in full asshole mode.

"You think I want this? You think I want to be with this monster? To have him touch me?" she screamed at me.

"It don't matter what I think. You are with him," I reminded her.

"Yes, but I don't want to be!" she pleaded, grabbing onto my arms again.

"Then answer me one thing: What was he doing there?" I asked.

"I didn't know he was getting out of jail," she said, steady lying again.

"Bullshit. So he happened to get out of jail, and he happened to be in your house that day? What you think, I'm a fool and I'm gonna buy this? What is your angle here?"

"But I didn't know he was getting out of jail. I had already broken up with him. I told him about you. I told him that I was in love with you," she said, begging me to believe her—except I didn't. I couldn't, because the evidence didn't back her up.

"You fucking think I'm crazy enough to believe this?" I fumed at Keisha for wasting my time with this bullshit and dredging up old wounds. I don't know if it was the job that had made me so cold, but even looking at Keisha's damaged face, I couldn't let down my guard and show her any sympathy.

"Niles, I'm sorry. I'm sorry from the bottom of my heart. I am. You need to hear me when I say be careful. Majestic is crazy. He is insane and dangerous."

"I'm not worried about your baby daddy." I laughed in her face. She didn't seem to understand that her worry and her man were her problems.

"You should be," she said, shaking like a leaf. "Do you think if I had any choice I would have stayed with him? He threatened to kill me and then to give my baby a new mother, and he would have done it, and nobody would have ever found my body."

"Then you should have trusted me. You think I sweat bullets over some bully who's such a pussy he has to put his hands on a woman? You let your fear of him keep you from telling me the truth. See, what you don't seem to understand is that your fear of losing me should have motivated you," I told her.

"I know," she whimpered like a puppy that had just been kicked. "Just please be careful. He thinks you had something to do with his brother's death, and he may come after you, Niles."

"That would not be in his best interest to come looking for me right now," I warned her and then turned and went back into my house. My handlers at Dynamic Defense would have been proud. Somehow during my training, Bridget must have removed my heart and filled my veins with ice water, because this Niles was not the same man I used to be. The question was, did I miss the old one?

Bridget

53

I knew I should have been concentrating on the fact that less than an hour ago Jonathan had uttered the words no operative in our organization wanted to hear—code Alpha-Omega—but I could not stop myself from thinking about Niles and the fact that I was one kiss away from him fucking me just the way I needed it. My Agent Provocateur panties were sopping wet from desire for that man, but I had to pull it together before I reached my destination, because code Alpha-Omega was no joke.

A block away from the address Jonathan had given me, I ran right smack into the middle of a full-scale police investigation.

"Hello." I waved over an officer. "Can you tell me what's going on here?" There had to have been at least fifty people, including suits, standing around the yellow tape with long faces. I noticed the coroner's truck parked in the driveway.

"Uh, ma'am, this is an active investigation," he said, his eyes way too interested in my cleavage.

I flashed him the FBI credentials I carried around for just this occasion, because I needed to get in there and see Jonathan, who could tell me exactly what went down and why he felt I needed to be there.

"You're going to have to speak with Captain Meyer. He's the officer in charge." Once he saw my badge, the cop wouldn't stop talking until I rolled up the window.

"No problem," I said as I waved him off and parked. Checking out the faces as I sauntered past, I could see that people were shook. This certainly wasn't the kind of neighborhood where they were used to a full-scale police presence.

As I headed into the backyard where all the action seemed to be happening, another officer tried to cut me off. I retrieved my badge, gave it a quick wave, and kept stepping. I spotted Jonathan, who was talking to a white-shirt captain and a rather dapper detective. He nodded at both men then headed my way.

"We've got problems," Jonathan began without even looking up at me.

"What's going on?"

"Have you seen the crime scene yet? Have you seen it?"

"No, and who's the Alpha-Omega on?"

He gestured for me to follow him.

"If you haven't guessed yet . . ." He sighed, stepping over the yellow crime scene tape and pointing. "It's on you, Bridget."

I stopped dead in my tracks, following his finger until two dead bodies came into view across the yard next to the pool. When I got closer, I saw that it was a man and a woman, and each had taken one to the head. What I saw next made me take a step back.

"Fuck!" I stared at the bodies, sprawled out on the patio, where my name had been spray-painted in large red letters. "Who the fuck are these people?"

"The woman's name is Bonnie," Jonathan said. I could feel his stare. "The man, as you can see, no longer has a face. His name was Fuller. You may remember him as Detective Fuller."

"What the fuck is this all about?" I asked, suppressing the panic I felt rising in my chest. "How'd my name get down there?"

Jonathan shook his head. "I don't know, but this isn't good. You've been compromised."

"No shit, Sherlock. I just don't know how this happened. I covered my tracks. I know I did." The one thing I could never be accused of was being sloppy on the job.

"Then you need to try and fix this. You do not want the folks upstairs getting wind of this."

There was really no reason for his warning, because my ass was already worried.

This was a top level threat, and I knew to treat it as one. My bosses were a secondary concern, because the first had to be my fear of someone coming after me. If they were willing to kill for the information I had, then they weren't about to give up with just two dead bodies.

"I need to find out who talked and who they talked to. This was not supposed to happen. It was quick and dirty." My explanation sounded flat even to me.

Jonathan looked me sternly in the eyes. "Yeah, well, somebody sang like a goddamn canary, and there is no telling what Fuller said to the killer or killers before he died."

"Other than my name, I don't think he knew that much." My mind was already racing as I tried to remember exactly how it went down the last time I saw Fuller at the station.

"Well, one thing is certain: If our superiors find out about this, they will take Monroe from you, and they may put you on a desk—or worse."

I swear I saw a faint smile on his face, like he'd be happy for that shit to happen. I took a deep breath, my mind bouncing from this situation to

Niles. No way would I want to lose him, and for more reasons than Jonathan knew, but I was smart enough not to say anything about our "coworkers with benefits" situation.

"So you need to figure this shit out, Bridget, and quick," he pressed.

I started thinking about Niles and how he figured into this and, well, it really got me worrying. "I need to go," I told Jonathan as I took one more look at Fuller and his wife lying dead on the ground.

"And you better hope like hell that you're not the next one on their list," he quipped, but I knew for certain that there was someone else they'd be looking for. I only hoped they didn't have his name.

Bruce

54

Majestic and I were greeted with smiles and brotherly love as we stepped into B. Smith's restaurant on the pier in Sag Harbor for lunch. The brothers we were supposed to meet were already seated in the back of the restaurant, so we sat down across from them, even though both Majestic and I hated having our backs to the door.

"Hey, man, good to see you back out on the streets," said Vegas, the darker, more muscular of the Duncan brothers. He stood up and gave Majestic a quick hug as we approached him and his younger, more studious-looking brother, Orlando.

We'd been summoned out to the East End of Long Island to meet with our suppliers, and since it was off-season, the place was nearly empty. Coming out here was one of the only ways to stay off the radar, since the Duncans didn't like to be seen with criminals. These guys were part of the biggest and best-run drug distributors on the East

Coast, and after dealing with the janky-ass third string dealers, we'd graduated a few years ago and moved up to their level. Our business had boomed ever since, and them being brothers and having a family-run company only served to strengthen our alliance. They liked that we'd been lifelong friends who now worked together.

"Vegas Duncan, what's happening, baby?" Majestic sounded excited like a little kid.

"Just trying to make it happen, my brother," Vegas replied as we all took our seats.

"This place is known for their seafood, so go for it."

Majestic turned to the waitress, a cute bottled blonde with big tits and an aggressive smile who probably dreamed of one day landing herself a yacht owner with a penthouse in the city.

"Give us two seafood platters." Majestic ordered for both of us because he knew I'd never met a shrimp or a lobster I didn't love.

I handed her the menu. "And I'll take a Coke."

"Two," Majestic shot out then dismissed her, ready to get to down to business.

Vegas Duncan was a real no-bullshit guy who didn't mince words or play by anybody else's rules. For the most part, we'd always landed on the same side, but I was sensing he wasn't happy today. I glanced over at Majestic to see if he was worried, but he was so cool I couldn't get a read.

"My brother tells me you guys have increased your business twenty percent in the last year," Vegas said.

"Yeah, things have been good. My man Bruce here—" Majestic wrapped his arm around my shoulder—"really held things down while I was away."

"I ain't do anything you wouldn't have done, bro," I replied.

"Well, the Duncans appreciate your hard work. As an extra incentive, we'd like to extend you a discount of three less on all your future business," Vegas said.

Majestic and I turned to each other, grinning like we were ten years old and had just come downstairs to find new bikes under the Christmas tree.

"Wow, thanks, man. You know we appreciate it," Majestic answered.

"But there is one catch." Vegas's words poured cold water on my internal celebration.

"And what's that?" I asked, leaning toward him.

"We hear you have an issue with a woman by the name of Bridget St. John."

Majestic didn't seem at all surprised that word had gotten back to them. Hell, the Duncans ran New York. There wasn't shit that got past them, especially when you put a hundred grand on a woman's head.

"Hell, yeah. We think she had something to do with my brother's death." His tone left no question of his intent to do bodily harm to her.

The waitress dropped our drinks, and reading the energy, she quickly shot the hell out of there.

Orlando Duncan, who had stayed silent until then, spoke. "That's not good for business." There was something about his highbrow attitude and tailored suit that told me college boy had never spent a moment getting his hands dirty in the streets. I assumed the reason he was even there had to do with Vegas showing him the ropes.

Majestic ignored him and turned to Vegas. "You got three brothers, so no disrespect, but don't tell me that you'd let a motherfucker continue to breathe once they'd put one of y'all in the ground."

Vegas stared at Majestic for a moment, tensing his jaw muscles before he spoke. "I'm truly sorry for your loss, but we can't have varying factions that we do business with going to war. Bridget is connected to some folks who you don't want to make your enemies."

Majestic shot me a look that let me know he was not about to back down. I'd seen it too many times.

"Hey, she gives me no choice," he said in response to the gauntlet Vegas had just thrown down.

Vegas leaned in until they were damn near eyeball to eyeball. "That sweet deal and all, the one that made sure you only got six months, didn't have much to do with your lawyer. We needed you out on the street doing your job, selling our product. You understand?"

Majestic didn't even blink at the revelation that the Duncans had been behind his release. "And I really appreciate that, but none of it is going to bring my brother back or make the motherfuckers who took his life accountable. There is shit you do in life that calls for serious payback, and this qualifies."

"Then you need to understand that you and Bruce are on your own. I can't protect you if you don't heed my warning. This woman is connected to some very serious people."

"Then consider me warned," Majestic shot back, not giving a fuck about this threat.

"This means that you are no longer under the Duncan family protection. We can't get involved in this situation."

Majestic leaned back in the booth and spoke calmly. "Then you got to do what you gotta do."

Vegas motioned to Orlando, and they got up, but not before he dropped two crisp hundred-dollar bills on the table before the two of them bounced. "Your meal is on the Duncans."

The waitress, who now appeared slightly terrified, dropped our food as she stared at the money on the table. She might have been scared, but she wanted that tip.

"Anything else?" she asked, not as chirpy as earlier but trying her damndest to put a smile on her face.

I shook my head in response, and she got lost.

I was worried about Majestic. "Look, I know you two go way back," I said to him, "but you do know you just told the heir apparent to the biggest Black Mafia family in the country to kiss your ass, don't you?"

"Yeah, and? What did you want me to do? I'm not caving to the Duncans, the Russians, or anyone else."

"What are we gonna do now? They're not gonna sell us any product."

Majestic still didn't seem bothered at all. "The man in the west is our protection and our supplier now. We already buy our guns and swag from him; we might as well add dope. Long as we got him and his cousin Alejandro on our team, we don't have nothing to worry about."

"Even though the Duncans run the business in New York?" I asked, even though I already knew the answer.

"Not anymore. We about to be their competition, 'cause I'm not bitching up for nobody, and them thinking I should means they deserve us taking it all."

"Then we need to plan a trip to Los Angeles," I told him. "And we'll go straight to the source."

A gigantic smile spread across his face, as we both tucked into our seafood platters, which, I have to say, were damn tasty. "Set it up."

Niles

55

I felt a rush of euphoria as I peered out the window at the Empire State Building from my one-bedroom suite on the thirty-ninth floor. For the first time since I had joined the Army, I felt good about the direction my life was going in, regardless of everything that had gone down with Keisha. It almost seemed like I was living somebody else's life, but I had every intention of making it my own. I may not have wanted to be an assassin, but let's be honest: I was good at it, and they were paying me a hell of a lot of money to kill bad people.

"Hey!" I answered the phone when I saw the code for Willie's number. "What's up?"

"Bridget is on her way upstairs."

Even though I was expecting her, I felt an internal lurch of excitement knowing she'd be at the door in a few minutes

"Well, hello stranger," I said when I opened the door for her.

"Nice goatee," she said playfully, motioning to the new growth of hair on my face.

"Yeah, I decided to do something different." I took her coat and laid it across a chair.

She took a look around, her attention landing on the view. "This is really nice."

"I thought I'd get a place in the city, somewhere away from the family, where I can decompress and stay in character."

"That's smart. It's what I do," she told me.

"That's where I got the idea," I admitted. "There's only one thing missing in this place."

She did a slow turn around the room, stopping to look at the unparalleled view again. "What could possibly be missing?"

"This place hasn't been christened." I snatched her by the waist and pulled her close to me. I kissed her, sucking on her tongue as I unzipped her skirt. It dropped to the floor, and I massaged her ass as I slid down her panties. Imagine my surprise when I discovered that they were already sopping wet.

I lowered her to the bed, took hold of her butt cheeks, and brought her to my face. Her scent was of wildflowers, and I swear she tasted delicious.

"Oh my," she gasped.

I softly sucked the folds of her lips, making my way to her clit. Gently sliding back the hood to expose her throbbing love button, I latched my lips around it, sucking and flicking my tongue over it like it was a nipple. I felt her body begin to shake as an orgasm took over. "Oh, oh, oooh!" She pushed me away as a smug smile covered her face and she began to squirt.

"I want you," she whispered.

I didn't say a word as I laid her back on the bed, kissing and sucking her breasts, until she took control and pulled me closer.

"I said I want you," she commanded.

My rock hard penis didn't need any more encouragement. I ripped off my clothes and got on top of her. Next thing I knew, our bodies were wrapped together as I gripped her around the waist and pushed myself deeper.

Bridget threw her head back, and her pelvis rose to meet me as she grabbed my buttocks, guiding my movements. I had to grab on to the edge of the bed and breathe to hold back the orgasm threatening to overtake me, because I wanted to stay here like this.

"Do you like it?" she asked before I smashed my lips against hers.

I hadn't thought it was possible, but this was even better than the first time, because now, we both wanted this.

"Oh my God, Niles!" Bridget's yearning met mine, but I had to quiet her before she took me over. I covered her lips with mine, and damn if the sweetness of her kiss didn't make me want to come even more.

"Dammit!" I hollered, knowing I couldn't stop myself from exploding any minute.

"Niles, Niles, Niles." Bridget's breathing got heavy and came out in fast spasms. She gripped her fingers tightly around my base, and I knew she was about to come. I let go at that moment, and we both came to a swift orgasm together.

"Damn! Damn!" I pulled Bridget closer to me as our bodies writhed in the aftermath of the explosion. I felt so good when I looked at her. The smile on her face said everything. "That good, huh?"

I rose up, grabbed a towel, and got rid of all the evidence "We're just getting started."

I walked over to the bar and poured her a drink as she lifted up on one elbow to watch me.

"Grey Goose martini, two olives, and pass the vermouth over the glass, right?" I said, mimicking the order I'd heard her give countless waiters and bartenders during our training sessions. I poured myself a bourbon on the rocks and walked back over to hand Bridget her drink.

"Wow. I wasn't expecting that," she said.

I liked that, because Bridget wasn't an easy person to surprise.

"I took the liberty of ordering us dinner," I said, using a line she'd taught me in our training. "It should be here at 8:15, which gives us time," I said. Just looking at her lying there with that post-orgasm glow was turning me on again.

"Well, then, I'm sure we've got time to cook up our own dessert." She reached out and pulled me toward her.

I woke up at 5:30 every morning automatically, an occupational habit I'd inherited from my stint in the Army, but when I opened my eyes, Bridget was already awake with a cup of coffee in her hand. She was sitting on the bed, staring off into space. I watched her for a brief moment. To be honest, she looked a little lost. "What the heck? You don't sleep?"

"Not when I have a lot on my mind. But it was fun last night." She turned to me, wearing only my shirt, which seemed to fit her perfectly, if you know what I mean. She ruined that image when she got out of bed and returned with a folder from her briefcase. She handed it to me, but her expression told me that whatever was in the folder gave her concern. "I got a really big assignment for you. Your next target is a motherfucker."

"You say that about every job."

"Well, dammit, I mean it this time!" There was an intensity to her voice I'd never heard before. "Now pay attention."

"Fine." I sat up, ready for the full disclosure on my latest assignment. "Tell me about this bastard."

"We've been trying to take this guy down for years. So far he's managed to evade, overpower, and kill almost every operative we've ever sent," she said, growing increasingly somber.

"They must not have been that good at the job," I said, feeling cocky. Nobody was invincible, and whoever this target was, I was surely the guy to get the job done.

She stared at me a long time before answering. "Those operatives he either killed or almost killed weren't any third-string rejects. They were some of the best we've ever had in the company, and most of them were my friends."

I had never seen her lacking confidence like this, and now I was concerned too.

"I'm sorry," I said.

"Don't be. But understand that only one operative has ever gone after him and survived."

"Really?" Now she had my full attention.

"Yes, and that person is me." She gave me a look I'd never seen on her face before, and the words that followed confirmed that she was genuinely scared. "I'm lucky to be alive after fucking with that crazy bastard. I mean, I pulled out every trick in my arsenal, and he just wouldn't die."

"Shit. Did you get close enough to dot him?"

She laughed. "Yeah, I dotted him on three separate occasions. None of them worked."

"How the fuck did he do that?"

"Apparently he almost died from someone trying to poison him, so he takes small doses of poison to make him immune. He never even flinched."

I shook my head in disbelief. I was starting to understand why she was so serious about this one.

"Oh, and guns aren't going to work, at least not if you want to survive." She looked disgusted. "He's surrounded by bodyguards all brandishing state of the art weapons. I mean, shit that hasn't even hit the streets. He's also got his own advance team already perched wherever he goes, looking for would-be snipers."

"He's gotta have a weakness."

"Maybe, but I never found it. I was actually captured by the sadistic motherfucker. He had me in a vice hung up on his wall, just so he could see the woman sent to kill him. So when I say don't think this is going to be easy, you better hear me. Just the thought of sending you after him terrifies me, and that's just not how I am."

I put my hand out and took hers, and she was shaking.

"So tell me, who is this guy who's got you so worried?"

"His name is Frank Soto, but they call him El Gato, The Cat. Trust me, he ain't no pussy. Motherfucker has at least nine lives, 'cause every time we think we got him, he somehow manages to slip away, leaving more bodies than I care to remember. At least I managed to escape with my life, which makes it hard as hell to forget."

I pulled her close to me as she continued.

"He dabbles in drug smuggling and human trafficking, but what he's known for is arms distribution."

"Wait. So you and a whole buncha others have gone after him, and he's still breathing? What makes you think I can take him down?" I wasn't about to admit it to her, but shit, I was starting to question my own ability.

"Folks at the top think you're ready, and they want this guy eliminated," she said.

"And you?" I asked, watching her closely. Over the past months, I'd gotten to know her pretty well, and I knew when she wasn't being straight up.

"I know you can do it. You're the best operative I've ever seen; even better than me, as much as that pains me to say."

"Wait. Pause. I just want to savor that for a moment."

She rolled her eyes and granted me about three seconds to gloat. I threw up my hands when she opened her mouth to continue. "No, one more second."

She folded her arms and gave me a frown.

"All right, you can continue," I told "I just thought we could use a little levity for a minute."

The smile I'd just put on her face disappeared quickly behind a fog of worry. "I just want you to know this guy is dangerous and he's smart. He doesn't trust anyone."

"How could any man not trust a face like yours?" I asked before leaning in and kissing her slowly and deeply. I wanted to get back to what we were doing before this conversation, but she pulled back.

"Well, he didn't." She opened her mouth like she had more to say, but then closed it, looking like she was unsure of how to continue.

"Go ahead. Tell me."

"Niles, I want this to be your last assignment. Our last assignment." Her eyes started to water.

"Seriously? You kicking me to the curb?" I hadn't expected that to come out of her mouth. I mean, I thought we were solid.

"Us. I'm kicking us to the curb. We have money. Lots of it. I just don't want to do this anymore," she said, her revelation shocking the hell out of me. "I need us to get out while we still can."

"Then what do you want to do? 'Cause unless you've been hiding your true nature, you're not exactly the stay at home mom type." I hoped my response didn't offend her, but I was just keeping it one hundred.

"I could be," she said, and I could see her melting, softening.

"You're serious."

She sat up and wrapped her arms around me, but not like normal. This felt like we were in an ocean, and I was her life preserver.

"Hey. What's wrong? Tell me," I pleaded. She was holding something back, and I knew it.

"We need to get out. Go to Europe, the Caymans, somewhere. Get lost for a while and just disappear. The two of us. There's something going on that I'll explain when you return."

"I can't leave my moms," I told her. I didn't know what was at the root of all of this, but something had her shook, and she wasn't thinking clearly.

"Maybe she can come with us. Fresh air will do her some good."

That made me laugh. "I can't even imagine my moms outside of Long Island."

I felt unable to tell her what she needed to hear, and so I kissed her, hoping it would somehow comfort her. She had me so confused.

"I know. Just please be careful and remember everything you've learned. I want you back in one piece."

I agreed. "We'll finish this discussion later. Now, tell me more about this El Gato so I can figure out exactly how I'm going to be the one to take him down."

Majestic

56

The moment Bruce and I entered the private cigar club, a haven for rich men and their secrets, we were led over to our host. He was a sixty-year-old Mexican national surrounded by six of the most beautiful, provocatively dressed women I'd seen in my life. His son was seated beside him.

Bruce and I sat down next to them, and the party began when they handed us goblets of some of the smoothest cognac I'd ever tasted, along with hand-rolled Cuban cigars. Two hours later, the cognac was still flowing, and I was feeling real nice to the point where I almost forgot this was a business trip.

"I've gotta give it to you, old friend. I haven't had this much fun in quite a while. I appreciate the hospitality," I told him, puffing on my cigar while my man Bruce draped his arms around the two beauties on either side of him.

Frank, our host, responded in his thick Spanish accent, "Majestic, my friend, considering the order you just placed with us, the pleasure is all mine. But the night is not over. There is still plenty to do." He gestured at the young ladies.

"Man, you're spoiling me." I laughed, planning for the night ahead with at least two of these women.

"However, I didn't invite you to the West Coast purely for pleasure. We have a mutual problem," he informed me, pulling my attention away from the beauties before me. The mention of trouble changed everything.

"What kind of problem? If you need me to take care of something while I'm out here, Bruce and I can be like ghosts."

His son, a handsome, light-eyed model type interrupted me. "It's a little more complicated than that. When Bruce inquired about a woman named Bridget St. John last week, the name didn't ring a bell, but when I mentioned it to my Pops . . ."

We all turned in his father's direction. "You know this woman?"

He took a deep breath and spoke, his voice dripping with disdain. "Sí, I know this Bridget St. John very well. She is a very dangerous bitch. Three years ago, she killed twenty of my men and almost killed me. Back then she went by the name of Bridget Pierre. It was a good thing that like a cat, El Gato has nine lives."

I leaned in closer. "Well, El Gato, I have my own reasons for wanting to end her life, but I'm only too happy to add yours to the list. I swear, the pleasure will be all mine."

"Ours." Bruce chimed in.

A huge smile spread across El Gato's face. "I was so hoping you were going to say that."

"But first I think I need to work off my anger right now," I explained, staring at the bevy of beauties to drive home my statement.

"Of course. Take two, you and your partner," he said, motioning to Bruce.

When I pointed to the gorgeous brunette sitting closest to him, he made a slight motion toward two other women, an Asian and a buxom blonde. I understood his meaning: the brunette was off limits to me. I didn't know why, but I wasn't about to press the issue. No sense in ruining a good business relationship over some pussy. The Asian and the blonde stood up, while the Latina honeys stayed glued to Bruce.

El Gato stood up. "Then it is settled. Tonight, you will fuck, and tomorrow, you will come to my house and I will tell you everything I know of this bitch, so that you can kill her."

"I'll see you tomorrow," I told him before we all made our way out of the club, my thoughts traveling from the women to the job ahead of me. I couldn't wait to get my hands on Bridget St. John.

Niles

57

When I pulled up to the cigar bar in the canary yellow Lamborghini, all eyes turned to me, which was exactly what I had wanted. I stepped out of the car and handed the keys and a hundred-dollar bill to the valet before heading to the entrance. On my way, I accidently bumped into a brown-skinned brother, who was accompanied by a large, six-five football player–looking dude and some rather scantily clad women.

"You ever heard of excuse me, motherfucker?" the brother barked.

"Look, it was an accident, but there's no need to bring my mother in it. We're all gentlemen here, remember?" I pointed at the sign by the front door that read GENTLEMEN'S CLUB.

"If you step on my shoes again, you're gonna wish I was a gentlemen as I bust you upside your head."

I had to give it to him. He didn't back down, and from his stance, I could tell he'd had some type of training.

"Yo, Bruce, is there a problem?" His big-ass friend and the girls had stopped about twenty feet past us.

He glanced over at his friend. If he called him over, it was gonna be a problem, because both of them looked like they could handle themselves, which basically meant my plan was shot. He stared at me for a second, and I stared back.

"Nah, this punk ain't worth it."

I can't begin to tell you how relieved I was when he started walking. The last thing I needed to do was have my mission blown because of two puffed-up assholes looking to impress their bitches.

I strolled into the smoke-filled club and scoped out the wealthy, middle-aged ballers with the young, expensive arm candy. At the largest and most impressive table sat the man I'd come to see. Bridget's warnings were playing in a loop in my head.

"Every single thing about this assignment is high stakes. El Gato is dangerous, but then so is everyone he surrounds himself with. Taking him out means you must be prepared to take out all of them."

"Can I help you, sir?" A Mediterranean beauty greeted me. Reaching into my pocket, I pulled

out my thick wad of crisp hundred-dollar bills
and peeled off five, making sure she spotted the
expensive diamond bezel Cartier watch on my
wrist. She flashed me her million-dollar I'd-fuck-
you-for-some-of-that smile and led me to a table
with a RESERVED sign.

"This is perfect." I assured her as I took a seat.
Then I handed her a larger stack along with a
special request.

A few moments later, she returned with a two-
thousand- dollar bottle of Dom Perignon White
Gold for my approval. The game officially began as
I watched her deliver it to El Gato himself.

"What the fuck!" A loud roar came from El Gato
as I watched his men try to restrain him. Clearly
they failed, as he headed over to my table like a
bull charging his opponent in a ring. His men had
to run to keep up with him.

El Gato spat his words out at me. "You send me
a bottle like I'm some cheap whore? And you send
me a message that you wish to help me upgrade?
Do you know who the fuck I am?"

I sat there calmly studying him before I replied.
"At two thousand dollars a bottle, I wouldn't consider you cheap. Besides, it was a whole hell of a lot
better than that basic shit you were drinking."

He damn near leapt at me.

"A man of your stature deserves the best. Would you disagree with me, Mr. Soto? Or would you prefer I call you El Gato?"

He grunted in response, letting me know that if this wasn't a public place, I most likely would be dead by now.

"You don't exactly fly under the radar," I commented before leaning back confidently. He continued to stare daggers at me as I continued. "You could always send back the champagne, but then that might hurt my feelings. Then I might not feel so inclined to do business with you," I told him and watched his expression relax as his mood shifted.

"And who are you that I would even consider doing business with you?" he questioned.

I answered with my cover, "Wellington. Marcus Wellington. And since I'm not about to share this information with the entire world, I suggest you pretend we're old friends and have a seat," I said boldly, knowing how fine a line I was walking.

He sneered at me. "Why would I do that?"

"Because what I have to say just might make your day," I told him.

He seemed to consider this briefly before he nodded to his men, who posted up around the booth like sentries as he sat down.

I motioned to the bottle. "Try it. A man like you will appreciate the difference." I poured him a glass and handed it to him, but he didn't dare drink, probably fearing I was trying to poison him. Maybe he was afraid his immunity was wearing off or something. That would make him one very paranoid man, a weakness for sure.

"What do you want, Mr. Wellington?" he asked, and I could tell his patience was already running short.

"It's not what I want. It's what I have."

"And exactly what do you have?"

I steeled my voice. "I have the shipment that left Fort Bragg. Your people were planning on stealing it in North Carolina today. That's what I have."

His voice lowered to a whisper. "What shipment are you referring to?"

"Oh, just a few hundred of the highest grade assault weapons money can buy."

He remained completely still in his seat, but I could see his rage boiling just beneath the surface. "Those are my weapons. I have buyers for them. They have already been paid for," he informed me.

I felt relieved that we were in a public place, because the way his hands were gripping the edge of the table told me he wished it were my neck instead.

"No, those are the weapons you planned on stealing. My men stole them first, which makes them mine. I'm sure this isn't the first time you've heard that possession is nine tenths of the law."

This was not a man used to losing. "Since you were so kind to inform me of that, I'd like to inform you of something."

Instead of looking at him, I decided to drag this out by taking a sip of the champagne before answering. "What's that?" I said when I finally put down my glass.

"You are a dead man."

"Perhaps, but then I'd be a dead man with a truckload of weapons that you need, so killing me is not the answer, and we both know it."

"And what is the answer?" he questioned me.

"A partnership. I've got the guns; you've got the clients," I said, as if it were the greatest idea in the world. He sat back, thinking, and I waited with my stomach churning.

He cursed in Spanish, biting his upper lip. "Fine. I will see you tomorrow at noon. We will negotiate after I've had you and your story checked out."

He stood up and snapped his fingers. Almost immediately, a beautiful brunette appeared in front of him. "This is Dominique. She will keep you company this evening, and tomorrow she will escort you to my house—or if I find out you lied, she will kill you."

I had to admit she was probably one of the sexiest women I'd ever met. "I take it this is non-negotiable," I said, forcing myself to keep a steady voice.

"You are a very perceptive man. But please don't worry, she is also excellent company."

Dominique nodded her approval to El Gato, which made me realize she must be one of his women, because she definitely had a vote. She slid in close to me, until her lips were on my ear.

"Not only can I speak eight languages, but I can cook, discuss art, music theory, architecture, and I am also skilled enough to suck a golf ball through a straw."

Yeah, this is going to be a very interesting night, I thought as El Gato drained his glass and picked up the bottle.

"Then I shall see you tomorrow," he said before taking the bottle back to his table, followed by his bodyguards.

Bridget

58

I'd always thought of myself as a bad-ass, never needing anybody, particularly not anybody attached to a penis, unless it was sliding between my legs. That was why this whole new experience with Niles had caught me off guard. My need for him was so out of the ordinary that, like my shrink had suggested, I just stopped questioning it. I just knew that this man was the one. He was the first one to come along who I allowed to soften the edges I'd grown so used to. Like some naïve schoolgirl, I allowed all my walls to disintegrate. And how could they not? Not only was he genetically superior, but Niles had my back. As soon as he got back we were going to have a talk and make some real changes. Fantasies of this new life swirled in my head, distracting me to the point that I didn't hear the doorbell, until it was being repeatedly rung.

"What are you doing here?" I opened the door, staring at the one person capable of ruining my mood.

"I've been doing a lot of covering up for you lately. I'm not sure how long I can keep this Detective Fuller thing from the director." Jonathan stormed into my apartment as if he'd been invited.

"I want to know what the hell kind of security I'm paying for that allows you to just waltz into my apartment." I was going to have a little talk with the doorman as soon as Jonathan was gone.

He folded his arms across his chest, studying me. "Really? That's what you're focused on?"

"I'm working, so I'm focused on a lot of things, Jonathan, including you leaving so I can get back to doing my job." I refused to play nice during this impromptu visit.

"I need to know what you're going to do about your problem. The fact that someone wrote your name down at a crime scene, big and bold for everyone to see, means this is huge."

Of course he was right, but I wasn't about to let him know my level of concern. "I'm working on it."

"I'm sure you are. Let me help you. We used to be a good team," he offered in a way that I'm sure he thought was gracious—except we both knew he didn't do anything without a motive.

"So what's it going to cost me?" I sneered at him, waiting for the catch.

He reached out and slid his hand around my waist. "I'm thinking the same thing you gave me for Niles," he said, breathing heavily in my ear.

I took a step back to create some distance between us, making sure I was out of the reach of his greedy hands. "No, thank you. I've already got a partner," I shot back, knowing it would burn him.

"Niles?" He burst out laughing like I'd said something hysterical. "You better pray he even comes back. That job was way over his pay grade, so I wouldn't hold out much hope for his return."

"You need to stop underestimating him, because when he does come back, we're leaving the business together. I'm done." As soon as I said it, I could see that my words pierced him like a blade.

"What? Quitting? Are you having some kind of feelings for this guy? Like you think you're in love or something?" Jonathan yelled, hovering over me until I was backed against a wall. "I thought you were smarter than this." He sounded disappointed that I wasn't the heartless bitch of his dreams.

"What if I do? I don't have to answer to you or anyone about my private life," I reminded him.

He leered at me. "You don't get to have a private life. Everything about you is transparent."

I shoved him away from me. "Stop acting so weird. I told you that when Niles returns, he can help me with this problem."

"You sure about that?" he challenged me. "'Cause a lot of bad things can happen when you put your trust in the wrong person."

"Of course I trust Niles. Not only is he capable, but I trust him with my life," I snapped back, hating his smug superiority.

"Stop being so stupid. Let me help you with this. I have the resources to find out who is after you, and when I find them, I can make this whole thing go away." Somehow, his pledge to help me came out sounding more like a threat.

"As long as I let you fuck me?" I questioned with attitude.

"And is that suddenly so distasteful? I mean, it's not like you haven't had my dick inside of you before, and from what I remember, you seemed to enjoy it."

"Well, not anymore. There is only one cock I'd like to suck, fuck, and have in my life from now on. This job doesn't allow for monogamy, and since I'm not try'na fuck for checks or respect anymore, I need to leave," I stated with finality, hoping that he would drop the hard-ass routine and leave. I did not want to admit to him that whoever was after me had me running scared.

"You're making a mistake," Jonathan seethed.

I stormed over and opened the door. "You can leave now. Like I said, I don't need your help any longer. I have Niles."

"Bridget, you take this route, and I may not be able to come to your rescue when your boy toy lets you down."

"He won't," I promised him before I slammed the door after him.

Niles

59

Two armed bodyguards met us as we pulled up in front of a twenty thousand square foot mansion. Each of the bodyguards opened a door for us, but mine had to wait, because I needed to do something. I reached into my pocket and pulled out a prescription bottle. Dominique gave me a questioning stare as I popped one of the pills.

"Xanax. It calms my nerves before a big meeting," I explained apologetically before we exited the car.

She led me through an impressively furnished house, into an outdoor courtyard. El Gato held court with several Latino men. Most of them were armed, with their weapons exposed. I wondered if it was for my benefit. I thought that Dominique would stay, but after kissing El Gato she quickly disappeared.

El Gato stood to greet me. "Mr. Wellington. Come, come, please sit."

"Thank you." I took the seat across from him, and he sat back down.

"Mr. Wellington, why didn't you mention that you work with Jose Rivera?" He asked me, his mood a whole lot more congenial than the night before. But we weren't besties just yet.

"So now that you know who I work with, you also know I have what you want."

"I do," he answered.

I reached into my breast pocket, removed an envelope, and slid it across the table.

"I'm sure you have a busy schedule, so I'd like to cut to the chase. Here are our terms." I sat quietly as he took the paper and read it.

Then he lowered it and stared at me a full minute before responding, "Wow! You got some pair of balls on you, don't you?"

"A closed mouth has never gotten fed, so I learned early to ask for what I want. We can supply you with anything you need, but you should know that our ultimate goal is to become your new supplier."

His eyes grew big. "Let me make sure I heard you correctly. You steal this shipment right from under my nose, and then you expect me to pay you double for it?"

I nodded. "Yes. That's exactly what I expect. We left you room to make a tidy profit."

"Go fuck yourself. I don't pander to extortion." He was furious, but I just played it cool and acted like this was all part of the negotiation.

"Look, we thought the right thing to do was to give you the first option, but please understand that you are in no way our only interested buyer. I will inform my people that you have passed. Good day, Mr. Soto." I stood up, ready to leave.

El Gato snapped his fingers twice, and two bodyguards pointed their guns at my head.

He sauntered over to me, threatening, "You are not going anywhere. Those are my weapons. Now, make arrangements to get them to me, or you die!"

I raised my wrist to look at my watch. The bodyguards glanced at their boss for an answer. El Gato waited patiently for me to reply, but all I did was smile, because I knew something they didn't. When I passed the bodyguards earlier, I had placed a tiny sticker on each of their necks, just the way I'd been taught.

"Why the fuck are you smiling?" El Gato shouted at me.

"Because the poison should be kicking in right about now," I informed him just as his men began to crumble to the ground. Suddenly, it was just the two of us, face to face.

"What have you done to them?" he screamed as he looked around at all of his men squirming for their lives.

"Poison dart frog toxin. Real lethal, fast-acting shit," I told him. "I had to take a pill before coming in here just to handle the stuff."

"You think you can kill me?" He lunged for the gun of the bodyguard closest to him, but I wasn't about to let that happen. I kicked it out of his reach.

As I went to reach for El Gato, his arm caught me in the chin. He almost kneed me in the nut sack, but I twisted my body just enough for the blow to land on my leg. I grabbed his leg in the air and pushed hard so that he fell backward. Just as I went to jump on him, he flipped up and landed on his feet. He was pretty spry for an old guy.

"If one of us is going, it won't be me!" I promised, and I meant it. A roundhouse, a couple of karate chops later, and I was on top of him, with a gun pointed at his head. "My girl Bridget sends her love."

"Fuck you and that bitch. I am El Gato," he bragged, but I already saw that without his swarm of men, he was almost helpless. "You can't kill me. I have nine lives." That was the last thing he said as I pumped two bullets into him.

"Yeah, well, I guess you should have counted, 'cause that was your ninth life."

Stepping away from the bloody scene, I grabbed the case full of money, shoved the gun in my waist, and hurried through the house toward the front door.

"Everything okay? I thought I heard gunfire?" Dominique stood blocking my exit.

"You might need a new employer, but other than that, things are just fine," I told her, and that's when I heard a gun being prepared. She came flying at me, arms and fists flailing, but I was in no mood. I hated fighting women, but I knew she was going to try to avenge her boss. It was her job.

We went at it, and I had to admit this girl was a real bad-ass. With every hit, she met me. Finally, I'd had enough, and I grabbed her in a chokehold and twisted, stopping just before the point of snapping her neck.

"Please. Didn't we have a great time last night?" She begged for her life, and I could feel myself softening. "I can show you an even better time today." She started stroking her breasts in a gesture meant to be sexual, but it was just grotesque.

"Please don't flatter yourself. That was business. I've got something much better waiting for me at home." I slammed the butt of the gun against her head, knocking her out. Yeah, I was ready to get home.

Willie

60

"What's up, boss? How'd it go?" I asked Niles when I answered my phone. I was thankful that he was alive, but hoping this would be a quick call and I could get back to business. With him being on the West Coast, I had at least six hours to get my groove on.

"Will you stop calling me boss?" Niles asked for the millionth time, but when someone gives you a job that changes your life and upgrades your lifestyle, what else would you call them to show respect? I have to admit, though, half the time I called him that just to fuck with him.

"What you want me to call you, pipsqueak? Like I did when you were a kid? That's what you want?" I joked.

"Where are you?" he asked.

I wasn't about to tell him the truth, not when I was puffing on one of his fine cigars. "Uh . . . I'm in the city." I admitted half the truth, not wanting to tell a bald-faced lie. He wasn't stupid enough to believe me.

"Are you in my suite?" he asked, full of suspicion.

I decided it was best to stay silent. For all I knew, he had some kind of hidden camera in the place and was watching my every move as we spoke.

"Got nothing to say, huh? Mm-hmm. Just like I thought. Wearing my robe too?" he added, which I was. "Drinking my two-hundred-dollar-a-bottle spring water?"

That one might have been a lucky guess, I thought. After all, he knew I was committed to staying sober so I wouldn't be drinking his fancy champagne.

"With your woman on my silk sheets in my bed?"

I glanced over at the bed, where Tanya was lying half-naked, giving me a look that told me she had something for me that I wanted.

"Niles, where's the trust, brother? Would Batman accuse Robin of sneaking a woman into the Batcave?"

He laughed. "He would if he had a horny-ass partner like you."

"Hey, at least I keep it one hundred," I told him. Niles knew exactly who I was at all times.

"Look, I'm sorry, but I'm gonna need you to put the party on pause for a few minutes. I've got something important I need you to handle for me."

I looked over at Tanya, and damn if I didn't want to hang up and get busy, but I couldn't let

him down. "No problem. What you need, boss?"
I gave Tanya an apologetic look, but I already
knew she wouldn't complain. That's one thing I
really appreciated about her. She understood my
priorities.

"I've been trying to get a hold of Bridget just to
check in, but she's not answering any of her phones.
You think you could check in on her, maybe call
Winston so it doesn't look like I'm sweating her?"

"Sure, I got you. Don't wanna look like you're
pussy whipped, even though you are." I laughed,
but he didn't.

"Not funny," Niles replied seriously.

"It was a joke. Shit, I'll call him right now." I
didn't like it when my nephew was like this. It
meant something deep was going down—possibly
something dangerous—and that always made me
nervous. I might like to fuck with him time and
again, but I didn't want anything to happen to
Niles.

"Great. Thanks, Unc. I'm about to get on this
plane. I'll see you at the usual spot in about six
hours."

As soon as Niles hung up, I dialed Winston.

"Winnie the Pooh," I teased as soon as he picked
up. "This your boy Willie. What's up?"

"Hello, Willie. Nothing much. Just watching
the game. How are you?" Despite his stuck-up

demeanor when he was at work, Winston was actually a cool cat who had given me pointers about how to deal with this sidekick driving shit. We'd actually gone to a couple of Mets games together.

"So you're not with Bridget?" That actually concerned me a little.

"No, I haven't spoken to her since this morning. She gave me the day off. Why do you ask?" I could almost hear him get up out of his seat. He had obviously picked up on my unease.

"Niles thinks something may be wrong with her. He called her cell and she didn't answer."

"Let me call you right back," he said. "Maybe she'll answer me."

I held tight and waited for Winston to call me back, hoping this was a false alarm and I could get back to my business with Tanya. A few seconds later, my phone rang.

"She didn't answer me neither," Winston said. "I'm going to her place in Chelsea. That's where I left her this morning."

"I'm not that far. I'll meet you at her place."

I said a quick good-bye to Tanya then hit the elevator and shot down to get the BMW out of the parking garage. I drove to Bridget's place, pulling up right behind Winston, who was getting out of the Rolls.

"I got a key," he said as we went to the entrance. "I'll talk to the doorman to see if he saw her leave anytime today."

It turned out that conversation was not going to be possible. The door to the building was ajar, and the doorman was nowhere to be seen. Something did not feel right. One look around and we spotted the doorman on the floor behind his station, blood seeping out of his forehead.

"Shit! Winston, man, we're on tape," I said, pointing to the security camera I spotted in the corner.

"Not a problem." He pulled out his cell phone and made a call.

"Yeah, it's Winston," he spoke into the phone. "I need you to crash the server on the Chelsea apartment building."

He ended the call and said to me, "Let's go."

I double-checked to make sure my piece was easy to grab before I went any farther. Winston did the same. Instead of taking the elevator, we headed up the stairs, which made me glad for all the training I'd gotten and the booze I'd gotten rid of in my life.

When we arrived at Bridget's floor and got to the apartment, we saw that her door was ajar. He reached for his gun; I did the same, and we entered quietly. The place had been ransacked, furniture overturned, stuffing pulled out of the cushions in the couch. Things were in complete disarray. Now our real concern had become finding Bridget alive.

We separated and moved stealthily through the apartment when we heard a sound coming from the back of the apartment. Winston picked up a large piece of broken glass off the floor then raised his fingers, silently counting. On the count of three, Winston tossed the glass against the wall as I ducked behind the couch and he ducked behind a wall. If Bridget was safe and she'd heard the glass, she'd come out or at least say something to alert us that she was all right. Instead, we heard a male voice.

"What was that?" Two thug-looking dudes came running from the back of the apartment, guns drawn, looking around for the source of the noise.

I slid around from the side of the couch, unnoticed by the intruders. Just as I was getting ready to make a move, Winston motioned for me to hold still. He had a clear shot from where he was. I watched as the bullet pierced his chest and one guy fell to the floor.

"Fuck!" the other guy shouted as he turned around to try to figure out what had happened. He saw me, then his dead boy slumped on the floor, and then his eyes went to the gun in my hand. He and the dead guy must have been real close, because I saw the fury in his eyes as he aimed his gun at my face.

As I braced myself for a gunfight, Winston tried to sneak up behind the guy to disarm him before he got off any shots. The guy must have seen Winston out of the corner of his eye, because he quickly turned in Winston's direction and fired two shots. Then he started running toward the front door. I raised my gun and let off a shot. He dropped like a sack of potatoes.

"Winston, where the fuck are you, man?" I looked around the living room, and when I finally spotted him through all that mess, I realized he'd been hit.

"Winston. Ah, shit. Man, please don't be dead. Please!" I shouted as I leaned over him.

"It's just my shoulder. I'll be all right," he said, trying to reassure me. "Willie, you got to find her."

"I gotta get you to a hospital, man."

"No, I'll be all right. I've been her driver for years. No one will question me being here. But they'll just hold you up, and you have to get Niles and find her."

"I can't leave you here, man," I insisted.

"Yes, you can. You have to get out of here quick."

I reluctantly stood up to go.

"Here. Take my phone. I put a tracker on all her cars. She's probably in the Porsche. It's her favorite. Once you activate it, you'll know where she is."

He took the phone out of his pocket and handed it to me.

"Now go before the police come. Get out of here," he ordered me. "Go. Please find my girl."

I raced out of the apartment and down the stairs. By this time, a crowd had gathered around the doorman's body, but I slipped past and kept moving to the car.

Inside the BMW, I took out Winston's phone and activated the tracker. It felt like forever waiting for the location to come up, but as soon as I saw the address pop up on the GPS, I headed out, hoping it was not too late.

As luck would have it, I hit every light from Columbus Circle to SoHo, and as a black man driving a BMW, I couldn't risk getting pulled over and wasting more time, so I had to stay within ten miles of the speed limit. Folks were out in the streets en masse, so the traffic was bumper to bumper when I finally got downtown. What should have been a fifteen-minute ride took me thirty-five.

I had tried calling Bridget multiple times, but she still wasn't answering her phone, which confirmed for me that something was very wrong.

"Where are you?" I said out loud as I raced around the parking lot looking for Bridget's car. I finally spotted it, but she was nowhere in sight. I got out of my car, my gun close at hand.

"Bridget!" I called out to her only to be met with silence.

As I got closer, I found her phone, purse, and packages sprawled on the ground between two cars.

"Shit." This was really bad. I grabbed her things and took them with me as I got back in the BMW.

For a split second, I thought of calling Niles on the plane, but I knew this wasn't the kind of information he'd want to receive over the phone, especially thousands of feet in the air where he really couldn't do anything. The only thing I could do was head back through Manhattan traffic to make sure I would be at the airport when his plane landed, so I could break the bad news to him.

Majestic

61

"That shit is funny as hell," I said, laughing at the ridiculousness up on the screen. A beat later, the three half-naked ladies draped around me in the screening room all followed my lead. It made me laugh again at just how anxious these hoes were to make me happy. Who could blame them? I was real generous to the people in my life, especially when they were as fine and accommodating as these lovelies, ass and tits out, sucking and fucking the way they had for the last twelve hours.

"Majestic, we still going out tonight?" China, my newest friend, asked as she stroked my arm like she wanted another round. Before I could answer, Bruce stepped into the room with a massive scowl on his face.

"We got problems."

His words hit me hard, because with the shit we were into, it could have been anything. Raising my right hand, I snapped my fingers, and as if I had performed a magic trick, all three ladies swiftly disappeared to give us privacy. I clicked off the screen, tied up my robe, and sat up straight to hear what had my partner so concerned.

"What is it?"

"Those two guys we sent over to that address El Gato gave us. They're both dead."

"Get the fuck outta here. Those were two first-class killers. This bitch is as good as El Gato said," I replied, concerned. "Thank God we sent outside talent to get her instead of our own people. They'll never trace it back to us."

"Well, maybe, but it gets worse. I just got a call from Cali. Literally right after we left and headed back to New York, someone hit El Gato." He delivered the news and then sank down in the chair next to mine from the weight of this revelation.

"You're shitting me. In that fortress he's got?" I sputtered, my thoughts darting all over the place. Hell, he had ten times the security that I did.

"I know, right. It was definitely professional. Dude killed everyone but that chick Dominique."

We exchanged a look. "You think it was her?" It wouldn't be the first time someone in this business got taken out by his own people.

Bruce shook his head, "Nah. She was really hurt, but I guess the person took pity on her or some shit and let her live."

"This is not good for business." My mind went to all of the work we had been planning to do together. "Who the hell did this? This shit's gonna cost us millions, and who knows if we'll ever recover," I explained to him, although I was sure he had already done the math. There were a lot of people that took that kind of hit and never came back.

Bruce pulled out his cell phone and fiddled with it a minute, then he handed it to me. "Dominique sent me this."

It was a picture of a guy sleeping like a fucking baby, not a care in the world.

"This the guy that got El Gato?" He looked like a lightweight to me.

Bruce seemed ready to blow. "Yep, he's the hitter. Dominique took this while he was sleeping. Apparently El Gato didn't trust the dude, so he made her spend the night to keep an eye on him. Notice anything familiar about him?"

"Nah, can't say I do. Why?"

"That's the guy I had beef with outside the club."

"Damn, this is fucked up, man. If we had only stayed in town a little longer, we could have dealt with him. Now we're royally screwed."

"We gonna have to start all over, or damn near," Bruce fumed, pounding his fist into the thick leather armrest. "We may have to go to the Duncans, hat in hand."

My phone rang, and I raised my hand for Bruce to put his rant on pause. I checked the caller ID and picked up the call. "Yo, Pooh, what's up?" I'd put him on a sensitive assignment.

"You see those pictures I sent you last night?" he asked, no doubt to make sure I knew he was doing his job. I had sent him over to Keisha's to keep an eye on her and to document anything suspicious. Something hadn't seemed quite right with her ever since I got home from camp.

"Man, I was a little indisposed last night. I had three of the best side-pieces over here try'na out-fuck each other. Bitches wore me out." I laughed just thinking about how crazy things had gotten. One went to suck my dick, and it was like the other two had to prove just how valid their dick-sucking skills were, and on and on. Some regular-season chicks vying to win the title of MVP.

"Yeah, well, you should take a look at those flicks," Pooh said, not interested in stories about last night's marathon sex. Usually he was the first one to ask for details, so I knew this was something important.

"What's going on?" I asked.

"I told you Keisha's trying to play you. I found some pictures of her and some dude hidden in her dresser."

"What? Hold on a sec." I scrolled through my phone, looking for his text. I swiped it open and what I saw nearly blew my mind.

"Get the fuck outta here," I mumbled to myself.

"You're never going to believe this shit, man." I turned the phone toward Bruce so that he could have my view. Then he picked up his own phone and stared at the photo Dominique had sent him.

"Wait. That's the same guy . . .?" he asked.

I nodded.

"Where'd you get that picture?"

I motioned to the phone. "Pooh. I had him keeping an eye on Keisha, and look who she's hanging with."

"Dammnnnnn!" Bruce whistled, bugging the fuck out.

"Pooh, I want you to go and get that bitch Keisha and bring her ass over here now."

Bridget

62

The sounds around me in what I assumed by the dampness was a basement were exaggerated because of the mask over my eyes and the gag in my mouth. When one or more of your senses are compromised, the rest overcompensate and become stronger. I tried with all my might to see through the mask, but the shit they had used blocked out everything.

I had to figure a way out of this. Whoever had snatched me in the parking garage couldn't be as smart or as dangerous as El Gato. They were just damn lucky. They certainly weren't showing any signs of being in the same league as that sadistic prick, or else I would have been in serious pain already. God, if Jonathan and them ever found out I'd been taken down by two stun gun toting thugs, they'd laugh me out of the agency—that is, if I survived this mess.

Thinking of El Gato made my thoughts turn to Niles. Hopefully he'd survived the mission, and if so, he was probably looking for me, which gave me a little bit of comfort. However, as much as I liked the idea of being a damsel in distress, right now that wasn't doing me a whole lot of good. How would he know how to get in touch with the organization and let them know that I was missing now that I was code Alpha-Omega? Even Winston didn't have that intel once they coded me. This convinced me that I had to go back to thinking like myself, my hard-ass, take-no-prisoners, don't-depend-on-nobody-for-nothing self, because I was the only one who could save me. Hell, I had survived worse, which made me feel a modicum of hope that somehow I'd figure a way out of this situation. The fact that I was still alive meant something. Maybe they needed to get something from me.

I thought I heard a noise. Then I became sure I could hear footsteps far off. As they came closer, I knew the person was male by the heaviness and size of each step he took. He kept coming closer, until he was right there in front of me. That's when I felt his hands on my face, rubbing against my cheek as he removed my gag.

"Take off this blindfold so that I can see who the hell you are, you coward," I shouted, relieved that I was able to speak.

He gave me no answer. Instead, he took four steps away from me, and I heard a chair in front of me move as he sat down like this was going to be some kind of fucking show.

"I don't know who you are, but you best fucking believe I'm going to kill you when I get these off," I shrieked as I tried to wriggle out of the restraints. If he thought I was going to be some complacent victim, he had totally underestimated Bridget St. John.

He began tapping his foot on the floor as if he was just waiting for me to finish trying to escape.

"Who are you? You have no idea who you are dealing with. I will have your ass for this," I warned him, still trying to loosen those damn restraints.

I felt terrified but knew better than to show it. "Tell me why I'm here. Tell me, goddammit."

Still, there was no answer from my captor. When I realized my threats were hollow in my current position, I decided to use some of the tactics I'd learned to manipulate him into revealing himself.

"So, you like your women tied up. Is that what you like? You're too weak to deal with a real woman, so you need one who is helpless? Is that your thing?" I pushed, trying to see if he'd react but all he did was continue that annoying tapping of his foot "I like real men, the kind who like strong, smart women. Do you know any of those?" Still nothing, no response, which was making me nervous. I was trying my damndest to keep up the tough girl thing, but all I wanted was to get out of there and to get back to Niles. I just wanted to be with him.

I needed to figure out who was holding me captive, in order to come up with a plan to get out of there. Who would want to get to me? Sure, I had a lot of enemies, but it was a pretty sure bet that this all had something to do with the murder of Fuller and my name written in his blood at the crime scene. I started talking again to see if I could incite this guy to finally talk.

"Congratulations. You finally found me," I said. "Wasn't very smart of you to leave a trail. Actually, it wasn't smart at all. You basically told me you were looking for me. What? You don't think I prepared myself for this?" I lied. "That I didn't make certain that there were people who could find me? Yeah, I'd say you fucked up." I laughed, hoping like hell he bought my little act.

"Plus the whole killing-a-cop thing? Wow! I mean, technically a retired cop, but you know the 'bleed blue' thing and how they stick together. Seems cops don't really like cop killers, so there are a lot of people looking for you.

"But, instead of being scared shitless, you come looking for me. That's some set of balls. And all this is over a worthless, piece-of-shit gangbanger."

All of a sudden he stopped tapping his foot. Game on, Bridget. Girl, that's it.

I couldn't believe it. With all the hits I'd done throughout my career, I would have expected to be kidnapped over the death of some international arms dealer or a head of state. Instead, I was being held captive because of some low-level street thug. This was about Niles and street justice. If only I'd paid closer attention, I would have figured that out as soon as I saw Fuller and his wife lying in a pool of blood with my name in it. I had been slipping big time, distracted by my feelings. This was just further confirmation that I needed to get the hell out of this career—as soon as I could get myself out of this basement.

"So you're pissed about your hustler buddy getting killed, is that it?" I asked him. "Well, understand something: When my man finds out about this, he's going put all you droopy-drawer motherfuckers to sleep, so if I were you, I'd fucking let me go."

I heard the chair hit the floor and I thought I must have hit a sensitive nerve. The gag was slapped back over my mouth, and whoever this person was, he got up and walked away.

"Let me go! Let me go!" I tried to scream through the gag, but the only response I heard was the slamming of the door.

Willie

63

During the whole ride from the house out to Teterboro Airport to scoop up Niles, I kept replaying the events of the last few hours in my head. I'd done everything I could think of to try to find Bridget, but the trail went cold at her car, and I didn't have a clue what to do next.

Winston was in Lenox Hill Hospital being treated for complications from the gunshot wound. The bullet had hit a couple of bones, so he needed to have a gang of tests to make sure that was the extent of the damage. The cops treated the thing as a basic breaking and entering with the intent to steal, and he was considered a hero thwarting the would-be robbers. He told me he made sure they knew he was the only one in the apartment and that he had reacted in self-defense, which wasn't that hard to convince them of, since the assailants had murdered the doorman on the way into the building. There were lots of questions about what they could have been looking for, but Winston was a pro, so I had no doubt that he answered those questions without raising any suspicion. It probably helped that he looked like a kind, elderly grandfather. He'd probably told them he served in Vietnam and a whole bunch of other bullshit. It made me realize I needed to have a story too, in case I ever found myself in that position.

By the time I got to the airport, Niles's plane had just landed. It seemed like it took forever for the stairs to be lowered. Then there was Niles in the doorway, carry-on in hand, looking very worried. When he hit the bottom step, I was waiting.

"What's up, Unc?" Niles greeted me in what he probably thought was a cheerful voice, but I could see the anxiety in his eyes. We hugged.

I hated to be the bearer of bad news, but I didn't have time to sugarcoat anything. "We got a problem." I got straight to the point as I took his bag and led him to the car.

"Tell me everything when we get in the car." His scratchy voice sounded like he'd stayed awake worrying for the entire six-hour flight.

He threw his carry-on in the trunk and got in beside me.

I began telling him the details. "After you called me, I hit up Winston, and the two of us met at Bridget's apartment."

"Uh-huh," he answered, his head doing a slow bob as he waited for more information.

"We get there, and the door to the building is open, and then we find the doorman on the floor in a pool of his own blood, which we can see is fresh—like this guy was smoked in the past few minutes. We run up the stairs, and soon as we hit her floor, we can see that her door is open.

"Now we sneak in, and then a couple of guys come running out of the back of her apartment, but the place is a mess, like they were looking for something."

Niles reacted. "Shit. This is not good."

"I know. Believe me. But you guys had prepared us for this, so it took me less than five seconds to know what to do. Winston took out the first one; shot his ass dead with one bullet. Then the other one comes for me, and I wasn't having that, so I fired off a shot and dropped him," I said, leaving out the part about what happened to Winston before I shot the guy.

"Look at you, all James Bond and shit." Niles cracked a smile, and I could see he was proud of me. As much as I hated to ruin this moment, he needed to hear the complete story. I couldn't help feeling like I had let him down.

"Hold on. That's not everything, though."

The smile fell from Niles's face. "Go ahead."

"Winston got shot. He took a bullet to the shoulder. The doctor said he's gonna make a full recovery, but he never should've been hurt. I'm sorry, man. " I was staring out the window, not wanting to see my nephew's disappointment.

His next words surprised me. "You kidding, man? You really stepped up for me. Now tell me the rest, and don't leave out the smallest detail."

I hated to have to tell him the worst part. "Well, I'm almost one hundred percent sure someone snatched Bridget."

"What makes you so sure? She's a pretty resourceful girl, and you didn't find her in the house. She could be laid up somewhere, just waiting for things to blow over."

"So Winston put a GPS on all of Bridget's cars, and he didn't tell her because, well, you know Bridget. She's her own army in her mind. But he knew that it was his job to try to keep her safe, in case something like this happened."

"Dude is smart—and devoted," Niles commented.

"Damn straight," I agreed. "So before I left the apartment, I tracked her car to a parking lot in SoHo. I found her car, but she was gone, and all her stuff was lying on the ground near her car. Her phone, keys, and her purse. Like it had just happened. If he had only thought about the tracker before we went to her apartment, we could've gone straight there first, and we may have been able to stop them," I said, feeling guilty that we hadn't been smarter about things.

"Fuck!" Niles slammed his fist on the dashboard. "She'd been acting all skittish lately, talking about getting out, like she was afraid and didn't want to worry me; but I should have been worried. I should have been a lot more worried. I should have never left her." Niles pulled out his phone and dialed, but when no one answered, he hung up and turned to me.

"Where to now?"

"To get some goddamn answers," he told me

Out of the corner of my eye, I could see that Niles's face was a mash-up of emotions, none of them good. Bridget had become more than his boss, and I knew she felt the same way about him. It was one thing to lose someone you work with, and another to lose the woman you're in love with. Yeah, I was really worried about my nephew. I knew that determined look on his face. Somebody was about to be in real shit.

"What are you gonna do?" I asked.

"I'm going to find out who has my girl," he told me, sounding serious and determined. "Take me to the city, Unc."

"Okay," I answered as I got on the highway headed into New York City, wishing things had gone differently.

Thirty minutes later, I pulled the BMW into a parking spot in front of a tall skyscraper. We sat there for a while, staring at the building, until I said, "Where the fuck are we?"

"Dynamic Defense," he said quietly.

"So, this is headquarters?"

Niles reached for the door handle without answering.

"Want me to come with you?"

"Nah, stay here. I'll be right back. Just stay here and stay ready to go," he told me as he jumped out.

"Niles!" I yelled out before he ran off. He looked at me and waited in silence, "Whoever took her was a professional."

"That's why we're here, Unc," was all he said before he darted into the building.

Majestic

64

Pooh's loud footsteps sounded like a team of Clydesdales riding through the hallway as he approached. "Get your ass in there!" he snarled as he shoved Keisha into the screening room, where Bruce and I kicked back, watching ESPN.

Whack! I reached out and backhanded Keisha's face. She grabbed her mouth in shock. She was lucky I didn't kick her ass—or worse.

"You fuckin' bitch!" I screamed at her. Everything in my being wanted to do a whole lot more than give her one slap. Pooh, knowing his job was done, nodded to me, backed up, and left the room. Bruce grabbed the remote and shut off the television, but he didn't move.

Keisha's voice was shaking when she spoke. "What was that for? I didn't do anything," she cried out, looking confused. My more violent tendencies were usually reserved for my work, but lately, she'd been making me cross that line.

I glared at her, struggling to contain myself. "Yes, you did, you fuckin' lying bitch."

Her eyes darted away from me, which told me she had an idea what this was about. "When have I ever lied to you? I don't, and if anybody is telling you otherwise, then they're lying." She crossed her arms over her chest as if to make her point.

"Oh, really?" I dangled those simple words in the air to see what the hell she would do with them. The ones who are guilty always struggle to convince you of something, while innocent people usually stand their ground. Now, this wasn't an exact science or nothing, but most times I found it to be a good indicator of whether someone was full of shit.

"Yes. You're the father of my child. You take care of us and provide a good life. Why would I ever lie to you?" Her voice was shaking as she tried to convince me of her loyalty. Too bad for her that it was too late to try to feed me that story. That bitch hadn't come to visit me once while I was locked up, and ever since I'd come home from jail, she'd been acting differently. Hell, even her pussy didn't feel the same; but I kept all those thoughts to myself.

I pulled out my phone and flashed the picture of her and the guy. The bitch looked like a trapped animal in a cage, desperately searching to find a way out.

"Majestic . . ." she started before I put my hand up to interrupt.

"I don't want to hear no more lies. I'm gonna ask you one time: Who is he, Keisha? Who the hell is he?" My voice took on a don't-fuck-with-me tone that I really hoped she was smart enough, and valued her life enough, to respect. She just stared like a deer in headlights, her eyes going from me to the picture and back again.

That's when I lost it. "Bitch, you better fucking answer me!"

She burst out sobbing, barely able to form words, like she expected that shit to work. Did she really think her tears were going to melt me or something?

"A friend. He's just a friend," she lied. That was enough for me to smack her across the face again, and this time I didn't care if it disfigured her.

I had to step back before I killed her. I started pacing around the room. "This motherfucker murdered my brother?"

Bruce stood up, obviously worried that this was going south.

"It's cool. I got this covered, man," I told him, and he sat back down.

Keisha shot him a look like she wanted him to jump up and rescue her or something. Dumb,

cheating bitch just didn't understand how deep
her troubles were right now. There was no way my
man was gonna take her side.

"No. He didn't kill Rodney, Majestic," she insisted.

I couldn't fucking believe that she was still up in
my face, defending this guy. "Then who did? If he
didn't kill my brother, who did? Answer me that.
Better yet, you bring that guilty motherfucker to
me," I challenged her.

Of course she had no defense. "I don't know
who did it," she said, sounding weak as hell. "And
I haven't talked to him in a while, so I can't bring
him to you."

"Bullshit! You're going to tell me who he is and
where the hell I can find him." I got in her face
and took hold of her arms, leaving no doubt that
I meant to cause her harm. Instead of spilling, the
bitch actually had the nerve to stand her ground.

"I'm not going to help you kill an innocent man."
She shook her head like she had some options.

"Really? Then I guess you'd rather die in his
place." I let her go and reached for my gun, aiming
it straight at her. The fear sprang to her eyes
immediately.

"Please!"

"Tell me his name!"

"No, I can't," she whispered, wincing like she
expected this to be the end for her and she was all
right with that.

I cocked the gun, pressing it into Keisha's temple. "You always was ride or die, but you just fucked up. I've already accepted the fact that I'm going to be a single parent, so I hope that motherfucker was worth it."

The terror in her eyes was painful to watch, but she left me no choice she had to die.

"Please. Majestic, please," she cried out, her eyes pleading, but she had pushed me past the point of having zero fucks to give.

"You got one last chance. Tell me his name or you're dead. And remember, ain't nobody gonna care when you're gone."

"My son will care. MJ will care," she blurted out, thinking that my son was going to sway me into feeling something. It was too late. My veins were pumping icicles, and she was shit out of luck.

"He's young," I said. "Hell, I'm betting in a year he won't even remember you. Shit, maybe I'll get him a new momma. Or a whole lot of mamas." The thought made me laugh, because I knew these hoes would be working overtime to win the coveted position of new baby mama to my son.

"Please!" she begged, clinging onto me.

"Now, I'm going to ask you one more time."

"I can't. Don't you understand that?" she cried. "I'm not going to be responsible for his death."

I smacked her so hard across the face that she crumpled to the floor. Then I pointed my gun at her, ready to end it. If Bruce hadn't gotten in between us, she would have been dead.

"Majestic, I got this. Gimme a couple hours to get you that info . . . then you can kill her ass."

I lowered my gun and turned to him. He'd never let me down, so I had to at least listen to him. Besides, he was still looking out for me, making sure I didn't catch another case for killing this deceitful ho. "A'ight, man," I said.

I looked back at this bitch, still groveling and crying at my feet. "While he's gone, you better figure out if this guy is worth dying over."

Niles

65

I jumped out of the car and sped inside the building, past the heavyset guard who looked like he had taken the job just so he could sit his ass down all day long.

"Excuse me!" he called out, huffing and puffing as he came hurrying behind me. "You need to check in first."

I backed up and went to the desk.

"Where you going?" he asked, pen in hand, ready to write my answer on the guest ledger in front of him.

"Dynamic Defense, LLC. Thirteenth floor," I recited from memory, anxious to get there.

The guard scrunched up his face and looked down at his directory. "We don't have a Dynamic Defense, LLC . Or a thirteenth floor."

This guy must have been new, but I didn't have time to school him. "Yes, you do. I was there a few months ago."

He leaned across the counter. "Look, most buildings don't have a thirteenth floor. Some people are suspicious, you know? Hell, in China their buildings don't have the number four anywhere." He acted like I had time for his lame-ass explanation.

Instead of listening to him, I turned and headed to the elevator bank.

"Sir, you can't go up there," he shouted after me. I could hear him moving toward me, but there was no way I was leaving, not before I got the answers I had come for.

When I felt his hand on my shoulder, I lost it. In one move, I bent his arm behind his back and had him totally defenseless, wincing in pain.

"Mister, you don't want any of this," I warned him because he was innocent, but not if he got in my way. "Not today. We clear?"

"Yeah, crystal clear," he stuttered.

I released him and got on the elevator. There was no number thirteen button, but I knew it was up there somewhere, and I had to find answers. I got off the elevator and raced to the stairwell, taking them three at a time, until I got to twelve. I opened the door and peeked down the hallway. It did not look familiar, so I moved to the next landing, but it was fourteen. It made no sense. I exited on fourteen only to find myself in a plastic surgeon's office.

A beautiful albeit plastic-looking receptionist sat behind the desk in a pristine white reception area. "Why, hello!" she said. She gave me the Botox version of a smile, revealing her veneers as she pushed out her double Ds. I guess her boss gave her good discounts, because she looked like all her parts were man made.

I returned my most charming smile. "How long has this office been here?"

"Long time. I've been here at least eleven years. I mean, I was a baby when I started, but the perks are just too good to leave." She flashed that Colgate smile again.

"So you'd know if there was ever a thirteenth floor? I'm looking for Dynamic Defense."

She shook her head. "You probably have the wrong building."

Don't ask me how the floor that I'd been to last time seemed to not exist anymore, but I knew damn well that I was at the right building, no matter what she said. Something was off, way off, and I was starting to become even more concerned about Bridget.

"Thanks," I said as I headed out.

"Hey, I hope you'll come back. I'd love to see you again," she called after me, but I was already out of there.

When I passed the security guard, he had a smug look on his face, but at least he was smart enough not to say "I told you so."

Willie stood ready to open the door when I exited the building. I was sure the look on my face told him everything.

"I can't find them anywhere," I said when I got in the car. "This is impossible. A whole company can't just up and disappear."

"That's crazy. Like you said, they can't just disappear."

"Neither could Bridget, but she did. Take me back to the house. I need to think. I need to find her, Willie."

My mind was racing as Willie drove me back home. If I had known that Bridget was in trouble, I never would have left. This must have been what she promised to tell me when I got back. Now I had no idea where she could be. Dynamic Defense seemed to have vanished into thin air, and I had no idea where to turn for clues. Even going through her purse hadn't revealed any information that could help me find her.

My phone vibrated, and for a second I thought it might be Bridget, but then I remembered we had her phone. I pulled my cell of my pocket, feeling defeated.

"Hello."

"Hello, Niles. This Frank Bush from Dynamic Defense. I hear you've been looking for us," he said calmly, like I hadn't been searching for an entire business that vanished.

"Yes, sir. You're a hard office to locate," I said, keeping my tone steady.

"I think if you give it some thought, you'll understand why we need to stay under the radar, which means we never stay at the same place for long. How can I help you?"

"I'm looking for Bridget. I think she's in trouble."

He didn't answer. Suddenly, a new voice came on the line.

"Niles, this is Jonathan Green. I'm Frank's boss. I work closely with Bridget. You and I need to meet in person. There are some things going on that I don't feel comfortable talking about over the phone. I'll be in touch."

Before I could ask any questions, the line went dead.

"Anything?" Willie asked as I sat holding my phone, feeling powerless.

"Not yet."

Bruce

66

"Um, Keisha's not here." Debra answered the door, acting all jumpy, like I was going to force her to produce Keisha on the spot. "She went somewhere with that boy Pooh."

I gave her my most disarming smile. "That's good, 'cause I'm not here for her."

"You're not?"

"Nah, I came by to see you—unless that's not okay," I took her in like she was my next meal. If she could have snapped her fingers and made her clothes fall off, she would have.

"You came to see me?"

I nodded. "Yeah, Deb. I been thinking about that phat ass of yours a lot lately. You got the kinda hips a brother could ride all night." Well, you would have thought I had offered her a diamond ring and a wedding date from the size of the smile on her face.

"So what's up? You gonna leave me standing out here, or you gonna invite me in so I can tighten your fine ass up?"

"Shit, if you gonna put it that way, come on in, baby." She stepped out of the way, twisting and posing, trying to look cute as I entered. She took my arm and led me into the living room, where she sat so close to me that she might as well have been in my lap. She was making my job easy for me.

"I hope this isn't weird for you," I said, pretending to be a sensitive thug, although I'm not sure Deb even cared.

"Baby, let me tell you, the only thing weird about this is the fact that you ain't came over here to do it sooner," she teased. "But I wish I knew you were coming. I would have put on something nicer than this old sundress." She started smoothing out her dress. I ran my fingers over her bare arm and felt her whole body tingle with desire.

"Deb, it don't matter what you have on, as long as you don't have a problem with me taking it off." I leaned in to let my lips graze her neck. Next thing I knew, she was all over me, like it had been way too long since she'd gotten any and she was pressed to make up for lost time.

My hands found her waist, and I brought her closer to me as our kiss grew more passionate. Yeah, I was looking forward to being inside of her.

"Wait! Hold up!" she cried out and then pushed me away. "I'm not some young girl hooking up with every brotha on the block. I don't wanna be just some side bitch. I wanna be your only bitch."

I had to stifle a laugh. "Have I ever treated you like you were some side bitch? I'm tired of being alone out here with all these chicken heads who just want my money. I want a real woman. Somebody who is down for me. You think you can be that for me? My ride or die?" I asked with all the sincerity I could muster.

Her head was bobbing up and down. "Yes. Yes and yes. I can be that for you."

God, she was making this so easy for me, I thought.

"Then why don't you show me the kind of woman you plan to be to your man?" I said.

She took my hand and led me into her bedroom, and the next thing I knew, she had removed all my clothes and was down on her knees, giving me a level of head that could only be learned through experience. This woman knew what to do with a dick in her mouth. She had her hands moving up and down, and the perfect amount of saliva and suction on my dick, like she was putting in her bid for ownership.

"Okay, I've shown you what I can do," she said after a while. "Let's see what you're working with."

She crawled up on the bed and backed that ass up. I wasted no time granting her request.

"Oh, shit! That's what I'm talking about!" she screamed as I pumped away from behind, slapping her ass as it met me with every motion. Damn if she wasn't giving those twenty-somethings a run for their money. I'd forgotten how much better sex could be with an equal who knew how to get down.

"Damn!" The word slipped out of me as she tightened the walls of her pussy and then started loosening and tightening them while I rode her.

"You like that?" Her voice, husky with desire, drove me further to the edge.

I slapped my hand over her mouth. "Please. Don't speak." I kept entering her until I couldn't take it, and then I pulled out, exploding my wad all over her ass. The whole thing was almost like an out-of-body experience, because as soon as I released, any positive feelings about her were gone, and I was my old self again. I might have appreciated her a minute ago, but now Deb was just another ho, and I was there with only one thing really on my mind: business.

"Damn! That was the best sex I ever had," Debra gushed, totally unaware that my mood had changed.

She got off her hands and knees and sat next to me on the edge of the bed, finally noticing my somber expression. "What? Didn't you enjoy that?" she asked, looking worried.

"Nah, baby, that was off the chain. But I need to know that I can trust you. That you're really going to look out for me."

"Of course." The words spilled out of her so fast that I almost felt sorry for her. She was so damn eager to please. The information I needed, though, was much too important for me to waste time with feelings.

I picked up my pants and took my phone out of the pocket to show her the photo. "So who is this?"

Her eyes started darting around the room like she was scoping out the emergency exits or something. It took her a while to speak up, and then she basically said nothing.

"You know I like to stay out of Keisha's business."

That was a bald-faced lie. I had heard her telling that girl what to do too many times before. I needed to push a little harder. "You know, this ain't what I call ride or die." I got up and started to put on my clothes.

She grabbed my arm and tried to pull me back onto the bed. "Bruce, please. I have to show some loyalty. She's my kid, you know."

"And you want me to be your man. Ride or die, remember?"

She hesitated then finally said, "Yeah, I remember. Look, ain't nothing going on with that man and Keisha. She used to be friends with his sister, and then he left to go in the military. When he came back in town, he got in touch to see how she was doing. They may have hooked up a few times while Majestic was locked up, but ain't nothing went down since Majestic's been home. I swear."

"Okay, baby, if that's all it is, then cool." I leaned down and kissed her. "So what's this dude's name, anyway?"

"Niles Monroe. He used to live over on Twentieth Street in that blue house, but I think he moved. You need me to find out where?"

"No, that's good. That's real good," I told her as I peeled off five hundred-dollar bills. "Buy yourself something nice."

She beamed like I was her knight in shining armor. "I can make you something to eat. You think I got skills in the bedroom, you should see me in the kitchen." She hopped up, ready to show off her other talents.

"Next time. Right now I gotta make a couple of phone calls. These streets ain't gonna make money on their own."

"All right, then," she said happily. "You go take care of business. I'll be right here waiting for you whenever you get done with your calls."

"Yeah," I said gruffly. "I'll be back. I gotta make sure I take care of you real good before I leave."

Niles

67

"So Winston says this guy Jonathan is legit. He was Bridget's partner and her boss for years. But he also said she didn't trust him all the way, so you shouldn't either," Willie warned me as we passed a sign on the highway informing us we'd just entered Connecticut.

His words barely fazed me enough to elicit a reaction. My mind was laser-focused on only one thing.

"Let's see what the guy has to say." If this guy had information that would help me get her back, I wouldn't care if he was Satan himself.

I pulled out my phone and looked at the photo of Bridget I'd taken the night before I left town. We'd just finished making love, and she was lying on top of the covers looking so peaceful that I had to snap a picture. She looked beautiful and innocent and sexy all at once, and I think it made me start to fall in love with her right then and there.

"This is the exit. We should be there in five," Willie announced as he maneuvered the car off the highway and took a sharp right. "You a'ight?"

"Yeah, I'm good," I assured him as he parked the car at the foot of the bridge and let me out.

As I started across the bridge, I looked up and spotted a handsome guy, about forty, waiting at the top.

"Niles." He spoke my name as we shook hands.

"Do you have any information on Bridget?" I asked him eagerly.

He handed me a folder from under his arm. "Take a look at this," he said and then stood there staring at me as I read the contents of the file.

It was filled with Dynamic Defense internal documents, most of them dealing with interior and exterior investigations of Bridget's activities. According to these documents, she was not just a big-time thief, but a spy and a traitor to her country.

"I'm supposed to just believe this?" I questioned. Bridget had taught me to approach everything I heard and read with a healthy dose of skepticism, and the shit that I was reading in here, I definitely did not want to believe. These documents did not describe the Bridget that I knew. This person was a complete stranger. It had to be a mistake.

"I don't know you from Adam," I said, challenging him. "This could all be bullshit. Show me some real proof."

He gave me a pitiful look, shaking his head. "Wow. She really put that Kama Sutra shit on you, didn't she? I bet she even told you she wanted to run away with you," he said. "She did that with all her marks. It was like her signature, for Christ's sake."

I felt my blood pressure rising, and I didn't know if it was because he was talking bad about a woman I cared for, or if it was because part of me feared there could be some truth to what he'd just said. Was it possible she'd been using sex to lull me into a false sense of security?

"C'mon, Niles," he said, sounding like he thought we were buddies or something. "Admit it. She's been acting a little funny lately. Am I right?"

My mind flashed back to our recent conversation, when all of a sudden she had started talking about getting out of the business.

Jonathan had an explanation for that too. "That, my friend, is because the noose was starting to tighten around her neck."

"This seems impossible," I said, fighting the sinking feeling that it wasn't, in fact, all that impossible. The words in those pages and what I knew of Bridget didn't add up, except there it was in black and white.

And if I was being honest with myself, I hadn't really trusted her all that much in the beginning. The way she roped me into taking the job, the way she tricked me into fucking her the first time . . . those were the actions of someone who would do anything to get what she wanted.

"Still think it's impossible?"

"I don't know what to think," I answered.

"When was the last time you checked your bank balance?"

"Not since last night. Why?"

"Because this morning Bridget wired five million dollars from her last three partners' private accounts into her personal Cayman Islands account. I don't know about you, but I trusted her with my personal account information, and this morning the bitch wiped me out."

"Bridget wouldn't do anything like that," I said, hoping like hell I was right.

"Yeah, I told myself the same thing, and now I'm three million dollars light. Look, I'm not here to force you into anything, but if you agree to help us, Mr. Monroe, we will make sure that you are more than compensated, including being reimbursed for any money Miss St. John might have stolen from you. And then, I promise you will be free to walk away from the agency if you choose."

It felt like I was having an out of body experience when I found my voice. "Help you how?" I asked.

"We need you to take out Bridget and her accomplice," he said.

In this job, I'd gotten used to receiving assignments where the murder of another person was talked about as calmly as if they were just placing a lunch order. Hearing talk of murder associated with Bridget, though, was another story. "I need to think about it," I said. "This is a lot to take in."

He kept talking. I guess he wanted to help me make up my mind faster than I was. "People who do this job, they are able to be whoever the other person needs them to be. It's like being an actor, and every job, every exchange, is just another role."

"So you're telling me that I didn't know her at all?" I asked, my voice rising.

"None of us knew her. She fooled all of us, if it makes you feel any better. She was one of our very best operatives, smart enough and cunning enough, but I promise you that she will pay for what she did to you and to us." Again, his voice took on that aura of camaraderie, only this was not a brotherhood I wanted to belong to: a group of men duped by the same woman.

"I don't know. This just doesn't make any sense." Despite his efforts, I still couldn't see myself hurting Bridget. "She told me she wanted to get out of the business and retire."

"Of course she did, because she realized we were on to her. We've already been over this," he said, a little impatience creeping into his voice, like he thought I was stupid. "You think if you were to meet and she knew that we sent you she wouldn't take you out without a second thought?" he challenged me. "You're just another job to her, and the sex and the fake emotions, it was all a distraction so that she could steal your money without you becoming suspicious."

He tilted his head and looked at me with curiosity. "You gotta be smarter than this—or was the sex just that good? I know for me it was, but it wasn't good enough to let her take advantage of me."

Man, I wanted to smash him in the face. "Look, I said I need to think about it." My voice was trembling, and I felt myself getting ready to flip. "I'm not even sure any of my money has been taken."

"Well, I hope it hasn't," he shot back, "but I wouldn't be too optimistic on that." He waited for a second, and when I still didn't give him the answer he wanted to hear, he said, "I understand your reluctance. I'll call you tomorrow, give you a chance to check your accounts." He turned and walked away.

I had to take a moment, staring out at the water, to get myself together. It felt as if I'd been punched in the gut. I couldn't believe that the woman I'd been falling in love with had been using me like I was just a fucking mark!

Willie read the disturbed look on my face when I got back in the car. "You don't look so good. What did he say?"

I handed him the folder. "It's all here in the file. They're saying she's a thief and most likely she set up her own abduction to fly the coop. She's been ripping them and me off from the start."

"You believe him?" Willie looked like he wanted to say something more.

"I don't know what I believe. I mean, he's been working with her a long time. I've known her less than a year. Maybe I really didn't know her at all. Plus, she has been acting a little weird lately. He said it's because she was feeling the heat."

Willie was scanning the paperwork as he listened to me. He looked up and said, "I hate to believe that about our girl, but I have to admit that there is some logic to it."

I took out my phone and opened my bank app so I could check my account balance. I felt like my heart was breaking in pieces when I saw the row of zeroes.

"Fuck! Fuck! Fuck! Fuck!"

"What?"

"She took my fucking money, Willie. Bridget stole my money!"

"Shit! What are you gonna do, man?"

I clamped my mouth shut. I did not want to admit to him the assignment Jonathan wanted me to accept. This was all just too ugly for words.

"Niles, man. Talk to me. What are you gonna do?"

"I don't know, Unc. That guy wants me to take her out—her and her accomplice."

He gave a low whistle. "That's fuckin' deep, man. Do you think you could really do that?"

I shook my head. "I really don't know. Right now, the only thing on my mind is that my mother needs me to take care of her, and I can't do that without my money."

"Well, shit," he said, starting the engine. "Then let's go find this bitch and get your money back."

Bridget

68

It had been at least a day since I was kidnapped. The man who I'd obviously pissed off the first day hadn't shown up again, but I had figured out that there were two other men guarding me on a steady rotation, because their footsteps were different. Whoever these people were, I could only assume they were holding me hostage because they were trying to flush out Niles. Why else would I still be alive? The only time that I had ever kidnapped a person was to get to whoever pulled the strings. In this case, they were probably trying to get to the person that they thought killed Rodney.

I was sure that Niles—and, I would hope, the people from Dynamic Defense—were already searching for me. I just hoped Jonathan didn't fuck this up with his extravagant ego and incompetence.

The door opened and I heard footsteps, two sets to be exact.

"Take it off," I heard one of them tell the other.

I felt someone touch my face then the sudden pain of the duct tape covering my eyes and eyebrows being ripped off.

It took me a few seconds to get past the pain and become accustomed to the light, but I still couldn't identify them, because they were wearing masks.

"Mmm! Mmmmm!" I tried to speak, but I was still gagged.

The door swung open, and I swear time stopped for a minute. I had to be dreaming—or maybe having a nightmare—because there was no way that what I was seeing could be real. His appearance left me feeling even more disoriented than I had been.

He moved across the room and took a seat directly across from me. I tried to squirm out of my seat, my eyes blazing with rage, but Jonathan simply smiled in that smug way I had seen way too many times.

"Why, hello, Bridget. I must say I'm really enjoying your predicament. You see, with you it's always been difficult to get a word in."

"Mmmm! Mmmm! Mmmm! Mmmm!" I struggled to get out all the motherfuckers, assholes, and limp-dicks I wanted to.

He laughed at me, enjoying this way too much. "I'm sorry, but I'm having kind of a hard time understanding you."

"Mmmmm! Mmmmm!" I said in response. I didn't give a shit if I couldn't form the words. I was sure he knew exactly what I was saying to him.

"Oh, you want to know why you're here? Of course. Well, aside from you being a huge bitch who believes the world revolves around you . . . Oh, and aside from you thinking you are always the smartest person in the room. Yes, that can all be quite grating, but it's not those things. It's actually quite simple. Me and my guys have decided to expand our retirement funds." He laughed, exchanging looks with the two masked men, who joined in.

"Mmmmm! Mmmmm!" In a perfect world, the roles would have been reversed, and I would have just shot him dead.

"You see, me and my team are sick of watching you and your golden boy get rich and take the glory while we get shit."

Fucking asshole! I couldn't say it out loud, but I sure was thinking it.

"Remember that case a few years back where you recovered almost five million dollars? Well, I removed more than a million, and guess who is going to take the fall for that?" he bragged.

"And that's not all. Now that your boy has taken down El Gato, we picked up even more. After your boy Niles did our dirty work, my men cleaned out his coffers and netted another fifteen million in cash. And guess who I linked it to? You!" he said, sounding almost gleeful. "I'm such a genius . . . but you wouldn't know that, would you, because you think you're the only smart one."

He leaned back in his chair and put his hands behind his head. "If you had really played things smart, though, you wouldn't be in this position right now, Bridget. When I dreamed up this whole plan, I thought you were going to be the woman by my side. I was going to cut you in on the whole thing. I was really in love with you, and I thought you were falling for me, too—until that pretty boy came along and you stopped giving up the goods to me."

My eyes went wide as I came to the realization that not only was Jonathan a thief, but he was also fucking crazy.

"Don't give me that look," he said. "You knew I would have done anything for you. But once you started fucking that rookie, your disloyalty needed to be punished.

"You know, you probably should never have opened that offshore account of yours, or at least you should have hidden it better. It was way too easy to find, and now that I've deposited a couple million in there, it was so easy to build a paper trail that makes it look like you are a low-down, dirty thief."

"Mmmmmm!" I struggled against my restraints, wanting to break free and strangle him. After all the years of hard work I'd put in for the agency, I could not go out with my reputation shot to hell by this psycho.

"Ah, but I haven't even told you the best part yet." He smiled, enjoying my panic. "You're sleeping with your operative, which makes him the perfect patsy to take the fall when they find your dead body. Crime of passion and all that. Remember, I did warn you that he had a bad temper. I'm thinking murder/suicide would be a nice touch. Us regular-looking guys don't need competition like Niles around anyway, you know what I mean?"

I struggled and failed to hold back tears at the mention of Niles, as I thought of the life I'd been envisioning for us—the life we wouldn't have if I couldn't get out of there. Jonathan must have seen my distress, and he had the balls to get up and kiss me on my forehead. Then he actually removed the gag and kissed my mouth before I could stop him.

My words came out in a rush. "You don't have to kill him, Jonathan. Just leave him out of this," I said. "You and I can be together, and no one ever has to know about the money. We can disappear together."

He frowned. "See, you really do think you're smarter than me, don't you? You expect me to believe that you want to be with me, but that you also want to save Niles's life? I like the old, cold-hearted Bridget better, the one who didn't give a fuck about anyone but herself. She would never have tried to save Niles. But this new Bridget wants to save Niles for only one reason: You're in love with him." He spat the last few words like they tasted poisonous in his mouth.

Damn it! I had let my feelings speak for me, and it might have cost me dearly this time.

He turned to the other two guys, who had been standing behind him the whole time. "Oh, please. Will you take off those silly masks?" he said. "You might as well let her know who you are. She's never going to get the chance to tell anyone."

At this point, I wasn't surprised at all when they removed the masks and I saw that it was Frank and Lance. I should have known that if anyone else from Dynamic Defense had been in on it with him, it would be those two.

"I'm going to kill you, Jonathan," I growled at him.

"I doubt that," he said, turning back to give Frank and Lance instructions. "Tomorrow, take her to the suite he keeps in Manhattan and kill her brutally. I'll take her boyfriend out right after I goad him into killing the director." He started heading up the basement steps, stopping halfway to look down at me one more time. "This whole thing is working out like a dream. Tomorrow I'll take over the director's job, and from there we're going to be beyond rich. Thanks, Bridget."

"I'm going to kill you! I'm going to kill you, Jonathan!" I screamed as he left. I didn't know how, but I would make good on that threat if it was the last thing I ever did.

Bruce

69

By the time I headed out of Debra's house, Pooh was just pulling up in his Escalade, with Majestic in the passenger's seat. Eddie was there too, waiting in my Navigator. I jumped in the Nav and pulled out, with Pooh following behind me.

"How was the pussy?" Eddie asked as I drove down into the winding roads of Huntington.

"It was better than you'd expect."

"So you not gonna hit it again?"

"Nah, man, I got what I needed from that old bitch. As far as I'm concerned, she's as good as dead," I said with a smirk.

Eddie laughed. "Yeah, and Majestic feels the same way about her daughter, too. She back there at his crib with Li'l Frog guarding her until we get back. I don't know if he's gonna let her live this time, Bruce."

I shrugged, not interested in talking about Keisha or her momma anymore. We rode the rest of the way in silence, until I pulled the Navigator in front of a relatively new colonial house set back on a quiet, tree-lined street.

"This where that motherfucker lives?" Pooh asked when he got out of his Escalade.

"Yeah," I answered. "Right after I called you, I made a couple other calls. I talked to my man who works at PSEG, and he said the only electric account with the name Niles Monroe on Long Island was at this address."

"Let's go," Majestic said, coming up behind Pooh.

They followed me up to the front door, and I rang the bell. I knew we were at the right place when Keisha's BFF, Tanya, opened the door. The bitch hated me and Majestic so much she could barely fix her mouth into a smile whenever she saw us. Now she couldn't hide her disgust, or her shock.

"What are you doing here?"

Ignoring her, we pushed our way inside. She tried unsuccessfully to block our entrance as we fanned out across the living room. An older lady who was sitting on the couch watching television got all agitated when she saw us come in. She tried to stand up too quickly and fell back in her seat.

Tanya rushed over to her and grabbed her arm, trying to comfort her.

Majestic stepped toward them, and the old lady spoke.

"Oh my God, Tanya, I think it's the Incredible Hulk, 'cept he's not green." She stared at him, bug-eyed.

"What are you doing here. Majestic?" Tanya asked.

"We're looking for someone."

"Well, there's no one here but us," she said, "so y'all can just go."

I stepped forward and got up in her space. "Niles Monroe. Where the fuck is Niles Monroe?" I hissed in the kind of tone that should be answered immediately. Tanya's ass wanted to act all big and bad, though, so she refused to say anything. The old lady looked like she started to open her mouth to say something, but Tanya squeezed her arm real hard, until all she said was, "Ouch!"

"Yo, Bruce," Majestic said. "Check this out." He was holding up a framed picture he'd taken off the mantel. In the photograph was the lady who was here with Tanya, smiling next to a dude in a military uniform.

"You put that down right now!" the lady cried out. "I love that picture of me and my boy, so you need to take your dirty hands off it!"

Tanya hadn't shut her up fast enough this time, and now we knew something that might help us: This old broad was Niles Monroe's mother. She also seemed to be bat-shit crazy.

Majestic put the picture down and approached her slowly. "No problem, ma'am. I just wanna know where my friend is. You see, we were old Army buddies, and I just wanna know that he's doing okay."

She tilted her head and stared at Majestic like she was trying to figure out if she should believe him. I thought we might actually be able to get his location out of this crazy lady, but Tanya tried to put a stop to the whole thing.

She stepped in front of Niles's mother to shield her. "Look, we don't want no trouble. Niles isn't here. Please, just leave. This isn't good for her." Tanya, who stood there quaking in her boots, was begging us to stop scaring the old woman, who didn't look scared at all. In fact, she had a lot of fire left in her.

The old lady focused on me. "You are ugly, and God don't like ugly."

Majestic started laughing. "You hear that, man? She called you ugly."

"Shit, I always been ugly," I said, stepping up to her, "but I would rather be ugly than be your son. God ain't gonna be able to help him."

"Don't you touch my son, you ugly gorilla." She was still feisty. "He ain't scared of you, none of you. If you know what's good for you, you won't be here when he gets home. He has a gun."

Majestic turned to me, still laughing. "You hear that, man? Her son has a gun. Woooo!" I pretended to be shaking with fear for a minute, then he dropped the act and his voice turned deadly serious.

"Well, I have a gun too." He pulled out a huge .44-caliber handgun, brandishing it right in her face.

This old bird was so fucking crazy that she stared down his gun like it was some kind of toy. "Judas!" she screamed at Majestic. By now, Pooh and Eddie had joined in on the laughter, but Majestic was no longer amused.

"And I plan on killing that piece of shit son of yours with this gun. Shoot him dead like a dog in the street."

SLAP! That damn lady slapped him right across the face. You could have heard a piece of cotton hitting the carpet; that's how quiet it got up in that house.

"Lady, my momma don't hit me," Majestic told her with pure hatred in his voice.

She was too dumb, or too crazy, to know who she was fucking with. "Maybe she should have. You look like you need some home training." Then the old bat hauled off and slapped him again.

"Lorna, please!" Tanya jumped in front of the old lady again, desperate to protect her. She started to plead on her behalf. "Majestic, she's a sick lady.

The doctor changed her medication and it's not strong enough. She don't know what she doing. The reason I'm here is because I'm her nurse and she needs her medication."

Now, I could have told her that she was wasting her breath. After the first slap that lady didn't have a chance in hell, but I decided to stay quiet and let him handle it.

Majestic turned to the guys, who were still in shock after witnessing someone hit him and still be standing there breathing. "Put her in the car," he ordered. "And tie up her goddamn arms."

Eddie grabbed Lorna, who was kicking and screaming as he dragged her out of the house. Tanya tried to stop him, but Pooh snatched her up pretty quick, and held her so tight that the only thing she could do was scream out for the old lady.

"Lorna! No! Leave her alone!"

I motioned toward Tanya and asked Majestic, "What about her?"

He looked at her like she was less than nothing. "What about her? She don't have any value. In fact, she's useless. Not even worth a bullet." With the quickness of a cat, Majestic grabbed Tanya by the neck. Pooh released her from his arms, and Majestic lifted her off the ground above his head. He tightened his grip, and she struggled wildly, trying her best to loosen his grip. Majestic squeezed his hands even harder, and her eyes began to bulge.

"Don't fight it, baby," he whispered. "Just go to sleep. Go on and take you a dirt nap. Nobody's gonna miss you."

Together we watched the life leave her body. Then he lowered her, and she slumped to the ground, dead. I did what I considered to be the right thing: I closed her eyes before we left.

Bridget

70

Once Jonathan left, I sized up the situation, realizing that if I was ever going to get out of there, it was now or never. Frank and Lance were basically flunkies who wouldn't know their heads from their assholes without someone like Jonathan to lead them around.

"I have to go to the bathroom," I said. Just like I had expected they would, they stared at each other, neither knowing what to do with this information.

So I pushed a little harder. "Please. I have to go, unless you want me to piss and shit on myself. That's not going to be pleasant for whoever has to ride over to the suite with me and clean up the mess."

"Fine. But do not try anything," Frank said, trying to sound threatening. I could take him, win, and not even mess up my hair.

He turned to Lance, acting authoritarian. "Pat her down," he snapped gruffly, like an actor in a cop movie.

Lance looked at me like I was contagious or something. How these assholes had made it this far in the organization was a mystery.

He started whining to Frank. "I patted her down before. She's not carrying anything."

Frank obviously did not want to be questioned in front of me. "Just do it," he barked with enough bass in his voice that Lance jumped to attention. He patted me down, and I wanted to kick him in the balls when he lingered a little too long on my backside.

"She's good," he told Frank.

"So take her over to the bathroom, then," he answered.

In front of the bathroom door, I held up my hands, which were still in restraints. "Um, can I get a little help here? Unless you want to come in and wipe my ass when I'm done."

Lance scrunched up his nose like the idea sickened him. He looked to Frank for permission to release the restraints.

"Go ahead," Frank said, cocking his gun as he warned me, "Don't try nothing funny." He followed behind us as they took me up the stairs to the bathroom.

Inside the dirty, windowless room, I unsnapped my bra and let the left flap fall. Right there in the seam there was a hole, where I had slid the row of poisonous tags. I took out a few, tucked them in my sleeve, and slid the rest back in their hiding place. Men always underestimated women, even the ones who killed for a living. Did they think I wouldn't have a plan?

When I stepped out of the bathroom, both idiots were lurking outside the door, waiting for me. It just made my job all that much easier to accomplish. I reached out a hand to each of them and said, "You mind helping me back to my chair? I'm kinda weak after being tied up for so many days."

Lance didn't hesitate for a second to move in against me on one side. Frank did it begrudgingly, but he also let me put an arm around his shoulder and lean against him for support as I fake-stumbled back to my dungeon.

"Can't you move any faster?" Frank complained. I was moving as slowly as I could get away with, because I wanted the poison to take effect before they had a chance to tie me up again. They came to a stop, opening the basement door. It had been about three minutes since I'd tagged them, and I was getting worried that they still seemed fine.

"I don't feel too good." Frank spoke first.

"Me either," Lance chimed in.

These two were so stupid that neither one seemed to have a clue what was going on. Finally it must have dawned on Frank, but by then it didn't matter.

"How did you . . .?" were the last words Frank spoke before he fell to the ground helplessly. Poor Lance raised his weapon, or at least tried to, but unfortunately for him, his faculties were compromised.

Locating the keys, I removed my cuffs and ran out of the house, squinting my eyes against the sunlight that I hadn't seen in days as I looked around to get my bearings. The house that I'd been in was surrounded by trees, but I could hear cars not too far away, so I started running in that direction. I couldn't risk taking the car that was parked out front, because Jonathan would definitely be tracking it through the GPS system once he figured out that Frank and Lance had failed to execute me.

Shortly after I found my way to the road, I saw a truck headed toward me. I ran out into the roadway, waving my arms wildly, because I knew this might be my only chance to escape. The truck slowed to a stop, and the female driver rolled down the window.

"Honey, you need a ride?" she asked.

"Yes, please!" I said, sounding as frantic as I felt. "You going anywhere near the city?"

"Sure am," she answered, and I climbed into her truck.

"Where exactly are we?" I asked.

"Stanford, Connecticut." She took a good look at me, concern evident on her face. "You okay? You look like you had a hard night. Have a fight with your old man?"

"Something like that," I muttered, letting her believe whatever she wanted.

"Fuckin' men!" she said. I just nodded in agreement. I wasn't really capable of holding a conversation at the moment. I closed my eyes and prayed that this trucker drove fast so I could get back into the city before it was too late to stop Jonathan from getting to Niles.

Keisha

71

"You a'ight?" Li'l Frog asked me for the hundredth time as he guarded me. He tried to act tough, but I knew he was really just a fatherless kid looking for some direction from a male figure. Unfortunately, Majestic and his crazy-ass sidekick Bruce had decided to take Li'l Frog under their wings, so he did whatever they told him to do, but he seemed to have at least a little bit of a heart.

Majestic, on the other hand, had an empty black hole where his heart should have been. It didn't matter that I was the mother of his child. If he hadn't gotten a call from Bruce telling him that they knew where Niles lived, then he would have killed me. Now I was here with Li'l Frog, like a sitting duck waiting for the hunter to come back and blast me. I decided to use Li'l Frog's weakness to try to escape.

"Yeah, I'm okay, I guess. Thanks for asking. I'm kinda hungry, though."

His eyes went wide. "You want to eat? I'm surprised your stomach can handle it after the beating Majestic put on your ass. That nigga's crazy," he said, sounding almost proud of the level of his boss's depravity.

I waved my hand, continuing to act unfazed, even though he was right; I really was sick to my stomach. "Please, you think this is bad? You should have been here the last time I cheated on him." I laughed a little. "I'm his son's mother. It ain't like he's gonna kill me or nothing."

"If you say so, Keisha," Li'l Frog responded. "That dude you was messin' with, though. He got some serious problems. He ain't gonna be breathin' too much longer."

I fought back the bile that rose in my throat at the thought of Majestic murdering Niles, because I couldn't let Li'l Frog know my true feelings. I had to continue my performance if I was going to get out of there and save myself, and maybe even Niles.

"Yeah, sucks for him, huh? So anyway, you want something to eat, Frog? I'm gonna go in the kitchen and see what Majestic got," I said.

"Yeah, you can make me something," he replied as he sat down and started watching the game on the TV.

In the kitchen, my first thought was to just run straight out the kitchen door, but Majestic lived on this crazy-ass hill ten miles from my house. It wouldn't have been hard at all for Li'l Frog to track me down. So instead, I searched every kitchen drawer, trying to locate the spare keys to one of the cars. I held back a little squeal of joy when I finally located them.

Next I had to figure out a way to distract Li'l Frog so I could get out to the car. I banged around some pots and pans so he would think I was cooking as I formulated a plan. Then the answer hit me. There was one easy and obvious way to distract someone young and gullible like Li'l Frog: sex.

Thank God Majestic hadn't taken away my cell phone before he left. I pulled it out and dialed my girl Denise. I wasn't really close to her like I was with Tanya, but Denise was the kind of girl who would do anything for the right price.

"Dee, I need a favor," I whispered into the phone, my heart racing.

She laughed. "Girl, you know if you want to creep, I'm your backup."

"Uh, yeah, cool," I said, my mind formulating a plan as we spoke. "I need you to come over Majestic's and give Li'l Frog a blow job. It has to be right now, and I need you to take him down in the basement."

"Keisha!" Her voice thundered on the other end. "You know I'm not doing that no more. 'Sides, his ass is so cheap. Last time I fucked him, I asked him to take me to get something to eat, and he took me to fucking White Castle. Hell, nah. I ain't messing with that type of dick no more."

I tried appealing to her sisterhood. "Please, D. I really need you. Majestic made him my babysitter, and I need you to help me get outta here. You know how that go."

She still wasn't convinced. "I don't know . . ."

So I went for her sweet spot. "I'll pay you a hundred."

"Well, don't let me get in the way of my sister getting no good dick," she answered crassly. "But I want two hundred."

"Done. Now get your ass over here—and don't block the driveway."

It really helps to know your friends, I thought. Had I told her what was really going on, she wouldn't have wanted no part of it, but if it was about me fucking, then Denise was down to help me.

Just as I hung up, Li'l Frog walked in. "What's up with that food?"

I walked over to the freezer and took out a frozen pizza. "I was gonna make some sandwiches but he ain't got no cold cuts. You want some pizza instead?"

"Sure," he said. "I'm gonna go finish watching the game."

"Okay," I answered, feeling like my heart was going to burst right out of my chest. "I'm going to pop these in the oven and go upstairs and change my shirt. He got blood on it."

Li'l Frog didn't reply. He just walked back into the den to watch the game.

I threw the pizzas in the oven then made my way upstairs to Majestic's bedroom. Some people might call me crazy for what I was about to do, but hell, he was going to kill me anyway because of Niles. Even if he caught me, he couldn't kill me twice. So, I went into the closet where he kept his safe, and entered MJ's birthday on the keypad. Thank God he hadn't changed the code since the last time he sent me in there to get something out of it, back in the days when he trusted me.

What I was doing scared the shit out of me, but I had a son to take care of, and once I left this house, I was going to be the most wanted woman in Long Island, possibly the whole state. I wasn't going to get far if I didn't have some money to take me there. I threw five large bricks of cash into a pillowcase, closed the safe, and rushed back down to the kitchen.

"Yo, when's that pizza gonna be done?" Li'l Frog yelled from the den.

"About ten more minutes," I answered, stuffing the pillowcase in the pantry out of view.

I paced around the kitchen nervously until the pizza was done, and then I carried the plate to Li'l Frog in the den.

"Here you go," I said as I set it in front of him.

He looked up at me. "Yo, I thought you was gonna change out of that bloody shirt. That shit is nasty."

"Yeah, I guess Majestic must be really mad this time, 'cause he got rid of all the clothes I used to keep up there," I answered, feeling weak in the knees from fear.

"Damn, you fucked up this time for sure, girl," he said, laughing at me.

I shrugged. "You want something to drink?"

"Yeah, get me a beer or something."

I turned to go get his drink, and I nearly collapsed from relief when the doorbell rang. Li'l Frog got up to answer the door, and I heard him talking to Denise as I headed back to the kitchen.

Say what you want about Denise being a ho, but that girl sure knew how to make them brothers come back for more. By the time I started heading back into the den a few minutes later to bring Li'l Frog his drink, she was already half naked and dragging him toward the basement.

"Come on, Frog," she said playfully. "Let's go downstairs and do it on the pool table."

He reached out and smacked her ass. "Yeah, girl, I'm gonna show you a set of balls, all right."

Denise turned around and closed the basement door behind her, and I made my move. On my way to the kitchen, I grabbed the pillowcase out of the pantry, then went into the garage and jumped into Majestic's Mercedes.

I drove like a bat out of hell to get to my house. I wanted to pack a bag for me and MJ, go get my son from school, then get the fuck out of Wyandanch for good. On the way, I tried to call Niles to warn him, but he didn't pick up the phone.

I was so glad that MJ was at school and not at the house with my mother. If I had to try to get him out of the house, she would fight me. No matter how many times Majestic beat me, she was only ever worried about losing her meal ticket. How was I going to convince her that this time, if she didn't let us go, this would be the time he killed me? Shit, he was so crazy, I couldn't even be sure MJ was safe from him anymore. The whole ride, I was already having an argument with my mother in my head.

I ran into the house and headed straight for my bedroom, where I threw together enough clothes for a few days. Then I put together a bag for MJ, including a couple of his superhero figurines. It broke my heart to think about how scary this was all going to be for my baby. When I finished packing, I took a deep breath and prepared myself to go talk to my mother. For a split second, I thought about leaving without even saying anything to her, but no matter how cold she was, she was still my mother. Beneath it all, I at least I knew she loved MJ, so I thought she deserved to know that she wouldn't be seeing us again.

"Ma," I said as I pushed open her bedroom door. She was lying under the covers in a really uncomfortable-looking position. How the hell could she sleep like that? I wondered. Not to mention the fact that it was past noon. She didn't usually sleep so late.

"Ma, you sick?" I asked as I went closer to the bed. She didn't move, so I put a hand on her shoulder to turn her toward me. She was ice cold, and when I nudged her body, her head flopped to the side in a completely unnatural position.

I let out a scream. My mother was dead, her neck snapped by someone as she was lying there in her own bed.

"Oh, God! Ma! Oh my God!" I felt myself reaching a state of hysteria as I screamed and bawled, but then my survival mode kicked in. I raced into my room and grabbed the bags I'd packed then ran out in the driveway. By the time I got to the car, my insides exploded and I threw up all over the driveway.

I jumped into the car and sped away with only one thing on my mind. I had to get to MJ's school before Majestic found out that I was missing.

"Mommy, where are we going?" MJ asked me as he played with his superhero toys in the back seat. I'd never pulled him out of class before. I'd told the school that we had a family emergency, but I tried to play it off as if everything was fine in front of MJ when he came down to the school office to leave. I couldn't risk falling apart in that office. The way I was feeling, they would have called an ambulance to take me away to a mental hospital for sure.

"Far away, baby. We're going far away," I said as I got on the highway heading God knows where.

Bridget

72

"You certainly seem like you're in a rush, darling," the truck driver said as she pulled over to let me out. After being silent and practically comatose during most of the ride, I became jittery and anxious as soon as we entered Manhattan, and she had obviously noticed the change. I was hoping it wasn't too late to reach Niles before he went ahead and did Jonathan's dirty work. I was playing against time today, but I'd be damned if I didn't win this one. One way or another, I was going to make Jonathan pay.

I gave her arm a little squeeze, my way of thanking her for rescuing me. "Yeah, I have an important appointment to make."

"Really? I sure hope that appointment includes some hot water and some soap," she said, waving her hand in front of her nose. "No offense, girl."

"None taken. Thanks for putting up with me and my smell," I told her as I opened the door and hopped out of the truck. She blasted the horn as she drove away, making heads turn in my direction.

All around me, people were hustling to and from work, so the streets were busy as fuck. I hurried into the new building, full of my take-no-prisoners attitude. I had two things on my mind: the first was saving Niles from the trap Jonathan had set before it was too late, and the other was making damn sure he paid for it with his life.

I entered Dynamic Defense's new headquarters, punched in my pass code, and headed straight for the elevator. I was being watched by damn near everyone in the lobby. When I saw my reflection in the elevator doors, I understood why they'd given me such strange looks. I looked like a tragic ex-fashionista. Even though my outfit was high-end, it had seen better days. My hair—well, my hairstylist would cry if she saw me looking this bad.

I got on the elevator, pressed the button for my floor, and started imagining all kinds of scenarios where I eviscerated that psychopath. I couldn't wait to see the look on Jonathan's face when he saw that I was alive.

From the elevator, I stormed through the doors into the executive suites. I didn't even acknowledge the director's secretary. She tried to get up to stop me, but by then I had let myself in.

"Douglas!" I shouted for him, but he wasn't there. I was surprised to see Senator Stove sitting on Douglas's desk, talking to Nadja of all people. For a low-level bitch, she seemed to have no problem finding herself in high-level places, but I certainly wasn't there to worry about her right now.

"Bridget," she chirped. Judging from the look on her face, she thought we were peers.

"Nice to see you, Miss Saint John," the senator added in greeting, giving me the once over.

"Senator." I nodded in response then turned toward Nadja. "I'm gonna need a double shot of espresso, pronto."

I turned back to the senator, but Najda didn't budge. I still couldn't understand why she was even there. Did they really let this bitch suck and fuck her way up the food chain that fast? I would have to talk to Douglas about that. To have her inefficient ass as an assistant was a real rookie move, if you ask me.

"Senator, I really need to speak to Douglas. It's a matter of life and death."

"I'm sorry, Bridget, but that's impossible." Nadja smiled too warmly for me.

I turned to address her. "Didn't I send you to get coffee? And can't you see two adults are talking and this is important? Like I said, this is a matter of life or death."

"Well, that's impossible," Nadja answered in a tone that said she thought she was in charge.

"She's right," the senator chimed in, which really pissed me off. Somehow, it seemed, they'd become best friends. "Douglas isn't here, and he can't be reached for at least the next two hours. He's in a closed door meeting with some top Canadian border officials."

"Maybe you should call Jonathan and talk to him. Let him deal with whatever problem you're having," Little Miss Sunshine suggested.

"That won't work," I said, standing my ground. I didn't have time for this shit. "Jonathan is the last person I want to deal with, so if he calls, don't even mention that I was here."

The senator stood up, looking concerned. "You're having a problem with Jonathan? I thought you two were close." He and Nadja shared a look I couldn't quite read.

Nadja was the one who piped in with a response. "Bridget, if you're upset with Jonathan, I'm sure it's something you two can work out. Let's not burden the senator with office dynamics."

I narrowed my eyes at that bitch. "You're a part of this, aren't you?"

"I'm not part of anything," she said with no expression on her face. "I have no idea what you're talking about."

"Neither do I, so I suggest you start talking right now!" The senator's anger matched my own now.

"Gladly," I said, sitting down on the leather couch in the waiting area. "Let me tell you about your favorite employee. He kidnapped me and tried to have me killed."

"What?" the senator yelled. Clearly I had his attention.

"You think I look like this for some other reason? I don't exactly make it a habit of, shall we say, dressing down," I shot back. "I've been in a basement somewhere in Connecticut for the past two days. Too bad for that motherfucker that his little flunkies failed to finish me off. . . . Oh, by the way. You shouldn't expect Lance or Frank to show up for their next shifts."

Another look passed between the two of them. What the fuck was going on here?

I continued my story. "So, yeah, Jonathan thought I would be dead by now. I guess that's why he felt comfortable telling me all the details of his plan to fill his bank account with stolen funds and then take over the director's job."

The senator stared at me, taking in everything I was saying.

Nadja, on the other hand, had to throw in her two cents again. "How did Jonathan plan to take Douglas's job?"

The thing that threw me off was that she didn't ask it like she was doubting me, but more like she was gathering information. But why?

"What the hell is going on here?" I finally asked when Nadja and Senator Stove gave each other yet another one of those knowing looks.

"We've suspected for a while now that something was going on with Jonathan," Senator Stove explained. "That's why we brought Nadja in from our Western European office, to see what she could flush out. We expected this to be a fairly long investigation, but it looks like what you're telling us has just moved our timeline up."

I looked at Nadja with a newfound respect. I had thought she was nothing more than a bimbo sleeping her way up the food chain. The girl sure knew how to keep her cover.

"She's a highly trained agent, just like you," the senator said when he noticed the way I was staring at Nadja.

I nodded at Nadja to let her know there was no beef between us.

"So tell us whatever you know," Nadja said.

"Jonathan has the whole thing planned. Right now he has the stolen funds—including Niles's money—planted in my account. Once I was dead, he was going to frame me for the theft."

"And what about the director's job?" Senator Stove asked. "How does that play in to all of this?"

"He didn't tell me all the details, but he cooked up some sort of plan to manipulate Niles, to give him a reason to take out the director. With Douglas gone, I guess Jonathan figures he's next in line for the director's job."

The senator stated the obvious. "This is bad. Very bad."

I jumped up from my seat. "Yeah, it is bad. But enough talking now. I need to know where Douglas is meeting with the Canadians. Jonathan plans on taking over the director's job today, which means he's probably already talked to Niles. If I know my student at all, then Niles will be on a rooftop waiting for Douglas to come out of that meeting. We need to get to him before he can take a shot."

The senator nodded to Nadja. "Take her over there."

"I got this," I said, not ready to relinquish my spot as top bitch in the organization.

"She's a highly trained agent, Bridget, just like you," the senator reminded me again.

"Believe me, I can more than handle myself in the field," she said and then opened her jacket so that I could see she was strapped.

"Ladies, handle this!" the senator commanded.

"All right," I answered, staring at Nadja in disbelief. "Then let's go."

Niles

73

Dropping my bag on the ground, I set up my equipment then tested the wind to line up my scope for the perfect shot. Jonathan had called me the night before and named Director Bonaventura as Bridget's accomplice, and that information just put me over the edge. The two of them had cooked up the whole scheme and made a fool out of me. I could have come home from the Army and lived a nice, quiet life if they hadn't dragged me into Dynamic Defense and all this other bullshit.

Now I was one pull of the trigger away from revenge. Once I took out the director, Bridget would be the next one on my list, as soon as I figured out where that bitch had gone into hiding. Jonathan had already promised that he would help me get my money back once I took care of those two, so I could rest easy knowing I could still afford to get my mother the care she needed.

Unfortunately, as much as I wanted to focus on the job at hand, my thoughts kept traveling back to the reason for it: Bridget. How the hell could I have been such a chump? Every woman I'd ever been close to, except my mother, had somehow ended up fucking me. I was pissed at myself for letting my guard down, but now that I could see the bigger picture, it all made sense. The bitch was a master manipulator. First she made sure my only choices in life were jail or Dynamic Defense. Then she worked hard to win my confidence. Seduced me with some crazy ancient sexual voodoo, and then played my emotions until I thought I was in love with her. I thought I'd felt wounded by Keisha, but this shit with Bridget was on a whole other level. As far as I was concerned, I was swearing off women from now on and just doing my job, making money and taking care of Mom.

I checked my watch. If the director's meeting with the Canadians was on schedule, then I had less than five minutes before my target would appear. The black Town Car was already sitting at the curb. I lined up the shot and waited for him to step out of the building.

"Don't do it!"

I recognized the voice right away. Turning my head from the scope, I saw Bridget burst through the rooftop door. She looked a hot mess. As much as I hadn't expected to see her, I wasn't surprised either. If anyone was good enough to find me, it was Bridget.

"When I have a job to do, I do it." I said angrily. "You should know. You were the one who trained me to finish whatever I started."

"Niles, don't do this," she said again.

"Jonathan said you might try to stop me."

"Jonathan is using you," she said, still out of breath from running upstairs.

"And you weren't?" I spat.

"Niles, he's jealous of us. Of what we have together. Don't throw it all away, please."

I laughed derisively. "What we have together! That's a joke. Why the fuck would I believe you? You've been lying to me from the beginning. I was just too stupid to see what was right in front of my face."

"It's not what you think," she insisted.

"What I think? I think you were the one using me to fatten your own pockets. You didn't care about me," I said, the bitterness spilling off my tongue.

I glanced through the scope, knowing the director could be coming out at any time. "I'm not gullible anymore, Bridget. From this day forward, I'm the one who's going to be fucking people over."

"No, I swear. It's not like that. Niles, I love you."

"You don't love me!" I shouted. She had me so furious that I couldn't focus on my target the way I needed to. I turned around to look at her.

"Yes, I do. I swear. I love you," she said.

"If you loved me, you wouldn't have stolen my money."

She looked surprised, and maybe even a little confused. I'd caught her off guard with that statement.

"Why, Bridget? If you love me, then why did you steal from me?"

"I wasn't trying to steal from you, baby. I did take your money, but I took it for us. I put it in an account for us in the Caymans. Look, I've seen what happens when someone who is not used to having money suddenly has access to such a large amount."

"What are you saying? I'm not mature enough to handle my own money? Fuck you." I spat out at her.

I turned back to my scope to see some men in suits exiting the building. I realized that the meeting must have been ending. Director Bonaventura could be coming out at any moment.

"Niles, God dammit! Please don't make me use this," she said. I was sure she had a gun aimed at me, but I refused to take my eyes off the scope. She kept talking, filling the air around us with her lies. "Yes, I took the money, but I did it so that you would have a future, so we would have a future. I know I shouldn't have, but I did. I'm sorry."

"That money was for my sick mother and you knew it!" I shouted, my back still turned to her.

"What are you talking about?" she asked. "I left you plenty of money to care for your mother. I only took ten percent for your retirement."

"Don't listen to her. She's a lying bitch. She took your money and mine." Jonathan appeared on the roof, throwing off my concentration again.

"Well, Bridget," he said, "when I found Frank and Lance in their unfortunate state, I knew I wouldn't have to look far to find you. I knew you'd be up here trying to talk your way out of this mess you created."

I spun around for a second, trying to understand what was going on. What the hell was he saying about Frank and Lance? Something wasn't adding up, but I couldn't quite put my finger on it.

"Don't worry about her," he said to me. "I got your back. Take the shot! Take the damn shot! If you want your money back—"

That was all he had to say. I turned around again to watch for the director's exit from the building. Bridget and Jonathan continued their war of words behind me.

"You bastard, you took his money, didn't you?" Bridget hissed at him.

"Niles knows who took his money. He's seen the proof."

"Proof? Look at me! I'm a billboard for proof. Did you tell him that you held me hostage? Kidnapped me?" She was screaming, but it only made him burst out into laughter. This shit was getting weirder by the second.

"Why would I kidnap you, Bridget?"

"Because you're jealous of me and Niles."

"Man, she really thinks her twat is that good; that you're stupid enough to believe her lies," he goaded me.

"There's the director," I said as I looked through the scope and saw him coming out of the building with two other men.

"You've got your target. Take the damn shot!" Jonathan screamed. I lined up my shot, wishing Bridget was my target instead. I wanted nothing more than to blow her away for her lies.

"Niles, you kill that man and they will hunt you down," she said.

I tried to pull the trigger, but my finger wouldn't move. I didn't know exactly what it was, but something still didn't feel right about this whole situation. I dropped my arms to my sides as I watched the director get in the car.

"What the fuck did you just do?" Jonathan screamed.

"You did the right thing, Niles," Bridget said, lowering her gun.

Jonathan appealed to me. "Who you gonna believe: me, or this lying bitch who had a gun pointed at you? If you're not going to kill him, then kill her. Take the shot."

I glanced from one to the other, growing more confused by the minute, but then I changed my target and aimed my gun at her.

"Go ahead. Do it. I don't care what happens to me if I've lost you already, Niles," she said.

"What the fuck are you waiting for? Kill her!" Jonathan yelled.

"Why don't you kill me yourself, you fuckin' pussy?" Bridget yelled at him, shocking the hell out of me.

I looked at Jonathan, and I could see the truth in his eyes: He couldn't pull the trigger. Maybe he really did love her.

"Don't do it, Mr. Monroe. Bridget is telling the truth."

I turned in the direction of the voice and saw a very attractive Middle Eastern woman standing in front of the entrance to the roof.

"Who the fuck are you?" I asked.

"She's nobody," Jonathan said. "A damn secretary. She don't know anything. Pull the fucking trigger."

"My name is Nadja," the woman said, ignoring Jonathan. "I'm an operative out of the Western Europe office. I was sent here to investigate Jonathan." There was something honest about her voice, something real, that made me trust her more than either of the other two.

Jonathan damn near lost his mind. "What the fuck! You're investigating me? You traitorous bitch!"

Again, Nadja ignored him, totally unfazed by his tirade. "Niles, I don't know what's going on with you and Bridget, but she's not the bad guy here. Jonathan is."

"What about the money? She stole your money," Jonathan continued, jumping around like a madman. He really looked like he was losing his mind. "You gonna let her get away with that?"

"We'll figure your money situation out. I promise," Nadja said, as calm as can be.

"Shut up!" Jonathan reached behind his back with his right arm, and when he brought it forward, he was raising a weapon. He quickly let off a shot.

BANG! I watched as Bridget crumbled to the ground.

"I told you to take the goddamn—"

Before he could finish his sentence, I put two shots right between his eyes; then I turned to Nadja angrily. "You better not be lying."

"I'm not." She ran over to Bridget.

I nudged Jonathan's body with my foot to confirm that he was dead then walked over to stand next to Nadja. Bridget had been hit in the arm.

"Niles," she said softly.

"I just wanna know two things," I said, feeling absolutely no sympathy for her.

"Anything." She was crying, and I didn't think it was because of the gunshot.

"Did you kill Rodney and them so you could recruit me?"

She hesitated for quite a while before she finally admitted, "Yes, I killed them, but it was for your—"

"Save it, okay? I've had enough of your bullshit." I glanced over at Nadja. "You got this?"

"Yes, I've got it," she said calmly.

I walked away. Bridget called out to me as I approached the door. I stopped with my hand on the knob, keeping my back to her.

"You said there were two things you wanted to know. What was the second?"

I opened the door and stepped into the stairway. "When am I gonna get my fucking money back?" was the last thing I said before I shut the door behind me.

Majestic

74

"Put her ass in that room with no windows down the hall and lock the fucking doors," I ordered as soon as we walked back into my house. That crazy old hag was working my nerves.

Bruce shot me a look that let me know he'd had about enough of her crazy ass too. There was something about the smug way this woman was acting that made me want to torture her son even more. She kept promising he was coming to rescue her, telling me he was going to walk in here like a goddamn black Jason Bourne or some shit. For a little while all her big talk about her bitch-ass son was funny, but eventually she started to drive us nuts with that shit, so midway to my place, we had to pull over and duct-tape her mouth, 'cause I couldn't hear one more thing about her son the fucking hero.

"Done, boss," Pooh said, pulling her down the hall.

"Yo, I thought you said you left Li'l Frog here with Keisha," Bruce said, plopping down on the sofa.

"I did."

"Where they at? I don't need her popping up home and finding her momma's body before we get rid of it. I don't know what you plan on doing with Keisha, but she ain't gonna take too kindly to what I did to her mom."

"Man, that bitch is gonna be on her way to the same place as her momma real soon. Ain't no room for disloyalty with all these fine-ass bitches running around here." I stuck my arm out, and we fist-bumped.

"Yo, Frog! Frog! Where the fuck you at?" I hollered, annoyed that he hadn't been front and center when we arrived. Now he came running out of the basement, buttoning up his pants like he just took a shit.

"Uh, yeah, boss." He couldn't look me in the eyes, which was a bad sign.

"Where the fuck is Keisha?" I took a step closer to him, but then I couldn't stand looking at him, so I just smashed his head into the wall. I didn't have time for this bullshit.

"She's right here," Li'l Frog said, looking around like a fool.

"Is she fucking invisible? 'Cause I don't see her!"

Bruce jumped in between us, snapping at him. "You were supposed to be watching her. Now where the fuck she at?"

Li'l Frog started cowering like he was waiting to be swung on again, but he wasn't moving, just looking stupid. "I don't know. . . . She was right here. All I did was go handle my business."

I wanted to break his fucking neck. "What fucking business do you have? You don't have any business! The only business you have is my business. Now, when was the last time you seen her?"

The fool had the nerve to check his watch. "Maybe thirty, forty minutes ago. She was in the theater watching a movie."

I grabbed him by the neck and threw him against the wall, and instead of pleading, the motherfucker just stood there looking guilty. He knew he had fucked up, and I was willing to bet he'd been down in that basement a hell of a lot longer than he was saying. I turned to Bruce, who must have thought the same thing, because he swung open the door to the basement, and we both saw why he'd been distracted. That ho Denise was standing on the stairs. She was the business he had taken care of.

Damn it! Keisha had set this shit up; I just knew it. Why the hell had I left this pussy-hungry child to do a man's job?

"Hey, Majestic! Bruce!" Denise came out of the basement, grinning like we was all cool and shit, not like she had just helped my baby mama escape.

Bruce grabbed her up and pushed her toward the door. "Get the fuck out, bitch!"

She knew enough to get out while she still could. You ain't never seen nobody hit the door as quick as she did.

"I'm sorry," Li'l Frog wailed, falling on the floor. He was in fear for his life, rightfully so. He was another thing I'd have to handle later.

"Go lock his ass up," I told Bruce.

I made a move to the garage. If that bitch had taken any of my cars, her ass was mine. I'd been so busy getting that old broad into the house that I hadn't paid attention when we were in there before. Now I saw that sure enough, my Mercedes was gone. That's when it hit me. If she had the balls to take my car, she might have taken something else.

"Shit!" I hurried to the bedroom to make sure my shit was where it was supposed to be. When I punched in the code and opened the safe to find an empty space, I turned around and punched a hole in the wall.

"Fuck! Bruce!" He came into my room and I told him, "That bitch took all my cash."

He stepped into the closet and looked into the empty safe. "Damn, man, that bitch is bold."

"I should have just killed that ho the same way you did her momma."

Bruce nodded his head. "But don't worry, man. We'll get to Keisha. Where the fuck is she going that we can't find her?"

"You're right," I said, thinking about Keisha's dumb ass trying to get away from me.

"We need to be worrying about this Niles cat. From everything I saw in that house, dude's a professional killer. Let's not forget he took out El Gato," my partner reminded me. "How about you take your anger out on him? 'Cause he's gonna be coming for us."

I nodded, walking out of the closet and heading toward the living room. "Call all the guys. We need to assemble an army of motherfuckers, 'cause if he's coming, we got to be ready. Tell everybody to get here not in ten minutes, but right fuckin' now. I want everyone locked and loaded. If that bastard shows a hair around here, I want his head blown the fuck off."

"Exactly. Let's do this," Bruce said.

Willie

75

Niles spent most of the afternoon down at the Dynamic Defense offices being debriefed by a bunch of stuck-up soldiers of fortune in suits. On the ride back home, I could tell that he was upset about a whole bunch of shit, but I'd learned to let him talk about things at his leisure. To be real clear, I was pissed about whatever kind of game Bridget had played with Niles's feelings, especially coming on the heels of Keisha. Maybe Bridget didn't steal all his money, but that bullshit about putting ten percent of it away for his retirement was a crock of shit. She'd been skimming off the top way before the two of them became an item. I just didn't want to upset Niles by saying it. Not that it mattered anyway. She wasn't going to be invited to Thanksgiving dinner anytime soon.

"So, do you think either of them ever really loved me, Unc?" Niles spoke for the first time in our forty-five minute drive. He was still staring out the window, but at least he was speaking.

"I don't know, Niles. I never really understood women other than wanting to fuck 'em, until I met Tanya. I'm probably not the best person to ask," I told him honestly as we pulled off the highway at our exit.

"You should marry her," he told me out of nowhere.

"Excuse me?"

He turned in my direction and gave me a stern look. "You should marry Tanya. She's a good woman, and she's one hundred percent in your corner."

"Yeah, she is, isn't she?" I think I was talking to myself more than him.

"Mm-hmm. Besides, you're gonna need somebody to change your Depends in a few years, and I'm certainly not doing it," he joked.

"Later for you." We were both laughing as I pulled into the driveway. No way was I going to admit that I'd already been looking at rings. I hadn't said the L-word yet, but that was only because I was scared to jinx it, 'cause I damn sure felt it.

We got out of the car and made our way to the door.

"Tanya? Lorna?" I called out as we came through the door. Not getting any answer was concerning. "Doesn't look like they're home," I told Niles.

"They gotta be home. Both cars are in the driveway." There was a split second where neither of said anything, then panic set in. We both knew something had to be wrong.

Niles started yelling, "Ma! Ma!" But again we heard nothing in response, not one sound as we rushed around to search the house.

"Shit. . . . Shit! Noooooooo! " I heard a voice when we entered the kitchen, but I was too emotional to realize that it was my own voice. There on the floor was Tanya. I ran over to her, dropping down and cradling her head, but it was too late. She was gone. The woman I planned to spend the rest of my life with was dead.

"Fuck! Fuck! Fuck!" I could hear Niles racing throughout the rest of the house.

"No! No! Nooooooo!" I wailed, lifting Tanya from the floor and carrying her ever so delicately from the kitchen to the sofa. I couldn't help myself; I was crying like a baby as I lovingly placed Tanya's body on the sofa "Who would do this to her? Who, Niles? She wouldn't hurt anyone."

"I don't know," he answered, "but whoever it was must have taken Ma too."

I was so distraught over Tanya that I had completely forgotten about my sister.

"Man, I can't take this shit!" I got up and walked over to the cabinet where Niles kept the booze, and took out a bottle of whiskey. I screwed off the top and took a deep breath, raising the bottle.

"What the fuck are you doing?" Niles shouted just at the moment the bottle was about to reach my eager lips. He shoved my arm so the whiskey ended up spilling all over the front of my shirt.

"What?" I growled at him, pissed that he'd interrupted my self-sabotage.

"She wouldn't want this," he said, forcing me to think about all the good Tanya had brought into my life. This shit just wasn't fair.

"I can't, man. I can't go on without her," I cried out, breaking down as he came toward me. I fell into his arms.

He just hugged me and let me cry for a long time, until I had worn myself out. "You can't do this, Unc. She loved you, and she would never want to see you lose the life you were just starting to rebuild."

"But that life was because of her. She was the reason I worked so hard. I wanted to be a man she could love." I was sobbing now.

"I know," he said meekly. No matter what he said, it wouldn't do anything to lessen the pain I was feeling, and he knew it.

"She was a good girl. She was my everything." I started sobbing again.

"I know, and whoever did this, we are going to make them pay," he promised, and I felt my pain transforming into anger. "But Willie, I need you to get a hold of yourself right now, because we've got to get Ma back."

"You're right," I said, drying my tears. "Someone's got my sister, and we need to go kill that motherfucker."

Niles

76

I wasn't sure what the hell was going on, but this day had just gone from bad to being the worst day of my life. Willie's wails of pain over finding Tanya dead were the nightmare soundtrack playing in the background as I raced from room to room. At this point, all I wanted was to find my mother safe and bring her home, but first I needed to figure out who had taken her. The first place my mind went was to Bridget and the organization. Could this be someone related to the jobs I had done for them or, God forbid, one of El Gato's people? I may have killed him, but I left an important loose end by allowing Dominique to live; not to mention the fact that his son was out there, probably hell bent on revenge. What if they had figured out my real identity and taken Ma?

I was yanked out of my thoughts when the house phone rang. Nobody had the number. I went into the kitchen to answer it.

"Hello?" I said, all my senses on high alert. Willie stopped wailing and stared at me as I took the call, No doubt he was also alarmed by the unexpected call.

"Are you missing something?" A deep male voice spoke, sounding like the caller thought he was cracking a joke. "I've been trying to call you all day."

"Who is this?"

"I'm your worst fucking nightmare. You think I wasn't going to find you? You think you could hide from me?" he yelled. He sounded like he wanted to murder me, but I didn't back down from the threat in his voice. I matched his fury with my own.

"You have my mother?" I hissed.

He gave me an answer that made we want to come through the phone and choke him to death. "You damn right I have your mother, and I'm going to do to her what you did to my brother Rodney, only a lot more painful and a whole lot longer."

That's when I knew who I was dealing with: it was Keisha's boyfriend Majestic.

"You fucking touch her and I'll kill you and the rest of your Neanderthal family," I raged.

"I'd like to see you try," he taunted.

I couldn't keep threatening him when he had my mother. I needed him to stay calm until I could find out where they were, so I tried a different tactic. I lowered the tone of my voice. "Look, I did not kill your brother. Last time I saw him he was alive. You have to believe me."

He laughed out loud, but I knew he wasn't amused. "Yeah, well, I don't believe you. Now you get to see how it feels to have your own flesh and blood killed."

"Look, this is about me, not my moms. I'm asking you—please—to exchange me for my mother." I was begging at this point, desperate to save Ma. "She's sick, man. She doesn't deserve this."

"Hmmmm. That's a thought. Let me think about it," he said sarcastically. "I'll get back to you. Oh, and if you call the cops, I kill her. I ain't got nothing to lose."

The phone went dead.

"Fuck!" I slammed the phone back on the receiver. I hated the helpless way I felt. I had gotten used to being the one who rode into difficult situations and fixed shit. Willie, who had gotten the gist of the conversation, was already at my side.

"Call Keisha. She'll know where that motherfucker lives. We need to go and get Lorna back," he said, spurring me to make the call because I was too fucked up to figure out what to do next.

Keisha

77

"Good night, Mommy," MJ said as I kissed him good night and put him to bed in the motel in a small town called Dunn, North Carolina.

I'd driven for eight hours straight before I felt safe enough to stop there. Majestic was on a rampage now that he knew I was missing. He'd called my phone about a hundred times in the span of an hour. It got so bad that I had to turn off my phone because MJ kept asking me who was calling and why I wouldn't answer my phone. I drove until I just couldn't keep my eyes open any longer, because I wanted to be as far away from New York as possible. My plan was to get up in the morning and start driving again, maybe to Mississippi or Louisiana, someplace Majestic would never think to look, and where I wouldn't bump into anyone he knew.

When MJ was asleep, I turned on my phone, wishing I could call someone to find out what was going on back on Long Island, but there was no one I could talk to. I still couldn't believe my mom was dead, and by now Niles probably was too. Why had my life turned out like this?

As soon as it powered on, my phone chirped repeatedly, notifying me that I had forty-three new text messages. I decided not to read the texts or listen to my voicemail, because I was sure they were full of hate and threats anyway. I really just wanted to use the phone to check the news back home and see if anyone had mentioned my mom or Niles on Facebook. The first thing I was going to do the next day was ditch this phone and get a pay-as-you-go phone from Walmart.

Not surprisingly, the phone rang in my hand. I was just about to hit IGNORE, until I realized it wasn't Majestic who was calling. It was Niles.

"Hello." My breath caught in my throat as it dawned on me that I might have just made a huge mistake. What if Majestic had killed Niles and was using his phone to get me to answer? If he had, then I'd fallen right into his trap.

"Keisha." I exhaled when I heard Niles's voice.

"Niles. Thank God," I said, babbling so fast I was not even sure he could hear me. "I thought you were dead. Majestic knows where you live. You can't stay at your house. He's gonna kill you. He's already killed my mother—"

He cut me off. "He killed Tanya too." He might as well have punched me in the face like Majestic had done earlier that morning. I had to sit down on the bed, because my legs were about to give out on me.

"Keisha, are you there?"

"He killed Tanya?" I repeated.

"Yes. I know how close you were. I'm sorry," he said, but his voice was flat. There was no warmth there.

"I hate him," I cried. "I hate him so much."

"I know you do, but I need your help right now," he said calmly.

"Anything—but I'm not going back there. I'm not going back to Long Island ever again."

"I'm not asking you to. It's Majestic. He took my mother, and I need to find him so I can get her back."

I gasped. First my mother, and now Niles's mom. Nothing in this world was sacred to Majestic.

"Niles, you can't go after him. Look what he's already done. He killed my mother; he killed Tanya. I don't want him to kill you too. He's an animal."

"He has my mother!" Niles shouted. "Don't worry about me. I learned how to handle myself in the Army."

I took a deep breath, knowing that he would go after Majestic whether I helped him or not. I might as well give him the address to save him some time. Maybe it would help him get to his mother before it was too late. "Okay," I said, "but you can't tell anyone that you spoke to me. I took MJ and left, and we're not coming back." I gave him Majestic's address, as well as the address of the house he'd bought for his mother, in case he was hiding out there.

"One more thing: Don't approach his house from the front. He's got all kinds of surveillance equipment. Go up the hill in the back. I remember Bruce saying that he didn't like the blind spots in the backyard security cameras. You might be able to slip in through that way."

"Good to know. And Keisha, you be safe."

"I'm sorry for everything, Niles."

He ended the call without responding. I lay back on the bed and, for the first time since I'd left New York, I allowed myself to cry.

Niles

78

The sun was just about to rise when we reached the top of the hill behind Majestic's mini mansion. Willie had wanted to hit the place last night as soon as we got the address from Keisha, but I'd learned a few things in the Army about attacking a stronghold, and having Majestic's guys stay up all night, making them antsy and sleep-deprived, was probably the best way—not to mention having the sun in their eyes as we attacked east to west.

"You don't have to do this. I can go in by myself," I said to Willie, who was carrying so many guns he looked like a caricature of a soldier.

"He has my sister," he answered, raising one gun in solidarity, his expression determined. I should have known he'd insist on helping me save my mother, the same way he'd always been there for both of us. "And that motherfucker killed Tanya," he added, and I knew he needed to get at this guy as bad as I did.

I looked at the house through the scope of my rifle and spotted six heavily armed guards posted around the backyard and another two standing by windows. I glanced at Willie. "You ready, Unc?" He nodded, and I pointed at a patch of trees near the house before firing six silenced shots from my rifle.

Thunk, thunk, thunk, thunk, thunk, thunk. All six guards fell.

We ran like hell toward the house, not stopping until were in the cover of the trees. "You okay?" I asked.

"Yeah. Just give me a sec," he replied, gasping for air. "I ain't as young as I used to be."

While he was catching his breath, I used my scope to check on the six targets I had taken out. All appeared dead, and it looked like none of the people in the house had noticed a thing.

I gave Willie the signal, and we made moves to the back door. I looked around for cameras and saw one or two, but we circumvented them in order to enter through a side door somebody had left unlocked.

We moved slowly from room to room, taking out these amateurs like fish in a barrel, until the place was eerily empty and strangely silent.

"This one?" Willie whispered as we approached a set of closed double doors at the end of the hallway. I nodded as I tiptoed toward the handle and pushed it open. It was one of those home theaters, and sitting in there were three guys. Two of them were huge, and the third was just crazy-looking.

My heart dropped when I realized my mother was in there with them.

The biggest dude stood up when he saw me, and put a gun to my mother's head. The other two jumped up and aimed at me. I raised my gun and pointed at the guy near my mother. Willie stepped up beside me and aimed his piece at the second big dude.

"You come to watch me kill your mother?" the guy with my mother said, and I knew that this was Majestic.

I glanced at my mother. Her mouth was taped shut, her hands were tied behind her back, and her eyes were wide with fear. I felt myself one second from going ballistic on his ass, but I knew the other two dudes would start blasting, and my mother would get caught in the crossfire.

Majestic had the nerve to look calm, like we were invited over to have a cup of tea. "I see you had no trouble finding the place. I guess those military skills came in handy. Bravo." He seemed to know a lot about me, which put me at a disadvantage. Then again, there was only one thing I needed to know about him: This piece of shit was threatening my mother's life.

"Step away from her." I moved closer.

He smirked. "Sorry, but that ain't gonna happen. I'm gonna do to her what you did to my brother, except in this case, you're gonna watch. The only reason you're alive right now is so you can see her die."

"I swear, if you hurt my mother, there will be no place in this whole world you can run."

He laughed. "Yeah, I'm not the running type. Bitches run from me." His crew joined him like shit was really funny.

I was boiling over. "Take that tape off of her mouth. Take it off!" I yelled, hating everything about seeing my mother like this. I had every intention of making him suffer. If I could take out El Gato, imagine what I would do to this motherfucker.

He looked down at my mother and shook his head. "All the squawking this bitch do, you should be thanking me."

Calling my mother a bitch was almost worse than kidnapping her, tying her up, and holding a gun on her. I took a step forward.

"One more inch and I will blow her away. Won't even give you a chance to say good-bye. Then I'm gonna turn this gun on you and blow you away. After that, I'm gonna go upstairs and have myself a peanut butter and jelly sandwich with some milk, watch a little ball, and have one of my lady friends give me a blow job."

"Yeah, that's exactly what a coward would eat," I shot back. "At least your brother was a man. At least when we had an altercation, he wasn't afraid to fight me. He wasn't hiding behind his weapon or his flunkies."

He puffed up his massive chest, probably thinking he'd intimidate me.

"Oh, you think I'm afraid, you punk? What kind of guy picks on women when there are grown-ass men for him to fight? Yeah, you. A punk and a coward, killing an innocent woman and going after my mother. Hell, if you ask me, the wrong brother is dead." I taunted him, fully expecting it to rile him up, and, of course, it did.

"You gonna wish you didn't say that!" he threatened.

One of his thugs moved in my direction like he had every intention of taking me down, but I already knew how to deal with his ass. As soon as he came close enough to touch me, I flipped his ass halfway across the room, slapping a dot on the back of his neck.

"So what? You his big protector? Figures," I said to the guy, changing my stance like I was ready for him to get up and fight again.

Majestic finally stepped up to fight his own battle. "I done took all I can out of you," he said. "Let's go. Mano a mano."

"Yo, Bruce. Watch this bitch while I handle him."
Majestic handed my mother off to the other big guy,
who put a gun to her head; then Majestic tossed his
gun to the side. I handed mine to Willie.

"You wanna fight? Let's fight. I'll show you what
really happened to your brother."

He started to jab, taking swings at me, but I
was relentless, wanting blood for the crimes he
committed against my family. I caught his fist
in mid-air and slammed him to the ground. As
he was getting back up to come at me again, the
crazy-looking flunky fell to the ground. The poison
had taken effect.

Majestic freaked out, stumbling in confusion.

"Ma," I said, turning to her for a quick second,
"that guy's just going to sleep while we have our
little fight." I lied because no way did I want my
mother to know I'd just killed a man in front of her.

Majestic got himself together and started delivering a series of punches, but I was matching him
throw for throw. I'm not gonna lie; he had training,
but it was still no match for my will and my anger.
Three quick hits to the throat and he was wobbly;
one more and he was on the floor.

Willie tossed me my gun. I stood over Majestic
and pressed it into his forehead.

"Don't do it, man, or your moms is dead." It
was the other big dude, the one he'd called Bruce,

talking to me. I turned to look at him, my adrenaline pumping faster at the sight of his gun against my mother's temple. The shock and fear I saw on her face caused me to lower my gun. She'd never seen me for the professional killer I'd become.

Willie descended on me, which told me he'd seen it too. Next thing I knew, he had his gun trained on Majestic. I knew Willie wanted to finish him off. I went over to rescue my mother, raising my gun to point it directly at Bruce.

"Niles! You take one step closer and I'll blow her brains out," he said.

"I'm gonna give you one chance. Let her go and walk away, 'cause if you don't, I can promise you, you're going to die today."

"Fuck that. I got her, so I'm the one in change. How the hell you making the rules?" Bruce ripped the tape off my mother's mouth. I cringed when I saw how much pain it caused her. "Tell your son to put down his gun."

"Baby," my mother said.

"Yeah, Ma?"

"Shoot him."

"Gladly." I smirked, pulling the trigger and landing a shot right between his eyes. Bruce's body slumped to the ground.

"Mom, I'm so sorry," I said as I took off the tape and undid her restraints.

"I told him my son was gonna kill him," she bragged as relief flowed through me. I loved my mother.

"Come on, Ma, let's go," I said, leading her out, but not before Willie mouthed to me exactly what I needed to hear: *I got this.* My smile widened as we left the room. A few seconds later, I heard the sound of a shot. I knew he'd done that for Tanya, but I planned to celebrate by taking my mom home.

Niles

79

I'd just come in from feeding the horses when I noticed a black SUV sitting in the driveway. The driver stepped out and opened the back door. I recognized his passenger as soon as I saw her. It was Nadja from Dynamic Defense. I felt the stress building up in my neck immediately at the sight of her, even though she had been very instrumental in covering up the details of my mother's rescue from the police. It's not every day the Long Island police find a house with a dozen dead bodies scattered around, so without her help there would have been one hell of an investigation, and I did not need that kind of scrutiny.

I headed to the porch to meet Nadja. Willie must have seen the car too, because he stepped out from the house and came to stand beside me.

"Good afternoon, Niles." She reached down and picked a daisy from the garden. "Beautiful place you have here."

"Thanks. We like it," I replied, feeling very stand-offish. "How can I help you?"

"Well, I'm headed back to Europe, and I just wanted to say good-bye and give you this." She reached into her pocket and handed me an envelope.

"What's this?" I asked, not giving a shit that I sounded suspicious.

"The director wanted to make sure you were reimbursed for every dime that was taken from you, including that last job."

I opened the envelope and studied the check that was inside. There were a hell of a lot of zeros.

"Mr. Monroe, I'd like to offer you a job," she said. I had expected this day to come.

"Tell the director I'm not interested," I said. "I'm done with Dynamic Defense. Have a nice flight." I turned to go into the house, but she wasn't done.

"Tell me you don't miss it: the thrill, the excitement, the rush of adrenaline?"

"I don't miss the lies and the bullshit your company put me and my family through."

"I can't say I blame you, but hear me out."

I suppose I could have listened to her. After all, she had just hand delivered to me a very solid future, but I swear I'd had enough of people like her, and my temper got the best of me.

"For what? You want to try and seduce me too, so you can mess with my mind? I'm not stupid. I've been there."

She narrowed her eyes and stared intensely before answering quietly. "Sex is not part of my job description. In my culture, the women are pure. I hate to disappoint you, Mr. Monroe, but I'm a virgin." She said this without a hint of irony or venom, just matter of fact. Her words shocked the hell out of me.

"She got you on that one, didn't she, nephew?" Willie laughed, and I shot him an evil look.

"Look, my father runs the company's Western European office. I'm just here to offer you a job because you're good at it. That's all."

My mother came out and walked over to my side. "What kind of job?" she asked suspiciously. She made no pretense of her protectiveness over her only son. I would never get tired of that.

"The kind of job your son is very good at," Nadja answered cryptically, instead of telling my mother that I killed people for a living.

She turned back to me and explained, "But this job is different, because it's working solely with an international clientele as a freelancer. You'll see that life outside of America is a different experience. I think you'd all like living abroad." She finished confidently and then opened her bag.

This time she pulled out three plane tickets and handed them to me.

"Three first class tickets. You have my number. Just let me know what you decide," she told me before getting back into her car.

As soon as the SUV pulled away, I turned to Mom and Willie.

"Willie? What do you want to do?"

He looked from me to Mom. "I don't know," he answered, but my mother had already made her decision.

"Europe's beautiful this time of year, and we could all use a fresh start."

Epilogue

Five Years later

"Niles! Niles!" Willie yelled, bringing me back into reality.

Within a matter of seconds, my life had flashed before me, giving me a glimpse at just how crazy it had been. For the two years following my departure from the United States, I'd worked relentlessly for Nadja, taking out target after target throughout Europe by day and mindlessly screwing every halfway decent woman I met by night, until I ran into Paris.

She'd broken down my walls of resistance and taken my heart in what seemed like no time. Hell, I'd only loved two women up until then, and both Keisha and Bridget had betrayed me in some form or fashion, so I should have known Paris would be no different.

I gazed down at the humming bomb, acknowledging that their betrayal hadn't remotely compared to what Paris had done.

"Niles, God dammit, answer me!" my uncle shouted at me again.

"I'm here, Unc," I said, dropping the bag containing the bomb and quickly heading toward the rear of the plane. "Like I said before, Unc, if I don't make it, I want you to kill her. Do you understand me? I want you to kill her."

"Sure, sure, I understand, but let's concentrate on getting you off that plane and away from that bomb."

"Yeah, let's." I quickly strapped on a parachute, taking a quick breath before grabbing hold of the latch for the rear door. I turned it until I heard the hissing sound of the seal being broken, then I opened the door completely. I glanced over at the bag one last time, a vibrating symbol of Paris's ultimate betrayal, shaking my head before I jumped from the plane.

I made it, I thought the moment I began to drop from the sky, but I wasn't quite safe yet. I'd just barely cleared the plane when I heard the bomb go off, and I was immediately propelled by the violent heat of the explosion. I flew wildly out of control for what felt like an eternity. The heat was so intense I worried I could be on fire. I reached for the pull for my parachute, knowing that I was in so much pain I was on my way to blacking out, *Shit, this could be the end.*